Praise for *The American*

'An enticing ...ction . . . Tav... ...an formality ... pre-Victorian laxity in social an... ...ual matters; he is adept at historical recreation, and allows a heady décor to work in his favour by having his mysteries come wrapped around by a creepy London fog or embedded picturesquely in a Gloucestershire snowdrift'
TLS

'Possibly the best book of the decade is Andrew Taylor's historical masterpiece, *The American Boy*. A truly captivating novel, rich with the sounds, smells, and cadences of nineteenth-century England'
Glasgow Herald

'Long, sumptuous, near-edible account of Regency rogues – wicked bankers, City swindlers, crooked pedagogues and ladies on the make – all joined in the pursuit of the rich, full, sometimes shady life. A plot stuffed with incident and character, with period details impeccably rendered'
Literary Review

'Taylor spins a magnificent tangential web . . . The book is full of sharply etched details evoking Dickensian London and is also a love story, shot through with the pain of a penniless and despised lover. This novel has the literary values which should take it to the top of the lists'
Scotland on Sunday

'It is as if Taylor has used the great master of the bizarre as both starting-and finishing-point, but in between created a period piece with its own unique voice. The result should satisfy those drawn to the fictions of the nineteenth century, or Poe, or indeed to crime writing at its most creative'
Spectator

'Andrew Taylor has flawlessly created the atmosphere of late-Regency London in *The American Boy*, with a cast of sharply observed characters in this dark tale of murder and embezzlement'
Sunday Telegraph

'Madness, murder, misapplied money and macabre marriages are inter... ... . an enjoyable

The American Boy

Andrew Taylor is the author of a number of crime novels, including the ground-breaking Roth Trilogy, which was adapted into the acclaimed TV drama *Fallen Angel*, and the historical crime novels *The Fire Court*, *The Ashes of London*, *The Silent Boy*, *The Scent of Death* and *The American Boy*, a No.1 *Sunday Times* best-seller and a 2005 Richard & Judy Book Club Choice.

He has won many awards, including the CWA John Creasey New Blood Dagger, an Edgar Scroll from the Mystery Writers of America, the CWA Ellis Peters Historical Award (the only author to win it three times) and the CWA's prestigious Diamond Dagger, awarded for sustained excellence in crime writing. He also writes for the *Spectator* and *The Times*.

He lives with his wife Caroline in the Forest of Dean.

@AndrewJRTaylor
www.andrew-taylor.co.uk

ANDREW TAYLOR

The American Boy

HarperCollins*Publishers*

HarperCollins*Publishers* Ltd
1 London Bridge Street,
London SE1 9GF

www.harpercollins.co.uk

This paperback edition 2018
1

First published in Great Britain by Flamingo 2003

A catalogue record for this book is available from the British Library

ISBN: 978-0-00-830075-3 (PB b-format)

This novel is entirely a work of fiction.
The names, characters and incidents portrayed in it are
the work of the author's imagination. Any resemblance to
actual persons, living or dead, events or localities is
entirely coincidental.

Typeset in Fournier MT by Palimpsest Book Production Ltd, Falkirk, Stirlingshire

Printed and bound by CPI Group (UK) Ltd, Croydon CR0 4YY

MIX
Paper from
responsible sources
FSC™ C007454

This book is produced from independently certified FSC™ paper
to ensure responsible forest management.

For more information visit: www.harpercollins.co.uk/green

For Sarah and William.
And, as always, for Caroline.

I would not, if I could, here or to-day, embody
a record of my later years of unspeakable
misery, and unpardonable crime.

From 'William Wilson' by Edgar Allan Poe

CONTENTS

The Wavenhoe family, 1819

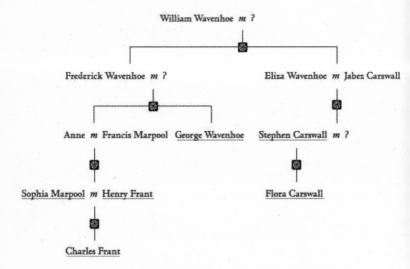

N.B. The names underlined are of those members of the family who were alive in September 1819

THE NARRATIVE OF THOMAS SHIELD

8th September 1819 – 23rd May 1820

CHAPTER ONE

W E OWE RESPECT to the living, Voltaire tells us in his *Première Lettre sur Oedipe*, but to the dead we owe only truth. The truth is that there are days when the world changes, and a man does not notice because his mind is on his own affairs.

I first saw Sophia Frant shortly before midday on Wednesday the 8th of September, 1819. She was leaving the house in Stoke Newington, and for a moment she was framed in the doorway as though in a picture. Something in the shadows of the hall behind her had made her pause, a word spoken, perhaps, or an unexpected movement.

What struck me first were the eyes, which were large and blue. Then other details lodged in my memory like burrs on a coat. She was neither tall nor short, with well-shaped, regular features and a pale complexion. She wore an elaborate cottage bonnet, decorated with flowers. Her dress had a white skirt, puffed sleeves and a pale blue bodice, the latter matching the leather slipper peeping beneath the hem of her skirt. In her left hand she carried a pair of white gloves and a small reticule.

I heard the clatter of the footman leaping down from the box of the carriage, and the rattle as he let down the steps. A stout middle-aged man in black joined the lady on the doorstep and gave her his arm as they strolled towards the carriage. They did not look at me. On either side of the path from the house to the road were miniature shrubberies enclosed by railings. I felt faint, and I held on to one of the uprights of the railings at the front.

'Indeed, madam,' the man said, as though continuing a conversation begun in the house, 'our situation is quite rural and the air is notably healthy.'

The lady glanced at me and smiled. This so surprised me that I failed to bow. The footman opened the door of the carriage. The stout man handed her in.

'Thank you, sir,' she murmured. 'You have been very patient.'

He bowed over her hand. 'Not at all, madam. Pray give my compliments to Mr Frant.'

I stood there like a booby. The footman closed the door, put up the steps and climbed up to his seat. The lacquered woodwork of the carriage was painted blue and the gilt wheels were so clean they hurt your eyes.

The coachman unwound the reins from the whipstock. He cracked his whip, and the pair of matching bays, as glossy as the coachman's top hat, jingled down the road towards the High-street. The stout man held up his hand in not so much a wave as a blessing. When he turned back to the house, his gaze flicked towards me.

I let go of the railing and whipped off my hat. 'Mr Bransby? That is, have I the honour –?'

'Yes, you have.' He stared at me with pale blue eyes partly masked by pink, puffy lids. 'What do you want with me?'

'My name is Shield, sir. Thomas Shield. My aunt, Mrs Reynolds, wrote to you, and you were kind enough to say –'

'Yes, yes.' The Reverend Mr Bransby held out a finger for me to shake. He stared me over, running his eyes from head to toe. 'You're not at all like her.'

He led me up the path and through the open door into the panelled hall beyond. From somewhere in the building came the sound of chanting voices. He opened a door on the right and went into a room fitted out as a library, with a Turkey carpet and two windows overlooking the road. He sat down heavily in the chair behind the desk, stretched out his legs and pushed two stubby fingers into his right-hand waistcoat pocket.

4

'You look fagged.'

'I walked from London, sir. It was warm work.'

'Sit down.' He took out an ivory snuff-box, helped himself to a pinch and sneezed into a handkerchief spotted with brown stains. 'So you want a position, hey?'

'Yes, sir.'

'And Mrs Reynolds tells me that there are at least two good reasons why you are entirely unsuitable for any post I might be able to offer you.'

'If you would permit me, I would endeavour to explain.'

'Some would say that facts explain themselves. You left your last position without a reference. And, more recently, if I understand your aunt aright, you have been the next best thing to a Bedlamite.'

'I cannot deny either charge, sir. But there were reasons for my behaviour, and there are reasons why those episodes happened and why they will not happen again.'

'You have two minutes in which to convince me.'

'Sir, my father was an apothecary in the town of Rosington. His practice prospered, and one of his patrons was a canon of the cathedral, who presented me to a vacancy at the grammar school. When I left there, I matriculated at Jesus College, Cambridge.'

'You held a scholarship there?'

'No, sir. My father assisted me. He knew I had no aptitude for the apothecary's trade and he intended me eventually to take holy orders. Unfortunately, near the end of my first year, he died of a putrid fever, and his affairs were found to be much embarrassed, so I left the university without taking my degree.'

'What of your mother?'

'She had died when I was a lad. But the master of the grammar school, who had known me as a boy, gave me a job as an assistant usher, teaching the younger boys. All went well for a few years, but, alas, he died and his successor did not look so kindly on me.' I hesitated, for the master had a daughter named Fanny, the memory of whom still brought me pain. 'We disagreed, sir – that was the long and the short of it. I said foolish things I instantly regretted.'

5

'As is usually the case,' Bransby said.

'It was then April 1815, and I fell in with a recruiting sergeant.'

He took another pinch of snuff. 'Doubtless he made you so drunk that you practically snatched the King's shilling from his hand and went off to fight the monster Bonaparte single-handed. Well, sir, you have given me ample proof that you are a foolish, headstrong young man who has a belligerent nature and cannot hold his liquor. And now shall we come to Bedlam?'

I squeezed the thick brim of my hat until it bent under the pressure. 'Sir, I was never there in my life.'

He scowled. 'Mrs Reynolds writes that you were placed under restraint, and lived for a while in the care of a doctor. Whether in Bedlam itself or not is immaterial. How came you to be in such a state?'

'Many men had the misfortune to be wounded in the late war. It so happened that I was wounded in my mind as well as in my body.'

'Wounded in the mind? You sound like a school miss with the vapours. Why not speak plainly? Your wits were disordered.'

'I was ill, sir. Like one with a fever. I acted imprudently.'

'Imprudent? Good God, is that what you call it? I understand you threw your Waterloo Medal at an officer of the Guards in Rotten-row.'

'I regret it excessively, sir.'

He sneezed, and his little eyes watered. 'It is true that your aunt, Mrs Reynolds, was the best housekeeper my parents ever had. As a boy I never had any reason to doubt her veracity or indeed her kindness. But those two facts do not necessarily encourage me to allow a lunatic and a drunkard a position of authority over the boys entrusted to my care.'

'Sir, I am neither of those things.'

He glared at me. 'A man, moreover, whose former employers will not speak for him.'

'But my aunt speaks for me. If you know her, sir, you will know she would not do that lightly.'

For a moment neither of us spoke. Through the open window came the clop of hooves from the road beyond. A fly swam noisily through the heavy air. I was slowly baking, basted in sweat in the oven of my own clothes. My black coat was too heavy for a day like this but it was the only one I had. I wore it buttoned to the throat to conceal the fact that I did not have a shirt beneath.

I stood up. 'I must detain you no longer, sir.'

'Be so good as to sit down. I have not concluded this conversation.' Bransby picked up his eye glasses and twirled them between finger and thumb. 'I am persuaded to give you a trial.' He spoke harshly, as if he had in mind a trial in a court of law. 'I will provide you with your board and lodging for a quarter. I will also advance you a small sum of money so you may dress in a manner appropriate to a junior usher at this establishment. If your conduct is in any way unsatisfactory, you will leave at once. If all goes well, however, at the end of the three months, I may decide to renew the arrangement between us, perhaps on different terms. Do I make myself clear?'

'Yes, sir.'

'Ring the bell there. You will need refreshment before you return to London.'

I stood up again and tugged the rope on the left of the fireplace.

'Tell me,' he added, without any change of tone, 'is Mrs Reynolds dying?'

I felt tears prick my eyelids. I said, 'She does not confide in me, but she grows weaker daily.'

'I am sorry to hear it. She has a small annuity, I collect? You must not mind me if I am blunt. It is as well for us to be frank about such matters.'

There is a thin line between frankness and brutality. I never knew on which side of the line Bransby stood. I heard a tap on the door.

'Enter!' cried Mr Bransby.

I turned, expecting a servant in answer to the bell. Instead a small, neat boy slipped into the room.

'Ah, Allan. Good morning.'

'Good morning, sir.'

He and Bransby shook hands.

'Make your bow to Mr Shield, Allan,' Bransby told him. 'You will be seeing more of him in the weeks to come.'

Allan glanced at me and obeyed. He was a well-made child with large, bright eyes and a high forehead. In his hand was a letter.

'Are Mr and Mrs Allan quite well?' Bransby inquired.

'Yes, sir. My father asked me to present his compliments, and to give you this.'

Bransby took the letter, glanced at the superscription and dropped it on the desk. 'I trust you will apply yourself with extra force after this long holiday. Idleness does not become you.'

'No, sir.'

'*Adde quod ingenuas didicisse fideliter artes.*' He prodded the boy in the chest. 'Continue and construe.'

'I regret, sir, I cannot.'

Bransby boxed the lad's ears with casual efficiency. He turned to me. 'Eh, Mr Shield? I need not ask you to construe, but perhaps you would be so good as to complete the sentence?'

'*Emollit mores nec sinit esse feros.* Add that to have studied the liberal arts with assiduity refines one's manners and does not allow them to be coarse.'

'You see, Allan? Mr Shield was wont to mind his book. *Epistulae Ex Ponto*, book the second. He knows his Ovid and so shall you.'

When we were alone, Bransby wiped fragments of snuff from his nostrils with the stained handkerchief. 'One must always show them who is master, Shield,' he said. 'Remember that. Kindness is all very well but it don't answer in the long run. Take young Edgar Allan, for example. The boy has parts, there is no denying it. But his parents indulge him. I shudder to think where such as he would be without due chastisement. Spare the rod, sir, and spoil the child.'

So it was that, in the space of a few minutes, I found a respectable position, gained a new roof over my head, and encountered for the first time both Mrs Frant and the boy Allan. Though I marked a slight but unfamiliar twang in his accent, I did not then realise that Allan was American.

Nor did I realise that Mrs Frant and Edgar Allan would lead me, step by step, towards the dark heart of a labyrinth, to a place of terrible secrets and the worst of crimes.

CHAPTER TWO

B EFORE I VENTURE into the labyrinth, let me deal briefly with this matter of my lunacy.

I had not seen my aunt Reynolds since I was a boy at school, yet I asked them to send for her when they put me in gaol because I had no other person in the world who would acknowledge the ties of kinship.

She spoke up for me before the magistrates. One of them had been a soldier, and was inclined to mercy. Since I had indeed thrown the medal before a score of witnesses, and moreover shouted 'You murdering bastard' as I did so, there was little doubt in any mind including my own that I was guilty. The Guards officer was a vengeful man, for although the medal had hardly hurt him, his horse had reared and thrown him before the ladies.

So it seemed there was only one road to mercy, and that was by declaring me insane. At the time I had little objection. The magistrates decided that I was the victim of periodic bouts of insanity, during one of which I had assaulted the officer on his black horse. It was a form of lunacy, they agreed, that should yield to treatment. This made it possible for me to be released into the care of my aunt.

She arranged for me to board with Dr Haines, whom she had consulted during my trial. Haines was a humane man who disliked chaining up his patients like dogs and who lived with his own family not far away from them. 'I hold with Terence,' the doctor said to me.

'*Homo sum; humani nil a me alienum puto.* To be sure, some of the poor fellows have unusual habits which are not always convenient in society, but they are made of the same clay as you or I.'

Most of his patients were madmen and half-wits, some violent, some foolish, all sad; demented, syphilitic, idiotic, prey to strange and fearful delusions, or sweeping from one extreme of their spirits to the other in the *folie circulaire*. But there were a few like myself, who lived apart from the others and were invited to take our meals with the doctor and his wife in the private part of the house.

'Give him time and quiet, moderate exercise and a good, wholesome diet,' Dr Haines told my aunt in my presence, 'and your nephew will mend.'

At first I doubted him. My dreams were filled with the groans of the dying, with the fear of death, with my own unworthiness. Why should I live? What had I done to deserve it when so many better men were dead? At first, night after night, I woke drenched in sweat, with my pulses racing, and sensed the presence of my cries hanging in the air though their sound had gone. Others in that house cried in the night, so why should not I?

The doctor, however, said it would not do and gave me a dose of laudanum each evening, which calmed my disquiet or at least blunted its edge. Also he made me talk to him, of what I had done and seen. 'Unwholesome memories,' he once told me, 'should be treated like unwholesome food. It is better to purge them than to leave them within.' I was reluctant to believe him. I clung to my misery because it was all I had. I told him I could not remember; I feigned rage; I wept.

After a week or two, he cunningly worked on my feelings, suggesting that if I were to teach his son and daughters some Latin and a little Greek for half an hour each morning, he would be able to remit a modest proportion of the fees my aunt paid him for my upkeep. For the first week of this instruction, he sat in the parlour reading a book as I made the children con their grammars and chant their declensions. Then he took to leaving me alone with them, at first for a few minutes only, and then for longer.

'You have a gift for instructing the young,' the doctor said to me one evening.

'I show them no mercy. I make them work hard.'

'You make them wish to please you.'

It was not long after that he declared that he had done all he could for me. My aunt took me to her lodgings in a narrow little street running up to the Strand. Here I perched like an untidy cuckoo, mouth ever open, in her snug nest. I filled her parlour during the day, and slept there at night on a bed they made up on the sofa. During that summer, the reek from the river was well-nigh overwhelming.

I soon realised that my aunt was not well, that I had occasioned a severe increase in her expenditure since my foolish assault with the Waterloo Medal, and that my presence, though she strove to hide it, could not but be a burden to her. I also heard the groans she smothered in the dark hours of the morning, and I saw illness ravage her body like an invading army.

One day, as we drank tea after dinner, my aunt gave me back the Waterloo Medal.

It felt cold and heavy in the palm of my hand. I touched the ribbon with its broad, blood-red stripe between dark blue borders. I tilted my hand and let the medal slide on to the table by the tea caddy. I pushed it towards her.

'Where did it come from?'

'The magistrate gave it to me for you,' she said. 'The one who was kind, who had served in the Peninsula. He said it was yours, that you had earned it.'

'I threw it away.'

She shook her head. 'You threw it at Captain Stanhope.'

'Does not that amount to the same thing?'

'No.' She added, almost pleading, 'You could be proud of it, Tom. You fought with honour for your King and your country.'

'There was no damned honour in it,' I muttered. But I took the medal to please her, and slipped it in my pocket. Then I said – and the one thing led to the other – 'I must find employment. I cannot be a burden to you any longer.'

At that time jobs of any kind were not easy to find, particularly if one was a discharged lunatic who had left his last teaching post without a reference, who lacked qualifications or influence. But my aunt Reynolds had once kept house for Mr Bransby's family, and he had a kindness for her. Upon threads of this nature, those chance connections of memory, habit and affection that bind us with fragile and invisible bonds, the happiness of many depends, even their lives.

All this explains why I was ready to take up my position as an under-usher at the Manor House School in the village of Stoke Newington on Monday the 13th of September. On the evening before I left my aunt's house for the last time, I walked east into the City and on to London Bridge. I stopped there for a while and watched the grey, sluggish water moving between the piers and the craft plying up and down the river. Then, at last, I felt in my trouser pocket and took out the medal. I threw it into the water. I was on the upstream side of the bridge and the little disc twisted and twinkled as it fell, catching the evening sunshine. It slipped neatly into the river, like one going home. It might never have existed.

'Why did I not do that before?' I said aloud, and two shopgirls, passing arm in arm, laughed at me.

I laughed back, and they giggled, picked up their skirts and hastened away. They were pretty girls, too, and I felt desire stir within me. One of them was tall and dark, and she reminded me a little of Fanny, my first love. The girls skittered like leaves in the wind and I watched how their bodies swayed beneath thin dresses. As my aunt grows worse, I thought, I grow better, as though I feed upon her distress.

CHAPTER THREE

O NCE AGAIN, I walked to save money. My box had gone ahead by carrier. I followed the old Roman road to Cambridge, Ermine-street, stretching north from Shoreditch, the bricks and mortar of the city creeping blindly after it like ants following a line of honey.

About a mile south of Stoke Newington, the vehicles on the road came to a noisy standstill. Walking steadily, I passed the uneasy, twitching snake of curricles and gigs, chaises and carts, stagecoaches and wagons, until I drew level with the cause of the obstruction. A shabby little one-horse carriage travelling south had collided with a brewer's dray returning from London. One of the chaise's shafts had snapped, and the unfortunate hack which had drawn it was squirming on the ground, still entangled in her harness. The driver was waving his blood-soaked wig at the draymen and bellowing, while around them gathered a steadily expanding crowd of angry travellers and curious bystanders.

Some forty yards away, standing in the queue of vehicles travelling towards London, was a carriage drawn by a pair of matching bays. When I saw it, I felt a pang, curiously like hunger. I had seen the equipage before – outside the Manor House School. The same coachman was on the box, staring at the scene of the accident with a bored expression on his face. The glass was down and a man's hand rested on the sill.

I stopped and turned back, pretending an interest in the accident, and examined the carriage more closely. As far as I could see, it had only the one occupant, a man whose eyes met mine, then looked away, back to something on his lap. He had a long pale face, with a hint of green in its pallor and fine regular features. His starched collar rose almost to his ears and his neck cloth tumbled in a snowy waterfall from his throat. The fingers on the windowsill moved rhythmically, as though marking time to an inaudible tune. On the forefinger was a great gold signet ring.

A footman came hurrying along the road from the accident, pushing his way through the crowd. He went up to the carriage window. The occupant raised his head.

'There's a horse down, sir, the chaise is a wreck and the dray has lost its offside front wheel. They say there's nothing to do but wait.'

'Ask that fellow what he's staring at.'

'I beg your pardon, sir,' I said, and my voice sounded thin and reedy in my ears. 'I stared at no one, but I admired your conveyance. A fine example of the coach-builder's craft.'

The footman was already looming over me, leaning close. He smelt of onions and porter. 'Be off with you, then.' He nudged me with his shoulder and went on in a lower voice, 'You've admired enough, so cheese it.'

I did not move.

The coachman lifted his whip.

Meanwhile, the man in the carriage stared straight at me. He showed neither anger nor interest. There was an impersonal menace in the air, as pungent as gas, even in broad daylight and on a crowded road. Like an itch, I was a minor irritant. The gentleman in the coach had decided to scratch me.

I sketched a bow and strolled away. I did not know the encounter for what it was, an omen.

CHAPTER FOUR

STOKE NEWINGTON WAS a pretty place, despite its proximity to London. I remember the trees and rooks with affection. The youngest boy in the school was four; the oldest nineteen and so nearly a man that he sported bushy whiskers and was rumoured to have put the baker's girl with child. The sons of richer and more ambitious parents were prepared for entry at the public schools. Most, however, received all the learning they required at Mr Bransby's.

'The parents entrust their sons' board and lodging to us as well as their tuition,' Mr Bransby told me. 'A nutritious diet and a comfortable bed are essential if a boy is to learn. Moreover, if a child lives among gentlefolk, he acquires their ways. We keep strictly to our regimen. It is an essential foundation to sobriety in later life.'

The regimen did not affect Mr Bransby and his household, who lived separately from the rest of the school and were no doubt sufficiently sober already. I was expected to sleep on the boys' side, as was the only other master who lived at the school, the senior usher.

'Mr Dansey has been with me for many years,' Bransby told me when he introduced us. 'You will find him a scholar of distinction.'

Edward Dansey was probably in his forties, a thin man, dressed in black clothes so old and faded that they were now mottled shades of green and grey. He wore a dusty little wig, usually askew, and had a cast in one eye, which, without being actually oblique, approached nearly to a squint. Both then and later, he was always perfectly civil. His manners were those of a gentleman, despite his shabby clothes. He had the great merit of showing no curiosity about my past history.

When I knew Dansey better I found he had a habit of looking at the world with his chin raised and his lips twisted asymmetrically so that one corner of the mouth curled up and the other curled down; it was as though part of him was smiling and part of him was frowning so one never really knew where one stood with him. The cast in his eye accentuated this ambivalence of expression. The boys called him Janus, perhaps because they believed his mood varied according to the side of his face you saw him from. They were scared of Bransby, who kept a cane in every room of the school so he could flog a boy wherever he was without delay, but they were terrified of Dansey.

On my second Thursday at the school, the manservant padded along to the form room as the boys were streaming out to their two hours of liberty before dinner and requested me to wait on his master.

My immediate fear was that I had somehow displeased Mr Bransby. I went through the door that separated his quarters from the rest of the house, which was like stepping into a different country. Here the air smelt of beeswax and flowers and the walls were freshly papered, the panels freshly painted. Mr Bransby had silence enough to hear the ticking of a clock, a luxury indeed in a house full of boys. I knocked and was told to enter. He was staring out of the window, tapping his fingers on the leather top of his table.

'Sit down, Shield. I must be the bearer of sad news, I'm afraid.'

I said, 'My aunt Reynolds?'

Bransby bowed his heavy head. 'I am truly sorry for it. She was an excellent woman.'

My mind was blank, an empty place filled with fog.

'She charged the woman with whom she lodged to write to me when she was gone. She died yesterday afternoon.' He cleared his throat. 'It appears that it was very sudden at the end, or else they would have sent for you. But there is a letter. Mrs Reynolds directed that it should be given to you after her death.'

The seal was intact. It had been stamped with what looked like the

16

handle of a small spoon. I thought I could make out the imprint of fluting. My aunt had probably used the small silver spoon she kept locked in the caddy with her tea. The wax was streaky, a mixture of rusty orange and dark blue. Economical in all things, she saved the seals of letters sent to her and melted the wax again when she sent a letter of her own.

The mind is an ungovernable creature, particularly under the influence of grief; we cannot always command our own thoughts. I found myself wondering if the spoon would still be there, and whether by rights it was now mine. For an instant the fog cleared and I saw her there, in my mind but as solid as Bransby himself, sitting at the table after dinner, frowning into the caddy as she measured the tea.

'There will be arrangements to be made,' Bransby was saying. 'Mr Dansey will take over your duties for a day or two.' He sneezed, and then said angrily, 'I shall advance you a small sum of money to cover any expenses you may have. I suggest you go up to town this afternoon. Well? What do you say?'

I recalled that my sanity was still on trial, and now there was no one to speak for me so I must make shift to speak for myself. I raised my head and said that I was sensible of Mr Bransby's great kindness. I begged leave to withdraw and prepare for my journey.

A moment later, I went up to my little room in the attic, a green hermitage under the eaves. There at last I wept. I wish I could say my tears were solely for my aunt, the best of women. Alas, they were also for myself. My protector was dead. Now, I told myself, I was truly alone in the world.

CHAPTER FIVE

MY AUNT'S DEATH drew me deeper into the labyrinth. It brought me to Mr Rowsell and Mrs Jem.

Her last letter to me was brief and, judging by the handwriting, written in the later stages of her illness. In it, she expressed the hope that we might meet again in that better place beyond the grave and assured me that, if heaven permitted it, she would watch over me. Turning to more practical matters, she informed me that she had left money to defray the expense of her funeral. There was nothing for me to do, for she had decided all the details, even the nature of her memorial, even the mason to cut the letters. Finally, she directed me to wait on her attorney Mr Rowsell at Lincoln's Inn.

I called at the lawyer's chambers. Mr Rowsell was a large, red-faced man, bulging in the prison of his clothing as though the blood were bursting to escape from his body. He directed his moon-faced clerk to fetch my aunt's papers. While we waited he scribbled in his pocketbook. When the clerk returned, Rowsell looked through the will, glancing up at me with bright, bird-like eyes, his manner a curious compound of the curt and the furtive. There were two bequests of five pounds apiece, he told me, one to the maid of all work and the other to the landlady.

'The residue comes to you, Mr Shield,' he said. 'Apart from my bill, of course, which will be a charge on the estate.'

'There cannot be much.'

'She drew up a schedule, I believe,' said Rowsell, reaching into the little deed-box. 'But do not let your hopes rise too high, young man.' He took out a sheet of paper, glanced at it and handed it to me. 'Her goods and chattels, such as they were,' he continued, staring at me over his spectacles, 'and a sum of money. A little over a hundred pounds, in all probability. Heaven knows how she managed to put it by on that annuity of hers.' He stood up and held out his hand. 'I am pressed for time this morning so I shall not detain you any longer. If you leave your direction with Atkins on your way out, I will write to you when we are in a position to conclude the business.'

A hundred pounds! I walked down to the Strand in a daze similar to intoxication. My steps were unsteady. A hundred pounds!

I went to the house where my aunt had lodged and arranged for the disposal of her possessions. Of the larger items, I kept only the tea caddy with its spoon. The landlady found a friend named Mrs Jem who was willing to buy the furniture. I suspected I would have got a higher price if I had been prepared to look elsewhere, but I did not want the trouble of it. Mrs Jem also bought my aunt's clothes.

'Not that they're worth more than a few shillings,' she said with a martyred smile; she was a mountainous woman with handsome little features buried in her broad face. 'More patches and darns than anything else. Still, you won't want them, will you, so it's doing you a favour. I've only thirty shillings. Will you wait while I fetch the rest of the money?'

'No.' I could not bear to stay here any longer, for I wanted to contemplate both my loss and my good fortune in peace and quiet. 'I will take the thirty shillings and collect the balance later.'

'As you wish,' she said. 'Three Gaunt-court. It's not a stone's throw away.'

'A long throw.'

She gave me a hard stare. 'Don't worry, I'll have the money waiting for you. Six shillings, no more no less. I pay my debts, Mr Shield, and I expect others to pay theirs.'

I could not resist a schoolboy pun. 'Mrs Jem,' I said solemnly, 'you are indeed a pearl of great price.'

'That's enough of your impudence,' she replied. 'If you're going, you'd better go.'

The balloon of mirth subsided as I walked away from the house where my aunt had lived. So this was all that a life amounted to – a mound of freshly turned earth in a churchyard, a few pieces of furniture scattered among other people's rooms, and a handful of clothes that nobody but the poor would want to buy.

There was also the small matter of the money which would come to me. For the first time in my life, I was about to be a man of substance, the absolute master of £103 and a few shillings and pence. The knowledge changed me. Wealth may not bring happiness, but at least it has the power to avert certain causes of sorrow. And it makes a man feel he has a place in the world.

CHAPTER SIX

WEALTH. THAT BRINGS me to Wavenhoe's Bank. It was Mr Bransby who first mentioned its name to me. I never went there, never met old Mr Wavenhoe himself until he was on his deathbed, but Wavenhoe's was the chain that bound us all together, the British and the Americans, the Frants and the Carswalls, Charlie and Edgar. Money plays its own tune, and in our different ways we all found ourselves dancing to it.

Early in October, I applied to Bransby for leave to go up to town. It was on that occasion that he mentioned Wavenhoe's. I needed to visit London because Mr Rowsell had papers for me to sign, and I wished to collect the few shillings that Mrs Jem owed me. He made no difficulty about my request.

'Upon one condition, however,' he went on. 'I should like you to go on Tuesday. Then you may undertake two errands for me while you are there. Not that you will find them onerous – quite the reverse, I fancy. When you travel up to town, you will take the boy Allan with you and leave him at his parents' house in Southampton-row. Number thirty-nine. His father writes that his mother desires to have him measured for a suit of clothes against the winter.'

'Will I collect him on my way back, sir?'

'No. I understand he is to return later in the evening, and that Mr Allan will make the arrangements. Once you have left him at his father's house, you may discharge your own business. But afterwards I wish you to call at a house in Russell-square so that you may convey a new pupil to the school. Or rather, he will convey you. The boy's father tells me he will order the carriage.' Bransby leaned back in his chair, his body pressing against his waistcoat buttons. 'His name is Frant.'

I nodded. I remembered the lady who had smiled at me at the gate of the school, and also the man who had nearly set his servants on to me as I walked up Ermine-street. I felt my pulse beating somewhere among the fingers of my clasped hands.

'Master Frant should suit us very well. His father is one of the partners of Wavenhoe's Bank. A very sound concern indeed.'

'How old is the boy, sir?'

'Ten or eleven. As it happens, this school was commended to Mr Frant by Allan's father. He is an American of Scottish descent, but resident in London. I understand that he and Mr Frant have conducted business together. Mark this well, Shield: first, a satisfied parent will share his satisfaction with other parents; second, Mr Frant is a gentleman-like man who not only moves in good society but meets wealthy men in the course of his business. Wealthy men have sons who require an education. I would wish you to make a particularly good impression, therefore, on Mr and Mrs Allan and Mr and Mrs Frant.'

'I shall endeavour to do so, sir.'

Bransby leaned forward across the desk so that he could study me more closely. 'I am confident that your manner will be everything that is appropriate. But I must confess – and pray do not take this amiss – that some alteration to your dress might be desirable. I advanced you a small sum for clothing, did I not, but perhaps not enough?'

I began to speak: 'It is unfortunate, sir, that –'

'And, indeed,' Bransby rushed on, his colour darkening, 'you have now been with us for nearly a month and your work has, on the whole, been satisfactory. That being so, from next quarterday I propose to pay you a salary of twelve pounds a year, as well as your board and lodging. It is on the understanding, naturally, that your dress will be appropriate to an usher at this establishment and that your conduct continues to give satisfaction in all respects. In the circumstances, I am minded to advance you perhaps half of your first quarter's salary so that you may make the necessary purchases.'

Three days later, on Tuesday, 5th October, I travelled up to London. Young Allan sat as far away as possible from me in the coach and replied in monosyllables to the questions I put to him. I delivered the boy into the care of a servant at his parents' house. I had taken but a few steps along the pavement when I felt a hand on my sleeve. I stopped and turned.

'Your pardon, sir.'

A tall man in a shabby green coat inclined his trunk forward from the waist. He wore a greasy wig, thick blue spectacles and a spreading beard like the nest of an untidy bird.

'I am looking – looking for the residence of an acquaintance.' He had a low, booming voice, the sort that makes glasses vibrate. 'An American gentleman – a Mr Allan. I wonder whether that might be his house.'

'It is indeed.'

'Ah – you are most obliging, sir – so the boy you were with must be his son?' He swayed as he spoke. 'A handsome boy.'

I bowed. The man's face was turned away from me but his breath smelt faintly of spirits and strongly of rotting teeth or an infection of the gums. He was not intoxicated, though, or rather not so it affected his actions. I thought he was perhaps the sort of man who is at his most sober when a little elevated.

'Mr Shield, sir!'

I turned back to the Allans' house. The servant had opened the door.

'There was a message from Mrs Allan, sir. She wishes to keep Master Edgar until tomorrow. Mr Allan's clerk will bring him back to Stoke Newington in the morning.'

'Very good,' I said. 'I will inform Mr Bransby.'

Without a word of farewell, the man in the green coat walked rapidly in the direction of Holborn. I followed, for my next destination was beyond it, at Lincoln's Inn. The man glanced over his shoulder, saw me strolling behind him and began to walk more quickly. He knocked against a woman selling baskets and she shrieked abuse at him, which he ignored.

He turned into Vernon-row. By the time I reached the corner, there was no sign of him.

I thought perhaps the man in the green coat had mistaken me, or someone behind me, for a creditor. Or he had accelerated his pace for quite a different reason, unconnected with his looking back. I dismissed him from my mind and continued to walk southwards. But the incident lodged itself in my memory, and later I was to be thankful that it had.

At Mr Rowsell's chambers in Lincoln's Inn, his clerk had the papers ready for me to sign. But as I was about to take my leave, the lawyer himself came out of his private room and shook me by the hand with unexpected cordiality.

'I give you joy of your inheritance. You are somewhat changed, Mr Shield, if I may say so without impertinence. And for the better.'

'Thank you, sir.'

'A new coat, I fancy? You have begun to spend your new wealth?'

I smiled at Mr Rowsell, responding to the good humour in his face rather than the words. 'I have not touched my aunt's money yet.'

'What will you do with it?'

'I shall place it in a bank for a few months. I do not wish to rush into a venture I might later regret.' I hesitated, then added upon impulse: 'My employer Mr Bransby happened to mention that Wavenhoe's is a sound concern.'

'Wavenhoe's, eh?' Rowsell shrugged. 'They have a good name, it is true, but lately there have been rumours – not that that means anything; the City is a perfect rumour mill, you understand, turning ceaselessly, grinding yesterday's idle speculations into tomorrow's facts. Mr Wavenhoe himself is an old man, and they say he delegates much of the day-to-day business of the bank to his partners.'

'And that is a cause of unease?'

'Not exactly. But the City does not like change, it may be no more than that. And if Mr Wavenhoe retires, or even dies, his absence may have an effect on confidence in the bank. That is no reflection on the bank itself necessarily, merely on human nature. If you wish, I shall make some inquiries on your behalf.'

I dined at an ordinary among plump lawyers and skinny clerks. My business had taken longer than I had anticipated, and I resolved to postpone my visit to Mrs Jem in Gaunt-court. After dinner, comfortable with beef and beer, I made my way up Southampton-row, passing the Allans' house. It was a fine autumn afternoon. With my new coat, my new position and my new fortune, I felt I had become a different Tom Shield altogether from the one I had been less than a month before.

As I walked, I observed the passers-by – chiefly the women. My eyes clung to a face beneath a bonnet, a pretty foot peeping beneath the hem of a dress, the curve of a forearm, the swell of a breast, a pair of bright eyes. I heard their laughter, their whispers. I smelt their perfume. Dear God, I was like a boy with his face pressed against the pastry-cook's window.

One struck me in particular, a tall woman with black hair, a high colour, and a fine full figure; as she climbed into a hackney I thought for an instant that she was Fanny, the girl I had once known, not as she had been then but as she might have become; and for a moment or two a cloud covered my happiness.

CHAPTER SEVEN

T HE FRANTS' HOUSE was on the south side of Russell-square. I rang the bell and waited. The brass plate sparkled. The paint was new. If a surface could be polished, it had been polished. If it could be scrubbed, it had been scrubbed.

A manservant answered the door, a tall fellow with a fleshy, hook-nosed face. I told him my name and business, and he left me to kick my heels in a big dining room overlooking the square. I walked over to the window and stared down at the square garden. The curtains were striped silk, cream and green, and the green seemed to have been chosen to match exactly the grass outside.

The door opened, and I turned to see Mr Henry Frant. As I did so, I looked for the first time at the wall beside the door, which was opposite the window. A portrait hung there, Mrs Frant to the life, sitting in a park with a tiny boy leaning against her knee and a spaniel stretched on the ground at her feet. In the distance was a prospect of a large stone-built mansion-house.

'You're Mr Bransby's usher, I collect?' Frant walked quickly towards me, his left hand in his pocket, bringing with him a scent of lavender water. He was the man I had seen at the carriage window in Ermine-street. 'The boy will be down in a moment.'

There was no sign of recognition on his face. I was too insignificant for him to have remembered me, of course, but it was also possible to believe that my own appearance had changed in the last month. Frant made no move to shake hands; nor was there an offer of refreshment or even a chair. There was an air of excitement about him, of absorption in his own affairs.

'The boy has milksop tendencies, fostered by his mother,' he announced. 'I particularly desire that these traits be eradicated.'

I bowed. In the portrait, Mrs Frant's small white hand toyed with a brown ringlet that had escaped the confines of her bonnet.

'He is not to be indulged, do you hear? He has had enough of that already. But now he is grown too old for the softness of women. It is time for him to learn to be a man. Behaving like a blushing maiden will be no good to him when he goes to Westminster. That is one reason why I have determined to send him to Mr Bransby's.'

'So he has never been to school before, sir?'

'He has had tutors at home.' Frant waved his right hand as though pushing them away, and the great signet ring on his forefinger gleamed as it caught the light from the window. 'He does well enough at his books. Now it is time for him to learn something equally useful: how to deal with his fellows. But I will not detain you any longer. Pray give my compliments to Mr Bransby.'

Before I could manage even another bow, Frant was out of the room, the door snapping shut behind him. I envied him: here was a man who had everything the gods could bestow including an air of breeding and consequence that sat naturally upon him, as though he were its rightful possessor. Even now, God help me, part of me envies him as he was then.

I waited another moment, studying the portrait. My interest, I told myself, was both pure and objective. I admired the painting as I might a beautiful statue or a line of poetry that spoke with both elegance and force to the heart. The brushwork was particularly fine, and the skin was exquisitely lifelike. Such beauty was refreshing, too, like a drink to a thirsty traveller. There was, therefore, no reason why I should not study it as much as I wished.

Ah, you will say, you were falling in love with Sophia Frant. But that is romantic nonsense. If you want plain speaking, I will give it you as

I gave it to myself on that fateful day: leaving artistic considerations aside, I disliked her because she had so much I lacked in the way of wealth and the world's esteem; and I also disliked her because I desired her, as I did almost any pretty woman I saw, and knew she could never be mine.

I heard footsteps outside the door and a high voice speaking indistinctly but loudly. I moved away and feigned an intense interest in the ormolu clock upon the mantel-shelf. The door opened and a boy rushed into the room, followed by a small, plain woman, dressed in black and with a wart on the side of her chin. What struck me immediately was that there was a remarkable resemblance between young Frant and Edgar Allan, the American boy. With their lofty brows, their bright eyes and their delicate features, they might almost have been brothers. Then I noticed the boy's attire.

'Good afternoon, sir,' he said. 'I am Charles Augustus Frant.'

I shook the offered hand. 'And I am Mr Shield.'

'And this is Mrs Kerridge, my – one of the servants,' the boy rushed on. 'There was no need for her to come down with me, but she insisted.'

I nodded to her and she inclined her head. 'I wished to ask if Master Charles's box had arrived at the school yet, sir.'

'I'm afraid I do not know. But I'm sure its absence would have been marked.'

'And my mistress desired me to say that Master Charles feels the cold. When the weather begins to turn, perhaps a flannel undershirt next to the skin might be advisable.'

The boy snorted. I nodded gravely. My mind was on the lad's clothes, though not in a way that Mrs Kerridge or indeed Mrs Frant would have liked. Whether at his own request or at his mother's whim, Master Charles was wearing a beautifully cut olive greatcoat with black frogs. He carried under his arm a hat from which depended a long and handsome tassel; he clutched a cane in his left hand.

'They're bringing the carriage round, sir,' Mrs Kerridge said, 'and Master Charles's valise is in the hall. Would you like anything before you go?'

The boy hopped from one leg to another.

'Thank you, no,' I said.

'There's the carriage.' He ran over to the window. 'Yes, it is ours.'

Mrs Kerridge looked up at me, squeezing her face to a frown. 'Poor lamb,' she murmured in a tone too low for him to hear. 'Never been away from home before.'

I nodded, and smiled in a way I hoped the woman would find reassuring. When we opened the door, a footman was waiting by the front door and a black pageboy, not much older than Charles himself, hovered over the valise. Charles Frant, smiling graciously at his father's servants, marched down the steps with a dignity befitting the Horse Guards, a dignity only slightly marred by the way he skipped up into the carriage. Mrs Kerridge and I followed more slowly, walking behind like a pair of acolytes.

'He is very young for his age, sir,' Mrs Kerridge muttered.

I smiled down at her. 'He's a handsome boy.'

'Takes after his mother.'

'Is she not here to say goodbye to him?'

'She's away nursing her uncle.' Mrs Kerridge grimaced. 'The poor gentleman's dying, and he ain't going easy. Otherwise Madam would be here. Will he be all right, sir? Boys can be cruel little varmints. He don't realise. He don't know many boys.'

'It may not be easy at first. But most boys find there is much to enjoy at school as well. Once they are used to it.'

'His mama frets about him.'

'It often happens that an event is more distressing in anticipation than it is in actuality. You must endeavour to –'

I broke off, realising that Mrs Kerridge was no longer looking at me. She had been distracted by the sight of a carriage whirling into the square from Montague-street. It was an elegant light chariot, painted green and gold, and drawn by a pair of chestnuts. The coachman slipped between two carts and brought the equipage to a standstill behind our own, the wheels neatly aligned within a couple of inches of the kerb. He sat back on the box with the air of a man well pleased with himself.

'Oh Lord,' muttered Mrs Kerridge, but she was smiling.

The glass slid down. I glimpsed a pale face and a mass of auburn curls partly concealed by a large hat adorned with grogram.

'Kerridge!' the girl called. 'Kerridge, dearest. Am I in time? Where's Charlie?'

Charles jumped out of the Frants' carriage and ran along the pavement. 'Do you like this rig, Cousin Flora? Mighty fine, ain't it?'

'You look very handsome,' she said. 'Quite the military man.'

He held his face up for her to kiss him. She leaned down and I had a better view of her. She was older than I had thought – a young woman; not a girl. Mrs Kerridge came forward to be kissed in her turn. Then the young woman's eyes turned to me.

'And who is this? Will you introduce us, Charlie?'

He coloured. 'I beg your pardon. Cousin Flora, allow me to name Mr Shield, an usher at Mr Bransby's – my school, you know.' He swallowed, and then gabbled, 'Mr Shield, my cousin Miss Carswall.'

I bowed. With great condescension, Miss Carswall held out her hand. It was a little hand that seemed to vanish within my own. She wore lilac-coloured gloves, I recall, which matched the pelisse she wore over her white muslin dress.

'You were about to convey my cousin to school, no doubt? I shall not detain you long, sir. I merely wished to say farewell to him, and to give him this.'

She undid the drawstring of her reticule and took out a small purse which she handed to him. 'Put it somewhere safe, Charlie. You may wish to treat your friends.' She bent down, kissed the top of his head, and gave him a little push away from her. 'Your mama sends her best love, by the by. I saw her for a moment at Uncle George's.'

For an instant the boy's face became perfectly blank, drained of the fun and excitement.

Miss Carswall patted his shoulder. 'She cannot leave him, not at this moment.' She looked over the boy to Mrs Kerridge and myself. 'I must not delay you any longer. Kerridge, dearest, may I drink tea with you before I go? It would be like old times.'

'Mr Frant is within, miss.'

'Oh.' The young lady gave a little laugh, and a look of understanding

30

passed between her and Mrs Kerridge. 'Good God, I had almost forgot. I am promised to Emma Trenton. Another time, perhaps, and we shall have a good old prose together.'

Miss Carswall's departure was the signal for ours. I followed Charlie into the Frants' carriage. A moment later we turned into Southampton-row. The boy huddled into the corner and turned his head to stare out of the far window. The tassel on that ridiculous hat swayed and bounced behind him.

Flora Carswall could never have been called beautiful, unlike Mrs Frant. But she had a quality of ripeness about her, like fruit waiting to be plucked, demanding to be eaten.

CHAPTER EIGHT

I FOUND IT difficult to sleep that night. My mind was possessed with a strange excitement that would not let me rest. I felt that during the day I had crossed from one part of my life into another, as though its events formed a river between two countries. I lay in my narrow bed, my body twitching and turning and sighing. I measured the passage of time by the striking of clocks. At last, a little after half-past one, my restlessness drove me from the warmth of my bed to smoke a pipe.

Mr Bransby held that snuff was the only form of tobacco acceptable to a gentleman so Dansey and I found it necessary to smoke outside. But I knew where the key to the side door was kept. A moment later I walked down the lawn, my footsteps making no noise on the wet grass. There were a few clouds but the stars were bright enough for me to see my way. To the south was a faint lessening of the darkness, a yellow haze, the false dawn of London by night, the city which never went to sleep. Beneath the trees it was completely dark. I smoked in the shelter of a copper beech, leaning against the trunk. Leaves stirred above my head. Tiny crackles and rustles near my feet hinted at the passage of small, secretive animals.

Then came another sound, a screech so sharp and hard and unexpected that I jerked myself away from the tree and almost choked on the smoke in my mouth. It came from the direction of the house. There was another, quieter noise, the scrape of metal against metal, followed by a smothered laugh.

I crouched and knocked out the pipe on the soft, damp earth. I moved forward, my feet making little sound on the leaf mould and the husks of last year's beech nuts. By now my eyes had grown accustomed to the near darkness. Something white was hanging from an attic window in the boys' wing. The room behind it was in darkness. I veered aside into the slightly deeper darkness running along the line of a hedge.

The attic was not in the same wing of the house as my own and Dansey's. Most of the boys slept in dormitories, with ten or twelve of them crammed together in one of the larger rooms below. But in this part of the attic storey, two or three boys might share one of the smaller rooms if their parents were willing to pay extra for the privilege.

Once again, I heard the gasp of laughter, snuffed out almost as soon as it began. Suddenly, and with an anger so sharp that it stabbed me like a knife, I knew what I had seen. I went quickly into the house, lit my candle and made my way to the stairs leading to the boys' attics. I found myself in a narrow corridor. By the light of the candle I saw five doors, all closed.

I tried the doors in turn until I found the one I wanted. I saw three truckle beds in the wavering glow of the candle flame. From two of them came the sound of loud, regular snoring. From the third came the broken breathing of a person trying not to cry. The window was closed.

'Which boys are in this room?' I demanded, not troubling to lower my voice.

One boy stopped snoring. To compensate, the other snored with redoubled force. The third boy, the one who had been trying not to cry, became completely silent.

I pulled the blankets from the nearest bed and tossed them on the floor. Its occupant continued to snore. I held the candle close to his face.

'Quird,' I said. 'You will wait behind after morning school.'

I stripped the covers from the next bed. Another boy stared up at me, making no pretence at sleep.

'You will accompany him, Morley.'

My foot caught on something on the floor. I bent down and made

33

out a length of rope like a basking snake, most of it pushed beneath Morley's bed.

With a grunt of anger, I threw off the covers from the third bed. There was Charlie Frant, his nightshirt rucked up above his waist and a handkerchief tied round his mouth.

I swore. I placed the candle on the windowsill, lifted the boy up and pulled down the nightshirt. He was trembling uncontrollably. I untied the handkerchief. The lad spat out a rag they had pushed inside his mouth. He retched once. Then, without a word, he fell back on the bed, turned away from me and buried his head in the pillow and began to sob.

Morley and Quird had hung him out of the window. The older boys had lashed his ankles round the central mullion to prevent him from breaking his neck on the gravel walk below.

'I will see you tomorrow,' I heard myself saying to them. 'At present, I cannot see any reason why I should not flog you twice a day and every day until Christmas.'

I wondered whether I should remove young Frant from his tormentors, but what would I do with him? The boy had to sleep somewhere. But the nub of the matter was that, sooner or later, by day or by night, young Frant would have to face up to Quird and Morley. Punishing them was one thing; but trying to shield him was another.

I went back to my own room. I did not sleep until dawn. When I did, it seemed only moments before the bell rang for another day of hearing little savages construe Ovid's *Metamorphoses*.

CHAPTER NINE

I WATCHED CHARLIE Frant in morning school, both before breakfast and after it. The boy sat by himself at the back of the room. I doubted if he turned a page of his book or even saw what was written on the one in front of him. His coat was now too bedraggled to have a military air. He had tear tracks on his cheeks, and his nostrils were caked with blood and mucus. Smears on the sleeve showed where he had wiped his nose.

At breakfast, I told Dansey what had happened in the night. The older man shrugged.

'If the boy goes to Westminster School, he'll get far worse than that.'

'But we cannot let it pass.'

'We cannot prevent it.'

'If the older boys would but exert some authority over the younger ones –'

Dansey shook his head. 'This is not a public school. We do not have a tradition of self-governance by the boys.'

'If I went to Mr Bransby, might he not expel them or at least discipline them – Quird and Morley, I mean?'

'You forget, my dear Shield: the true aim of this establishment is not an educational one. Considered properly, it is nothing but a machine for making money. That is why Mr Bransby has sunk his capital in it. That is why you and I are sitting here drinking weak coffee at Mr

Bransby's expense. Both Quird and Morley have younger brothers.' Dansey's lips twisted into their Janus-like frowning smile. 'Their fathers pay their bills.'

'Then is there nothing to be done?'

'You can beat the wretched boys so soundly that you reduce their ability to persecute their unfortunate friend. At least I can be of assistance in that respect.'

At eleven o'clock, after the second session of morning school, I flogged Morley and Quird harder than I had ever flogged a boy before. They did not enjoy it but they did not complain. Custom blunts even pain.

Later, I caught sight of Charlie Frant in the playground. Half a dozen boys had grouped around him in a ragged circle. They tossed the hat from one to the other, encouraging him to make ineffectual grabs for it. The hat had lost its tassel. Some wag had contrived to pin it on the back of the olive-green coat.

'Donkey,' they chanted. 'Who's a little donkey? Bray, bray, *bray*.'

When lessons resumed after dinner, Frant was not at his desk. He had hidden himself away to lick his wounds. I decided that if Lord Nelson could turn a blind eye to matters he did not wish to see, then so could I. I did not, however, turn a blind eye to either Quird or Morley. Their work, never distinguished, withered under the unremitting attention that I bestowed upon it. I gave them both the imposition of copying out ten pages of the geography textbook by the following morning.

Towards the end of afternoon school, the manservant came from Mr Bransby's part of the house and desired Dansey and myself to wait upon his master without delay. We found him in his study, pacing up and down behind his desk, his face dark with rage and a trail of spilt snuff cascading down his waistcoat.

'Here's a fine to-do,' he began without any preamble, before I had even closed the door. 'That wretched boy Frant.'

'He has absconded?' Dansey said.

Bransby snorted.

'Not worse, I hope?' There was the barest trace of amusement in

Dansey's voice, like an intellectual whisper pitched too low for Mr Bransby's range of comprehension. 'He has – harmed himself?'

Bransby shook his head. 'It appears that he strolled away, as cool as a cucumber, after the boys' dinner. He walked a little way and then found a carrier willing to give him a ride to Holborn. I understand that Mrs Frant is away from home but the servants at once sent word to Mr Frant.' He waved a letter as though trying to swat a fly. 'His stable boy brought this.'

He took another turn in silence up and down the room. We watched him warily.

'It is most vexing,' he continued at length, glowering at each of us in turn. 'That it should concern Mr Frant – the very man we should study to please in every particular.'

'Has he settled on withdrawing the boy?' Dansey asked.

'We are spared that, at least. Mr Frant wishes his son to return to us. But he demands that the boy be suitably chastised for his transgression so that he apprehends that the discipline of the school is firmly allied to paternal authority. Mr Frant desires me to send an under-master to collect his son, and he proposes that the under-master should flog the boy in his, that is to say Mr Frant's, presence and in the boy's own home. He suggests that in this way the boy will realise that he has no choice but to knuckle down to the discipline of the school and that by this he will learn a valuable lesson that will stand him in good stead in his later life.' Bransby's heavy-lidded eyes swung towards me. 'No doubt you were about to volunteer, Shield. Indeed, my choice would have fallen on you in any case. You are a younger man than Mr Dansey, and therefore have the stronger right arm. There is also the fact that I can spare you more easily than I can Mr Dansey.'

'Sir,' I began, 'is not such a course –?'

Dansey, standing behind me and to the left, stabbed his finger into my back. 'Such a course of action is indeed a trifle unusual,' he interrupted smoothly, 'but in the circumstances I have no doubt that it will prove efficacious. Mr Frant's paternal concern is laudable.'

Bransby nodded. 'Quite so.' He glanced at me. 'The stable boy has ridden back to town with my answer. The chaise from the inn will be

37

here in about half an hour. Be so good as to discuss with Mr Dansey how he should best discharge your evening duties as well as his own.'

'When will it be convenient for me to wait upon Mr Frant?'

'As soon as possible. You will find him now at Russell-square.'

A moment later, Dansey and I went through the door from the private part of the house to the school. A crowd of inky boys scattered as though we had the plague.

'Did you ever hear of anything so unfeeling?' I burst out, keeping my voice low for fear of eavesdroppers. 'It is barbaric.'

'Are you alluding to the behaviour of Mr Frant or the behaviour of Mr Bransby?'

'I – I meant Mr Frant. He wishes to make a spectacle of his own son.'

'He is entirely within his rights to do so, is he not? You would not dispute a father's right to exercise authority over his child, I take it? Whether directly or in a delegated form is surely immaterial.'

'Of course not. By the by, I must thank you for your timely interruption. I own I was becoming a little heated.'

'Mr Frant and his bank could purchase this entire establishment many times over,' Dansey observed. 'And purchase Mr Quird and Mr Morley as well, for that matter. Mr Frant is a fashionable man, too, who moves in the best circles. If it is at all possible, Mr Bransby will do all in his power to indulge him. It is not to be wondered at.'

'But it is hardly just. It is the boy's tormentors who deserve chastisement.'

'There is little point in railing against circumstances one cannot change. And remember that, by acting as Mr Bransby's agent in this, you may to some degree be able to palliate the severity of the punishment.'

We stopped at the foot of the stairs, Dansey about to go about his duties, I to fetch my hat, gloves and stick from my room. For a moment we looked at each other. Men are strange animals, myself included, riddled with inconsistencies. Now, in that moment at the foot of the stairs, the silence became almost oppressive with the weight of things unsaid. Then Dansey nodded, I bowed, and we went our separate ways.

CHAPTER TEN

I COME NOW to an episode of great significance for this history, to the introduction of the Americans.

Providence in the form of Mr Bransby decreed I should witness a scene of comings and goings in Russell-square. A man believes in Providence because to do otherwise would force him to see his life as an arbitrary affair, conducted by the freakish rules of chance, no more under his control than a roll of the dice or the composition of a hand of cards. So let us by all means believe in Providence. Providence arranged matters so that I should call at Mr Frant's on the same afternoon as the Americans arrived.

The shabby little chaise from the inn brought me to London. The vehicle creaked and groaned as though afflicted with arthritis. The seat was lumpy, the leather torn and stained. The interior smelt of old tobacco and unwashed bodies and vinegar. The ostler who was driving me swore at the horse, a steady stream of obscenity punctuated by the snapping of the whip. As we drove, the daylight drained away from the afternoon. By the time we reached Russell-square, the sky was heavy with dark, swirling clouds the colour of smudged ink.

My knock was answered by a footman, who showed me into the dining room to wait. Because of the weather and the lateness of the afternoon, the room was in near darkness. I turned my back on the portrait. Rain was now falling on the square, fat drops of water that smacked on to the roadway and tapped like drumbeats on the roof of the carriages. I heard voices in the hall, and the slam of a door.

A moment later the footman returned. 'Mr Frant will see you now,' he said, and jerked his head for me to follow him.

He led me across the marble chequerboard of the hall to a door which opened as we approached. The butler emerged.

'You are to desire Master Charles to step this way,' he told the footman.

The footman strode away. The butler took me into a small and square apartment, furnished as a book-room. Henry Frant was seated at a bureau, pen in hand, and did not look up. The shutters were up and candles burned in sconces above the fireplace and in a candelabrum on a table by the window.

The nib scratched on the paper. The candlelight glinted on Frant's signet ring and the touches of silver in his hair. At length he sat back, re-read what he had written, sanded the paper, and folded it. As he opened one of the drawers of the bureau, I noticed that he was missing the top joints of the forefinger on his left hand, a blemish on his perfection which pleased me. At least, I thought, I have something that you have not. He slipped the paper in the drawer.

'Open the cupboard on the left of the fireplace,' he said without looking at me. 'Below the shelves. You will find a stick in the right-hand corner.'

I obeyed him. It was a walking-stick, a stout malacca cane with a silver handle and a brass-shod point.

'Twelve good hard strokes, I think,' Mr Frant observed. He indicated a low stool with his pen. 'Mount him over that, with his face towards me.'

'Sir, the stick is too heavy for the purpose.'

'You will find it answers admirably. Use it with the full force of your arm. I desire to teach the boy a lesson.'

'Two older boys set on him at school,' I said. 'That is why he ran away.'

'He ran away because he is weak. I do not say he is a coward, not yet; but he might become one if indulged. Pray make it clear to Mr Bransby that I do not expect the school to indulge his weaknesses any

40

more than I do.' There was a knock on the door. He raised his voice. 'Come in.'

The butler opened the door. The boy edged into the room.

'Sir,' he began in a small, high voice. 'I hope I find you in good health, and –'

'Be silent,' Frant said. 'Wait until you are spoken to.'

The butler stood in the doorway, as if waiting for orders. In the hall behind were the footman and the little Negro pageboy. I glimpsed Mrs Kerridge on the stairs.

Frant looked beyond his son and saw the servants. 'Well?' he snapped. 'What are you gaping at? Do you not have work to do? Be off with you.'

At that moment the doorbell rang. The servants jerked towards it, as though attached to the sound by a set of strings. There was another ring, followed immediately by knocking. The footman glanced over his shoulder at the butler, who looked at Mr Frant, who squeezed his lips together in a tight, horizontal line and nodded. The footman scurried to the front door.

Mrs Frant slipped into the hall before the door was more than a foot or two ajar. A maid followed her in. Mrs Frant's colour was high as if she had been running, and she clutched her cloak to her throat. She darted across the squares of marble to the door of the book-room, where she stopped suddenly on the threshold, as though confronted by an invisible barrier. For a moment nobody spoke. Mrs Frant's grey travelling cloak slipped from her shoulders to the floor.

'Madam,' Frant said, standing up and bowing. 'I'm rejoiced to see you.'

Mrs Frant looked up at her husband but said nothing. He was a tall, broad man and beside him she looked as defenceless as a child.

'Allow me to name Mr Shield, one of Mr Bransby's under-masters.'

I bowed; she inclined her head.

Frant said, 'You are come from Albemarle-street? I hope I should not infer from this unexpected visit that Mr Wavenhoe has taken a turn for the worse?'

She glanced wildly at him. 'No – that is to say, yes, in that he is no worse and may even be slightly better.'

41

'What gratifying intelligence. Now, Mrs Frant, I do not know whether you are aware that your son has chosen to pay us an unauthorised visit from his school. He is about to pay the penalty for this, and then Mr Shield will convey him back to Stoke Newington.'

Mrs Frant glanced at me, and saw the malacca cane in my hand. I looked at the boy, who was shaking like a shirt on a washing line.

'May I speak with you, sir?' she said. 'A word in private?'

'I am afraid that at present I am not at leisure. Pray allow me to wait on you in the drawing room when Mr Shield and Charles have left us.'

'No,' Mrs Frant said so softly that I could hardly hear her. 'I must ask you —'

There came another ring on the doorbell.

'Confound it,' Frant said. 'Mr Shield, would you excuse us for a moment? Frederick will show you into the dining room. Close the door of this room, Loomis. Then see who that is. Neither Mrs Frant nor I are at home.'

I propped the cane against a bookcase and went into the hall. Mrs Kerridge moved towards the back of the house, shooing the maid before her. Loomis pulled open the front door. I glanced over his shoulder.

For an instant, I thought it was much later than it really was. Rain was now falling heavily over the square from a sky as black as coal. Through the doorway came the smell of freshly watered dust, and the hissing and pattering of the rain. The brief illusion of night was reinforced by an enormous umbrella stretching across the width of the doorway. Below it I glimpsed a small, grey man in a snuff-coloured coat.

'My name is Mr Noak,' announced the newcomer in a hard, nasal voice. 'Pray inform Mr Frant that I am here.'

'Mr Frant is not at home, sir. If you would like to leave your —'

'Nonsense, man. They told me at his place of business he was here. He is expecting me.'

The little man stepped into the hall and Loomis gave ground before him. Beside me, Frederick drew a sharp intake of breath, presumably at this breach of decorum, this frontal assault on Mr Loomis's authority. Noak was followed by another man, much taller and perhaps twice his weight, who backed into the hall, lowering, collapsing and shaking the umbrella. He turned round, holding out the dripping umbrella to Frederick. This fellow was a Negro, though not so dark as the pageboy and with a more European cast of features. He took off his hat, revealing close-cropped grey hair. His dark eyes examined the hallway, resting for a moment on me.

'Convey my card to Mr Frant,' Noak said, unbuttoning his coat and feeling in an inner pocket. 'Stay a moment. I shall write a word on the back.'

The butler did not even try to dissuade him. The little man had a natural authority which any schoolmaster would have envied. He found a pencil in his waistcoat and scribbled briefly on the back of the card. The Negro waited, his hat in his hands. The umbrella dripped on the floor. Frederick craned his neck, trying to see what Noak was writing. I edged nearer Mrs Kerridge to get a better view of proceedings. She glanced up at me and rubbed the wart on the side of her chin.

Noak handed the card to Loomis. 'I'm obliged to you.' He passed his hat to Frederick.

Loomis tapped on the book-room door and went inside. No one spoke in the hall. Noak turned his back towards Frederick and raised his arms, so the footman could help him out of his coat. The Negro was as still as a post, his eyes now fixed on a spot behind Mrs Kerridge's head.

The book-room door reopened, and to my surprise Mr Frant himself emerged, his face illuminated with a smile of welcome. The Negro's head swivelled towards Mr Frant, and the expression on his face had an element of calculation which reminded me of the way farmers at market look when assessing a calf or a mare. At the time it did not strike me as significant – but how could it have done? Only later did I realise what was really happening in the hall of the house in Russell-square.

'My dear sir,' Frant said, advancing towards Noak with his hand outstretched. 'This is indeed an honour. And I had not expected you so soon, though I left word with my clerk in case we were fortunate. You travelled post from Liverpool, I collect?'

'Yes, sir. We arrived a little after noon.'

'But I forget my manners.' Frant released Noak's hand and turned towards Mrs Frant, who was now standing in the doorway behind him. 'My dear, allow me to present Mr Noak of Boston, in the United States. You have often heard me speak of him – he is acquainted with the Allans and many of our other American friends. And this, sir, is Mrs Frant.'

She coloured becomingly and curtsied. 'How do you do, sir. You must be exhausted after your long journey.'

'And here is my son,' Frant continued before Noak could reply. 'Come, Charles, make your bow to Mr Noak.'

You must allow the gentry this, if nothing else: they know how to close ranks in front of strangers. You would never have guessed from their behaviour that the Frants were not the happiest of families. Mrs Frant smoothed her son's hair and smiled first at her guest and then at her husband. I fancied that the only symptom of her underlying agitation was her breathing: it seemed to me that her bosom rose and fell more rapidly than was natural.

'Charles is about to return to his school,' Mr Frant said. 'Pray excuse him.'

Noak inclined his head. 'I should not like to be the cause of interrupting a young man's education.'

He glanced briefly and incuriously in my direction; Frant had not considered me worth introducing. Mrs Frant smiled dazzlingly at Mr Noak, took the boy by his shoulders and steered him towards Mrs Kerridge.

'Charlie and Mr Shield will leave now,' Mrs Frant murmured. 'Make sure they take something to eat with them.' She added in a sudden rush, still in a whisper, 'But they must leave at once, Kerridge, the hour is already late. We have detained Mr Shield from his duties for too long.'

Mrs Kerridge curtsied.

Mrs Frant turned to me. 'I confide my son to your charge, sir. I regret we have inconvenienced you.'

I bowed, sensing that my own colour was rising. What you must realise is that she was beautiful, and her beauty had the power to invest the simplest words with charm. In her company I was like a man in the desert who stumbles on a pool of clear water fringed with palms. You will understand nothing of what follows unless you understand that.

'How did you come here?' she asked me.

'In a hired chaise, madam. It is outside.'

'Tell them to have it brought round to the area door. It – it will be quicker than using the hall door.'

Quicker, and more discreet. She hugged her son. Her husband and Mr Noak were chatting about the inconvenience of travelling post, at the mercy of other people's worn-out horses. I stared at the angle between her neck and shoulder and wondered how soft the skin would be, and what it would smell of.

She pushed Charles gently away from her. 'Go with Mr Shield, Charlie. And write to me often.'

'But Mama –'

'Go, dearest. Go quickly now.'

'This way, Master Charles.' Mrs Kerridge placed an arm over the boy's thin shoulders and urged him away from the front of the hall. Looking back at me, she added, 'If you would be so kind as to come this way, sir.'

She smiled at Mr Noak's man, still standing, still watching with grave interest.

'I am Mrs Kerridge, sir.'

'Salutation Harmwell, ma'am. At your service.'

'Come and dry out in the servants' hall. Perhaps we can offer you a little refreshment while you wait?'

He paused for a moment, as if contemplating the meaning of her question; then he bowed his assent, and for an instant his gravity dissolved into what was almost a smile.

I wondered how well Harmwell spoke English. He was undoubtedly a fine figure of a man, though, in any language. Aye, and Mrs Kerridge thought so too; I could tell that from the way she stumbled on the stairs and clung to his arm and thanked him so prettily for his support. It struck me for the first time that, though by no stretch of the imagination was she a handsome woman, she had a fine, mature figure and a pleasing smile when she chose to use it.

In the basement, the cook emerged and lured young Frant into her kitchen to select the contents of our hamper for the drive back to school.

I waited in the shadows by the staircase, ignored and feeling somewhat of a fool. Mrs Kerridge showed Mr Harmwell into the servants' hall. A moment later she returned, demanding a decanter of Madeira and a plate of biscuits. Unaware of my presence, she raised a finger to detain Frederick, who was about to fetch the chaise.

'What did that scrawny little fellow write on his card?' she muttered. 'Did you see?'

He glanced from side to side, then spoke in a low voice to match hers. 'Can't have been more than two or three words. I could only read one of them. Carswall.'

'*Mr* Carswall?'

Frederick shrugged. 'Who else?' He gave a snort of amusement. 'Unless it was Miss Flora.'

'Don't be pert,' Mrs Kerridge said. 'Well, well. You'd better fetch that hackney.'

As the footman was leaving, I shifted my weight from one foot to another. My boot creaked. Mrs Kerridge looked quickly in my direction, and then away. I kept my face bland. Perhaps she wondered whether I had marked the oddity of it. If Mr Frant had been eagerly awaiting the arrival of Mr Noak, why had not Mr Noak simply sent in his card? And why had the name of Carswall acted as his Open Sesame?

The page came clumping down the stairs with indecorous speed.

'Don't run, Juvenal,' snapped Mrs Kerridge. 'It ain't genteel.'

'The mistress told Mr Loomis to have the carriage brought round,' the boy gasped. 'Mr Wavenhoe's, that is, she come in that. She's a-going back to Albemarle-street.'

Frederick grinned. 'I wouldn't want to linger here if it was my uncle a-dying, and him as rich as half a dozen nabobs.'

'That's more than enough from you,' Mrs Kerridge said. 'It's not your place to go prattling about your betters. If you want to keep your situation, you'd better mind that tongue of yours.' She turned to me, no doubt to alert the others to my presence. 'Mr Shield, sir, I'm sorry to keep you waiting down here. Ah, here's Master Charles.'

The lad came out of the kitchen holding a basket covered with a cloth. Frederick called out that our chaise was at the door. A moment later, the boy and I were driving back to Stoke Newington. I unstrapped the hamper and Charlie Frant wept quietly into the napkin that had been wrapped round the warm rolls.

'In a year's time,' I said, 'you will smile at this.'

'I won't, sir,' he retorted, his voice thick with grief. 'I shall never forget this day.'

I told him all things passed, even memories, and I ate cold chicken. And as I ate, I wondered if I had spoken the truth: for how could a man ever forget the face of Mrs Frant?

CHAPTER ELEVEN

THE NEXT INCIDENT of this history would have turned out very differently if there had not been the physical resemblance between young Allan and Charlie Frant. The similarity between them was sufficiently striking for Mr Bransby on occasion to mistake one for the other.

On the day after my return from London, I gave Morley and Quird another flogging after morning school. I made them yelp, and for once I derived a melancholy satisfaction from the infliction of pain. Charlie Frant was pale but composed. I believed they had let him alone during the night. Morley and Quird were uncertain how far they could try me.

After dinner, I took a turn about the garden. It was a fine afternoon, and I strolled down the gravel walk to the trees at the end. On my left was a high hedge dividing the lawn from the part of the garden used as the boys' playground. The high, indistinct chatter of their voices formed a background to my meditations. Then a shriller voice, suddenly much louder than the rest as if its owner were becoming heated, penetrated my thoughts.

'He's your brother, isn't he? Must be. So is he a little bastard like you?'

Another voice spoke; I could not make out the words.

'You're brothers, I know you are.' The first voice was Quird's, made even shriller by the fact that it would occasionally dive deep down the register. 'A pair of little bastards – with the same mother, I should think, but different fathers.'

'Damn you,' cried a voice I recognised as Allan's, anger making his American twang more pronounced than usual. 'Do not insult my mother.'

'I shall, you little traitor bastard. Your mother's a – a nymph of the pavey. A – a fellow who knows her saw her in the Haymarket. She's nothing but a moll.'

'My mother is dead,' Allan said in a low voice.

'Liar. Morley saw her, didn't you, Morley? So you're a bastard and a liar.'

'I'm not a liar. My mother and father are dead. Mr and Mrs Allan adopted me.'

Quird made a noise like breaking wind. 'Oh yes, and I'm the Emperor of China, didn't you know, you Yankee bastard?'

'I'll fight you.'

'You? You little scrub. Fight me?'

'One cannot always fight with the sons of gentlemen,' said the American boy. 'Much as one would prefer it.'

There was a moment's silence, then the sound of a slap.

'I *am* a gentleman!' cried Quird with what sounded like genuine anguish. 'My papa keeps his carriage.'

'Steady on,' Morley intervened, croaking like a raven. 'If there's to be a fight, you must have it in the regular manner.' Morley was older than his friend, a hulking youth of fourteen or fifteen. 'After school, and you must find yourself a bottle-holder, Allan. I shall act for Quird.'

'He'll have the other little bastard,' Quird said, 'the one we put out of the window. That was famous sport, but this will be even better.'

I could not intervene. From time immemorial, fighting had been commonplace in schools. The little boys aped the bigger ones. An establishment such as Mr Bransby's aped the great public schools. The public schools aped the noble art of pugilism on the one hand and the mores of the duel on the other. It was one thing for me to intervene in an episode of nocturnal bullying, but quite a different one for me to seek to prevent a fight conducted with the tacit approval of Mr Bransby. I own that I was surprised by the tenderness of my own feelings. I was perfectly accustomed to the knowledge that boys are rough little animals and maul each other like puppies.

There was a good deal of whispering during afternoon school. The older boys, I guessed, had seized with enthusiasm the opportunity to organise the fight. I consulted with my colleague Dansey, who told me, as I knew he would, that I must leave well alone.

'They will not thank you, Shield. Boys are morally fastidious creatures. They would consider you had interfered in an affair of honour.'

By the time supper came, nothing had happened. That was plain from the unmarked countenances of Quird and Allan, and from the buzz of excited whispering that spread up and down the long tables.

'It will be after supper, I fancy,' Dansey observed. 'There will still be enough light, and Mr Bransby will be safe in his own quarters. They should have well over an hour to beat each other into pulp before bedtime.'

I did not know the result of the fight until the following morning. It did not come as a surprise. There are cases when Jack kills the Giant to universal approbation, but they are few and far between. Quird was at least a head taller than Allan and a couple of stone heavier. Arm in arm with Morley, Quird swaggered into morning school. Edgar Allan, on the other hand, sported two black eyes, a grazed cheekbone and swollen lips.

I looked for, and found, reasons for me to give impositions to Morley and Quird which would keep them occupied after prayers every evening for a week. Sometimes it is easier to punish the wicked than to defend the innocent.

Gradually I discovered that the defeat was widely recognised as having been an honourable one. Dansey told me that he had overheard two older boys talking about the fight at breakfast: one had said that the little Yankee was a well plucked 'un, to which the other had replied that he had fought like the very devil and that Quird should be ashamed of himself for picking on such a youngster.

'So you see there's no harm in it,' Dansey said. 'None in the world.'

CHAPTER TWELVE

OVER THE NEXT few days I did not pay much attention to Charlie Frant and the American boy. I saw them, of course, and noted that they showed no further marks of mistreatment, or rather no more than one would expect to find on small boys in their situation. I was aware, however, that they often sat together and played together. Once I overheard two older boys pretending to mistake one for the other, but in a jocular way that suggested that the resemblance between them had become a source of friendly amusement rather than mockery.

The next event of importance to this history occurred on Monday the 11th October. The boys were more or less at leisure during the period between the end of morning school at eleven o'clock and their dinner two hours later. They might play, write letters, or do their preparation. They were also allowed to request permission to make excursions to the village.

Their movements outside the school, however, were strictly regulated, at least in theory. Mr Bransby had decreed, for example, among other things, that boys should patronise certain establishments and not others. Only the older boys were permitted to purchase liquor, for which they required special permission from Mr Bransby. The older boys ignored the condition, usually with impunity, and were frequently drunk at weekends and on holidays; and some of the younger ones were not slow to follow their example. But I own I was surprised when I saw Charlie Frant ineffectually attempting to conceal a pint bottle beneath his coat.

I had walked into the village in order to buy a pipe of tobacco. On my way back to the school, I happened to pass the yard entrance of the inn which hired out hacks. There was really no avoiding the meeting. Looking as furtive as a pair of housebreakers, Frant and Allan edged out of the yard immediately in front of me. I was on their left, but their attention was to their right, towards the school, in other words, the direction from which they expected trouble. Frant actually knocked into me. I watched the shock spreading over his features.

'What have you got there?' I asked sternly.

'Nothing, sir,' replied Charlie Frant.

'Don't be a fool. It looks remarkably like a bottle. Give it me.'

He passed it to me. I pulled out the cork and sniffed. The contents smelled of citrus and spirits.

'Rum-shrub, eh?'

The boys stared up at me with wide, terrified eyes. Rum-shrub was something of a favourite among the older boys at the Manor House School, for the combination of rum with sugar and orange or lemon juice offered them a cheap, sweet and rapid route to inebriation. But it was not a customary beverage for ten-year-olds.

'Who told you to purchase this?' I inquired.

'No one, sir,' said Frant, staring at his boots and blushing.

'Well, Allan, is your memory any better?'

'No, sir.'

'In that case, I shall be obliged if you would both wait on me after supper.' I slipped the bottle into my coat pocket. 'Good day.'

I walked on, swinging my stick and wondering which of the older boys had sent them out. I would have to beat Allan and Frant, if only for the look of the thing. Allan and Frant followed me round the corner. I glanced back, in time to see a man coming up behind them. He was a tall figure, clad in a blue coat with metal buttons.

'Boy,' the man said, taking Charlie by the arm with a large hand and bending down to peer into his face. 'Come here – let me look at you.'

His face was turned away from me, but it was the voice that was somehow familiar – deep, husky and audible though the man spoke little above a whisper. He must have seen me ahead but cannot have realised my connection with the boys.

'Let go,' Charlie said, trying to tug himself away.

'You'll do as I ask, my boy, because –'

'Let him go, sir,' snapped Allan in his high voice. He took hold of Charlie's other arm and tried to pull him away.

Charlie saw me. 'Sir! Mr Shield!'

The man raised his stick. I was not sure which boy he intended to hit. I did not wait to find out but shouted and broke into a run.

'That is enough, sir. Leave the boys alone.'

He released his grip on Charlie and swung towards me. 'And who the devil are you?'

'Their master.'

He screwed up his forehead. His eyes were hidden by dark glasses. I could not tell whether he recognised me or not.

'Damn you,' he said.

'Be off with you. Or I shall call the constable.'

The man's face changed: it was as though the features were dissolving into a puddle of discoloured flesh. 'I meant no harm, sir, I take my oath on it. Won't you pity an old soldier? All I hoped was that these two young gents might be able to oblige me with the price of a little refreshment.'

I suppressed the temptation to give him the bottle of rum-shrub. Instead I raised my stick. He muttered a few words I could not catch and walked rapidly away, his shoulders rounded.

Charlie Frant looked up at me with his mother's eyes. 'Thank you, sir.'

'I suggest you return to school before you fall into more mischief,' I said.

They scuttled down the lane. I wondered if I should accost the man but he was already out of sight. So I followed the boys, walking slowly and cudgelling my brains to find an explanation while wondering whether an explanation was in fact required. Here was an old reprobate, I told myself, a drunkard lurking in the environs of an inn in the hope of cadging a drink. No doubt he had seen the two little boys with their bottle of rum-shrub leaving the tap and he had followed them as a hunter follows his prey.

It was the most natural thing in the world, a man would think, nothing strange about it. But to me there was something strange. I could not be sure but I believed I might have seen the fellow before. Was it he who had accosted me the previous week outside Mr Allan's house in Southampton-row? The coat and hat were different, and so was the accent; but the voice itself was similar, and so were the blue spectacles and the beard like an untidy bird's nest.

CHAPTER THIRTEEN

I TOOK THE coward's way out and did not pursue the matter. After supper I flogged the little boys as lightly as I could while preserving the decencies. Both of them thanked me afterwards, as custom dictated. Allan was pale but apart from grunting when the blows fell gave no sign of pain; Frant wept silently, but I turned my eyes away so that he would not know that I had seen his moment of weakness. He was the gentler of the two, who followed where Edgar Allan led.

Mr Bransby usually exchanged a few words with Dansey and myself when we waited upon him before evening prayers. That evening I took the opportunity of this meeting to mention to him that Frant and Allan had been accosted by a drunk in the village during the afternoon. I added that I had been on hand to deal with the man, so no harm had been done.

'He pestered young Frant, you say?' Bransby was in a hurry (he never lingered before or after evening prayers because he dined immediately afterwards). 'Well, no harm done. I'm glad you were at hand to deal with him.'

'I believe I may have seen the vagabond in town the other day, sir. He claimed acquaintance with Allan's father.'

'These fellows try their luck everywhere. What are the magistrates doing, to let them roam the streets and pester honest folk?'

Mr Bransby said nothing further on that occasion. But there was a sequel the following week. On the twentieth, he desired me to wait upon him after morning school.

'Sit down, Shield, sit down,' he said with unusual affability, taking a pinch of snuff and sneezing. 'I have had a letter concerning you from Mrs Frant. It seems that Master Charles sent her a highly coloured account of your dispute with the vagabond the other day. You are quite a hero among the little boys, I find.'

I inclined my head but said nothing.

'There is also the point that tomorrow is the fourteenth anniversary of the Battle of Trafalgar, and therefore a half holiday for the school.'

I was well aware of this, as was everyone else in the school. Mr Bransby had a cousin who had distinguished himself in the service, who had seen action at Trafalgar, and who had once shaken Lord Nelson himself by the hand. As a result, Mr Bransby had a great respect for the achievements of the Royal Navy.

'Mrs Frant proposes that the boy spend his half holiday with her in London. She has invited Allan as well. I understand he too performed heroically in the great battle of Stoke Newington.'

Bransby looked expectantly at me. He was neither a subtle humorist nor a habitual one, and I found his efforts so unnerving that all I could manage was a weak smile.

'Furthermore,' he continued, 'Mrs Frant suggests that you accompany the lads. I trust you will not find that an inconvenience?'

I bowed again, and said that it would be no trouble in the world.

The following afternoon, the carriage was waiting for us after the boys' dinner. Both Charlie Frant and Edgar Allan were in an ebullient mood, and eager to be away from school.

'Shall you call on your parents while you are in town?' I asked the American boy.

'No, sir. They are away from home.'

'And they are not his parents, sir,' said Charlie, squirming with the excitement of being privy to information that he believed I lacked. 'They are his foster parents.'

I glanced at Edgar. 'Indeed?'

Charlie reddened. 'Should I not have said? You do not mind, Edgar?'

'There is no secret.' Allan turned to me. 'Yes, sir, my parents died when I was an infant. Mr and Mrs Allan took me into their home and have always treated me as a son.'

'I'm sure you repay their kindness,' I replied and gestured at random at the world beyond the window of the Frants' carriage. 'Is that a swallow or a house-martin?'

The distraction was clumsy but effective. We talked of other matters for the remainder of the journey. When we got to Russell-square, I went into the house with the boys to discover when Mrs Frant wished me to return for them. Loomis, the butler, desired me to step upstairs with the boys. He showed us into the drawing room. Mrs Frant was seated by one of the windows with a book in her hand. Charlie, no doubt aware of the presence of Allan and myself, was very cool and composed with her, submitting to her embrace rather than returning it. A moment later, she turned to me, her hand outstretched.

'I must thank you, sir,' she said. 'I shudder to think what might have happened to Charlie had you not been at hand to help him.'

'You must not magnify the danger he was in, madam,' I said, thinking that her hand was soft and warm like a living bird.

'But a mother can never exaggerate the dangers that face her child, Mr Shield. And this is Edgar Allan?'

As she was shaking hands with him, Charlie piped up: 'His grandpapa was a soldier, Mama, like mine. They might have fought each other. He was a general in the American Revolutionary army.'

Mrs Frant looked inquiringly at Edgar.

'Yes, ma'am. That is to say, he is widely known as General Poe among his friends and neighbours, but my foster father Mr Allan has informed me that he did not in fact hold that rank. I believe he was a major.'

'And his mama was a famous English actress,' Charlie went on, though I could see the conversation was causing Edgar some embarrassment.

'How charming,' Mrs Frant said. 'You come from a talented family. What was her name?'

'Elizabeth Arnold, madam. Though English, she acted mainly in the United States. And it was there that she died.'

'You poor boy.' She turned the conversation: 'Perhaps you should visit cook before you do anything else. I shouldn't be at all surprised if she had baked something for you.'

The boys clattered out of the room, relieved to be away from the company of their elders. For the first time I was quite alone with Mrs Frant. Her dress rustled as she crossed the room from the window and sat down upon a Grecian sofa of carved mahogany. The air moved around me as she passed, and I smelt her perfume. I was seized by a crazy desire to kneel at her feet, throw my arms around her and bury my head in the sweet softness of her lap.

'Would you care for some tea, Mr Shield?' she asked.

'Thank you, madam, but no.' I had spoken abruptly, and I hastened to smooth the refusal with a lie. 'I have several errands I must complete. When would you like me to return?'

'I have ordered the carriage for half-past six o'clock. If you wish to come earlier, perhaps at six, the boys will be having their supper and I'm sure you could join them.' There was a delicious touch of pink to her pale complexion, and she began to speak faster. 'I would ask you to dine with us, but my husband prefers to sit down at a later time.'

I bowed my acknowledgement of her condescension and a moment later said goodbye. When the door of the drawing room was safely closed behind me, I dabbed my forehead and felt the sweat. I was terrified by the strength of my own desire.

I walked slowly down the stone steps to the hall. Loomis was waiting at the bottom. As I drew nearer, he gave a gentle cough.

'Mr Frant desired me to ask you to step in and see him on your way out, sir.'

I followed the servant to the book-room at the back of the hall. He knocked at the door, opened it and announced me. Mr Frant was seated at his bureau, as he had been on the other occasion I had visited him here. This time, however, my welcome was altogether more cordial. He looked up from a letter he was reading, and a smile spread across his pale features.

'Mr Shield – I am rejoiced to see you. Pray sit down. I will not delay you long.' He folded the letter and locked it away in a drawer. 'My wife informs me that you rendered us a considerable service the other day.'

'It was nothing of consequence, sir,' I said, embarrassed that the Frants were making so much of the incident.

'Nevertheless, I am obliged to you. Tell me, would you describe to me exactly what occurred?'

I explained that an older boy had sent Frant and Allan upon an errand – I did not judge it prudent to enlarge upon its nature – and that the man had approached them on their way back. I added that I had been fortunate enough to witness the moment when the man accosted the boys.

'What exactly did he do, Mr Shield?'

'He took Charles by the arm.'

'Why would he do that if he were a beggar? Would he not ask for money instead?'

'I think it likely his wits were disordered, sir. He had been drinking. I cannot say whether he intended to offer violence or whether his design was simply to attract the boys' attention and demand money. Young Allan tried to drag Charles away.'

'A brave lad. The man was carrying a stick, I understand?'

'Yes, sir.'

'And he offered you violence?'

'Yes, sir, but it didn't signify – I had a stick myself and I fancy that even without it I would not have been in difficulties.'

'My son told his mama the man was somewhat larger than you.'

'True, sir, but on the other hand I am somewhat younger.'

Henry Frant turned aside to sharpen a pencil. 'Would you indulge my curiosity a little further and describe him?'

'He was well above the middle height and had an ill-trimmed beard. He wore blue spectacles, and a blue coat with metal buttons and I think brown breeches. Oh, and a cocked hat and a wig.' I hesitated. 'There's one more thing, sir. I cannot be absolutely certain, but I believe I may have seen him before.'

'The devil you have. Where?'

'In Southampton-row. It was on the day I came to collect your son when he first went to school. I took Edgar Allan to his parents' house on the way. The man was loitering, and asked me when I was leaving if that was Mr Allan's, and then he hurried away.'

Frant tapped his teeth with the pencil. 'If he were interested in Allan's boy, then why should he attach himself to mine? It makes no sense.'

'No, sir. But the two boys are not unlike. And I noticed the man stooped to look at me.'

'So you formed the impression he might be short-sighted? Perhaps. I will be candid, Mr Shield. A man in my situation makes enemies. I am a banker, you understand, and bankers cannot please everybody all the time. There is also the point that a certain type of depraved mind might consider stealing the child of a wealthy man in order to extort money. This attack may be no more than a chance encounter, the casual work of a drunkard. Or it may be that the man was more interested in Mr Allan's boy. But there remains the third possibility: that he nursed a design of some sort against my son, or even in the long run against myself.'

'To judge by what little I have seen of him, sir, I would doubt that he could put any design successfully into action, apart, perhaps, from that of raising a glass or a bottle up to his lips.'

Frant gave a bark of laughter. 'I like a man who speaks plain, Mr Shield. May I ask you not to mention what we have discussed to my wife? Speculation of this nature must inevitably distress her.'

I bowed. 'You may depend on me, sir.'

'I take this kindly, Mr Shield.' Frant glanced at the clock on the mantel-shelf. 'One more thing, for my own private satisfaction I should like to meet this fellow and ask him a few questions. Should you come across him again, would you be good enough to let me know? Now, I must not keep you any longer from your half holiday.'

He shook hands cordially with me. A moment later I was walking down to Holborn. My mind was in a whirl. There is something intensely gratifying about being treated civilly by people of wealth and indeed fashion. I felt myself a fine fellow.

Perhaps, I thought as I strolled through the autumn sunshine, my luck was changing. With Mr and Mrs Frant as my patrons, where might I not end?

CHAPTER FOURTEEN

T HE AFTERNOON UNEXPECTEDLY changed its course as
I was walking down Long Acre on my way to Gaunt-court and
Mrs Jem's six shillings, the balance of the price we had agreed for
my aunt Reynolds's possessions. I stopped to buy a buttonhole and,
while the woman was fixing it to my lapel, I glanced over her shoulder
along the way I had come. I saw some twenty-five yards away, quite
distinctly, the man with the bird's-nest beard.

As if aware I had recognised him, he ducked into the shadow of a
shop doorway. I gave the girl a penny and hurried back along the street.
He plunged out of the doorway and blundered into one of the side roads
leading down to Covent Garden.

Without conscious thought, I set off in pursuit. I acted upon impulse
– partly, no doubt, because Mr Frant wanted to know more about the
man, and I welcomed an opportunity to oblige Mr Frant. But there was
both more and less to it than that: I was like a cat chasing a rope's end:
I chased the man not because I wanted to catch him but because he
moved.

The market was drawing to its close for the day. We pushed our way
into a swirling sea of humanity and vegetables. There was a tremendous
din – of iron-shod wheels and hooves on cobbles, of half a dozen barrel
organs, each playing a different tune, of people swearing and shouting
and crying their wares. Despite his age and weight and condition, my

quarry was remarkably agile. We zigzagged through the market, where he tried to conceal himself behind a stall selling oranges. I found him out, but he saw me, and off he went again. He leapt like a hunter over a wheelbarrow full of cocoa nuts, veered past the church and swerved into the mouth of Henrietta-street.

It so happened that there was a pile of rotting cabbage leaves on the corner and this, quite literally, was his downfall. He slipped and went down. Though he tried at once to scramble up, his ankle gave way and he sank back, swearing. I seized him by the shoulder. He straightened his spectacles and looked up at me, his face red with exertion.

'I meant no harm, sir,' he panted in that absurdly deep voice. 'As God is my witness, I meant no harm.'

'Then why did you run away?'

'I was afraid, sir. I thought you might set the constables on me.'

'Then why did you follow me in the first place?'

'Because –' He broke off. 'It does not matter.' His voice took on a richer note and the words that followed fell into a rhythm, like words often repeated: 'I give you my word, sir, as one gentleman to another, that I am as innocent as the day is long. It is true that I have fallen upon evil times but the fault has not been mine. I have been unlucky in the choice of my companions, perhaps, and cursed by a generous spirit, by a fatal tendency to trust my fellow men. Yet –'

'Enough, sir,' I interrupted. 'Why have you been following me?'

'A father's feelings,' he said, beating himself on the breast with both fists, 'may not be denied. The heart which beats within this breast is that of a gentleman of an old and distinguished Irish family.'

By now he was kneeling in the gutter and a knot of spectators was gathering around us to enjoy the spectacle.

'Bloody clunch,' an urchin cried. 'He's dicked in the nob.'

'Which, you may ask, has been the worst of my many losses?' my companion continued. 'Was it the loss of my patrimony? My enforced departure from my native heath? Was it the bitter knowledge that my reputation has been unjustly besmirched by men not fit to brush my coat? Was it disappointment in my profession and the loss, through the intemperate jealousy of others, of my hopes of regaining my fortune by my own exertions? Was it the death of the beloved wife of my bosom? No, sir, bad though all these things were, none of them was the worst blow to befall me.' He raised his face to the sky. 'As heaven is my witness, no sorrow compares with the loss of my little cherubs, my beloved children. Two fine sons had I, and a daughter, destined to be the delights of my maturity and the supports of my old age. Alas, they have been snatched away from me.' He paused to wipe his eyes with the sleeve of his coat.

'If that was a play,' observed another of our audience, 'I wouldn't pay a penny to see it. I wouldn't pay a bloody ha'penny. A bloody farthing.'

'You repugnant rapscallion!' the man roared, shaking his fist at the boy. Once more he lifted his face to the sky. 'Why, heaven?' he inquired. 'Why do I bare my innermost heart before the vulgar herd?'

'Who are you calling names then?' said another voice.

'The gentleman is unwell,' I said firmly.

'No, he ain't. He's half-cocked.'

'Perhaps his wits are a little disordered,' I conceded, helping my captive to his feet.

The big man began to weep. 'The lad speaks no more than the truth, sir,' he said, leaning so heavily on me that I could scarce bear his weight. 'I'll not deny that in my sorrow I have occasionally found consolation in a glass of brandy.' He brought his lips close to my ear. 'Indeed, now you mention it, a drop of something warming would be a most effective prophylactic against this autumn chill which even now I feel creeping over me.'

I led him, mumbling, down Henrietta-street. The crowd dropped away from us for the man was no longer amusing. In Bedford-street, he steered me to a tavern where we sat opposite each other in a corner. My guest thanked me kindly for my hospitality and ordered brandy and water. I asked for porter. When the girl brought the drinks, he raised his glass to me and said, 'Your health, sir.' He drank deeply and then looked inquiringly at me. 'You do not drink.'

'I am wondering whether I should have you arrested and given in charge,' I said. 'I regret that I shall be compelled to do so if you do not tell me the nature of your interest in myself and in the boys you waylaid in Stoke Newington.'

'Ah, my dear sir.' He spread his hands wide. He was calmer now, almost at his ease, and the mellifluous tone of his voice was oddly at variance with his dishevelled appearance. 'But I have already explained. Or rather I was in the middle of doing so when that pack of ruffians interrupted me.'

'I am at a loss to understand you.'

'The boy, of course,' he said impatiently. 'The boy is my son.'

CHAPTER FIFTEEN

I RETURNED TO Russell-square shortly after six o'clock, having missed my six shillings from Mrs Jem; in fact, thanks to Mr Poe, I was poorer than before and had acquired a slight headache. The door was answered by the footman, Frederick, whom I had met before. I desired him to inquire whether his master was at leisure. A moment later, Mr Frant came down the stairs, asked me how I did with the utmost cordiality, and led me into the book-room.

He looked keenly at me and seemed to divine in my countenance the reason for my presence. 'You have intelligence of the man who assaulted Charles?'

'Yes, sir. After leaving you, I was walking down to Leicester-square. It appears he had been loitering in the neighbourhood, and followed me.'

There were spots of colour in Frant's sallow cheeks. 'Why should he do that? Are you the reason for his interest?'

'I believe not. I chanced to see him behind me. He ran off but I gave chase.'

Frant made an impatient movement with his hand, which warned me to be brief.

'The long and the short of it is I brought him down and then gave him a drink afterwards. He confided that he is an Irish-American who has fallen on hard times. His name is Poe, David Poe. His family believe him dead.'

'And what does he want with you and the boys?'

'The object of his interest is Edgar Allan, sir, and he hoped I might lead him to the boy this afternoon. He alleges that the Allans are merely foster parents – which I have heard from the boy's own lips, by the way – and that Edgar is in fact his son. He told me that circumstances forced him to leave his wife in New York, and that she shortly afterwards died in Richmond, Virginia, leaving three children.'

'Assuming he speaks the truth, what does he want from his son? Money?'

'Quite possibly. Yet he may not have acted entirely from self-interest.'

Frant gave his bark of laughter. 'You surely do not suggest that he has suddenly been overwhelmed by the weight of his paternal responsibilities?'

'No – yet a man may sometimes act from more than one motive. Perhaps he is curious. There may even be a streak of tender sentiment in him. He told me he merely wanted to see the boy, to hear him speak.'

Frant nodded. 'Once again, Mr Shield, I am obliged to you. Where does he lodge? Did you find that out?'

'He declined to give me his precise direction. He lives in St Giles. As you know, it is a perfect maze of alleys and courts and he doubted I could find his lodging even if he told me where it was. But he informed me he is often to be found in a nearby tavern, the Fountain. He plies his trade there.'

'He is gainfully employed?'

'As a screever.'

Frant shrugged. 'And takes his fees in gin, no doubt.'

He fell silent and took a turn about the room. In a moment, he said, 'So you have done me a second service, Mr Shield. May I ask you to do a third?'

I bowed.

'I would be obliged if you would preserve the utmost discretion about this. Considered in all its aspects, this is a delicate matter. Not so much for you or me but for others. I see a good deal of Mr Allan in the way of business, and I know he is fond of the boy, and treats him as his son. The arrival of someone claiming to be the lad's natural father would come as a profound shock. Indeed, I understand Mrs Allan is in delicate health and such a shock could kill her.'

'You think Mr Poe may be an impostor?'

'It is possible. Some reprobate American, perhaps, who knows of Mr Allan's wealth, and his generosity towards the boy and his affection for him. Then we must consider Mr Bransby, must we not? Should this matter become public, and should it also become known that an Irish rogue from St Giles preyed on boys while they were in the care of Mr Bransby, then I do not imagine the effect upon the school would be a healthy one. A school is like a bank, Mr Shield, in that there must be mutual trust between the institution and its customers, in this case between the school and the parents who pay the bills. A rumour of this affair, should it get out, would spread widely, and no doubt become exaggerated in the telling.'

'Then what is to be done, sir?' I was alive to the fact, as no doubt Mr Frant intended I should be, that my welfare was to some extent tied to the school's, and that if Mr Bransby's profits diminished, then so might the size of his establishment.

'I am also mindful that young Edgar Allan has been a friend to my boy,' Frant went on, as though thinking aloud, as though I had not spoken. 'So, taken all in all, I think we should encourage the *soidisant* Mr Poe to – ah – neglect his duties as a father. I shall make it worth his while, of course.' He gave me a sudden, charming smile. 'Mr Bransby is indeed fortunate in his assistants. Should you ever tire of the teaching profession, Mr Shield, let me know. There are always openings to be found for young men of parts and discretion.'

Twenty minutes later, the boys and I rattled away from that big, luxurious house in Russell-square. The boys chatted happily about what they had done and what they had eaten. I sat back in my corner, enjoying the feel of the leather and the faint smell of Mrs Frant's perfume. I confess that during the day my opinion of Henry Frant had changed considerably. Previously I had thought him a proud and disagreeable man. Now I knew there was a more amiable side to him. I toyed with a pleasant dream in which Mr Frant used his influence to obtain for me a well-paid sinecure in Whitehall or brought me into Wavenhoe's Bank to work as his secretary. Stranger things had happened, I told myself, and why should they not happen to me?

CHAPTER SIXTEEN

S UCH WAS MY naïveté, I believed that my aunt's attorney Mr
Rowsell had conceived a sudden liking for me. The apparent proof
of this came in the form of an invitation to dinner.

He wrote that there was another document to be signed in connection
with my aunt's estate. Moreover, he had devoted some thought to the
question of how I might lay out my modest nest-egg to best advantage.
He believed he was now in a position to offer me some advice, should
I wish to receive it. Unless I preferred to call on him in Lincoln's Inn,
Mrs Rowsell would be pleased if I would dine with them on any Saturday
I cared to name. He understood, of course, that my time was not at
present my own, but no doubt my employer would understand how
desirable it was that the disposition of my aunt's estate should be
completed as soon as possible.

The Rowsells lived at Northington-street in the neighbourhood of
Theobalds-road. On Saturdays, Mr Rowsell went to Lincoln's Inn during
the morning and they dined at five. When I arrived, Mrs Rowsell made
a brief appearance, her face flushed, wiping floury hands upon her apron.
She was a plump lady, considerably younger than Mr Rowsell. Having
greeted me, she made her excuses and returned to the kitchen.

Mr Rowsell seemed to have forgotten the original purpose of my
visit. He called for the children, who had been with their mother. There
were four of them, ranging in age from three to nine. Puffing with

exertion, he led us up to the sitting room on the first floor where I did my best to amuse the elder boy and girl with card tricks and the like.

The dinner was served in a parlour at the front of the house. Mrs Rowsell was plainly anxious, but as the dishes succeeded each other without accident she became more cheerful. After we had attacked an enormous suet pudding and retired defeated, the cloth was withdrawn and Mrs Rowsell left us to our wine. As she passed round the table to the door, her husband leaned backwards in his chair and, believing himself unobserved by me, pinched her thigh. She squealed – 'Oh la! Mr Rowsell!' – smacked his hand away and scuttled out of the room.

Mr Rowsell beamed at me. 'Man was born for the married state, Mr Shield. The benefits it brings are inestimable. A toast, sir! A toast! Let us drink to Hymen.'

It was the first of many toasts. By the time we had finished the second bottle of port Mr Rowsell was lying back in his chair, glass in hand, his clothes loosened, trying to recall the words of a sentimental ballad of his youth. He exuded benevolence. Yet his little blue eyes often stared at me in a fixed manner I found uncomfortable, and it occurred to me that perhaps he was less drunk than he appeared. I dismissed the idea almost at once because there was surely no reason for him to deceive me.

With the third bottle, he put music aside and talked with unexpected eloquence about money, a subject that interested him in the abstract: in particular he was fascinated by its ability to grow and diminish apparently of its own volition, without relation to the goods or services it theoretically stood for. This at last gave me an opportunity to bring the conversation round to the reason for my invitation to dinner.

'You wrote, sir, that you were in a position to advise me about how to lay out my aunt's money?'

'Eh? Oh yes.' He leaned back in his chair and looked at me with great solemnity. 'In your position I should avoid risk. I recall that at an earlier stage of our acquaintance, you mentioned that your esteemed employer had recommended Wavenhoe's Bank to you.'

'Yes, sir.'

'There is a personal connection of some sort, I collect?'

'We have a boy at the school whose father, Mr Henry Frant, is one of the partners.'

Mr Rowsell wiped his pink, moist forehead with a gravy-spattered napkin. 'Mr Frant is the youngest of the partners, I believe, but nowadays takes the leading part in the business.'

'I understand that Mr Wavenhoe himself is not well.'

'I remember your mentioning the circumstance. It is common knowledge that he is dying. They say in the City that it will be only a matter of weeks.'

I thought of Sophia Frant. 'I'm sorry to hear it, sir.'

'Things were very different when Wavenhoe was young. It was his father who founded the bank. City people, of course, tended to steer clear of those West End accounts. The further West you go, I always say, the higher the profits but the higher the risk. Of course he was lucky to get Carswall. In a private partnership you can do nothing without capital.' He looked sternly at me. 'Stephen Carswall may not be an agreeable man, but no one would deny he has capital. Shrewd, too. Sold his sugar plantations in the nineties, early enough to get a good price. Mind you, many men thought he was mad. But he could see the way the wind was blowing. Those damned Abolitionists, eh? Once you abolish the trade, it's only a matter of time before the institution itself is under threat. When the institution goes, as it will, the entire economic foundation of the West Indies will be destroyed. But Carswall was ahead of the game there. That's the beauty of banking: all you need is capital; none of the worry of land and other fixed property. They can't abolish money, thank God. Though I wouldn't put it past them to try.' He pushed the port towards me. 'Where was I?'

'You were describing how Mr Carswall became Mr Wavenhoe's partner, sir. Did he take an active part in the running of the bank?'

'He left that to Wavenhoe most of the time, as far as the City was concerned, at least. But what went on behind the scenes may have been another matter. Carswall has many friends in America, especially in the southern states, and they did a good deal of business over there. And they did very well in Canada, despite the late war.' Mr Rowsell was of course referring to that inconclusive and largely unnecessary squabble between Great Britain and the United States, not to the great war with France.

I said, 'So they had a finger in every man's pie?'

'Spread the risks, eh, increase the profits. It was Carswall who brought in young Frant. Not that he's so young any more. You have met him?'

'Yes, sir. I was able to do him a small service, and he was most amiable. He is very much the gentleman, of course.'

'The family fell on evil times, which forced him into trade. As for his amiability, I hear a different story. Frant has ability, I don't question that. It's just that – your glass, sir, your glass is empty.'

Breathing heavily, Mr Rowsell refilled the glass so well that it over-flowed. The diversion caused him to lose the thread of his discourse. He sipped his wine and stared with a frown at the polished mahogany.

'Is Mr Carswall married?' I asked after a moment or two.

'Married? Not now. There was a wife, I believe, but she died. Mind you –' He lowered his voice and leaned towards me. 'I'm not saying he hasn't found consolation. Stephen Carswall used to have something of a reputation, if you get my drift.' He tapped his nose to make his drift even clearer. 'He's kin to George Wavenhoe. You knew they were cousins?'

I shook my head.

'Stephen Carswall's mother was sister to George's father. So they are first cousins.' He laughed and stabbed his forehead once more with the napkin. 'Young Frant was a fly one. He came in as Carswall's man, and what does he do but marry Sophia Marpool, old Wavenhoe's niece? So there he is, with a connection to both partners. A love match, they say, but I wager that most of the love was on one side. Master Henry thinks he's the heir apparent, the crown prince. But it's ill luck to count your gains during the game, eh?'

Rowsell stood up, staggered to the door, opened it with difficulty, and bellowed for the servant to bring another bottle.

'Something went wrong? Something to do with Mr Carswall?'

'There was a host of reasons. First Carswall decided to withdraw his capital. He'd settled in the country, turned gentleman, wanted nothing to do with the bank. The story is that Wavenhoe was pressed to find the ready cash when it was needed. It was a large sum. Then Wavenhoe himself has not been well these last few years. He left more and more of the day-to-day conduct of business in the hands of Henry Frant. The City does not feel entirely easy with Frant. It is not just that he is a gentleman dabbling in trade. There are stories that he is fond of play, like his father before him. That was how the Frants lost their money.'

The maid brought another bottle. When it was opened, Rowsell recharged our glasses and drank deeply.

'It's a matter of confidence, you see. All business must depend on it, and banking more than most. If you lose the esteem of those you do business with, you might as well shut up shop. No, my boy, to return to your own case, if you wish to keep your money safe, there is much to be said for the Consolidated Funds.' Mr Rowsell stared glassily at me and at last continued to speak, though slowly and with elaborate care of his consonants. 'You will not become rich, but you will not become bankrupt, either.'

He stopped. He blinked rapidly. His mouth opened and closed several times but no sound came. He bowed like a great oak falling, stately even in ruin. His head hit the table, knocking over the glass. He began to snore.

CHAPTER SEVENTEEN

A S THE WEEKS slipped by and the weather grew steadily colder, the friendship between Charlie Frant and Edgar Allan flourished. Like many schoolboy friendships it was partly a defensive alliance, a strategy for dealing with a world full of Morleys and Quirds. Though similar in looks, they were different in temperament. The American was a proud boy who would not take insults lightly, who when teased would fly at his tormentors. Charlie Frant was gentler, and well supplied with pocket money. If you offended one of them, you had a taste of Edgar Allan's anger, which was formidable. If you pleased one or both of them, however, you were likely to be among the beneficiaries when Charlie Frant next paid a visit to the pastry-cook's.

As for myself, I felt the life of the school settle around me like an old coat. But one part of my life was incomplete. I own that I dwelt overmuch in my daydreams during this period. When I was in this unsatisfactory state I no longer thought much of Fanny, the girl whose ghostly presence had lingered in my mind for years. Instead, I frequently encountered both Miss Carswall and her cousin Mrs Frant. Daydreams have this advantage over real life: one is not obliged to be constant.

There was nothing to warn me of the troubles that lay ahead. One evening, however, Mr Bransby summoned Dansey and myself to his private room.

'I have had a disturbing communication from Mrs Frant, gentlemen,' he said. 'She writes that her son and young Allan have been accosted in the village by the ruffian who approached them before. The man's effrontery beggars belief.'

'We have heard nothing about this from the boys, sir?' Dansey said.

Bransby shook his head. 'He did not linger. And there was no unpleasantness. No, it seems that he simply came up to them in the High-street, gave them a half-sovereign apiece, told them to mind their book and walked away.'

'How extraordinary,' Dansey said. 'I gained the impression that he was not the sort of man who had a ready supply of half-sovereigns.'

'Just so.' Mr Bransby fumbled for his snuff-box. 'I have interrogated Frant and Allan, of course. Frant mentioned the meeting to his mother in a letter. They had nothing substantial to add to what they had told her, except to emphasise that the man's behaviour was noticeably more benevolent than on the previous occasion. Allan added that he was more respectably dressed than before.'

'So we may infer from all this that he is in more comfortable circumstances?'

'Indeed. But Mrs Frant is understandably somewhat agitated. She does not like the idea that boys of this establishment, and in particular her son, should be at the mercy of meetings with strange men. I propose to inform the boys that they must report any suspicious strangers in the village to me at once. Moreover, Mr Dansey, I would be obliged if you would alert the innkeepers and tradesmen to the danger. You and Mr Shield will circulate a description of the man in question.'

'You believe he may return, sir?'

'It is not a question of what I believe, Mr Dansey, but rather a matter of trying to allay Mrs Frant's fears.'

Dansey bowed.

I could have revealed the identity of the stranger. But it was not my secret to tell. Nor did I think it would be kind to Edgar Allan. The gap between father and son was too wide to be easily bridged, especially in that the boy had no knowledge whatsoever of his natural father and believed him to have died long ago in the United States. It could only come as a shock to the lad to learn that David Poe was an impoverished drunkard on his very doorstep.

I said, 'You do not think it likely he will venture to return, sir?'

'For my part, I doubt it. He will not show his face here again.'

In that, at least, Mr Bransby was entirely correct.

CHAPTER EIGHTEEN

A LL THIS TIME, George Wavenhoe lay dying in his fine house in Albemarle-street. The old man took his time, hesitating between this world and the next, but by November matters had come to a crisis, and it was clear that the end could not be far away. Once again I was summoned to Mr Bransby's private room, this time without Dansey.

'I am in receipt of another letter from Mrs Frant,' he said with a trace of irritation. 'You are aware that her uncle, Mr Wavenhoe, has been very ill for some time?'

'Yes, sir.'

'His medical attendants now believe him to be at death's door. He has expressed a wish to say farewell to his great-nephew. Mrs Frant requests that you convey her son to Mr Wavenhoe's house, where she and the rest of his family have gathered. And she further requests that you remain with him while he is there.'

I confess my heart leapt at the prospect of being under the same roof as Sophia Frant for a few days. 'But surely that will be most inconvenient for the conduct of the school, sir? Could she not send a servant instead to collect him?'

Bransby held up his hand. 'Mr Wavenhoe's establishment is in some disorder. Both Mrs Frant and the boy's old nurse are fully occupied in nursing Mr Wavenhoe. She does not wish her son to be neglected, or to mope, while he is with them.' He took a pinch of snuff and sneezed.

'As to the inconvenience, that is to some extent mitigated by the fact that Mrs Frant is prepared to pay handsomely for the privilege of having your company for her son. It should only be for a day or two.'

For an instant, a wild hope surged through me: could Mrs Frant have invited me for her own sake, rather than her son's? A moment's reflection was enough to show me my folly.

'You will leave this afternoon,' Bransby said. 'I could wish it otherwise. Sooner or later the boy must learn to stand on his own two feet.'

When Charlie Frant heard that I was to take him to his uncle Wavenhoe's, and why, his face aged. The skin wrinkled, the colour fled. I glimpsed the old man he might at some point in the future become.

'May Allan come with me, sir?' he asked.

'No, I'm afraid not. But you must bring your books.'

Later that day we drove up to town. Charlie resisted my efforts at conversation, and I was reminded of that other journey, when I had taken him back to school in disgrace. Although it was only the middle of the afternoon, it was such a raw, damp, grey day it felt hours later than it really was. When we turned from the noise and lights of the bustle of Piccadilly into Albemarle-street, what struck me first was the quiet. They had put down straw to muffle the sound of wheels and bribed the organ grinders, the beggars and the street sellers to take themselves elsewhere.

Mr Wavenhoe lived in a substantial house near the northern end of the street. The servant took our hats and coats in the hall. Men were talking in raised voices in a room on the right of the front door. There were footsteps on the stairs. I looked up to see Flora Carswall running towards us, her feet flickering in and out on the stone steps. She stooped and kissed Charlie who shied away from the embrace. She smiled at me and held out her hand.

'Mr Shield, is it not? We met briefly outside my cousin's house in Russell-square.'

I told her I remembered our meeting well, which was no more than the truth. She said she was come to take Charlie up to his mother. I asked after Mr Wavenhoe.

'I fear he is sinking fast.' She lowered her voice. 'These last few months have not been happy ones for him, so in some respects it is a blessed relief.' Her eyes strayed to Charlie. 'There is nothing distressing about it. Or rather, that is to say, not for the spectator.' She coloured most becomingly. 'Lord, my father says I let my tongue run away with me, and I fear he is right. What I mean to say, is that Mr Wavenhoe looks at present like one who is very tired and very sleepy. Nothing more than that.'

I smiled at her and inclined my head. It was a kindly thought. To see the dying is often disagreeable, particularly for a child. The sound of male voices became louder behind the closed door.

'Oh dear,' Miss Carswall said. 'Papa and Mr Frant are in there.' She bit her lip. 'I am staying here to help Mrs Frant with the nursing, and Papa looks in at least once a day to see how we do. But now I must take Charlie up to his mama and Kerridge or they will wonder where we are.' She turned to the footman. 'Show Mr Shield up to his room, will you? And he and Master Charles will need a room to sit in. Has Mrs Frant left instructions?'

'I understand the housekeeper has lit a fire in the old schoolroom, miss. Mr Shield's room is next door.'

We went upstairs. Miss Carswall led Charlie away. I looked after her, watching her hips swaying beneath the muslin of her gown. I realised the footman was doing the same and quickly looked away. We men are all the same under the skin: we fear death, and in our healthy maturity we desire copulation.

We climbed higher and the footman showed me first into a bedroom under the eaves, and then into a long schoolroom next to it. There were fires burning in the grates of both rooms, a luxury I was not used to. The man inquired very civilly if I desired any refreshment, and I asked for tea. He bowed and went away, leaving me to warm my hands by the fire.

A little later, there came footsteps on the stairs, followed by a knock on the door. I looked round, expecting Charlie or the footman. But it was Mrs Frant who entered the room. I stood up hastily and, made clumsy by surprise, sketched an awkward bow.

'Pray be seated, Mr Shield. Thank you for coming with Charlie. I trust they have made you comfortable?'

Her colour was up and she had her hand to the side, as though running up the stairs had given her a stitch. I said I was well looked after, and asked after Mr Wavenhoe.

'I fear he is not long for this world.'

'Has Charlie seen him?'

'No – my uncle is asleep. Kerridge took Charlie downstairs with her for something to eat.' Her face broke into a smile, instantly suppressed. 'She believes she must feed him every time she sees him. He will be with you directly. If you need any refreshment, by the way, you must ring the bell. As for meals, I thought it might be more convenient if you and Charlie had them up here.'

She moved to the barred window, which looked across an eighteen-inch lead-lined gully to the back of the parapet of the street façade. She wore greys and lilacs today, a transitional stage before the blacks she would don when her uncle died. A strand of hair had escaped from her cap, and she pushed it back with a finger. Her movements were always graceful, a joy to watch.

She turned towards me, clicking her tongue against the roof of her mouth as though impatient with herself. 'You must have lights,' she said almost pettishly, tugging the bell. 'It is growing dark. I cannot abide the dark.'

While we waited for the servant to come she questioned me about how Charlie was faring at school. I reassured her as best I could. He was much happier than he had been. No, he was not exactly industrious, but he coped with the work that was expected of him. Yes, he was indeed occasionally flogged, but so were all boys and there was nothing out of the way in it. As for his appetite, I rarely saw the boys eating, so I could not comment with any authority, but I had seen him on several occasions emerging from the pastry-cook's in the village. Finally, as to his motions, I feared I had no information upon that topic whatsoever.

Mrs Frant blushed and said I must excuse the fondness of a mother.

A moment later, the footman brought my tea and a lamp. When the shadows fled from the corners of the room, then so did the curious intimacy of my conversation with Mrs Frant. Yet she lingered. I asked her what regimen she would like us to follow while we were here. She replied that perhaps we might work in the mornings, take the air in the afternoons, and return to our books for a short while in the evening.

'Of course, there may be interruptions.' She twisted her wedding ring round her finger. 'One cannot predict the course of events. Mr Shield, I cannot –'

She broke off at the sound of footsteps on the stairs. There was a tap on the door, and Mrs Kerridge and Charlie entered.

'I saw him,' Charlie said. 'I thought he was dead at first, he lay so still, but then I heard his breathing.'

'Did he wake?'

'No, madam,' Mrs Kerridge said. 'The apothecary gave Mr Wavenhoe his draught, and he's sleeping soundly.'

Mrs Frant stood up and ran her fingers through the boy's hair. 'Then you shall have a holiday for the rest of the afternoon.'

'I shall go and see the coaches, Mama.'

'Very well. But do not stay too long – it is possible your uncle may wake and call for you.'

Soon I was alone again in the long, narrow room. I drank tea and read for upwards of an hour. Then I became restless, and decided to go out to buy tobacco.

I took the front stairs. As I came down the last flight into the marble-floored hall, a door opened and an old man emerged, wheezing with effort, from the room beyond. He was not tall, but he was broad and had once been powerfully built. He had thick black hair streaked with silver and a fleshy face dominated by a great curving nose. He wore a dark blue coat and a showy but dishevelled cravat.

'Ha!' he said as he saw me. 'Who are you?'

'My name's Shield, sir.'

'And who the devil is Shield?'

'I brought Master Charles from his school. I am an usher there.'

'Charlie's bear leader, eh?' He had a rich voice, which he seemed to wrench from deep within his chest. 'Thought you were the damned parson for a moment, in that black coat of yours.'

I smiled and bowed, taking this for a pleasantry.

The elegant figure of Henry Frant appeared in the doorway behind him.

'Mr Shield,' he said. 'Good afternoon.'

I bowed again. 'Your servant, sir.'

'Don't know why you and Sophie thought the boy ought to have a tutor,' the old man said. 'I'll wager he gets enough book-learning at school. They get too much of that already. We're breeding a race of damned milksops.'

'Your views on the rearing of the young, sir,' Frant observed, 'always merit the most profound consideration.'

Mr Carswall rested one hand on the newel post, looked back at the rest of us and broke wind. It was curious that this old, infirm man had the power to make one feel a little less substantial than one usually was. Even Henry Frant was diminished by his presence. The old man grunted and, swaying like a tree in a gale, mounted the stairs. Frant nodded at me and strolled across the hall and into another room. I buttoned up my coat, took my hat and gloves and went out into the raw November air.

Albemarle-street was a quiet, sombre place, lying under the shadow of death. The acrid smell of sea coal filled my nostrils. I crossed the road and glanced back at the house. For an instant, I glimpsed the white blur of a face at one of the drawing-room windows on the first floor. Someone had been standing there – staring idly into the street? or watching me? – and had retreated into the room.

I walked rapidly down towards the lights and the bustle. Charlie had said he wanted to watch the coaches, and I knew where he would have gone. During my long convalescence, when I was staying with my aunt, I would sometimes walk to Piccadilly and watch the fast coaches leaving and arriving from the White Horse Cellar. Half the small boys in London, of all conditions, of all ages, laboured under the same compulsion.

I stepped briskly into Piccadilly, dodged across the road, and made my way along the crowded pavement towards a tobacconist's. The shop was full of customers, and it was a quarter of an hour before I emerged with a paper of cigars in my pocket.

A few paces ahead of me walked a couple, arm in arm and muffled against the cold. The man raised his stick and hailed a passing hackney. He helped the lady in, and I think his hand must have brushed against her bosom, though whether on purpose or by accident I could not tell. She turned, half in, half out of the hackney, and tapped him playfully on the cheek in mock reproof. The woman was Mrs Kerridge, and the cheek she tapped had a familiar dusky hue.

'Brewer-street,' said Salutation Harmwell, and followed Mrs Kerridge into the coach.

There was nothing suspicious about that, of course, or not then. It was not unusual to see a white-skinned woman arm in arm with a well-set-up blackamoor. Dusky gentlemen were rumoured to have certain advantages when it came to pleasing ladies, advantages denied to the men of other races. But I own I was shocked and a little surprised. Mrs Kerridge had seemed so sober, so prim, so old. Why, I thought to myself, she must be forty if she's a day. Yet when she looked down at Harmwell, her face had been as bright as a girl's at her first ball.

I stared after the hackney, wondering what the pair of them were going to do in Brewer-street and feeling an unaccountable stab of envy. At that moment a hand touched my sleeve. I turned, expecting to see Charlie at my elbow.

'I always said Mrs Kerridge was a deep one,' said Flora Carswall. 'I believe my cousin sent her on an errand to Russell-square.'

I raised my hat and bowed. An abigail in a black cloak hovered a few paces away, her eyes discreetly averted.

'And where are you off to, Mr Shield, on this dreary afternoon?' Miss Carswall asked.

'The White Horse Cellar.' It did not seem quite genteel to confess that I had been looking for a tobacconist's. 'I believe Charlie may be there.'

'You are looking for him?'

'Not really. I am at leisure for an hour or so.'

'It is vastly agreeable to see the coaches depart, is it not? All that bustle and excitement, and the thought that one might purchase a ticket, climb aboard and go anywhere, anywhere in the world.'

'I was thinking something very similar.'

'Most people do, probably. How I hate this place.'

I stared at her for an instant. Why should a girl like Flora Carswall dislike a city that could gratify her every whim? I said, 'Then for your sake I hope your stay here will be brief.'

'That depends on poor Mr Wavenhoe. But it is not being in town that I dislike – quite the reverse, in fact – but the gloom of Albemarle-street and some of the people one is obliged to meet there.' She smiled at me, her outburst apparently forgotten. 'I wonder – if you are at leisure, might I request the favour of your company? Then I could send my maid home – the poor girl has a mountain of sewing. I have one or two errands to run; they will not take long.'

I could hardly have refused even if I had wanted to. Miss Carswall took my arm and we threaded our way through the crowds down St James's-street. In Pall Mall, she scanned the latest novels in Payne and Foss's for a few minutes and spent rather more time with Messrs Harding, Howell, & Co. The people there made much of her. She bought a pair of gloves, examined some lace newly arrived from Belgium, and inquired after the progress of a hat she was having made for her. She even asked my opinion about whether a certain colour matched her eyes and prettily deferred to my verdict. She was excessively animated; and the longer we were together the more I liked her, and the more I wondered whether our meeting had been coincidental.

On the way back to Piccadilly, neither of us talked much. Once she slipped in the mud, and would have fallen if I had not been there. For a moment her grip tightened on my arm and I saw her looking up at my face. When at last we returned to Albemarle-street, she removed her hand from my arm and we walked side by side but unattached. As we drew near to Mr Wavenhoe's house, she walked more slowly, despite the cold and despite the rain which had begun to fall.

'You have met my father?'

'Yes – as I was leaving the house just now.'

'I daresay you thought him a little brusque,' she said. 'Pray do not answer. Most people do. But I hope you will not allow his manner to offend you. He is naturally choleric, and the gout makes it worse.'

'You must not distress yourself, Miss Carswall.'

'He is not always as amiable as he might be.'

'I shall bear it as best I can.'

She looked sharply at me and stopped walking altogether. 'There is something I wish to tell you. No, not exactly: it is rather that I would prefer to tell you myself than have you discover it from someone else. I –'

'Sir! Cousin Flora! Wait!'

We turned to face Piccadilly. Charlie ran towards us. His cheeks were pink from the cold and the exercise. The side of his coat was covered with mud. As he came close, my nose told me that it was not mud but horse dung.

'Sir, that was the most famous fun. I rubbed down a horse. I gave the ostler sixpence and he said I was a regular out-and-outer.'

In his joy, he let out a whoop of delight. We were now standing beneath the very windows of the house where George Wavenhoe lay dying. I looked over Charlie's head at Miss Carswall. I think each of us expected the other to reprove the lad for making so much noise. Instead we smiled.

Then Miss Carswall went briskly into the house and left me to wonder what she had been about to tell me.

CHAPTER NINETEEN

I N MY ABSENCE, the schoolroom had filled with smoke. No one could remember the last time a fire had been lit in there. The flue of the chimney appeared to be partly blocked. The sweep was summoned for the following morning. In the meantime, Mrs Frant decided that Charlie and I should use the library on the ground floor for our lessons.

We sat at a table drawn near to the fire. I set Charlie to construe twelve lines of Ovid. He was willing enough but his mind could not stay on the task for long. I too found it hard to concentrate. Then the door opened, and the servant showed Mr Noak into the room. He wore evening dress, plain but respectable.

I sprang up, ready to withdraw with Charlie. The footman said sulkily that he had not realised that anyone was using the room.

'Pray do not disturb yourself,' Mr Noak said to me. 'If I may, I shall sit here and turn the pages of a book until Mr Frant is at leisure.'

The servant withdrew. Mr Noak advanced towards the fire holding out his hands.

'Good evening, sir,' Charlie said. 'We met at my father's house a few weeks ago.'

'Master Charles, is it not?'

They shook hands. Charlie was a well-bred little boy, and he now turned to me. 'May I present my – my tutor, Mr Shield, sir?'

Noak held out his hand to me too. 'I believe I saw you on the same occasion, Mr Shield. We were not introduced, and I'm glad to remedy the deficiency now.'

The words were gracious but Noak had a harsh, staccato way of delivery which made them sound almost insulting. I moved aside the table so he could warm himself at the fire. He looked down at the open book.

'I do not approve of Ovid,' he said in precisely the tone of voice he had used before. 'He may have been a great poet but I am told he was licentious in his mode of life.'

Charlie stared wide-eyed at Mr Noak.

I said, 'We choose passages which display his genius but do not dwell on his less agreeable qualities.'

'Then again, one must ask oneself what is the utility of studying the languages of antiquity? We live in a world where commerce is king.'

'Permit me to remind you, sir, that Latin is the language of natural science. Moreover, the study of the language and the literature of great civilisations cannot be wasted effort. If nothing else it must school the mind.'

'Pagan civilisations, sir,' Noak said. 'Civilisations that passed their peak two thousand years ago or more. We have come on a little since then, I fancy.'

'That we have been able to build so high is surely a tribute to the strength of the foundations.'

Mr Noak stared at me but said nothing. In my present position I could hardly afford to anger anybody. Yet he had talked such obvious nonsense that I felt it my duty to advance some counter arguments, if only for Charlie's sake. At this moment the door opened and Henry Frant came in. The almost foppish elegance of his dress was in stark contrast to Mr Noak's sober attire. Charlie caught his breath. I had the curious impression that he would have liked to shrink into himself.

'My dear sir,' Frant cried. 'How glad I am to see you.'

As he advanced to shake hands, I gathered up our possessions and prepared to leave.

'You have been renewing your acquaintance with Charles, I see, and with Mr Shield.'

Noak nodded. 'I am afraid I have disturbed them at their studies.'

'Not at all, sir,' I said.

Mr Noak continued as if I had not spoken. 'Mr Shield and I have been having a most interesting conversation concerning the place of the classical languages in the modern world.'

Frant shot me a quick glance but swerved away from this subject. 'I have kept you waiting – I am so sorry. It was kind of you to meet me here.'

'How does Mr Wavenhoe do?'

Frant spread out his hands. 'As well as can be expected. I fear he may not be with us long.'

'Perhaps you would prefer it –' Noak began.

'I would not on any account postpone our dinner,' Frant said quickly. 'Mr Wavenhoe is sleeping now, and I understand from his medical attendants that an immediate crisis is not to be expected. Nor is he expected to wake for some hours. They tell me the carriage is at the door.'

Noak lingered by the fire. 'I had wondered whether I might see Mr Carswall here,' he remarked. 'He is Mr Wavenhoe's cousin, is he not?'

'He has indeed been here today, and may look in again,' Frant said smoothly. 'But I believe he is not in the way at present.'

'I had the pleasure of meeting him and his daughter briefly the other evening. Though of course I knew him by reputation already.'

At the door, Noak paused, turned and said goodbye to Charlie and myself. At last the door closed and we were alone again. Charlie sat down in his chair and picked up his pen. All the colour and excitement of the afternoon had drained away from his face. He looked pinched and miserable. I told myself that a father must inspire awe in his children as well as affection. But Mr Frant always made it easier for Charlie to fear him than to love him.

'We shall shut up our books for the day,' I said. 'Is that a backgammon board on the table there? If you like, I will give you a game.'

We sat opposite each other at the table by the fire and laid out the pieces. The familiar click of the counters and the rattle of the dice had a soothing effect. Charlie became engrossed in the game, which he won with ease. I waited for him to set out the counters again so I might have my revenge, but instead he toyed with them, moving them at random about the board.

'Sir?' Charlie said. 'Sir, what is a by-blow?'

'It is a child whose parents are not married to each other.'

'A bastard?'

'Just so. Sometimes people will use words like that when they have no basis in fact, simply with the intention of wounding. It is best to disregard them.'

Charlie shook his head. 'It was not like that, sir. It was Mrs Kerridge. I overheard her talking to Loomis –'

'One should not eavesdrop on servants' tittle-tattle,' I put in automatically.

'No, sir, but I could hardly help overhearing, as they spoke loud and the door was open and I was in the kitchen with Cook. Kerridge said, 'the poor mite, being a by-blow', and afterwards when I asked her what it meant, she told me not to bother my head about it. They were talking about Uncle Wavenhoe dying.'

'And she said you were a by-blow?'

'Oh no, sir – not me. Cousin Flora.'

CHAPTER TWENTY

HENRY FRANT HAD miscalculated. While he was dining that evening at his club with Mr Noak, George Wavenhoe rallied. For a short time, the old man was lucid, though very weak. He demanded that his family be brought to him.

By then, the Carswalls had returned to the house and were dining with Mrs Frant. Charlie was in bed, and I was reading by the fire in a small sitting room at the back of the house. Mrs Kerridge asked me to wake Charlie and bring him down when he was dressed; she could not go herself because she was needed in the sickroom. A few minutes later, Charlie and I descended to the second floor, where we found Mrs Frant in whispered conversation with a doctor on the landing. She broke off when she saw Charlie.

'My love, your uncle desires to see you. I – he wishes to say fare-well.'

'Yes, Mama.'

'You understand my meaning, Charlie?'

The boy nodded.

'It is not at all frightening,' she said firmly. 'He is very ill, however. One must remember that soon he will go to Heaven, where he will be made well again.'

'Yes, Mama.'

She looked at me. Her face was very lovely in the soft light. 'Mr

Shield, would you be kind enough to wait here? I do not think my uncle will detain Charlie for long.'

I bowed.

She and Charlie went into the old man's room. The doctor followed them. I was left alone with a footman. The man was in his evening livery, his wig a great crest of stiff white powder, his calves like twin tree-trunks encased in silk. He examined his reflection surreptitiously in a pier glass. I paced up and down the passage, pretending to look at the pictures which hung there, though I could not have told you their subjects a moment afterwards. Somewhere in the house I heard the rumble of Stephen Carswall's voice, fluctuating yet constant, like the sound of the sea on a quiet summer night. The door of the room opened and the physician beckoned me towards him.

'Pray come in for a moment,' he murmured, waving me towards him.

He put his finger to his lips, lifted himself on to tiptoe and led me into the room. It was large and richly furnished in a style which must have been the rage thirty or forty years ago. The walls above the dado rail were covered with silk hangings of deep red. There was a huge chimney glass above the fire which made the room look even larger than it was. Candles on ornate stands burned at intervals around the walls. A large fire blazed in the burnished steel grate, filling the room with a flickering orange glow. What compelled attention, however, was the bedstead itself, a great four-poster with a massive carved wood cornice, hung with curtains of floral-patterned silk.

Amid all this outmoded magnificence, this Brobdingnagian grandeur, was a tiny old man, with no hair and no teeth, with skin the colour of an unlit wax candle, whose hands picked at the embroidery of the coverlet. My eyes were drawn to him, as though the bed were a stage and he the only player on it. This was strange, because in many ways he was the least significant person in the room. Besides the doctor and Mrs Kerridge, who kept back in the shadows, there were four people clustered round the dying man. Near the head of the bed sat Mr Carswall, his body spilling untidily out of a little carved wooden gilt bedroom chair. Standing at his shoulder was Miss Carswall, who looked up as I entered and gave me a swift smile. Facing them across the bed was Mrs Frant, seated in another chair, with Charlie resting on one of the chair's arms and leaning against her.

'Ah, Mr Shield.' Carswall waved me forward. 'My cousin wishes to add a codicil to his will. He would be obliged if you would witness his signature, along with the good doctor here.'

As I stepped forward into the light, I saw on the bed a sheet of paper covered in writing. A writing box lay open on the dressing table nearby.

'The lawyer has been sent for,' said Mrs Frant. 'Should we not wait until he arrives?'

'That would take time, madam,' Carswall pointed out. 'And time is the one thing we may not have. There can surely be no doubt about our cousin's intentions. When Fishlake comes, we shall have him draw up another codicil if necessary. But in the meantime, let us make sure that this one is duly signed and witnessed. I am persuaded that Mr Wavenhoe would wish it, and that Mr Frant would see the wisdom of such a course.'

'Very well, sir. We must do as my uncle desires. And thank you. You are very good.'

While this conversation was going on, the old man lay propped against a great mountain of embroidered pillows. He breathed slowly and noisily through his mouth, sounding like an old pump in need of grease. The eyes were almost closed.

Carswall picked up the sheet of paper from the coverlet. 'Flora, the pen.'

She brought the pen and the inkpot to her father. He dipped the nib in the ink, lifted Wavenhoe's right hand and inserted the pen between the fingers.

'Come, George,' he growled, 'here is the codicil: all that is required to make things right is that you sign your name here.'

Carswall lifted the paper in his other hand. Wavenhoe's eyelids fluttered. His breathing lost its regularity. Two drops of ink fell on the embroidered coverlet. Carswall guided Wavenhoe's hand to the space below the writing. With a slowness that was painful to watch, Wavenhoe traced his name. Afterwards the pen dropped from his fingers and he let himself fall back against his pillows. The breathing resumed its regularity. The pen rolled down the paper, leaving a splatter of ink-spots, and came to rest on the coverlet.

'And now, Mr Shield,' Carswall said. 'Pray oblige us by doing your part. Flora, hand him the pen. Sign there, sir, beside the writing box. No, stay, before you sign, write these words: "Mr Wavenhoe's signature witnessed by me" – then write your name, sir, your full name – "on the 9th day of November, 1819."'

While he gave his instructions, he folded down the top of the sheet so I could not see the codicil itself, only Mr Wavenhoe's signature. He handed the paper to Flora, who stood beside me, holding the candle so I could see what I was doing. I wrote what Mr Carswall required, and signed my name. Flora was standing very close to me, though without touching; but I fancied I sensed the warmth of her body.

'When you are done, be so good as to pass the paper to the doctor,' Carswall said.

I crossed the room and handed the codicil to him. Wavenhoe's eyes were fully open now. He looked at me and frowned.

'Who –?' he whispered.

'Mr Shield is Charlie's tutor, sir,' Flora said.

Wavenhoe's eyes drifted away from me and he turned his head so he could see the Frants on the other side of the bed. He looked at Mrs Frant.

'Anne?' he said in a firmer voice. 'I thought you were dead.'

She leaned towards him and took his hand. 'No, Uncle, I am not Anne, I am her daughter Sophie. Mama has been dead these many years, but they say I am very like her.'

He responded to the touch, if not the words. 'Anne,' he said, and smiled. 'I am rejoiced to see you.'

His eyelids twitched and he slipped into a doze. The doctor scratched his signature and gave the paper to Carswall, who flapped it in the air until the ink was dry and then folded it away in his pocketbook. No one told me I should leave. I think the little group around the bed had forgotten my existence. I withdrew and stood in the shadows by the wall with Mrs Kerridge and the doctor. Flora sat in the chair beside her father.

Mrs Frant picked up a Prayer Book from the side table beside her and looked inquiringly at Carswall who nodded. She opened it and began to read from Psalm 51:

But lo, thou requirest truth in the inward parts: and shalt make me to understand wisdom secretly. Thou shalt purge me with hyssop, and I shall be clean: thou shalt wash me, and I shall be whiter than snow. Thou shalt make me hear of joy and gladness: that the bones which thou hast broken may rejoice.

As I listened, I thought that we were all imprisoned in a place between light and darkness, life and death, and that the only sounds that mattered in the world were the slow rasp of Wavenhoe's breathing, the creak and sputter of coals in the grate and the rise and fall of Sophia Frant's voice.

After a few moments, Stephen Carswall pulled out his watch. He sighed loudly, pushed back his chair, the legs scraping on the oak floorboards, and stood up, snorting with the strain of manoeuvring his big, clumsy body. Mrs Frant broke off her reading at the end of a sentence. Carswall made no sign of apology or even acknowledgement.

'Shall we go down to the drawing room?' he said to his daughter.

'If you would not object, sir, I should prefer to remain here.'

He shrugged. 'You must please yourself, miss.' He glanced down at the little figure on the bed and nodded his head. It was a curious gesture: like the tip of the head a maidservant gives when she makes her obedience. He stamped across the floor and Mrs Kerridge opened the door for him. From the ground floor came a muffled knock on the front door and the subdued murmur of voices.

'Ah,' Carswall said, cocking his head, suddenly all attention. 'That lawyer fellow, at last, unless Frant's back early. If it's Fishlake, I'll deal with him.'

'My love,' Mrs Frant said to Charlie, 'it is time for you to go to bed. Kiss your uncle goodnight, and then perhaps Mr Shield will go upstairs with you. We must not inconvenience him any further, must we?'

Charlie detached himself from his mother's chair. I saw his face in that instant, saw him screwing up his courage for what had to be done.

He bent over the figure in the bed and brushed his lips against the pale forehead. He backed away and, avoiding his mother's embrace, walked unsteadily towards me.

George Wavenhoe coughed. Flora gasped, and all of us turned suddenly towards the bed. The old man stirred and opened his eyes. 'Goodnight, dear boy,' he said softly but with perfect clarity. 'And sweet dreams.'

CHAPTER TWENTY-ONE

I DREAMT ABOUT George Wavenhoe as I lay in my bed several floors above him: and in my dream I watched him sign the codicil yet again, and watched his little yellow fingers clutch the pen; and in my dream the nails had grown and become claws, and I wondered why no one had clipped them. I woke to the news that he was dead.

Mrs Frant summoned me to the breakfast room. Her face was pale, her eyes rimmed red with weeping, and she did not look at me but addressed the coal scuttle. She and Mr Frant, she said, had decided that Charlie should stay with them in Russell-square until after Mr Wavenhoe's funeral. She thanked me for my trouble and told me she had ordered the carriage to take me back to school.

The conversation left a sour taste in my mouth. She had made me feel like a servant, I told myself, which to all intents and purposes I was. I packed my few belongings, said goodbye to Charlie and was driven back to Stoke Newington.

As the days slipped past, I tried to absorb myself in the life of the school. But I found it hard not to think about the Frants, the Carswalls and Mr Wavenhoe. Mrs Frant and Miss Carswall filled my thoughts far more than was entirely proper. And there was much that puzzled me: what had Salutation Harmwell and Mr Noak to do with all this? Was it true that Miss Carswall was her father's natural daughter?

Nor could I ignore Mr Carswall's behaviour. Though Mr Wavenhoe had certainly signed the codicil which I had witnessed, and Mrs Frant and the physician had seemed perfectly satisfied as to the correctness of Mr Carswall's conduct, had the old man known what he was signing? I was not easy in my mind. There was nothing one could call suspicious, exactly, but there was much to arouse curiosity, to raise doubts.

To make matters worse, a trickle of intelligence from the newspapers and certain of Mr Bransby's correspondents revealed that Mr Rowsell's forebodings had been amply justified. Something was very wrong at Wavenhoe's Bank. There were reports that it might close its doors and refuse payments. Mr Wavenhoe's death had caused a crisis in confidence. I did not appreciate how swiftly events were moving until some ten days after I returned from Albemarle-street. By this time Mr Wavenhoe was buried, and Charlie had returned to school, wearing mourning but in other respects apparently untouched by the experience.

After morning school, I strolled into the village, as was my habit if the weather was dry. A green and gold carriage, drawn by a pair of chestnuts, pulled up beside me in the High-street. The glass slid down, and Miss Carswall looked out.

'Mr Shield – this is a pleasure I had not anticipated.'

I raised my hat and bowed. 'Miss Carswall – nor had I. Are you come to see your cousin?'

'Yes, indeed – Mr Frant wrote to Mr Bransby; he is to have a night in town. But I am somewhat early. I would not wish to arrive before my time. Schoolboys are such creatures of habit, are they not? I wonder if I might prevail upon you to show me a little of the village and the surrounding country? I am sure it will be better to keep the horses moving.'

I disclaimed any topographical information of value but said I would be glad to show her what I could. The footman let down the steps and I climbed into the carriage. Flora Carswall slid along the seat into the corner to give me room.

'How very obliging of you, Mr Shield,' she said, toying with an auburn curl. 'And how fortunate that I should encounter you.'

'Fortunate?' I said softly.

She coloured most becomingly. 'Charlie mentioned that you often take the air after morning school.'

'Fortunate for me, at least,' I said with a smile. 'As it was the other day, when we met in Piccadilly.'

Miss Carswall smiled back, and I knew my guess had hit the mark: she had followed me from Albemarle-street that afternoon. 'I suppose that sometimes one must give fortune a nudge,' she said. 'Don't you agree? And I own that I am glad to have the opportunity for a private conference with you. Would you – would you tell John coachman to drive out of the village for a mile or two?'

I obeyed.

She cleared her throat and went on, 'I am afraid the bank is in a bad way.'

'I have seen something of that in the newspapers.'

'It is even worse than is generally supposed. Pray do not mention this to a living soul but my father is quite shocked. He had not realised – that is to say, there is serious cause for alarm. It seems that a number of bills were due at about this time, some for very large sums of money, and in the normal course of affairs, they would have been extended. But no: the creditors wish to be paid immediately. And then, to make matters worse, we had assumed – indeed the whole world had assumed – that Mr Wavenhoe was a very wealthy man. But it appears that this was no longer the case at the time of his death.'

'I'm sorry to hear this. May I ask why –?'

'Why I am telling you? Because I – I was concerned about what happened on the evening Mr Wavenhoe died. My father often appears high-handed, I regret to say. He is a man who is used to his own way. Those of us who know him make allowances, but to a stranger it can seem – it can seem other than it really is.'

'I witnessed a signature, Miss Carswall. That is all.'

'You saw Mr Wavenhoe sign, did you not? And you yourself signed immediately afterwards? And you could testify that there was no coercion involved, and that Mr Wavenhoe was in his right mind and knew what he was doing?'

Until now her hands had been inside her muff. As she spoke, in her agitation, she took out her right hand and laid it on my sleeve. Almost immediately she realised what she had done and with a gasp she withdrew it.

'I can certainly testify to that, Miss Carswall. But surely others can do the same? The doctor's word would naturally carry more weight than mine, and Mrs Frant's, too.'

'It is possible that Mr Frant may dispute the codicil,' she said, colouring again, and more deeply. 'You know how it is with families, I daresay: a disputed inheritance can wreak the most fearful havoc.'

I said gently, 'This codicil, Miss Carswall: why should Mr Frant wish to dispute it?'

'I will be frank with you, Mr Shield. It concerns the disposition of a property in Gloucester which had belonged, I believe, to Mr Wavenhoe's grandmother, that is to say to the grandmother whom he shared with my father. Mr Wavenhoe was sentimentally attached to it on that account, for he had childhood memories of the place. I understand from my father that it is in fact the only one of his properties that is not encumbered with a mortgage. And the codicil now bequeaths it to me.'

'May I ask who would have received it if Mr Wavenhoe had not signed the codicil?'

'I'm not entirely sure. Perhaps my cousin Mrs Frant would have held it in trust for her son. There are a number of small bequests, but apart from those, she and Charlie are the co-heirs, and Mr Frant is appointed the executor. My father and Mr Wavenhoe had quarrelled over a matter of business, you see, so he was not mentioned in the will. Yet, in my uncle's last hours, when Papa represented to Mr Wavenhoe that he had no quarrel with me, my uncle was much struck by the force of the argument and desired the codicil to be drawn up there and then.'

'And Mr Frant?'

'Mr Frant was not there. Sophie was in and out of the room but her thoughts were otherwise occupied.' Miss Carswall hesitated and then added in a voice not much above a whisper, 'In fact, she put quite the wrong construction upon it. She thought that she was the beneficiary of the codicil.'

I remembered her words to Mr Carswall before Mr Wavenhoe had signed the codicil: *We must do what my uncle wishes. And thank you. You are very good.*

Miss Carswall edged a little closer to me and lowered her voice. 'I understand that Mr Frant does not believe my uncle was in a fit state to make a decision of this nature, that indeed he had no idea what he was putting his name to.'

I nodded without committing myself. Was it possible that Mrs Frant had been tricked, and that I had been an unwitting agent in a scheme to defraud her of an inheritance? Did that explain her altered behaviour to me on the morning after Mr Wavenhoe's death?

'It would not matter so much,' Miss Carswall burst out, 'if my uncle's affairs were not so embarrassed. My father believes that once his debts are paid there will be scarcely enough to settle the household bills. As for the bank – there is such a run on it at present that my father says there is sure to be a suspension of payments and perhaps even a commission of bankruptcy. It will go very hard on Sophie, I fear.'

'And on Mr Frant.'

'If the bank has run into difficulties, then he must be held at least partly responsible,' Miss Carswall said tartly. 'Since my father withdrew from the partnership, Mr Frant has been largely responsible for the conduct of business.'

The carriage had left the village, and was now proceeding down a country lane at a walk.

Miss Carswall looked up at me. 'I must go to the school.' Her voice had softened, had become almost pleading. 'I – I scarcely know how to say –'

'To say what?'

'It is so absurd,' she replied, speaking in a rush. 'And in any case it may be quite untrue. But Mr Frant is said to nurse a grudge against you.'

'But why should he do that?'

'It is said that he feels you should not have witnessed my uncle's signature.'

'It is said? By whom?'

'Hush, Mr Shield. I – I heard him talking with my father and the lawyer on the morning after my uncle died. That is to say, I was in the next room, and they did not trouble to lower their voices.'

'But why should Mr Frant object to my witnessing the signature? If I had not done it, someone else would have. Does he hold a grudge against the physician as well?'

Miss Carswall did not reply. She covered her face with her hands.

'Besides, your father was so pressing that I could hardly refuse him,' I said, my mind filling with the memory of Mrs Frant's cold, pale face in the breakfast room at Albemarle-street. 'Nor was there any reason why I should do so.'

'I know,' she murmured, peeping at me through her gloved fingers. 'I know. But men are not always rational creatures, are they?'

CHAPTER TWENTY-TWO

O N TUESDAY THE 23rd November, Wavenhoe's Bank closed its doors for ever. On the same day, two of its customers committed suicide rather than face ruin.

When a bank fails, the consequences spread like a contagion through society: fathers rot in the Marshalsea or blow out their brains, mothers take in sewing or walk the pavements, children are withdrawn from school and beg for pennies, servants lose their places and tradesmen's bills go unpaid; and so the plague spreads, ever outwards, to people who never heard of Wavenhoe's or Russell-square.

'Frant burned his fingers badly when the tobacco market collapsed,' Dansey told me as we smoked our evening pipes in the garden. 'I have it on good authority that he had to turn to the Israelites to keep his head above water. Oh, and the servants have left. Always a sure sign of a sinking ship.'

On Wednesday there were more suicides and we heard that the bailiffs had gone into that opulent house in Russell-square. Dansey and I stood at a window and watched Charlie Frant, arm in arm with Edgar Allan, marching round the playground and blowing plumes of warm breath into the freezing air.

'I pity the boy, of course. But take my advice: have nothing more to do with the Frants, if you can help it. They will only bring you grief.'

It was sound advice but I was not able to take it, for the very next day, Thursday, the sad history of the Frants and Wavenhoes reached what many believed to be its catastrophe. The first intelligence we had of the terrible events of the night came at breakfast time. The man who brought the milk communicated it to the maids, and the news set the servants whispering and swaying like a cornfield in a breeze.

'Something's afoot,' Dansey said as we sat with our weak, bitter coffee. 'One doesn't often see them so lively at this hour of the morning.'

Afterwards, Morley sidled up to us, with Quird hovering as usual at his elbow. 'Please, sir,' he said to Dansey, shifting from one foot to the other, his face glowing with excitement. 'Something horrible has happened.'

'Then I advise you not to tell me what it is,' Dansey said. 'It may distress you further.'

'No, sir,' Quird broke in. 'Truly, sir, you don't understand.'

Dansey scowled at the boy.

'I beg your pardon,' Quird said quickly. 'I did not mean to –'

'Someone's been murdered in the night,' Morley broke in, his voice rising in his excitement.

'They say his head was smashed into jelly,' Quird whispered. 'Torn limb from limb.'

'It might have been any of us,' Morley said. 'The thief could have broken in and –'

'So a thief has turned to murder?' Dansey said. 'Perhaps Stoke Newington is not such a humdrum place after all. Where is this interesting event said to have occurred?'

'Not exactly in the village, sir,' Morley answered. 'Somewhere towards town. Not a stone's throw from us, not really.'

'Ah. I might have known. So Stoke Newington remains as humdrum as ever. When there is news I shall be interested to hear it. In the meantime, I do not propose to waste my few remaining moments of leisure listening to second-hand servants' gossip. Good morning.'

Morley and Quird retreated. We watched them leaving the room.

'What tiresomely underbred creatures they are, to be sure,' Dansey said.

'I wonder if there is some truth in what they heard.'

Dansey shrugged. 'Very possibly. No doubt we shall be talking about it for weeks on end. I can imagine nothing more tedious.'

This was not affectation on his part. Dansey could be reticent to a fault but he rarely troubled to lie. Indeed, he rarely troubled much with anything; I sometimes wonder what might have become of him if he had.

I did not have to wait long to learn more. Part way through morning school Mr Bransby's servant came to fetch me. I found my employer in the parlour with a small man in grey, mud-stained clothes. Bransby was pacing up and down, his face redder than usual.

'Allow me to present Mr Shield, one of my ushers,' he said, pausing to help himself to a large pinch of snuff. 'Mr Shield, this is Mr Grout, the attorney who acts as clerk to the magistrates. I regret to say that a most shocking circumstance has come to light, one that may cast a shadow over the school.'

Mr Grout had a face that was an appendage of his nose, like a mole's. 'A man has been murdered, Mr Shield. His body was found early this morning by a watchman at a building plot not more than a mile and a half away. There is a possibility that you may be able to identify the unfortunate victim.'

I stared in consternation from one to the other. 'But I have never been there. I did not even know –'

'It is not the location which is our concern,' the clerk interrupted. 'It is the identity of the victim. We have reason to believe – I would put it no more strongly than that – that he may not be unknown to you.'

Bransby sneezed. 'Not to put too fine a point on it, Shield, Wavenhoe's Bank had an interest in this building projection.'

'The bank hold the head-lease on the land themselves. Or perhaps I should say *held*.' Grout wrinkled his nose. 'Owing to the scarcity of money at the present time, the man who holds the principal building-lease, a Mr Owens, was compelled to apply to them for a series of loans. Unfortunately the money the bank provided was not enough to meet his obligations. The poor fellow hanged himself in Hertford a few months ago.'

Bransby shook his head. 'And now poor Frant has gone to meet his Maker. Truly an unlucky speculation.'

'Mr Frant is dead?' I blurted out.

'That is the question,' Grout said. 'The watchman believes the body is Mr Frant's. But he met him only once, and that briefly, and he cannot be said to be a reliable witness at the best of times. At such short notice I have been able to find no one in the vicinity who knows Mr Frant. But I understand that he has – had, that is to say – a boy at the school, so I have driven over to see whether someone was able to identify the body; or not, of course, as the case may be. Mr Bransby tells me he has never met Mr Frant either, but that you have.'

'Yes, sir, on several occasions. Tell me, what of Mrs Frant? Has she been informed?'

Grout shook his head. 'It is a delicate matter. One would not like to tell a lady that her husband had been murdered, only to discover that the victim was in fact somebody else. Mr Bransby tells me you have been a soldier, sir, that you were in fact one of our glorious army at Waterloo. I hope I am correct in inferring that the sight of a man who has died a violent death may have fewer terrors for you than it would for a mere civilian.'

There was a glazed expression on Mr Bransby's face. He gave me a tight smile and nodded. I knew I had little choice but to accept the rôle that he had allotted me.

Mr Grout bowed to my employer. 'Mr Shield should be back in time for dinner.'

'Well, the sooner this is done the better.' Bransby fixed me with a glare. 'We can only hope and pray that the unfortunate man does not prove to be Mr Frant.'

A few minutes later, Mr Grout and I were driving briskly away in his whiskey. We rattled down Church-street and turned right into the High-street. It was on this road, not very far south from here, that I had met Mr Frant for the first time – in September, when I had walked to Stoke Newington to take up my situation at Mr Bransby's school. I remembered the meeting well enough – as one does when a man more or less threatens to set his servants on one – but he had never shown the slightest recollection of it. It occurred to me that now I had a possible explanation for his presence on the road that day, one that perhaps also accounted for Mr Frant's bad temper: he had been inspecting one of his failing investments.

We turned into a narrow lane between tall hedges. As we bounced and slithered along on a surface of rutted, frozen mud, I glimpsed market gardens and scrubby pasture over the tops of the hedges. Grout squeezed the whiskey into an opening on the left that led to a large field. There was little grass to be seen – merely heaps of sand and gravel, stacks of bricks, and above all mud. Few walls were higher than my waist. The plot looked as if it had recently suffered an artillery bombardment, leaving two rows of ruins separated by an immense heap of spoil. Grout pulled up beside a wooden shed. For a moment we looked out over the dismal scene.

'I believe the design is for twenty houses facing each other across a communal garden,' Grout said. 'Wellington-terrace. Mr Owens drew up the plans himself. According to the prospectus, Londoners will flock to benefit from the healthy air.'

'One can see why he felt obliged to hang himself,' I observed.

'I agree – it is not a happy place. Nothing has gone well for the scheme from start to finish.'

The door of the shed opened and a man came out, touching his hat.

'Ah, there is the constable.' Grout raised his voice. 'Well, where is he?'

'We brought him in here, sir, just as you said.'

Grout glanced at me. 'Are you ready, Mr Shield? Then let us wait no longer.'

We jumped down from the whiskey and followed the constable over the caked mud into the shed. My eyes adjusted slowly to the gloom. A small stove burned in the corner and filled the air with heavy, acrid fumes. A man huddled beside it, a clay pipe smouldering in his mouth. In the shadows at the back of the shed was the shape of a door laid upon trestles. On the door lay the long, dark mound of a body. I sniffed: in the smoke were other smells: the tang of spirits and the dark effluvium of the charnel house.

Grout indicated the man by the stove. 'This fellow's name is Orton, Jacob Orton.'

'Late of the Seventy-Third, sir,' said Orton in a mendicant's whine. 'And I have a testimonial from my company commander to prove it.' He raised the hand holding the pipe in a parody of a military salute and a shower of sparks flew like meteors through the air. 'They called me Honest Jake in the regiment,' he said. 'That's my name, sir, that's my nature.'

'Are there no more lights in here?' Grout demanded.

'It is a terrible dull day, to be sure,' Orton said, sucking on his pipe.

Grout darted towards him and seized his lapels. 'Are you sure you heard nothing in the night? Think carefully. A lie will cost you dear.'

'As God is my witness, sir, I was sleeping as sound as a babe in his mother's arms.' Orton snuffled. 'I could not help it, your worship.'

'You're not paid to sleep: you're paid to watch.'

'Drunk as a pig,' said the constable. 'That's what he means, sir.'

'I don't deny I took a drop of something to keep out the cold.'

'Drank so much the Last Judgement could have come without him noticing anything out of the way,' the constable translated. He nodded towards the silent shape that lay on the trestles. 'You've only got to look at him to see he didn't go quietly. Ain't that right, Mr Grout?'

The clerk ignored the question. He turned aside and tugged at the sacking over one of the windows, which were small and set high to dissuade thieves. The sacking fell away, revealing an unglazed square. Pale winter daylight spread reluctantly through the little cabin. Orton whinnied softly, as though the light hurt him.

'Stow it,' said the constable.

'He moved,' Orton whispered. 'I take my oath on it. I saw his hand move. Just then, as God's my witness.'

'Your wits are wandering,' Grout said. 'Bring the lantern. Why is there not more light? Perhaps we should have left the poor man where he lay.'

'There's foxes, and a terrible deal of rats,' Orton said.

Grout motioned me to approach the makeshift table. The body was entirely covered with a grey blanket, with the exception of the left hand.

'Dear God!' I ejaculated.

'You must brace yourself, Mr Shield. The face is worse.'

His voice seemed to come from a great distance. I stared at the wreck of the hand. I bent closer and the constable shone the light full on it. It had been reduced to a bloody pulp of flesh, skin and shockingly white splinters of bone. I fought an impulse to vomit.

'The top joints of the forefinger appear to be missing,' I said in a thin, precise voice. 'I know Mr Frant had sustained a similar injury.'

Grout let out his breath in a sigh. 'Are you ready for the rest?'

I nodded. I did not trust myself to speak.

The constable set down the lantern on the corner of the door, raised himself on tiptoe, took the top two corners of the blanket and slowly pulled it back. The figure lay supine and as still as an effigy. The constable lifted the lantern and held it up to the head.

I shuddered and took a step back. Grout gripped my elbow. My mind darkened. For an instant I thought the darkness was outside me, that the flame in the lantern had died and that the day had slipped with tropical suddenness into night. I was aware of a powerful odour of faeces and sweat, of stale tobacco and gin.

'He should think himself lucky,' Orton wheezed at my shoulder. 'I mean, look at him, most of him's hardly touched. Lucky bugger, eh? You should see what roundshot fair and square in the belly can do to a man. Now that's what I call damage. I remember at Waterloo –'

'Hold your tongue, damn you,' I said, obscurely angry that this man seemed not to have spent the battle cowering in the shadow of a dead horse.

'You block the light, Orton,' Grout said, unexpectedly mild. 'Move aside.'

I closed my eyes and tried to shut out the sights and sounds and smells that struggled to fill the darkness around me. This was not a battle: this was merely a corpse.

'Are you able to come to an opinion?' Grout inquired. 'I realise that the face is – is much battered.'

I opened my eyes. The man on the trestle table was hatless. There were still patches of frost on both clothes and hair. It had been a cold night to spend in the open. He wore a dark, many-caped greatcoat – not a coachman's but a gentleman's luxurious imitation. Underneath I glimpsed a dark blue coat, pale brown breeches and heavy riding boots. The hair was greying at the temples, cut short.

As to the face, it was everyone's and no one's. Only one eye was visible – God alone knew what had happened to the other – and it seemed to me that its colour was a pale blue-grey.

'He – he is much changed, of course,' I said, and the words were as weak and inadequate as the light from the lantern. 'But everything I see is consonant with what I know of Mr Frant – the colour of the hair, that is to say, the colour of the eyes – that is, of the eye – and the build and the height as far as I can estimate them.'

'The clothes?'

'I cannot help you there.'

'There is also a ring.' Grout walked round the head of the table, keeping as far away from it as he could. 'It is still on the other hand, so the motive for this dreadful deed appears not to have been robbery. Pray come round to this side.'

I obeyed like one in a trance. I was unable to look away from what lay on the table. The greatcoat was smeared with mud. A dark patch spread like a sinister bib across the chest. I thought I discerned splinters of exposed bone in the red ruin of the face.

The single eye seemed to follow me.

'Now take cavalry,' Orton suggested from his dark corner near the stove. 'When they're bunched together, and charging, so the horses can't choose where they put their hooves. If there's a man lying on the ground, wounded, say, there's not a lot anyone can do. Cuts a man up cruelly, I can tell you. You wouldn't believe.'

'Stow your mag,' said the constable wearily.

'Least he's got a peeper left on him,' Orton went on. 'The crows used to go for the eyes, did you know that?'

The constable cuffed him into silence. Grout held the lantern low so I could examine the right hand of the corpse. Like the left, it had been reduced to a bloody pulp. On the forefinger was the great gold signet ring.

'I must have air,' I said. I pushed past Grout and the constable and blundered through the doorway. The clerk followed me outside. I stared over the desolate prospect of frosty mud and raw brick. Three pigeons rose in alarm from the bare branches of an oak tree that survived from a time when the land had not been given over to wild schemes and lost fortunes.

Grout pushed a flask into my hand. I took a mouthful of brandy, and spluttered as the heat ran down to my belly. He walked up and down, clapping his gloved hands together against the cold.

'Well, sir?' he said. 'What is your verdict?'

'I believe it is Mr Henry Frant.'

'You cannot be certain?'

'His face . . . it is much damaged.'

'You remarked the missing finger.'

'Yes.'

'It supports the identification.'

'True.' I hesitated and then burst out: 'But who could have done such a thing? The violence of the attack passes all belief.'

Grout shrugged. His eyes strayed towards the nearest of the half-built houses.

'Would you care to see where the deed was done? It is not a sight for the squeamish, but it is as nothing compared with what you have already seen.'

'I should be most interested.' The brandy had given me false courage.

He led me along a line of planks that snaked precariously across the mud. The house was a house in name only. Low walls surrounded the shallow pit of the cellar, perhaps two or three feet below the surface of the field in which we stood. Grout jumped into it with the alacrity of a sparrow looking for breadcrumbs. I followed him, narrowly avoiding a pool of fresh excrement. He pointed with his stick at the further corner. Despite his warning, there was little to see, apart from puddles of icy water and, abutting the brickwork in the angle of the wall, an irregular patch of earth which was darker than the rest, darker because shadowed with Henry Frant's blood.

'Were there footprints?' I asked. 'Surely such a struggle must have left a number of marks?'

Grout shook his head. 'Unfortunately the scene has had a number of visitors since the deed was committed. Besides, the ground was hard with frost.'

'When did Orton make the discovery?'

'Shortly after it was light. When he woke, he found that while he slept someone had wedged the door of the shed. He had to crawl out through one of the windows. He came here to relieve himself, which was when he found the corpse.' Grout's nose wrinkled. 'First he alerted a neighbouring farmer, who came to gawp with half a dozen of his men. Then the magistrates. If there were footprints, or other marks, they will not be easy to distinguish from those which were made before or afterwards.'

'What of Mr Frant's hat and gloves? How did he come here? And why should he come at that time of evening?'

'If we knew the answers to those questions, Mr Shield, we would no doubt know the identity of the murderer. We found the hat beside the body. It is in the shed now, and has Mr Frant's name inside. And the gloves were beneath the body itself.'

'That is odd, is it not, sir?'

'How so?'

'That a man should remove his gloves on such a cold night.'

'The affair as a whole is a tissue of strange and contradictory circumstances. Mr Frant's pockets had been emptied. Yet the ring was left on his finger.' Grout rubbed his pointed nose, whose tip was pink with cold. 'The principal weapon might have been a hammer or a similar instrument,' he went on, the words tumbling out at such a rate that I realised that he, too, was not unmoved by the dreadful sight on the trestle table. 'Though it is possible that the assailant also used a brick.'

He scrambled out of the cellar and we walked slowly back towards the shed.

'They may have come here on foot,' Grout said. 'But more likely they rode or drove. Someone will have seen them on the way.'

'Ruined men can be driven to desperate measures, and it is not

111

impossible that one of those whom Mr Frant injured has had his mind overturned by his troubles, and has sought revenge.'

Grout gave me a long look. 'Or this might be the work of a jealous lover. Or a madman.'

There was nothing more for me to do at Wellington-terrace. As Mr Grout drove me back to school, I sat in silence beside him, my mind too full for conversation. We passed the flask to and fro between us. It was empty by the time we drew up outside the Manor House School.

I said, 'May I tell Mr Bransby what has passed?'

Grout shrugged. 'He either knows or surmises everything you or I could tell him. So will the whole neighbourhood in an hour or two.'

'There is the matter of the boy. Mr Frant's son.'

'Indeed. Mr Bransby must do what he thinks fit on that head.' He bobbed his nose towards me. 'I do not know how the magistrates will proceed, and if I did know, it would not be proper for me to tell you. However, there will be an inquest, and you may be required to attend. In the meantime, though –' he spread his arms wide '– there will be talk. That much I do know.'

CHAPTER TWENTY-THREE

I N THE EVENING of that terrible day, I smoked a pipe with Dansey in the garden after the boys were in bed. We walked up and down, huddled in our greatcoats. Soon after my return, Mr Bransby had summoned Charlie Frant. The boy had not been seen since. A message had been sent for Edgar Allan to take his friend's possessions to Mr Bransby's side of the house.

'It is said a man has been arrested already,' Dansey said softly.

'Who?'

'I do not know.'

I bowed my head. 'But why did the murderer mutilate the body?'

'A man in search of revenge is a man out of his senses. If it was revenge.'

'Yes, but the hands?'

'In Arabia, they cut off the thief's hands. We used to do it here, I believe, or something similar. Crushing the hands in the manner you described might be another form of the practice. Perhaps Mr Frant's killer believed his victim was a thief.'

Our pipes hissed and bubbled. At the foot of the garden, we turned, and stood for a moment under the shelter of the trees looking back at the house.

Dansey sighed. 'Come what may, this affair will make a considerable noise in the world. Pray do not think me impertinent if I speak for a moment in the character of a friend, but I would advise you to keep your own counsel.'

'I am obliged to you. But why do you make such a point of this?'

'I hardly know. The Frants are great folk. When great folk fall, they bring down smaller folk in their train.' He sucked on his pipe. 'It is a thousand pities you were called upon to identify the body. You should not have had to appear in this matter at all.'

I shrugged, trying unsuccessfully to push from my mind the memory of that bloodied carcass I had seen in the morning. 'Shall we go in? It grows cold.'

'As you wish.'

It seemed to me that there was a note of regret in Dansey's voice. We walked slowly back to the house – slowly, because his footsteps lagged. The moon was very bright, and our feet crunched on the silver lawn. The house reared up in front of us, the moon full on its garden front.

Dansey laid a hand on my arm. 'Tom? I may call you that, may I not? Pray call me Ned. I do not wish –'

'Hush,' I said. 'Look – someone is watching us. Do you see? The third attic from the left.'

The window belonged to the chamber Morley and Quird had shared with Charlie Frant. We quickened our pace, and a moment later passed into the house.

'Moonlight plays strange tricks,' Dansey said.

I shook my head. 'I saw a face. Just for a moment.'

That night I slept dreamlessly, though I had feared my nightmares of carnage would return after the sight I had seen in Jacob Orton's shed.

In my waking hours, the school itself was better than any medicine. For the next few days, our lives continued their placid course, seemingly unchanged. Nevertheless, news continued to reach us from the outside world. The man who had been taken into custody was the brother of the builder, Mr Owens, who had committed suicide. The brother was said to be subject to fits of ungovernable rage; reputable witnesses had heard him utter threats against Henry Frant, whom he held responsible for his brother's suicide; he was a violent man, and had nearly killed a neighbour whom he suspected of making sheep's eyes at his wife. But the following day, the magistrates ordered his release. It transpired that he had spent the evening of the night in question drinking at his uncle's house, and had shared a bed with his cousin; and so his family would give him an alibi.

The inquest came and went. I was not called to give evidence, much to my relief and to Mr Bransby's. Mr Frant's confidential clerk, a man named Arndale who had known him for the better part of twenty years, had no hesitation in identifying the body as his master's. The jury brought in a verdict of murder against person or persons unknown.

Despite the horrific manner of his death, there were few expressions of grief for Mr Frant or of sympathy for his widow. As information emerged about the collapse of Wavenhoe's Bank and the reasons for it, the public prints hastened to condemn him.

The extent of Frant's depredations was never known for certain, but I heard sums ranging from £200,000 to upwards of half a million. Many of the bank's customers, secure in the good name of Wavenhoe's, had appointed Mr Wavenhoe and Mr Frant as their trustees. As such, Frant had purchased hundreds of thousands of pounds' worth of stock in the three per cent Consols. In the last three years, he had forged powers of attorney enabling him to sell this stock. Mr Wavenhoe had signed the documents put before him, though doubtless he was unaware of their significance. The name of a third partner, another of the trustees, had been forged on all occasions, as had several of the subscribing witnesses. Mr Frant had converted the proceeds from these sales to his own use, retaining sufficient funds to allow him to pay dividends to the bank's customers, thereby preventing their suspicions from being aroused.

Arndale, Frant's clerk, claimed to have known nothing of this. (Dansey thought the man had avoided prosecution by co-operating with the authorities.) Arndale confirmed that the house had been badly hit by the withdrawal of Mr Carswall's capital. He also testified that the bank had made many advances to speculative builders, which had rendered necessary a system of discounting, and that Mr Frant had subsequently been obliged to make further advances to these persons, in order to secure the sums in which they already stood indebted. In addition, rumours continued to circulate to the effect that Mr Frant had been addicted to play, and that he had lost large sums of money at cards and at dice in private houses.

'Whoever killed him did the hangman a favour,' Dansey said. 'If Frant weren't already dead, they'd have tried him for forgery and sent him to the gallows for uttering.'

At the time there was much speculation as to whether Mrs Frant had been privy to her husband's schemes. Some found her doubly guilty by association, for was she not the wife of one partner and the niece of another? Not everyone agreed.

'A man does not discuss his business dealings with his wife,' Dansey argued. 'No, she is guilty merely by association. The public prefers a living scapegoat, if at all possible.'

What made matters worse was that Mrs Frant had no one to speak in her defence. Mr Carswall had given her the shelter of his roof but he remained silent on this head and on all others. She was said to be suffering from a fever, her spirits quite overthrown by the double tragedy of her husband's murder and the revelation of his crimes.

As for Charlie, he stumbled like an automaton through the days. I wondered that Mr Carswall did not remove him from the school. Boys are unpredictable creatures. I had expected his schoolfellows would bait him, that they would make him suffer for his father's crimes. Instead, most of them left him alone. Indeed, when they did not ignore him, they handled him with a certain rough kindness. He looked ill, and they dealt with him as though he were. Edgar Allan rarely left his side. The young American treated his friend with a solicitude and a delicacy of sentiment which was unusual in one so young.

Delicacy of sentiment, however, was not a characteristic which could be attributed to either Morley or Quird. Nor was common decency. I came across them fighting with Allan and Frant in a corner of their schoolroom. Morley and Quird were so much older and so much heavier that it was not so much a fight as a massacre. For once, I intervened. I flogged Morley and Quird on the spot and ordered them to wait on me that evening, so that I might flog them again.

'Are you sure you want to do that, sir?' Morley asked softly when he and Quird appeared before me at the appointed time.

'I shall beat you all the more if you don't take that insolent smile off your face.'

'It's only, sir, that me and Quird happened to see you and Mr Dansey the other night.'

'Quird and I, Morley, Quird and I. The pronoun is part of a compound nominative plural.'

'Smoking under the trees, you were.'

'Then be damned to you for a pair of snivelling, spying scrubs,' I snarled, my rage boiling over. 'And why were you not in bed, pray?'

Morley had the impudence to ignore my question. 'And we saw you and him, sir, on other nights.'

I stared at him, my anger rapidly subsiding. A show of anger has its uses when you are dealing with boys, but ungovernable passion must always be deplored.

'Bend over,' I ordered.

He did not move. 'Perhaps, sir, it is my duty to inform Mr Bransby. We must all listen to the voice of conscience. He abhors the practice of –'

'You may tell Mr Bransby what you like,' I said. 'First, however, you will bend over and I shall thrash you as you've never been thrashed before.'

The smile vanished from Morley's broad, malevolent face. 'This is most unwise, sir, if I may say so.'

The words were measured, but his voice rose into a squeak at the end when I hit him a backhanded blow across the mouth. He tried to protest but I caught him by the throat, swung him round and flung him across the chair that served as our place of execution. He did not move. I dragged up his coat-tails and flogged him. There was no anger in it now: I was cold and deliberate. One could not let a boy take such a haughty tone. By the time I let him go he could hardly walk, and Quird had to half carry him away.

Nevertheless the incident left me shaken, though Morley had richly deserved his beating. I had never flogged a boy so brutally before, or given way to my passions. I wondered if the murder of Henry Frant had affected me in ways I had not suspected.

What I did not even begin to suspect until later was that Morley may have known Dansey better than I did, and that his meaning had been quite other than I had supposed.

Nine days after the murder, on Saturday the 4th December, I received a summons to Mr Bransby's private room. He was not alone. Overflowing from an elbow chair beside the desk was the large, ungainly form of Mr Carswall. His daughter perched demurely on a sofa in front of the fire.

As I entered, Carswall glared up at me through tangled eyebrows and then down at the open watch in his hand. 'You must make haste,' he said. 'Otherwise we shall not get back to town in daylight.'

Astonished, I looked from one man to the other.

'You are to accompany Charles Frant to Mr Carswall's,' Bransby said. 'His father is to be buried on Monday.'

CHAPTER TWENTY-FOUR

'I AM A bastard,' Miss Carswall said to me on the Monday evening after Mr Frant's funeral.

I was so shocked by her immodesty I did not know how to reply. I glanced at the door, fearing it might be open, that her words had been overheard. At the time Miss Carswall and I were alone in the drawing room of her father's house in Margaret-street; Charlie had run upstairs to fetch a book.

She fixed me with her brown eyes. 'Let us call things by their proper names. That is what I wished to tell you in Albemarle-street. The day when Charlie interrupted.'

'It is of no significance,' I said, feeling I must say something.

She stamped her foot. 'Had you been a bastard yourself, you would know how foolish that sounds.'

'I beg your pardon. I did not make my meaning clear. I did not mean that it was of no significance to you, or indeed in the general scheme of things. I – I meant merely that it was of no significance to me.'

'You knew, sir, admit it. Someone had told you.'

Miss Carswall glared at me for a moment. She had the fair, almost translucent skin that so often goes with auburn hair. She looked captivating in a passion.

'My papa does not choose to advertise the circumstances of my birth,' she went on after a moment's silence. 'Which in itself has been a matter of some inconvenience to me. It can lead to situations in which people – that is to say – they may approach me under false pretences.'

'You need not trouble yourself on my account, Miss Carswall,' I said.

She studied the toes of her pretty little slippers. 'I believe my mother was the daughter of a respectable farmer. I never knew her – she died before I was a year old.'

'I'm sorry.'

'Don't be. When I was six, my father sent me to board at a seminary in Bath. I stayed there until I was fifteen, when I went to live with my cousin, Mrs Frant. Papa and Mr Frant were then on friendly terms, you see. Mr Frant was in America on the bank's business, so there were just the three of us, Mrs Frant, little Charlie and me. I wish . . . '

'What do you wish?'

'I wish I could have stayed there. But my father's wife died, so there was no longer an obstacle to my living with him. And he and Mr Frant had quarrelled, so it was not convenient for me to stay in Russell-square. So I came here.' She spoke jerkily now, as though pumping the words from a deep reservoir of her being. 'As a sort of companion. A sort of housekeeper. A sort of daughter. Or even – Ah, I scarcely know what. All those things and none of them. When my father brings his friends to the house, they do not know what I am. I do not know what I am.' She broke off and sat down on the little sofa by the fire. Her bosom rose and fell in her agitation.

'I am honoured you should take me into your confidence,' I said softly.

She looked up at me. 'I am glad the funeral is over. They always make me hippish. No one came, did they, no one but that American gentleman. You would not think it now but in his life Henry Frant had so many people proud to call him friend.'

'The American gentleman?'

'Mr Noak. He knew Mr Frant, it appears, and Mr Rush the American Minister introduced him to Papa and me a few weeks ago.'

'I have met him, I believe. Mr Noak, that is to say.'

She frowned. 'When?'

'He was at Russell-square once, just after his arrival from America.

I saw him later, too, in Albemarle-street on the night Mr Wavenhoe died.'

'But why should he come to the funeral? They do not appear to have been intimate friends, and Mr Frant's crimes have turned his other friends into strangers.'

'I do not know.' I looked into her face. 'Can you not ask him your-self?'

She shook her head. 'I scarcely know him. We were introduced, but he has no conversation. Anyway, why should he wish to waste his time talking nonsense to a chit of a girl?'

I made no reply, for none was needed, or not in words. The question hung in the air between us and she blushed. Our eyes met and we smiled at each other. Flora was never beautiful but when she smiled it made your heart leap.

'Poor dear Sophie – Mrs Frant,' she said suddenly, perhaps eager to steer the conversation elsewhere. 'She has nothing, you know, nothing left at all. Mr Frant even took the rest of her jewels. She had given him most of them already but on the day he went away he broke into a drawer of her dressing table and took what was left – the ones that were especially dear to her, that she hoped to save from the wreckage.'

'The jewels were not found?'

'No – it is presumed the murderer took them. Still, Sophie is not without friends, Mr Shield – not while I am here. She is as dear to me as an elder sister. My home shall be hers for as long as she needs it.'

There were running footsteps on the stairs. Miss Carswall darted a glance at me, as if to assess the effect of her edifying sentiments, and turned aside to thread a needle by the light of the candle on her work-table.

Charlie burst into the room, instantly slowing to the sedate, sober walk of one who has buried his father on that day. He wore deepest mourning but at unguarded moments his face gave the lie to his appear-ance of sorrow. I believed him deeply shocked by Mr Frant's murder – how could he not be? – but I do not think he ever grieved for his father. He sat down by the fire. Miss Carswall took up a piece of embroi-dery. I opened my copy of Boethius's *De Consolatione*.

Occasionally a page rustled or the hand with the needle would move, but I do not think any of us did much work. It had been very cold that day, and I was still chilled to the bone. The gloom of the occasion afflicted us all in our different ways. Mr Frant's funeral had been at St George the Martyr's near Russell-square, and now his body was interred in the burying ground north of the Foundling Hospital. Somewhere above our heads lay Mrs Frant, attended by Mrs Kerridge. The widow had insisted on attending her husband's funeral, which had brought a recurrence of the fever.

It had been at Mrs Frant's request that Charlie had been withdrawn from school for the rest of term, and that I had been hired to provide him with tuition and masculine company. According to Miss Carswall in one of her moments of indiscretion, Mrs Frant had worked herself into such a passion when Carswall initially opposed this plan that the doctors had feared for her life.

Now the three of us sat in silence, pretending to be usefully occupied but in fact lost in our thoughts and waiting for the footman to bring the tea-tray. But my thirst was destined to remain unquenched, for when the man appeared, he desired me to wait on Mr Carswall.

I went downstairs. The house was east of Cavendish-square, smaller in size and less fashionable in location than I had expected from Mr Carswall's reputation for wealth. I found him in the back parlour on the floor below. Cigar in hand, he was sitting in an armchair before a large fire.

'Shield, shut the door quickly, will you? It's damned cold. Funerals always give me a chill. Stand there, man, stand in the light where I can see you.' He looked me up and down for a moment. 'Charlie tells me you was a soldier. One of the nation's heroes at Waterloo.'

'I was there, sir, certainly.'

He brayed with laughter, opening and then snapping shut his mouth as though catching a fly. 'I could never see the purpose of lining up to be killed, myself. Still, I allow that it is valuable for the country if some of its young men think otherwise.' He took up a glass from a table at his elbow and sipped. 'They tell me you saw Harry Frant dead.'

'Yes, sir.'

'Lying where he fell, was he? Wellington-terrace, ha! That was an unlucky speculation if you like. And all to end in a dark and gloomy cellar.'

'The cellar was open to the sky, sir. The walls of the houses were not more than a few feet above the ground. Besides, though I saw where he had been killed, by the time I reached the place he had been moved. He lay in a shed nearby.'

'Oh.' Carswall cleared the phlegm from his throat with a great rumble. 'They never told me that. I understand the body had been much mutilated.'

'That is correct.'

'How? Spit it out, man. You need not mince your words. I may not have been a soldier but I am not lily-livered.'

'The public journals said he had been attacked with a hammer.'

'Very true. One was found in a hedgerow. There was blood on it, they said, and hairs. In your opinion, having seen the injuries, could that have been the instrument used?'

'Very possibly, sir. Mr Frant had been much beaten about the head. Indeed, one eye had been quite put out.'

'But you believe it was he?'

'I could not be sure. The hair, the height, the clothes – even the hands: everything supported that conclusion.'

'Yet the face was unrecognisable. That is the long and the short of it, is it not?'

'If it was not he, there was certainly a general similarity in appearance. The cast of features, the –'

'Granted,' Carswall interrupted. 'But what of the hands?'

'Mr Frant's ring was on his right hand. The top joints of the forefinger on the other hand were missing.'

'They were a gentleman's hands?'

I shrugged. 'It is hard to say. They too had been much marked. Nor did I have either the opportunity or inclination to examine them closely. Besides, the light was not good.'

Carswall consulted a watch he took from his waistcoat pocket. He sighed as though he did not like what it told him. For a moment, he stared into the depths of the fire. His cravat was loosened, his breeches were unbuttoned at the waist and the knee. His coat was crumpled and stained, his hair in disarray. But his mind was capable of such vigour, his habitual manner of speech was so emphatic, that one often forgot that he was an old, sick man.

Suddenly he glanced up and smiled at me and the effect was blinding. It was as though his daughter had smiled: a similar rearrangement of features into something so different from what had been before.

'You see where these questions are tending, do you not?'

'The finger.'

He nodded. 'Were you able to form an opinion as to whether the amputation had been of recent date or not?'

'In the circumstances I suspect even a medical man would have found it hard to decide.'

'What of the skin beneath the clothes?'

'I did not have an opportunity to examine it.' I hesitated. 'The skin of a cadaver is not like that of a living man. The body had been outside all night. It was very cold. Unless there were distinguishing marks, such as a scar or a mole –'

'There were not.'

Carswall brooded and drank wine. Only two candles were lit, one at either end of the mantel-shelf. The room was full of shadows. I thought of the cave that Plato describes in his *Republic*: here were the shadows and the fire; but would I ever be able to see what lay beyond the other side of the fire, in the sunlit real world? Or would the Frants and the Carswalls keep me for ever trapped in their cave?

'I will be plain with you,' Carswall said. 'But first I must ask you to respect my confidence. Will you give me your word?'

'Yes, sir.'

'Mrs Frant tells me that on two occasions a disreputable fellow came to Stoke Newington and pestered Charlie. And that on the first occasion, he tried to assault, or perhaps seize, the boy, and that you were at hand to effect a rescue. Is that true?'

'Yes, sir. Though –'

'And on the second occasion, the man was sufficiently in funds to give the lads a tip.' Carswall held up a hand, preventing me from speaking. 'Now here is something you don't know. On the Friday before he died, as Mr Frant was walking through Russell-square on his way home at about midday, he was accosted outside his house by a man who answered to the description that both you and Charlie had given of the stranger in Stoke Newington. Mrs Frant chanced to be looking out of the drawing-room window. She remarked the circumstance particularly, because at that time they were much plagued by creditors. This man did not seem to be a creditor, however, or a bailiff, or anyone of that nature. Though Mrs Frant could not hear the words of their conversation, it was clear from his gestures that Mr Frant was angry and that the other man was cowed by his anger. Mr Frant came into the house and the other man walked rapidly away. Mrs Frant asked her husband when he came up who the man had been. And here is the strangest circumstance of all: Frant flatly denied that he'd been talking with anyone.' Carswall paused, poked his forefinger through the gap between two buttons of his waistcoat and scratched his belly. 'Now why would he wish to do that, do you think?'

'I cannot say, sir.'

'I wonder. Mrs Frant believes you had private business with her husband.'

'It is true that on one occasion I was able to be of service to Mr Frant.' I turned away, so that he could not see my face. 'I confess I do not understand why you find this meeting that Mrs Frant witnessed to be of such significance in the matter of Mr Frant's death.'

'I should have been surprised if you had. I have not told you the whole of it yet. The drawing-room window was open, despite the cold, because Mrs Frant had been airing the room. The stranger raised his voice, and she heard him quite distinctly say the words *Wellington-terrace*. Moreover, she believes – though I do not know how much weight one should attach to this – that the man had an Irish or perhaps American accent.' Carswall tapped the arm of his chair with the base of the glass. 'I do not deny that her ears may have heard, at least in memory, what she wanted to hear. One more thing: she is convinced that the private business you had with her husband had to do with the stranger in Stoke

Newington. She is barely well enough to speak at present but she charged me to lay all this before you.'

I bowed my head. A wave of shame swept over me.

'You would not wish to make her suffering worse, I take it?' Carswall said.

'No, sir.'

'Then you can have no objection to disclosing whatever you know.'

'Very well. After the man's first visit to Stoke Newington, Mr Frant was naturally concerned for the safety of his son. I saw the man again, by chance, one afternoon in Long Acre. I gave chase and eventually ran him down and heard his story. He is an American, he told me, but of Irish descent. He called himself David Poe. The reason for his visit to Stoke Newington was not Charlie or Mr Frant. Charlie's friend Edgar Allan was the object of his interest.'

'Allan? The son of the American who lives in Southampton-row? The Mr Allan who was badly hit when the tobacco market collapsed?'

'I cannot comment on Mr Allan's business dealings, sir, but he is certainly the father of Edgar Allan – or rather the foster father. Young Edgar makes no bones about the fact that he has been adopted. This David Poe claimed to be his natural father.'

'Why should he turn up now after all these years?'

'He hoped for money.' I hesitated. 'I think, too, there may have been an element of paternal affection in him. Or at least of curiosity.'

Carswall blew his nose long and loud into a large yellow handkerchief. 'I do not understand. On the second occasion, he *gave* them money.'

'Yes, sir. I can only infer that in the interim Mr Poe's material circumstances had considerably improved.'

Carswall consulted his watch. 'There is another point: Mrs Frant made it quite clear that on that first occasion the man was interested in Charlie, not in the other boy.'

'I believe it probable that Poe made a mistake. I should make it clear that at the time the man seemed inebriated. Also, there is a certain resemblance between the two boys.'

'A double, eh?'

'Not precisely, sir. There is a similarity, no more than that.'

Carswall threw the butt of his cigar into the fire. 'Tell me, were you able to establish where the man lives?'

'In St Giles. He would not say exactly where, but he informed me that he is often to be found at the Fountain, where he works as a screever.'

'And you told Frant all this?'

'Yes, sir.'

'Some time after this, the man Poe reappears in Stoke Newington, with his circumstances miraculously changed for the better. Later, Mrs Frant sees her husband talking with a man, who may be this Poe, in Russell-square, an encounter her husband afterwards denies, and also overhears the words Wellington-terrace. Later still, a body which purports to be that of Mr Frant is discovered foully murdered in Wellington-terrace. Well? How does that strike you?'

'On the present evidence, sir, it is impossible to judge whether these circumstances are connected, whether they are in some way linked.'

Carswall hammered the heel of his left hand against the arm of the chair. 'Don't lecture me, young man. That's the trouble with you bumbrushers, you treat the world as your schoolroom. Now – how well do you know St Giles?'

'I have walked there on occasion.'

'For pleasure?' When I did not answer, he gave another of his laughs, a strange, hard, almost inhuman sound that could have come from the mouth of a great bird. 'Do you know the Fountain?'

'It's somewhere north of the church,' I said. 'Near Lawrence-street, I believe.'

'Will you go there tomorrow and seek out Mr Poe?'

'I am, sir, as you remind me, a schoolmaster, and –'

'Just so, just so, Mr Shield. You are also a man who has seen some-thing of the world. And you are the only person I am aware of, with the possible exception of Mrs Frant herself, who knows what this man Poe looks like.'

'But Mrs Frant has charged me to look after her son.'

'God damn it, am I not paying for the privilege of your presence?'

The rich assume we are in their power, and usually they are right.

For now, I was scarcely more than one of Carswall's servants. If I aroused his ire, he would speak to Mr Bransby and I would be out of my place.

He pressed the repeater button on his watch and it emitted a tiny chime. 'Besides,' he said gently, 'I am not asking you to do this for me. I am asking you to do this for Mrs Frant herself. And I know you will not refuse me.'

CHAPTER TWENTY-FIVE

THE FOLLOWING MORNING, I slipped out of the house, made my way through the market to Oxford-street, and walked eastwards towards St Giles. I had purchased an old, patched coat from the man who brought the kindling. I carried a heavy stick, borrowed from Mr Carswall.

It was a foul day, the air rendered almost opaque by a yellow fog that found its way into the mouth and tasted like soot. I blundered along the pavements colliding with my fellow pedestrians, and on one occasion nearly losing my life to a passing coal cart.

In the days of what they were pleased to call my lunacy, I would often wander in the Rookeries of St Giles-in-the-Fields. The worst parts were north of the church in that dark lozenge of courts and alleys and lanes that lay between Bainbridge-street, George-street and the High-street. I was never molested, though, even by the dogs that ran wild in the streets. Misery calls to misery. They had known I was one of them.

As I drew nearer the black heart of the place, the smells and the noise rose up to greet me, enveloping me, sucking at me, as though they were but extensions of the fog. The Rookeries were a place where the natural order of things was reversed: where victims became beasts of prey, and preyed in turn on their natural enemy.

I turned off the High-street into Lawrence-street. A woman wearing but a shift despite the cold tore at my coat with fingers as small as a child's. I brushed past her and in my hurry stumbled over a lean pig ambling through the pool of muck extending into the roadway from the mouth of an alley. A pair of urchins ran after the animal, shouting shrill obscenities in their excitement. I hurried on. I passed a woman swathed in grey blankets, huddled in a doorway, with a baby at her breast. She held out a bare, scrawny arm to me and beckoned. 'I'll make you happy, dearie,' she cried in a thin, reedy whine. And I heard her cursing me in the same, unchanging voice as I left her behind.

'And would you spare a copper for an old soldier to drink His Majesty's health?' a husky voice inquired from the level of my knees.

I glanced down and saw a red-faced man without legs, huddled on a low trolley.

'Would you direct me to the Fountain? It is not far from here, is it?'

'His Majesty's health,' the man insisted.

I found a penny in my pocket and dropped it into his waiting palm.

His fingers closed around the coin. 'There's an alley on the left halfway between Church-street and George-street: cut up there and you'll find it.'

But his eyes darted towards a knot of drinkers spilling from an alehouse. It was enough to put me on my guard and I hurried away, swinging my stick and looking as sour and formidable as I could. Philanthropy is a luxury. You do not find it in the Rookeries, where even the indulgence of a charitable impulse may exact a price.

I reached the entrance to the alley. The way was unpaved, no more than four feet wide, and its surface was thickly covered with a tide of mud and excrement, human and animal, part moist, part frozen. The passage was densely populated with sleeping, drinking and talking figures. Two little girls sat in the filth, nursing bundles of rags and making patties from dirt. Scarcely a yard away, a man and a woman groaned and grunted in an act of copulation that seemed to bring more pain than pleasure.

With my stick held menacingly before me, I waded through the crowd. From the fog-filled court at the end of the alley came a slow dancing melody, 'St Patrick's Day', played on a fiddle. I had heard that tune before, when we were quartered next to an Irish regiment. They called the Rookeries the Holy Land or Little Dublin because of the destitute Irish who drained into it from the rest of the city, and the rest of the kingdom.

I reached the gloomy little court at the end of the alley. The building on the right bore a crudely executed signboard showing a fountain. I pushed open the door and, stepping over yet another crawling infant, entered what appeared to be the taproom. It was low and dark, no more than twelve-foot square, and it must have contained at least thirty people. I pushed my way through the press until I came across a woman built like a guardsman with a great leather belt round her waist from which depended a leather pouch and a bunch of keys. I swept off my hat and executed, as best I could in the confined space, a courtly bow.

'Madam,' I said, 'perhaps you could help me. I am looking for Mr Poe the screever.'

She took a long swallow from a tankard in her hand and set it down on a nearby shelf. Turning back towards me, she wiped the foam from her moustache and said, 'I am afraid you are come too late.' Her eyelids fluttered over small brown eyes like specks of dried fruit in a pudding. 'A gentleman with a wonderful fund of poetry. Such recitations we had of an evening. And such a gentlemanly hand, too, he was never short of work. A petition here, a letter of advice and admonition to a beloved child there, a plea to an aged parent beyond the seas.' She took another swallow from her tankard. 'Mr Poe has a style for each eventuality.'

'But he is no longer with you, madam?'

'Alas, no, though he had the bed by the window in my second-floor front for so long he was like one of the family. "Maria, my love," he'd say to me, "you treat me like a king; you are my queen and this room is our palace."'

She brought her face close to mine and grinned at me, revealing a mouthful of pink, swollen gums. I smelled the sour tang of spirits and the rich, dark odour of rotting meat.

'Why, I could show you the room, if you liked, sir. "Such a comfortable bed," Mr Poe used to say, and he had no need to share it, not unless he wished to, if you take my meaning. Well? Should you like to see it with me?'

131

'You're too kind, madam. Unfortunately, I have pressing business with Mr Poe –'

'There's pressing and pressing, I always say,' Maria said, nudging me with her great bosom. 'Not so pressing, I hope, that you may not take a glass of something warm to keep out the chill? Once this fog gets in the lungs, it can do for a man in a matter of days. My first husband was consumptive, and my third.'

I recognised the force of the inevitable, and requested that she might do me the honour of taking a glass of spirits with me. She relieved me of a shilling, opened a hatch above her shelf and produced tumblers of gin and water.

Shortly afterwards, my hostess became indisposed. First she leaned back against the wall and, grasping my shoulders with a pair of muscular hands, informed me that I was a fine figure of a man. She attempted to kiss me, then drank some more gin and wept a little for her third husband, who she said had touched her heart more than the others.

'Mr Poe's direction, madam,' I broke in. 'You were so kind as to say you would let me have it.'

'Mr Poe,' she wailed, trying without success to throw her apron over her head. 'My Mr Poe has forsaken his little love bird. He has flown our happy nest.'

'Yes, madam – but where?'

'Seven Dials.' She sniffed, and suddenly she might have been as sober as a nun. 'Got himself a job clerking for a gent, he said, needed to move nearer his new place of employment. Truth was, Fountain-court wasn't good enough for him no more.'

'Where in Seven Dials?'

'He lodges in a house in Queen-street.' As she spoke, her legs gave way and she slithered slowly down the wall, with her knees rising like mountains until they touched the jutting precipices of her bosom. 'There's a man tells fortunes in the house. Ever so genteel. He has a parrot that talks French. Mr Poe said he looked at him – the man did, not the parrot – and told him he saw beautiful women at his feet, and riches beyond the dreams of avarice.'

CHAPTER TWENTY-SIX

BY THE TIME I left the Fountain, the fog had grown even worse. My eyes stung and watered. My nose streamed. I swam through the coughing, spluttering crowds down to Seven Dials. On the way, I passed through St Giles's churchyard. The church itself loomed like a great, smoke-stained whale on the ocean floor. It was as though I were travelling through a city at the bottom of the ocean, a drowned world.

The fancy had barely formed in my mind when I recalled that St Giles was indeed a place where people drowned. A few years before, within a stone's throw of the church, an enormous vat had exploded at the Horseshoe Brewery. Thousands of gallons of beer washed like a tidal wave through the parish, sweeping away stalls, carts, sheds, animals and people. In this locality, many people live in cellars. The beer flooded into these underground homes, and eight people were drowned in ale.

The thought of this vengeful wave sliding through the streets and lanes lent weight to a growing suspicion that I was pursued. The sensation crept upon me by imperceptible degrees, gradually more palpable like a hint of damp in one's sheets. Though I turned and looked over my shoulder again and again, the fog made it difficult for me to identify individuals in the mass of humanity that pressed immediately upon my heels.

I stopped at a street corner to get my bearings, and a set of footsteps behind me also seemed to stop. I turned right into New Compton-street, away from Seven Dials. By now I had convinced myself that someone truly was following me. I continued in a westerly direction, and then swung down and round into Lower Earl-street, and so towards Seven Dials. My conviction wavered. I could hear so many footsteps around me that I could not identify the ones that I thought had been following me.

I crossed Seven Dials and walked slowly up Queen-street, keeping to the left-hand side and peering into each establishment I passed. Roughly halfway down, I found a little shop with a parrot's cage discernible on the other side of its grimy window. I pushed open the door and went inside. The parrot squawked, a strange harsh call with three syllables, instantly repeated. In another instant the squawk became words and acquired meaning.

'*Ayez peur*,' cried the bird. '*Ayez peur*.'

The room was no more than eight feet square, and it stank of coal fumes and drains. For all that, it was a sweeter-smelling place than the street and certainly a warmer one. A man sat hunched over a stove at the back of the shop. He wore a coat that trailed to the ground, a muffler and a greasy skullcap of black velvet. A blanket covered his legs to shield him from the draughts. He turned to greet me, and I saw a clean-shaven face with fleshy features beneath a lined but lofty brow.

'Fortunes; ballads, whether political or amorous by nature; medicines for man and beast,' he intoned in a deep, cultivated voice, with a method of delivery that would not have been out of place in the pulpit; 'remedies for the afflictions of venery; charms of proven efficacy to satisfy all human desires in this world or the next; rooms by the week or by the day. Theodore Iversen is at your service, whatever your pleasure may be.'

Not to be outdone in the matter of civility, I took off my hat and bowed. 'Have I the pleasure of addressing the owner of this establishment?'

'*Ayez peur*,' said the parrot behind me.

'I hold the lease, though whether I shall be able to afford to do so next year is another matter.' Iversen laid down a pipe on the table beside the stove. 'You do not want to know the future, I suspect, nor do you want a charm. That leaves medicine and accommodation.'

'Neither, sir. I understand that one of your lodgers is an old acquaintance of mine, a Mr David Poe.'

'Ah, Mr Poe.' He turned aside to stir a small iron saucepan standing on the stove. 'A refined gentleman. A martyr to the toothache.'

'And is he at home at present, sir?'

'Alas, no. I regret to say he has left the shelter of my roof. Or so I assume.'

'May I ask when?'

Mr Iversen raised his eyebrows. 'Two days ago – no, I tell a lie: it was three days. He had kept to his room for a day or two before that with his toothache, a sad affliction at any age; to my mind, we are better off without teeth entirely. I offered to give him something to ease the pain, but he declined my assistance. Still, if a gentleman wishes to suffer, who am I to stand in his way?'

'And did he say where he was going?'

'He said nothing to me whatsoever. He stole away like a thief in the night except, unlike a thief, he stole nothing. No matter – he has paid for his lodging until the end of the week.'

'So he has not left the room for good?'

'That I cannot say. I have a number of infallible methods of revealing what the future holds – and as the seventh son of a seventh son, I am of course gifted with second sight as well as extraordinary powers of healing – but I make a rule never to use my skills of prognostication for my own benefit.'

'*Ayez peur,*' said the parrot.

'Damn that bird,' said Mr Iversen. 'There is a piece of sacking on the chair behind you, my dear sir. Be so good as to drape it over the cage.'

Turning, I caught the impression of movement in the corner of my eye. Had someone been peering at us through the window? The glass was grimy and contained impurities which made objects on the other side of it ripple as though under water. It was not impossible, I told myself, that my imagination had transformed such a ripple into a spy. I covered the cage and turned back to the shopkeeper.

'If you believe that Mr Poe may return,' I said, 'does not that suggest that his bags are still in his room?'

Mr Iversen smirked.

I said: 'I have a fancy to see my friend's room. Perhaps it contains some indication of where he has gone.'

'I make it another rule that only lodgers are allowed in my rooms. Present lodgers and, of course, *prospective* lodgers, who may quite reasonably express a wish to inspect the outlook, the dimensions, *et cetera*.'

'So there would be no objection to my seeing the room if I were a prospective lodger? If I had arranged, perhaps, to take the room for a day when it should become vacant.'

'None in the world.' Mr Iversen beamed at me. 'Five shillings a night for sole use of the room and the flock mattress. Shared pump in the yard. Extra charges should you wish the girl to bring you water or clean sheets and so forth.'

'Five shillings?'

'Including a shilling for sundries.'

I drew out my purse and paid his extortionate rate for a room I would never sleep in.

'Thank you,' he said, tucking the money away in his clothing. 'And now I shall require your assistance.'

He swept the blanket from his legs. I saw that he wore not a coat, as I had thought, but a long, black robe, like a monk's habit, upon which were embroidered alchemical or astrological symbols, though age and dirt had so obscured them that they were barely visible in the dim light of the shop. On his feet was a pair of enormous leather slippers. The removal of the blanket also revealed the chair on which he sat. A set of wheels had been fixed to the legs; a shelf on which Mr Iversen could rest his feet projected from the front; and a handrail had been attached to the top of the chair-back.

He unhooked a bunch of keys from the belt that encircled the robe. 'I would be obliged if you would be so good as to push me through that door. Fortunately Mr Poe's chamber is on the ground floor. The stairs are a sore trial to me.' He snuffled. 'My dear father's apartment is on the floor above us, and it grieves me deeply that I cannot run up and down to satisfy his little wants.'

Iversen was a heavy man, and it was no easy matter to push him through the doorway. Here we entered another world from the dusty little shop, one that was almost as heavily populated as Fountain-court had been. There were people visible in the kitchen at the back, and people on the stairs. Washing had been draped across the hall, so we had to struggle through grey curtains of dripping linen. Men were singing and stamping their feet on the floor above, and the sound of hammering rose from below.

'We have a shoe manufactory in the cellar,' my host told me. 'They make the finest riding boots in London. Would you care to bespeak a pair? I'm sure they would give you, as a fellow tenant, a very special price indeed.'

'I would not have a use for them at present, thank you.'

As we passed the foot of the stairs, Iversen called up: 'Pray do not agitate yourself, Papa. I shall be with you in a moment.'

There was no reply.

We stopped outside a door near the kitchen. He leaned forward and unlocked it. The room was a dark little cell, no more than a closet, with just space for a small bed and a chair. The glass in the tiny window was broken, the hole plugged with rags and scraps of paper. A full chamber-pot stood beneath a chair, with an empty bottle on its side next to it. The bed was unmade.

Iversen pointed under the bed. 'His valise is still there.'

'May I look inside?' I asked. 'It may contain some clue as to my friend's whereabouts, and it would be in his own interest if I could find him.'

He gave a laugh which turned into a cough. 'I regret it infinitely, but it will be another shilling if you wish to open it.'

I said nothing but gave him the money. The valise was not locked. I rummaged through its contents – among them a pair of shoes that needed re-soling, a patched shirt, a crayon drawing of the head and shoulders of a lady with large eyes and ringlets, her hair dressed in the fashion of twenty or thirty years before. There was also a volume containing some of Shakespeare's plays: the book had lost its back cover and had the name of David Poe on the flyleaf.

'Do you know where he found employment?' I asked.

Iversen shook his head. 'If a man pays his rent and makes no trouble, I've no cause to poke my nose into his business.'

'Where are his other belongings?'

'How should I know? Perhaps this is all he has. As a friend of his, you are no doubt better informed about his circumstances than I am.'

'Is there anyone here who might know where he has gone?'

'There's the girl who brings the water and takes the slops. You could ask her, if you wish. It'll cost you another shilling, though.'

'Have I not paid enough already?'

He spread his hands. 'Times are hard, my dear young friend.' I gave him the shilling. He bade me push him into the kitchen, where babies wailed and two women quarrelled obscenely over a heap of rags, then through a low-ceilinged back kitchen where three men played at dice while a woman boiled bones, and finally into the small yard beyond. The foetor rising from the overflowing cesspool made me reach for my handkerchief.

'There,' my guide said, pointing to a wooden shed the size of a commodious kennel, which leaned against the back wall of the yard. 'That's where Mary Ann lives. You may have to wake her. She's had a busy night.'

I picked my way through the rubbish-strewn yard and knocked on the low door of the shed. There was no answer. I knocked again and waited.

'I told you,' the shopkeeper called. 'She may be asleep. Try the door.'

The rotting wood of the door scraped on the cobbles of the yard. There was no window, but the light from the doorway showed a small woman huddled under a pile of rags and newspapers in the corner.

'No need for alarm, Mary Ann. I am a friend of Mr Poe's, and I wish to ask you one or two questions.'

Slowly she raised her head and looked at me. She gave a high, wordless sound, like the cry of a bird.

'I mean you no harm,' I said. 'Do you remember Mr Poe – who lodges in the room by the kitchen?'

She sat up, pointed her finger at her mouth and again emitted that wordless cry.

'I'm trying to discover where he has gone.'

At this, Mary Ann sprang to her feet, backed into the corner of her wretched dwelling and, still pointing at her mouth, made the same sound again. At last I understood what she was telling me. The poor girl was dumb. I bent down, so my eyes were level with hers. She was not wearing a cap, and her thin, ginger hair was alive with grey lice.

'Do you remember Mr Poe?' I persisted. 'Can you hear me? Nod your head if you do and if you remember him.'

She waited a moment and then slowly nodded.

'And he left here three days ago?'

Another nod.

'Do you know where he went?'

This time she shook her head.

'Or where his place of work was?'

She shook her head with even more vigour than before.

'Did he take a bag with him when he left?'

She shrugged. The light from the door was full on her face, and her eyes flickered to and fro. I thrust my hand in my pocket and pulled out a handful of coppers which I placed in a column on the floor beside her. To my intense embarrassment, she seized my hand in both of hers and covered it with kisses, all the while emitting her bird-like squeals.

'You must not agitate yourself,' I said awkwardly, tugging my hand free and standing up. 'Pray excuse me from disturbing your sleep.'

She made a gesture, requesting me to wait, and burrowed into the layers of clothing that armoured her frail body against the world. She squeaked and squealed continually, though now the sounds were gentler, reminding me of the murmuring of wood doves. At last, her face glowing, she handed me a crumpled sheet of paper which looked as if it had been torn from a memorandum book. On it was a pencil drawing of a boy's head and shoulders, that much was obvious, though not a boy who could have existed in real life. It was the sort of drawing a man does with his hand while his mind is occupied elsewhere.

I smiled as though the sight of it pleased me and tried to hand it back to Mary Ann. She squealed and cooed and made it clear with her hands that she wished me to keep it. I slipped the paper inside my coat and said goodbye. She smiled shyly at me, gave me the slightest of waves and dived back beneath her bedclothes.

Iversen was still waiting in his chair at the back door. 'You've made a conquest, my dear sir, I can tell that. We rarely have the pleasure of hearing Mary Ann so loquacious.'

I ignored this attempt at wit. 'Thank you. If there's nothing more you can tell me, I shall take my leave.'

'Now you're in the yard, it will be more convenient for you if you go down the entry.' Iversen indicated the narrow passage beside the privy, a noisome tunnel leading through the depth of the house to the street on the other side. 'Unless you want your fortune told, that is, or a charm to make the lady burn with passion for you.'

I shook my head and walked into the passage. I hurried along the entry towards the foggy bustle of the street beyond. The air smelled particularly dank and rotten. A great grey rat ran over my foot. I took a swipe at it with my stick but missed and hit the wall instead. My mind was full of pity for the girl and anger towards Iversen, who I suspected was her procurer.

The attack took me completely by surprise.

I was two-thirds of the way down when a man propelled himself out of nowhere into my right shoulder. I fell back against the opposite wall and tried to raise my stick. But the narrowness of the passage and the man's body itself impeded me. I had an instant in which to realise that a side door from the house opened into the passage. The door was recessed, with enough room for a man to lurk on the step.

Not just one man but two: the second flung himself at me. Both wore dark clothes. I twisted in the grasp of the first. Metal chinked on the brickwork. I smelled hot, stale breath. A voice swore. I heard footsteps running through the muck from the street.

'God damn you,' a man howled.

A great blow hit my head. Pain fogged my vision. The last thing I heard was another man yelling: 'Mother of Christ! Get the God-damned blackbird!'

CHAPTER TWENTY-SEVEN

I RETAIN LITTLE memory of what happened next. I lost all awareness of my surroundings for several seconds, perhaps longer. Nor, when I regained it, was I much the better for the achievement. It was only with an immense effort of the intellect that I was able to determine that the fog was as heavy as ever, and that for some reason someone was half carrying, half dragging me through a crowd of jostling people.

I gasped for air. A man shouted something very near to my ear, and a moment later I found myself being bundled into a hackney. I collapsed on to the seat.

'Brewer-street,' said a man beside me.

'He's foxed,' said a second voice.

'No. He's fainted. Nothing more.'

'If he flashes the hash in there –'

I heard the chink of coin, and the voices fell silent. A moment later the hackney began to move. Our progress was slow. I huddled in the corner with my head in my hands. The swaying of the carriage made me feel nauseous, and for a while I thought the coachman's fears would be justified. Time ceased to mean anything. The light hurt my eyes. My companion did not attempt to speak to me. I doubt if I could have answered him if he had.

The hackney pursued a zigzag course and in time its swaying became familiar, almost a source of comfort rather than of unease. I opened my eyes and squinted outside. There, looming out of the fog, was the unmistakable shape of St Ann's Church with its slatted belfry and swollen spire. The recognition gave my mind a jolt which seemed to free some internal mechanism: the cerebral processes began to flow smoothly once more.

What the devil was I doing in a hackney? Had I been kidnapped? Try as I might, I could remember nothing between being thrust into the carriage and, at some undefined point earlier, Iversen the shopkeeper watching me as I went through the contents of Mr Poe's valise. Slowly I turned my head, and the movement made the ache worse.

'Ah,' Salutation Harmwell said. 'The colour has returned to your face, Mr Shield. That is a good sign.'

'Mr – Mr Harmwell. I don't understand.'

'You remember nothing?'

'No – there seems a gap in my memory.' Even as I was speaking, that mysterious void disgorged a fragment of information. 'The blackbird.'

'I beg your pardon?'

'I remember someone – damned if I know who, or when, or why – an Irish voice, I think – someone saying something about a blackbird. And in St Giles, as I recall, the word is commonly used –'

'To describe a man of colour?'

'Precisely. Pray, Mr Harmwell, can you enlighten me as to how I come to be here?'

'I chanced to be walking down Queen-street when I heard the sound of an affray. I looked into the passage of the shop I was passing and saw you engaged in a struggle with two desperate ruffians. Not that I recognised you at this point – all I knew was that some poor innocent was in the process of being beaten and robbed. So I knocked one of them down. The other ran off and I judged it prudent that we should withdraw as soon as possible.'

I glanced down at his hand and saw that his knuckles were badly grazed. 'I am much obliged to you, sir.' I rubbed the side of my head where a bruise was already forming. 'I – I do not know what I would have done if you had not happened to be passing.'

'You have lost your hat, I am afraid. Indeed, I think it must have taken the full force of the blow, and you would have been in a much worse state if it had not been there. I believe you had a stick, too, but that has gone as well.'

I nodded. I had not noticed the absence of either. I bit back the observation that it was surely a remarkable coincidence that Harmwell should have happened to be passing. The fact that the coincidence had been of great service to me was neither here nor there.

'Do you still have your purse?'

I felt in my pocket. 'Yes.'

'That is something.'

I knew only that I must be cautious, not why. I said slowly, 'Perhaps I was passing along the street, and they dragged me into the passage in order to rob me.'

'That is unlikely,' Harmwell replied. 'I think I should have seen you, despite the fog. It is more probable that you entered the passage from the other side, or possibly from a side door of one of the houses it serves.'

The hackney moved steadily westwards, wriggling through the bustling streets into the heart of Soho. At last we reached Brewer-street. Harmwell directed the coachman to a house on the north side, near the corner with Great Pultney-street. He waved aside my attempt to pay the fare.

The dizziness returned when I stood up. Harmwell helped me down and lent me the support of his arm as we went into the house. A servant with a blank face and shabby livery conducted us upstairs. It appeared that Mr Noak had taken the whole of the first floor. There was a sitting room at the front, and Harmwell settled me on a sofa beside the fire and told the servant to bring me a glass of brandy. He went in search of his master. By the time he returned with Mr Noak, I had swallowed half the brandy and regained a few more of my wits. But I still could not remember what had happened in the interval of time between my being in Mr Poe's room in Queen-street and Harmwell bustling me into the hackney.

God-damned blackbird?

As I heard that coarse voice in my mind, an image from those lost moments of my life slipped into the forefront of my memory: that of a small, childlike creature seizing my hand and kissing it. The memory was so clear that I saw the grey lice moving in her sparse ginger hair.

I rose to my feet as Mr Noak entered and found I could stand without support. He gave me his hand and asked me how I did. I stumbled out my thanks to Harmwell for saving my life, and to Mr Noak himself for his hospitality.

'Harmwell did no more than his plain duty as a Christian,' Noak said in his hard New England voice. 'It was providential he should have been passing.'

'Indeed,' I said.

'Pray be seated.' Noak settled himself in an armchair on the other side of the fire. 'The last time we met, Mr Shield, we disputed about the value of reading Ovid. I do not know London well but I understand from my clerk that he came across you in a part of town which is not the usual haunt of schoolmasters.'

'Mr Carswall sent me there upon an errand.'

'Mr Carswall? Yes, I had the pleasure of seeing him recently, though on a melancholy occasion.' He looked sharply at me. 'Forgive my curiosity, but I thought you were employed at a school outside London.'

'I am, sir, but at the present I am staying with Mr Carswall in Margaret-street so that I may give lessons to Charles Frant.'

Noak's mouth tightened. 'We must applaud Mr Carswall's charity in providing a home for Mrs Frant and her fatherless boy.'

He paused, seeming plunged in gloomy reflection. Time passed. My own thoughts were scarcely happy either. Mrs Frant might not have needed Mr Carswall's charity if I had not witnessed George Wavenhoe's signature on his deathbed.

At length he continued: 'Are you able to remember who attacked you? No doubt you will wish to lay information against them in Bow-street.'

'I regret that I cannot remember the circumstances of the attack, nor of Mr Harmwell's rescue.'

'How very unfortunate. Still, you know where it happened, and Harmwell saw your assailants.'

Harmwell coughed. 'The passage was gloomy, sir. I did not have a clear view of them.'

'And St Giles is a lawless place,' I pointed out. 'The men who attacked me will no longer be there.'

Noak glanced from Harmwell to myself. 'What about the people of the house? Were they concerned in the attack?'

Harmwell shrugged.

I said, 'I recall nothing beforehand to show that they must have been.'

'But they might, eh?'

'It is impossible to say.' I winced from the pain in my head. 'I – I cannot remember. I shall consult Mr Carswall on my return, sir, but I believe it is likely that he would advise me to let sleeping dogs lie.'

'I see,' said Mr Noak, and I had the uncomfortable suspicion that he saw more than I liked.

'I must not trespass any further on your good nature,' I said. 'Mrs Frant and Mr Carswall will be becoming anxious.'

'Harmwell will take you back.'

'But I could not possibly trouble you or him any longer.'

'It is no trouble,' Noak said abruptly, rising to his feet. 'Or not to me. Even if it were, you have had a bad blow on the head and it is my duty as a Christian to ensure your safe return, just as it was Harmwell's duty to come to your assistance.'

He nodded farewell to me and left the room. Harmwell rang the bell for the servant. Within ten minutes we were in another hackney, moving so slowly through the fog that it would have been faster to walk. Neither of us spoke. After a while, the silence became oppressive and I blundered into speech.

'What are your impressions of London, Mr Harmwell?'

'Why, it is so vast and so varied that one scarcely has time to form an impression before another comes along and overturns it. There is so much wealth here, the mind can hardly comprehend it.'

'But you Americans have great wealth in the United States, too, I am sure.'

'I am not American, sir. I am from Canada. My father was from Virginia but he moved north with his master after the Revolution.'

'They were Loyalists? Did your father sustain severe losses by the move?'

'No, sir, he gained everything.' Harmwell turned and gave me a level stare. 'He gained his freedom. Mr Saunders was granted an estate in Upper Canada and my father continued to work for him. So did I until I enlisted in the army in the late war with the United States.' A harsh note entered his voice. 'If the family had not died out in the meantime, I should have returned to their employ on my discharge from the army.'

'I am sorry – yet you found another position?'

'Mr Noak was kind enough to offer me a clerkship.'

My curiosity had already led me considerably further than good manners allowed so I turned the conversation to more general subjects. We talked mainly about New York and Boston. Harmwell did not volunteer information easily but he showed himself a man of sense in his replies.

It was after three o'clock by the time we had crossed the restless river of humanity that filled Oxford-street. When we reached Margaret-street, I begged him to descend and take some refreshment. Harmwell hesitated, and then said that if there were no objection, he would pay a call on Mrs Kerridge, if she were at liberty, as she had promised to write out a receipt for him to send to his mother in Canada. He spoke so solemnly, his face a picture of filial piety, that I almost burst out laughing when I recalled the way his hand had brushed her breast that afternoon in Piccadilly, and how she tapped him on the cheek as a punishment.

Once we were in the warmth of the house, a servant took Harmwell down to see Mrs Kerridge. Mr Carswall was at home but I wished to wash my face and change my coat before I saw him. I went upstairs to my room and lit a candle because it was already so dark I could barely see the hand in front of my face. There was still an inch or two of cold water in the jug on my washstand. I poured it into the bowl. As I peeled off my coat, a scrap of paper fluttered to the floor. I bent down and picked it up.

It was a page torn from a memorandum book. I held it up to the flickering flame of the candle and saw a crudely executed pencil sketch of a boy's head and shoulders. Something stirred in my memory. The picture had no resemblance to any living child. Yet, the shape of the skull – the high forehead, the curve of the cheek – reminded me of both Charlie Frant and Edgar Allan.

The flame was now behind the paper and shining through from the other side were ghostly traces of writing. I turned it over. Written in ink were the words: *9 Lambert-place.*

There was no indication who had written the words, or when, or why. As I stared at them in the light of that candle, I was tempted to slide the tip of the paper into the flame and forget it had ever existed. My memory of those lost moments still had not returned. Nevertheless I sensed I was being drawn into a scheme whose nature, purpose and extent I could not begin to understand. The Wellington-terrace murder, Carswall's errand in St Giles, the attack on me outside Mr Iversen's shop, Harmwell's providential intervention – all these things must make a pattern, I told myself, and I found Dansey's words ringing uncomfortably in my mind: *When great folk fall, they bring down smaller folk in their train.*

The corner of the paper darkened and a wisp of smoke rose into the air. With a muffled cry, I snatched it from the flame. After all, I told myself, I needed something to show Mr Carswall for my day's work. There was also the fact that I did not like to own myself beaten.

Time reveals as well as conceals: it uncovers our lies, even those to ourselves. Now I think I rescued the paper for one reason alone. Because if I had nothing to show Mr Carswall, he would send me back to Stoke Newington; Charlie would be withdrawn from Mr Bransby's; and I would never see either Miss Carswall or Mrs Frant again.

CHAPTER TWENTY-EIGHT

'NOAK'S NIGGER,' SAID Mr Carswall, his mouth twisting in distaste. 'Shut your eyes and listen to him and you'd hardly know he wasn't as white as you or me. But it won't do. Never does. An educated nigger is an abomination in the sight of God. And why didn't you tell me you was here? I knew nothing of it until Pratt told me.'

It was Pratt, a weasel-faced footman, who had climbed unwillingly to my chamber and brought his master's summons. The man had smiles for the Carswalls, and sneers for everyone else.

'I beg your pardon, sir. When Mr Harmwell brought me back, I needed –'

'Harmwell!' Carswall interrupted, his mind returning to its former topic. 'There's a fine name for him. The trouble with these damned Abolitionists is they never study the nigger in his natural surroundings. I saw enough of them on my plantations. No better than animals. If these prating hypocrites took the trouble to find out what goes on in the slave quarters, they'd soon change their tune.'

Though it was not yet four o'clock in the afternoon, and Mr Carswall had not dined, he was not himself. He was not exactly drunk but he was not exactly sober, either. He was sitting before the fire in the tobacco-scented back parlour that served as his private sitting room. The shutters were across the window and the candles lit. He wore an embroidered dressing gown and slippers. I wondered whether Pratt had also told his master that Mr Harmwell was still downstairs, pursuing his filial researches into Mrs Kerridge's receipts.

Carswall fumbled in his waistcoat pocket and brought out his watch. 'You've taken your time about it, Shield, in all events. Well? What news? What the devil were you doing with the nigger?'

I summarised what I had discovered: that Mr Poe had left his lodgings in Fountain-court, apparently because he had found a new position, and moved down to Queen-street in Seven Dials. According to his landlord there, he had been suffering from the toothache. Three days ago, he had vanished, leaving at least some of his possessions behind.

'Three days?' Mr Carswall said. 'So he's been seen after the murder? So what of Noak's nigger?'

'Yes, sir. But to revert to Mr Poe for one moment more. There is the question of the toothache.'

'Ah – you mean his face was covered? So the man might not have been Poe?'

'It is at least a possibility. Unlike the woman in Fountain-court, Mr Iversen – Poe's landlord, that is to say – does not appear to have known him well, or for long.' I had a splitting headache and was finding it hard to order my thoughts and frame my words. On the other hand, since finding the sketch of the boy, my amnesia had receded like the fog rolling back, and I could now remember most of what had occurred in those missing moments. I told Mr Carswall about the dumb maidservant and handed him the sketch with the address on the back.

He studied the drawing of the schoolboy for a moment and then turned it over and examined the address on the back. 'Lambert-place? Where's that?'

'I am not sure, sir. But there is more: as I was walking through the passage that led from the yard at the back of the house to the street, I was attacked by two ruffians.'

'In league with the landlord?'

'Not necessarily. They could have come from the street. Fortunately my cries attracted the attention of Mr Harmwell, who came to my rescue.'

'Ah, the nigger. So we come to him again. What was he doing there?'

'He and Mr Noak would have me believe it was coincidence.'

'The alternatives are that he was in league with the landlord, or that he followed you.'

'At one point as I walked from Fountain-court to Seven Dials, I thought someone might be behind me. But the fog was so thick I could not be sure. And when I was in Mr Iversen's shop, I wondered whether someone was spying on us through the window to the street.'

Carswall tugged his lower lip and gave a great sigh. 'How did they treat you, he and Mr Noak?'

'Nothing could have been kinder. Mr Harmwell bore me off in the hackney to Mr Noak's lodgings in Brewer-street, and they gave me a glass of brandy. They did not press me for information. Then Mr Noak told Mr Harmwell to bring me back here. They would not even allow me to pay the fare.'

'In the morning, find Lambert-place and discover whether the people of number nine know anything of a visitor from Queen-street.'

'Should I be looking for Mr Frant, sir, or for Mr Poe?'

Carswall glared at me. 'How the devil should I know?'

'I thought perhaps the handwriting –'

'A couple of words? What use is that?'

'The drawing appears to be of a schoolboy.'

'Charlie, you mean? Or the American? Well, that gets us no further, does it? Nor is there anything to show that the hand that wrote the address is the hand that made the drawing. But perhaps Mrs Frant might know whether Frant amused himself with a pencil – yes, ring the bell there.'

I obeyed. A moment later the footman returned and Carswall inquired how Mrs Frant did. Pratt replied that she had come down to the drawing room for a few minutes, with Miss Carswall to keep her company. It was, I knew, the first time she had left her bedchamber for several days, apart from attending the funeral. Charlie was with her, too. With unchar-acteristic consideration, Carswall told the man to inquire whether it would be convenient for him to wait upon her.

While he was waiting for an answer, Carswall hauled himself to his feet. Swaying, he supported himself on the mantelpiece.

'We shall go down to the country in a few days' time,' he said. 'Mrs Frant and her son will of course go with us.'

'He is not to return to Mr Bransby's?'

Carswall shook his heavy head. 'I cannot see the justification for the extra expense, particularly as Mrs Frant will no longer maintain a London residence. I have discussed the matter with her, and she agrees with me: it will be kinder to the boy to remove him promptly from the school. The circumstances of his father's ruin and disappearance must weigh heavily against him there.'

The intelligence came as a blow to me, though I had half expected it. I stood in miserable silence while Carswall whistled tunelessly. Mrs Frant must know that Mr Carswall had cheated her out of her Uncle Wavenhoe's last bequest. Yet she was so reduced in her circumstances that she had no choice but to follow the advice of the man who had made her son a beggar.

At last the footman returned with a message from Mrs Frant. She begged to be excused: she did not yet feel equal to the exertion.

Mr Carswall muttered to himself, 'Still, it don't signify. She shall talk to me soon enough. They all like to tease.'

He stood there for a moment, scratching himself like an old pig in a sty. Then he appeared to recollect he was not alone. He sat down heavily in his elbow chair, looked up at me and smiled, disconcerting me again with that glimpse of Miss Carswall in his ugly face.

'I'm much obliged to you, sir, much obliged for all you have done. You have not had an easy time of it, I am afraid. And it is good of you to undertake to be my eyes and legs.' He felt in his waistcoat pocket for his watch. 'If only there were more time,' he said, staring at the dial. 'Still, I must not detain you any longer – you have your pupil to attend to. I shall see you on your return tomorrow.'

Thus dismissed, I made my way slowly upstairs. I was sadly out of humour. My spirits were depressed by the prospect of returning to the school which had so recently been a haven to me. As I reached the first-floor landing, however, the drawing-room door opened. A black dress fluttered and my nostrils caught the scent of Parma violets.

'Mrs Frant! I – I hope I find you better.'

'Yes, thank you, sir,' she said, closing the door behind her. 'I have been very ill, but I am now somewhat improved.'

Her face was white and hollow-cheeked, and her eyes blazed as though she was still in the grip of a fever. She glanced hurriedly along the landing and up the stairs.

I began to speak, hardly aware of what I was saying: 'I cannot say how much I regret –'

'Mrs Kerridge tells me you were hurt,' she interrupted in a low, urgent voice, and it was as well for me that she did not allow me to finish my sentence. 'That you were attacked by ruffians.'

My hand flew to the bruise on my head. 'It is of no significance, madam. Pray do not be concerned about it.'

'Oh, but I am. Come here, by the mirror – let me see it.'

A candelabrum stood on a marble-topped pier table, with its candle flames reflected in the tall mirror on the wall above it. I stood with my head bowed. Mrs Frant raised herself on tiptoe and peered at the spot on the right side of my temple where the blow had landed.

'A little closer,' she commanded. 'There, I see – there is swelling and a bruise. Fortunately the skin is grazed rather than broken.'

'My hat took the force of the blow.'

'Thank God!'

I felt the tips of her fingers brush against my forehead. A thrill ran through me, and I steadied myself on the table to conceal the tremor of excitement.

'Ah! It is still painful. Does your head ache?'

'Yes, madam.'

'You were on an errand for Mr Carswall, I collect?'

'Yes. Fortunately I lost nothing but my hat and my stick. Mr Noak's clerk was passing and came to my rescue.'

She drew away and I saw that her colour was rising, the blood vivid in her pale face. 'You must rest this evening. Charlie will stay with me for the present. I will have them send you up a cold compress and something to eat. Nothing too heavy, though. A little broth, perhaps, and a glass of sherry.' She looked at the drawing-room door, through which came the sound of voices. 'I trust you will be fully restored by the morning.'

'Thank you. Madam – Mr Carswall informs me that Charlie will not be coming back to school.'

She turned her face away from me. 'That is correct, Mr Shield. Charlie and I are in Mr Carswall's hands now, and he has decided that it will be better for Charlie and me to go down to the country for a time, after so great a change in our circumstances.' She hesitated and then rushed on. 'I am naturally desirous of sparing Mr Carswall any unnecessary expense.' She looked away and added with an unmistakable note of irony in her voice: 'He has done so much for us already.'

I bowed, sensible of the compliment she had paid me in speaking so frankly. 'We shall miss him at school.'

Her lips trembled. 'And he will miss you all. I am very much obliged to you.' She took a step away from me, turned and took a deep breath. 'You – you will not mind if I ask a question – one that may seem a little indelicate? But I hope a widow may be excused.'

'Pray ask me whatever you wish, ma'am, and I will answer to the best of my ability.'

'Am I correct in thinking that you were one of the first to see my late husband? After – after his body was found?'

I nodded.

'I believe that when he left the house that day, he had in his pocket a small box – made of mahogany, inlaid with tulip wood, with a shell pattern on the lid.'

I remembered what Miss Carswall had confided in me on the evening of Mr Frant's funeral. 'A jewel box, perhaps?'

'Yes – though the box itself is dearer to me than the contents. It was no longer in his pocket, but I thought it might have fallen on the ground.'

'I wish I had seen it, ma'am – but I did not.'

Mrs Frant gave me a wan smile. 'It doesn't signify, truly. It is merely that I had a foolish fondness for it, and for the memories attached to it. But I must not detain you – you must rest.'

We wished each other goodnight. Once again she moved away, and once again she paused and turned back.

'Pray – pray be careful, Mr Shield,' she murmured. 'Especially in your dealings with Mr Carswall.'

A moment later, I was alone on the landing with my headache and the smell of her scent. I had no reason to be happy, but I was.

CHAPTER TWENTY-NINE

L ONDON MAY BE the greatest city the world has ever known, but it is also a cluster of villages – flung together by the currents of history and geography, but each retaining its individual character. Even in newly built neighbourhoods, the pattern reasserts itself: mankind is drawn to the village and fears the metropolis.

I learned from the street directory that Lambert-place was in the network of streets west of the Tottenham Court-road, at no great distance from either Margaret-street or the Rookeries of St Giles. I walked there through the fog. A low, blood-red sun struggled in vain to dispel the murk but its feeble rays succeeded only in producing wild and singular effects of light. I was not perfectly recovered from the events of yesterday, and at times it seemed to me that I was wandering through a phantasmagoria rather than a city of bricks and mortar. My spirits had not yet emerged from the shadow of the attack in Queen-street, and I was painfully alert to the slightest circumstance that might betoken danger.

As I drew nearer my destination, the nature of the neighbourhood, of this accidental village, became apparent to me. Gentlemen lived in and around Margaret-street, and necessarily gave the vicinity its character. In the Rookeries were the worst examples of vice and poverty the capital could offer, and these left an indelible stamp upon the parish of St Giles. But the little district around Lambert-place was different again – quiet and respectable, given over to small tradesmen and artisans.

The street itself was a cul-de-sac containing twelve small houses and the entrance to a mews serving two larger streets running parallel to it. I knocked at the door of number 9. It was opened by a tired little woman with two children clinging to her skirts and a third in her arms. I inquired for my friend Mr Poe. The woman shook her head, and the baby began to cry. I described my friend as a well-set-up man perhaps with his face muffled against the toothache.

'Why didn't you say so before?' she demanded. 'It's Mr Longstaff you want.' She turned her head and called over her shoulder: 'Matilda!'

She stood back to allow me to enter. As I did so, a door opened at the back of the hall and an old woman emerged.

'There's a gent here for Mr Longstaff.' The younger woman towed her children towards the stairs. 'And I'll be obliged if you would remind him about the last week's rent, Matilda. I can't pay the butcher with hot air and promises for ever.'

'I'll speak to him.' The old woman looked up at me and her cracked voice rose to a polite whimper. 'You're fortunate, sir – it happens that Mr Longstaff is quite at leisure at present. Pray step this way.'

I followed her into a small room overlooking the yard at the back of the house. In front of the window was a high-backed elbow chair in which was sitting a man who seemed even smaller than the woman who had ushered me in. The chair was fixed to the floor with iron brackets.

Its occupant sprang to his feet as I entered, and I saw he was very much younger than the woman. He was short and broad-shouldered, with a crooked back and one leg shorter than the other. He gave a lopsided impression, like a man walking across a steep slope.

'Well, sir, whatever you desire for your teeth, you'll find it here,' he said in a rush. 'The cauterising of nerves, fillings, simple extractions performed with such skill and rapidity they are almost painless. Transplanting, though, is my speciality, sir – a practice endorsed by Mr Hunter, under whom I studied as a young man. I use only teeth from living sources, sir, those from corpses never take, though lesser practitioners will attempt to fob you off with them. Should you wish it, I can manufacture for you a complete set of false teeth that may be worn for years together, and are an ornament to the mouth, and greatly assist clarity of speech. I have made them from mother-of-pearl, silver and even enamelled copper in my time, sir. But I recommend walrus or human teeth, they discolour less than the others.'

As the torrent of words was tumbling out, Mr Longstaff approached very close to me. With a trembling hand, he put on a pair of spectacles with lenses as thick as penny pieces and looked fixedly at my lips.

'Pray open your mouth, sir.'

'I do not at present require treatment,' I said. 'I am come to ask after a friend of mine whom I believe you may have treated the other day.'

'The gentleman with the extraction,' the old woman said loudly, and so immediately that I suspected they had had no other patients within the last few days. 'You remember.'

'He did not give you a name, I suppose?' I asked. 'I am not fully persuaded that it was my friend.'

'Not that I recall.'

'Then what did he look like, sir – you will have seen his face.'

'I look in their mouths, sir, not at their faces; but his was not a pretty sight.'

I swung round to the old woman. 'And you, madam? Did you remark his appearance?'

She burst out laughing, exposing a fine set of false teeth, made of what might have been ivory. 'Bless you, sir, there's not much I see clearly nowadays.' She lifted her face to mine and the light from the window fell in full upon it. All at once, her meaning burst upon me. The eyes exhibited a singularly blurred and unfocused appearance, as different from healthy eyes as a stagnant pond is from running water.

I turned from one to the other, my frustration mounting. 'Pray, can you tell me what his voice was like?'

The man shrugged but the woman nodded vigorously. 'A deep voice. There might have been a brogue in it. Later he sounded more like a West End gentleman. But I don't know: all the time he was most indistinct.'

'Indeed, Mother, that was on account of the toothache.' The dentist snickered. 'Afterwards, he had no time for talking and too much blood in his mouth to speak at all.'

157

'He couldn't get away fast enough,' the dentist's mother confided. 'They're often like that. Bless you, sir, they're so terrified we have to strap them into that chair. And when we unstrap them, they're away like a startled rabbit.'

'If you know where he lodges, you could take his bag,' the dentist said.

'His bag, sir?'

'He had several with him. But he was in such a hurry to depart that he left a satchel behind.'

'Sobbing, he was,' the woman observed, and smacked her lips.

'Hush, Mother,' said the dentist, turning to me, and once again the torrent of words began to flow. 'In my profession, sir, it is inevitable that even the most skilled practitioner must inflict the occasional moment of pain upon his patient. Laudanum and brandy may blunt its edge, but they cannot resolve the difficulty altogether. And operations involving the removal of a wisdom tooth can be particularly painful. The posterior molars are invariably the most difficult to extract.'

I felt a sympathetic twinge in my own teeth. 'If you would like, sir, I will undertake to reunite my friend with his satchel.'

'You will be doing us a service, sir,' said the dentist.

'But you must give us a receipt,' the woman said sharply, turning those unsettling orbs towards me.

'Of course, madam.'

Taking out my memorandum book, I scribbled a receipt while the dentist fetched the satchel which had been hanging all this time from a peg on the back of the door. It was made of brown leather, much scuffed, and its straps had broken so the flap was now secured with string. I tore out the page with the receipt and took my leave. The dentist begged me to consider his services should I need treatment for my teeth, and even offered to give me an examination, *gratis*, upon the spot. I declined and hurried away.

I walked rapidly to a tavern in Charlotte-street, where I found an empty booth and ordered ale. When the girl had gone I tugged at the knots that secured the satchel. My hands were cold and the knots obstinate. I lost patience and sliced through the string with my penknife.

The fog outside seemed to serve as a pretty metaphor for the fog inside my own mind. I opened the satchel, and the first thing I saw, traced in blotched ink on the inside of the flap, was the name *David Poe*. The letters had faded to the colour of dried blood.

The satchel's contents spilled on to the scrubbed surface of the table. My fingers explored the little heap of possessions – a small flask which had once contained brandy, a shirt of fine quality but in need of a wash, a grubby neckcloth and a cigar case made of leather. I opened the case and shook out its contents.

As I did so, I was thinking that, every time I turned up what I thought was a fact, it seemed that the more I inspected it, the more it retreated into the realms of hypothesis. I longed for certainty, for indisputable facts. Now it seemed probable, but of course by no means certain, that the dentist's patient had indeed been David Poe, the American. In this case, of course, it followed that there was no longer any reason to suppose that the dead man in Wellington-terrace had been anyone other than Henry Frant. But such speculation was as fragile as a dandelion's feathery pappus. A breath of wind would suffice to destroy it.

Behind me, and above my shoulder, came a sharp intake of breath. I turned quickly. The girl had brought my ale. The tray was trembling in her hands. She was staring not at me but at an object on the table.

There followed a moment of superhuman clarity, of prodigious ratiocination: my mind accelerated and packed into an instant thoughts which would normally fill a minute, an hour, a day.

'I am a student of medicine,' I snapped. 'What are you gawping at? It is nothing but a rare specimen of *digitus mortuus praecisus* lent me by the professor himself. If you value your position, do not spill beer on it.'

I covered it with the neckcloth – casually, as though making room for her to set down her tray without risk of spillage. The girl laughed – still nervous, but the reassuring opacity of the Latin words had soothed her alarm. Despite my warning, though, a few drops of beer slopped on to the table. Her hand flew to her mouth; she muttered an apology and scuttled away.

I took a long pull of ale. When I was alone, and safe from observation,

I twitched aside the neckcloth. The object was rust-coloured in part, but mostly dirty yellow. On one end was a long fingernail spotted with what might have been ink.

The trouble with wishes is that they sometimes come true. I had at last found something which no matter how long I looked at it would not dissolve into a mere speculation. I had discovered an indisputable fact. And I wished with all my heart that I had not.

CHAPTER THIRTY

'MY DEAR YOUNG fellow,' said Mr Rowsell, bouncing to meet me with his hand outstretched. 'How delightful to see you. Mrs Rowsell was asking if I had news of you only the other day.'

He shook hands most cordially and pressed me to take some refreshment. My mind was in a whirl. At this juncture in my affairs I would have given much for the advice of a disinterested friend. I was sensible of Mr Rowsell's recent kindnesses to me, and I was sorely tempted to lay the whole matter before him. But I was not sufficiently intimate with him to know whether I might trust him entirely.

My own position had become delicate, and indeed susceptible to misinterpretation. In the last two days I had pursued the trail of David Poe, telling packs of lies as I went. I was by no means certain that I was not compounding a felony by my failure to alert the authorities to what I already knew and suspected. I needed the comfort of a friend's company, but not a friend's counsel. Or rather – I needed counsel badly, but I dared not ask for it. It was possible that Mr Rowsell would feel it his duty to alert the authorities himself. Nor would it be fair to him to ask him to keep a secret that might place him on the wrong side of the law.

'Well, dear boy, I must say – and do not think me impertinent, I beg – but you seem in low spirits.'

'It is the fog, sir. It gets into my lungs.'

'Very true,' he said comfortably. 'Is that a bruise I see upon your temple?'

'I – I must blame it once again upon the fog. I tripped and fell against a railing.'

'And what brings you here?'

I explained that I had been asked to spend a few days in London with Charlie Frant, and that we were staying at the house of his cousin, Mr Carswall, in Margaret-street. 'Mr Carswall sent me on an errand, and finding that I had a few moments I might call my own, I decided to see whether you were at leisure.'

'Mr Carswall? You are staying with him?'

'Not for long. The family intend to remove to the country in a day or two.'

'To Mr Carswall's estate in Gloucestershire, no doubt. And will the boy and Mrs Frant go with them?'

'I believe so, sir.'

Rowsell shook his head sadly. 'I feel for Mrs Frant and her son. How are the mighty fallen! I understand they have not sixpence to call their own.' Mr Rowsell opened a corner cupboard and took out a decanter and glasses. 'It is an unlucky family. Mr Henry Frant brought the bank down around his ears because of his appetite for gambling, and his father and his uncle were the same. Forty years ago, the Frants were considerable landowners, both here and in Ireland.'

I looked up sharply. 'I had not realised that the Frants had Irish connections.'

'Oh yes. I believe the Irish estate was the last to go.' Mr Rowsell set down the decanter and glasses on the table and stood there for a moment, stroking his stomach, which as usual looked as though it were on the verge of bursting out of his waistcoat. 'For your aunt's sake, Tom, I must tell you that Mr Carswall's reputation is not entirely unblemished. I would not wish you to injure your prospects by associating with him. He is very rich, of course, but riches are not everything, particularly riches gained as his are said to have been gained.'

I was calmer now, my agitation to some degree soothed by Mr Rowsell's familiar voice. On the floor by my chair, however, was David

Poe's satchel. Inside it was the cigar case with its dreadful contents. Mr Rowsell poured the wine and handed me a glass.

Before I drank, I said, 'They are withdrawing Charlie Frant from the school. There is no reason why I should see any of them again. So Mr Carswall has a reputation of being a gambler, as his partner was?'

'He's not so foolish as Frant. No, but there were rumours about his dealings during the late war with the United States. Nothing was ever proved, you understand, but it is certain that he came out of it much richer than he went in. As did Frant himself.'

We drank in silence for a moment. Then Mr Rowsell got up and went to the window, and peered down at the fog which lay as thick as clotted cream, as poisonous as choke-damp in a mine, obscuring even the ground below.

'Mr Frant acted as Wavenhoe's agent in North America for a while,' Rowsell said, picking his words with care. 'In the early years of the war. He was made a partner in the bank on his return. Then there was some sort of falling out, and Carswall withdrew his capital.'

'These rumours, sir: may I ask – what did they amount to?'

'There is no secret about it – the matter is widely spoken of. The bank purchased an army contractor's business in Kingston, in Canada, and it is said there were irregularities about the sale of supplies. And a story went the rounds – and I hardly like to repeat it in case walls have ears, for it would certainly mean an action for slander – a story that some of the supplies purchased for the use of our troops found their way eventually into the hands of the Americans. And not just supplies, either. In some quarters, accurate intelligence about our intentions and the dispositions of our troops commanded a very high price indeed.'

'Surely Mr Carswall –'

'Would not have been so foolish? On the other hand, Frant was in Canada and in those days Frant was Carswall's creature. In any case, that is why not everyone is happy to receive Mr Carswall.'

I promised I would be on my guard. Rowsell returned to his chair and his wine.

'Do not mind my saying so, Tom, but you look quite fagged. Mrs Rowsell has it that you do not eat enough. Which reminds me, if Mr

Bransby permits, would you care to eat your Christmas dinner with us? Mrs Rowsell was most pressing that I should attempt to secure your company.'

'My duty and best compliments to Mrs Rowsell, sir. I shall be happy to wait on her.'

'Good, good. It will be just ourselves and some of Mrs Rowsell's family.' He paused in raising his glass to his lips, and stared at me, a frown cutting into his smooth pink forehead. 'There is nothing amiss, I trust?'

'Nothing in the world, sir.'

'And you are quite settled at Mr Bransby's?'

'Yes, indeed.'

'I rejoice to hear it.' He swallowed a mouthful of wine. 'Should you ever desire a change of profession, you could do worse than try the law. I believe I could put you in the way of something with fair prospects of advancement. In Holborn, perhaps, or the City. It would take time and application, of course. As for the matter of lodgings, why, I am sure Mrs Rowsell would be glad to see a respectable person in our front garret.'

I was still weakened from the day before. I felt tears fill my eyes at this undeserved kindness. 'Thank you, sir,' I said and lowered my head.

Neither of us spoke. Mr Rowsell paced up and down, pausing to look at the fog when he reached the window. It seemed to me that for a moment my own inner fog had lifted.

CHAPTER THIRTY-ONE

'WHAT INFERNAL LUCK,' Stephen Carswall said. 'A man who looks only inside mouths, and a woman who sees the next best thing to nothing at all.'

'The woman thought she might have heard a brogue. And then the accents of a gentleman.'

'That's neither here nor there. Frant could slip into a brogue as soon as look at you. When he was a boy, he used to visit the family's place in County Wicklow, and he could sound like a regular Paddy if he wished. So the mere fact of a brogue does not allow us to distinguish between Frant and Poe. As for sounding like a gentleman, who is the judge? The mother of a tooth-puller? Her opinion is not worth having.' He paused and stared down at the object in his palm. 'But this is something else.'

'It does not appear to come from a gentleman's hand.'

'True. But there is nothing to say that it belonged to Poe, either.' Carswall tilted his palm and slid the finger into the cigar case, his face betraying no emotion other than weariness. He hobbled to the open bureau – his gout was painful that day – and slipped the case into a drawer. 'Let us assume that the man who had his tooth extracted is Frant, and that in order to make the world believe he was dead, he killed Poe and mutilated the corpse. But why should he hold on to the finger he had cut from Poe's hand?'

'That I do not know, sir. Unless he was biding his time until he found a safe place to destroy it.'

'No, no. He could have thrown something as small as that on the fire. Or into a cesspit. Or the river, for that matter. God damn it, we are no nearer proof, one way or the other.'

I thought, but did not say aloud, that this might have been just what the man who left the satchel had intended. Nor did I mention that the finger looked oddly shrivelled and yellow. What had happened to it since it had been parted from the rest of the hand? Was there some clue in its present appearance to where it had been kept? Could one even be sure it was a forefinger?

'I am obliged to you, nonetheless.' Carswall took out his watch. 'There is nothing more we can do at present.' Then without any change in tone he went on: 'I have written to Mr Bransby and told him you will be returning tomorrow.'

I bowed.

'I daresay you will be relieved to resume your normal duties. I shall make a point of saying to Mr Bransby that you have given satisfaction, and shown yourself trustworthy.' Carswall pawed his watch. 'I am awaited in the City. You may spend the rest of the day with Charlie.'

A moment later I trailed up the stairs to the drawing room, where Pratt, the footman I disliked, had told me I would find Charlie. There was no schoolroom in the house in Margaret-street, and in any case the drawing room was warmer and more comfortable. I will not disguise the fact that as I mounted the stone treads of the staircase my heart beat a little faster at the thought of whom I might find with Charlie.

Miss Carswall looked up as I entered the room, her face breaking into a smile. She was alone, sitting by the fire with a screen to shield her face. A folded newspaper lay upon her lap.

'I beg your pardon,' I said. 'They told me Charlie was here.'

'He will be down presently, Mr Shield. He has run up to his mama for a few moments. Pray come and wait by the fire. The cold is bitter, is it not?'

I was glad to fall in with this suggestion. I saw that she had been reading the *Morning Post* and my eye caught the word 'murder' on the page lying open before her.

'Am I to understand that Mrs Frant has had a relapse?' I asked. 'She seemed much improved when I saw her yesterday.'

'I am rejoiced to say that she is much better. But she tires easily, and her physician recommends that she rest in her room during the afternoon.' Miss Carswall looked directly at me – there was a frankness about her demeanour, an openness, which I found most appealing – and said: 'While we are on the subject of health, you are looking rather better than I feared you would. Mrs Frant told me that you were attacked.'

'It was unpleasant rather than serious.'

'I suspect you make light of it.' She shivered deliciously. 'We are none of us safe!'

'No harm was done. Mr Harmwell beat back my assailants, and then he was kind enough to escort me home in a hackney.'

Miss Carswall's smile broke out like the sun from behind clouds. 'Is it possible that his motives were not entirely disinterested, sir? Bearing in mind that touching scene we witnessed in Piccadilly?'

I grinned at her. 'I understand that Mrs Kerridge has been copying out receipts for Mr Harmwell's mother.'

The smile turned into a giggle. 'Tell that to the Marines.' As she spoke, Miss Carswall moved in her chair and the hem of her skirt rose up, exposing pretty ankles and elegant calves encased in French-silk stockings. 'Why, it seems unnatural for Kerridge to have a follower. She must be old enough to be my mother.'

At this, she coloured and fell silent, for the remark was not the best of taste, especially from one situated as Miss Carswall was. I wondered, not for the first time, if there was more than met the eye in Harmwell's interest in Mrs Kerridge. She was better placed than most to know exactly what was going on in this family. She was Mrs Frant's maid, the only servant who remained from that lost house in Russell-square. She had also looked after Miss Carswall when she had lived with her cousin for upward of two years while Mr Frant was in Canada, and of course she had known Charlie since he was a baby. The three of them held her in great affection, and often confided in her. On account of this, perhaps,

Mrs Kerridge wielded an influence over the other servants out of proportion to her official standing among them.

'Mr Carswall tells me you are soon to remove to the country,' I said, to break the silence before it grew awkward.

'We are indeed. Papa is so provoking. He talks of unnecessary expense, which is nonsense. But he will not listen to reason.' She spoke these words in a self-mocking manner, which converted them from a criticism of her father to a commentary on her own shortcomings.

'You prefer the town, I think, miss?'

'Oh, indeed. I remember how delightful it was when I first came to live with Sophie in Russell-square, and suddenly Bath itself seemed no more interesting than a village. I know town is practically empty now, and it will be even emptier after Christmas. But even in that condition, it is far more agreeable to me than the vacant prospects and unpolished inhabitants of the countryside. I – I shall miss my friends, too. In London, one knows so many people that one may to a large extent choose with whom one associates. But it is quite different at Monkshill. We have a very limited acquaintance.' She paused a moment and then added, with peculiar emphasis: 'Yes, I shall miss certain friends very much.'

She had been gazing at the paper on her lap, but when she spoke those last few words, she raised her face to mine, which gave what she said a particular force, and made it difficult not to place a particular construction upon the words. Miss Carswall smiled at me and was about to say something else. But at this interesting moment, the door of the drawing room flew open and Charlie burst in on us.

'Cousin Flora!' he cried. 'Mama says I do not have to go back to school!'

CHAPTER THIRTY-TWO

I RETURNED TO Stoke Newington on Thursday, the 9th December. As the month progressed, the weather grew worse. The cold and the lengthening nights were perfectly in tune with my gloomy spirits. Sometimes I slipped into a fit of wild despair. When my mind was unoccupied, two faces rushed to fill the vacancy, those of Mrs Frant and Miss Carswall. I was amazed by my own folly: if it were ludicrous to pine for one lady so far removed from my own sphere of society, then how much more absurd to pine for two? Yet however much I brought philosophy to my aid, I could not expel those two lovely images from my thoughts.

'You are out of sorts, Tom,' said Edward Dansey one evening as we sat over the dying fire.

'It is merely a fit of the dumps. I beg your pardon – I do not wish to be a plague.'

'One's spirits have their seasons, just as the weather has. What is it you are reading?'

I passed the book to him.

'The *Carmina* of Catullus?' He held the book up to the candle and turned over the pages. 'Charming, charming,' he murmured. 'All the passion of youth is here, and all its folly. I should not let Mr Bransby see you reading it, however.'

'I am re-reading the poems not for their matter but for their metre,' I said.

'Yes, there are elements of interest in Catullus's use of phalaecians and scazons. As for the hexametric poems, it is undeniable that he handles the metre with far more elegance than Lucretius contrives, though to my mind a greater employment of enjambment would have improved them still further. His elegiacs, on the other hand, do not merit the compliment of imitation, and his pentameters are often positively uncouth.' He looked up, saw my face and turned his lopsided smile on me. 'You must not mind me, Tom, I am a little out of sorts myself.' He returned the volume. 'Have you heard the news? Quird is to be withdrawn from the school.'

'I cannot say I am sorry to hear it.'

'It appears that his father was badly hit when Wavenhoe's collapsed. The family has lost nearly all it had.'

'It is, I'm afraid, a common enough story.' I held out my hands to the fire. 'I hope they are not in actual want?'

'Not quite. It is a dreadful business.' Dansey's eyes glowed orange in the candlelight. 'But of course few have suffered as Mrs Frant has suffered. Is it true that she is entirely dependent on the charity of her cousin Mr Carswall?'

'I believe so.' I heard a trace of agitation in my tone, for I remembered that fatal codicil that had removed, with my unconscious assistance, her last hope of financial independence. I forced myself to continue: 'And Charlie, too, of course.'

Dansey waved a long-fingered hand. 'At least he is young. Youth has astonishing resilience. But Mrs Frant's position must be truly wretched.'

I mumbled agreement, not trusting myself to speak.

'No doubt she loved him?'

I made no reply, though Dansey waited for one.

'Yes, but then love is a curious emotion,' he went on in a moment, as though I had answered in the affirmative. 'We commonly use one word where at least three are required. When poets speak of love, they describe a passionate attachment to another individual. It is perhaps less an attachment than a form of hunger. However they dress it up in the language of sentiment, it is at bottom a physical appetite for the sexual act, a desire to enjoy the last favour. It is an extraordinarily powerful

170

appetite, it is true, and one directed with remarkable intensity at a single individual, an intensity that may border on madness – as, perhaps, it did for poor Catullus with his Lesbia. Yet it is usually short-lived. I have known many young men who fall in love once a week. And when such a man marries the beloved of the moment, the passion rarely lasts at the pitch it attained before it was satisfied.'

I stared at the fire. Dansey's voice had taken on a slow, dreamlike quality. I wished I were alone in a silent room.

'As to the second meaning,' he said after another pause, another opportunity for me to speak. 'On many occasions love is little more than a respectable synonym for lechery, a universal appetite for copulation, for unbridled carnality. The word love casts a veil of propriety over it. It is an attempt to disguise its nature, to shield it from the strictures of moralists. But, truly considered, the phenomenon is no more lovely or unlovely than the behaviour of a pig at a trough.'

I stirred in my chair.

'Pray do not be uneasy,' he said quickly. 'The taxonomy of the emotions should be the province of the natural philosopher, as well as that of the poet. And, to the unbiased observer at least, it is clear that a mature person may feel for – for – another person a category of emotion which may properly be called love; indeed it may be argued that it deserves the appellation more than the previous categories. This would be my third definition of the word. I refer to an individual's calm and disinterested concern for the well-being of another.'

I suppressed a yawn. 'It sounds remarkably like friendship. Or a mother's feeling for a child.'

'No, Tom, not exactly. It does not exclude passion, you see. Passion may play a part, albeit guided by reason, by experience. One sees it sometimes in married couples, in whom it may flourish after their initial ardours have subsided. One sometimes sees it, too, in friendships between members of the same sex, very commonly in soldiers or sailors who have braved terrible dangers together. If one had to characterise this type of affection, one could, I think, usefully enter-tain the notion of *completeness*. The lover feels incomplete without the beloved. It is an emotion that may flourish unobtrusively in unexpected places. Though it may embrace the sexual sphere, it is not confined to it.'

He leaned forward, elbows on knees. I saw twin candle flames burning in his eyes. It is a terrifying thing to glimpse the depth of another's need.

I pushed back my chair and stood up. 'Ned – pray excuse me – it has been a long day. I shall fall asleep if I stay another moment. You will not take it amiss if I withdraw, will you?'

'No,' Dansey said. 'No, of course not. You were falling into a doze. I warrant you hardly heard a word I've been saying.'

I wished him goodnight. At the door, he called me back.

'You will want this,' he said. 'Your Catullus.'

CHAPTER THIRTY-THREE

NEITHER OF US referred to this conversation again. It was possible that Dansey believed, or affected to believe, that I had been on the edge of slumber during the latter part of it, and had not heard all he said, or comprehended the general drift of his remarks. So we lived and worked together on our old amicable footing. Yet something had changed. After that evening, I rarely sat with him late into the night beside the dying warmth of the schoolroom fire, or strolled smoking with him across the frosty lawn after the boys had gone to bed.

Nevertheless, I found my thoughts recurring to his remarks upon the subject of love on more than one occasion. If it were true that the tender passion could be divided into three categories, which category embraced what I felt for Sophia Frant – or, indeed, for Flora Carswall? I saw with peculiar vividness in my mind's eye the picture of Dansey's pig at his trough.

I could not say that I was looking forward to the end of term, to the six weeks of the school's Christmas holiday. Though a few boys would remain, the establishment would be considerably reduced, and Dansey and I would inevitably be thrown much together. I had agreed to eat my Christmas dinner with the Rowsells, but I had no other engagements or diversions in hand.

About a week before Christmas, I met young Edgar Allan on the stairs and he said to me, in that hurried and peculiarly breathless way that small boys have: 'Sir, please, sir, but Frant begs me to give you his compliments and hopes you may be able to accept.'

I stopped. 'Accept what, Allan? His compliments?'

'You have not heard, sir?'

'Unless I know what I am supposed to have heard, I cannot tell, can I?'

Something in the logic of this must have appealed to him, for the boy burst out laughing. When his mirth had subsided, he said: 'Frant wrote me to say that his mama is inviting me to stay at Mr Carswall's during the Christmas holiday. And Mr Carswall is to write to my ma and pa, and to Mr Bransby, requesting that you should be allowed to accompany me, though I should be perfectly safe in the care of the coachman, but Charlie says that women always fuss and sometimes it is wise to let them have their head.'

'I have as yet heard nothing of this projected expedition,' I said. 'I am not convinced that it will be perfectly convenient.' I watched Allan's face change, as though a cloud had passed over his good humour. 'However, we shall have to see what Mr Bransby has to say about it.'

The boy took this as a form of agreement. He bounded happily away, leaving me to wonder whether his information was accurate, and, if it were, whether Mr Bransby would permit me to go, and whether it would be wise for me to do so or not. Wise or not, I knew what I wanted. Lofty thoughts about the taxonomy of love in general, and about pigs and troughs in particular, were all very well in the abstract but I no longer had any desire to pursue them.

The following afternoon, Mr Bransby relayed Mrs Frant's invitation.

'There is some uncertainty as to when you will return,' Mr Bransby went on. 'Mr Carswall does not feel that young Frant has been minding his book with sufficient attention since he left us. He may desire you to remain longer with them, to coach the boys and perhaps to escort Edgar Allan back to school at the beginning of term – Charles Frant, of course, will not be rejoining us. You are not expected elsewhere, I suppose, on Christmas Day?'

'As a matter of fact, I was, sir. But it is of no importance.'

That evening, I sat down by the fire in the schoolroom to write to

Mr Rowsell, regretting that I would not be able to eat my Christmas dinner with them after all. I had hardly begun when Dansey came in.

'Mr Bransby tells me you are taking young Allan down to the country,' he said abruptly. 'Is it true you will remain there the entire vacation?'

'It's possible. Mr Carswall will decide.'

Dansey flung himself into a chair. 'Are you sure this is wise, Tom?'

'Why ever not?' I spoke with more heat than I had intended. 'A change of scene will be beneficial.'

'And a change of company, no doubt.'

I murmured that I was perfectly happy in my present situation.

'I beg your pardon,' Dansey continued after a moment. 'I have no right to advise you. You will go with young Allan, I collect?'

'I wonder that Mr Allan has permitted him to go. It is only a month since Mr Frant's death.'

'I imagine he did it to oblige Mr Carswall. Wealth is a passport to esteem. Forgive me; I do not mean to pry – but are you altogether easy in your mind about this?'

'Why should I not be?'

Dansey hesitated. 'I am a rational man, as you know. But sometimes I have an intuition when all is not well. I daresay I am being fanciful.'

He stood there for a moment, his lopsided mouth working in his Janus face as though he wanted to say something else but could not persuade his lips to mouth the words. He turned on his heel and slipped out of the room. I stared down at the sheet of paper, the few words on it flickering and shifting in the candlelight. It was another freezing evening, and I shivered.

Dansey had an intuition, but it occurred to me that I had more substantial grounds for caution: the manner in which first Mr Frant and now Mr Carswall had entangled me in their affairs; the codicil that had cost Mrs Frant an inheritance; the mutilated cadaver at Wellington-terrace; and the severed finger I had discovered in David Poe's satchel.

CHAPTER THIRTY-FOUR

I N 1819, CHRISTMAS Day was a Saturday. Mr Bransby decreed that term should officially end on the previous Tuesday. On the afternoon of that day, I travelled down to London with Edgar Allan. We put up for the night with his foster parents in Southampton-row. Mrs Allan, an anxious, vapourish woman with a hypochondriacal tendency, alternately caressed and ignored Edgar. In the late afternoon, Mr Allan returned from his place of business. He was a grim-faced man, much preoccupied. In their presence Edgar seemed to glow with vitality and intelligence; he was as different from them as chalk from cheese.

'If you go to Cheltenham,' Mrs Allan said over dinner in her high, wavering voice, 'you must stay at the Stiles Hotel. Do you remember, my love?' she said to her husband. 'The people there were most attentive.'

'But they're not going to Cheltenham,' Mr Allan said.

An uneasy silence settled over the dinner table, broken only by the clatter of cutlery and the footsteps of the servant. I had assumed until now that it was Charlie who needed Edgar's company. Now I recalled Edgar's enthusiasm for the proposal, and wondered if it might not be the other way round.

After dinner, Mr Allan retired to his private room on the plea of needing to cast up his accounts. Mrs Allan sat in the drawing room and played cards with Edgar. While she played, she talked incessantly of her friends and family, her homesickness for Richmond, Virginia, her fear of seasickness, and the number and nature of her ailments, which were, it seemed, matters of constant surprise and interest to her medical attendants.

After we had drunk tea, I made my excuses and went out. Like a sentimental fool, I walked up to Russell-square and stood for a moment on the pavement outside the house where the Frants had lived. There was a lantern above the door, and lights showed in the cracks between the shutters. A sense of my own folly overwhelmed me. I walked rapidly away, as though the faster I walked, the sooner I would leave my folly behind.

At length I found myself outside a tavern in Lambs Conduit-street. I spent forty minutes in the taproom, smoking and drinking brandy. All the while, I could not rid myself of the single thought that ran round my head like a rat in a trap: *tomorrow I shall see her.*

I walked back to the Allans' house, where I fell into a restless sleep. The human mind is a perverse creature. When I awoke, I realised the face I had seen most often in the magic-lantern show of my dreams was that of Flora Carswall.

CHAPTER THIRTY-FIVE

IN THE MORNING, I had time to call at Mr Rowsell's chambers in Lincoln's Inn. It seemed churlish to be so close to him and not to pay him a visit; and I wished to say farewell and send my apologies to Mrs Rowsell. He welcomed me with his customary good humour and sent out Atkins, his clerk, for coffee.

His face lengthened, however, when I told him where I was going.

'I cannot pretend I like this plan, Tom,' he said, 'though of course it is no concern of mine. But the children will miss you sorely on Saturday. Is Mr Bransby happy to see you go?'

'He is disposed to consider that on the whole the advantages outweigh the drawbacks.'

Rowsell nodded. 'There are financial considerations, no doubt, and he would be fully alive to their importance. How long do you stay?'

As I was answering him, there was a knock at the door and Atkins ushered in the boy with the tray. The clerk glanced at me with tiny eyes like specks of mud and averted his round, pale face. Rowsell sat in silence until we were alone. I knew him well enough to apprehend that he was not easy in his mind. I thought his solicitude as misplaced as Dansey's.

He poured the coffee and handed me a cup. 'You remember we were discussing Mr Carswall and Mr Frant's conduct in the late war with America?'

'Why, yes, sir.'

'I was in the City the other day and I heard another story about Wavenhoe's that I did not altogether like. In fairness, it may be no more than a story. But it came from more than one source, so I suspect there may be some truth in it.' He tasted his coffee and screwed up his face. 'It concerns what precipitated this entire ugly affair – the collapse of the bank, that is, the discovery of Mr Frant's criminal dealings and his eventual murder. It appears that the bank was liable for certain bills, amounting together to a considerable sum, that became due at the end of October. Most of them concerned building speculations in which the bank had invested.'

I nodded, for Miss Carswall had told me something of this when she waylaid me in Stoke Newington. 'There was no money to pay them?'

'That was not in itself the difficulty. In the normal run of things, Frant could quite reasonably expect to negotiate extensions to the terms of the bills. However, it appears that a few weeks before the debts became due, a number of the bills changed hands. They were purchased by a commercial house which often acts as a go-between in transactions where the principal does not wish to have his name known. At the end of the month, these bills were presented for payment, and Frant found he could not negotiate extensions to any of them.'

'So you believe that an enemy of Mr Frant's may have contrived his ruin?'

'Not contrived, not exactly – that's putting it too strong. Frant's corrupt dealings made the bank's eventual downfall inevitable. No, if true, what this circumstance suggests to me is that the collapse of the bank may have been brought forward, perhaps by several weeks, or even months.'

Rowsell paused to pour us more coffee.

'What would be the advantage in that?' I asked.

'At this point we cannot tell. But in order to put into effect such a scheme, a man would need to have the command of considerable wealth, and also to regard Mr Frant with inveterate malignancy. Why else would one buy control of the debts of a failing concern? On the face of it, the scheme's success would involve its perpetrator in considerable financial loss. Since Wavenhoe's closed its doors, those bills are hardly worth the paper they are written on.'

'Aye,' I said. 'I see what you are driving at, sir.'

'Not *what*,' Mr Rowsell said, spreading out his arms so vigorously that a few drops of coffee flew out of his cup and splattered in an arc of black spots on the floor. '*Who*.'

'Oh. You – you cannot mean Mr Carswall?'

Demure as a maiden, he looked at me over the brim of the tiny cup. His big pink face was empty of guile, empty of all emotions except a generalised benevolence and a mild curiosity.

CHAPTER THIRTY-SIX

IN THE FREEZING, fog-bound evening, Edgar and I boarded the Gloucester Mail. I was grateful that Mr Allan had indulged us in the luxury of inside seats. As we inched our way down Piccadilly, I stared at the throngs of people on the pavement, their faces lit by the unhealthy glare of the street lights. Edgar sat very still, his eyes huge in his face, watching and listening, yet deaf to my attempts at conversation; he was like one under an enchantment.

Slowly we picked up speed. By and by the motion and the monotony set the boy's head nodding to and fro on his shoulders, bouncing between me and a grocer's wife, between sleep and wakefulness. One by one, our fellow passengers followed his example. I wished I might do the same. A journey is full of excitement when one leaves or arrives, but the intervening period is commonly characterised by discomfort and boredom.

The coach whirled through the darkness. A dwarfish clergyman snored on the seat opposite mine. The windows were tightly closed, at the request of the grocer's wife, who slumbered steadily, rousing herself when she heard the screech of the horn at turnpike gates and recruiting her strength from a bottle in her reticule. The interior of the coach filled with the fumes of Jamaica rum and water. The clergyman had a nightmare; his limbs twitched helplessly; and his tiny feet pushed their way out of the blanket that covered him and kicked my shins.

The only moments of interest came as we clattered through the silent country towns along the road. I raised the blind, rubbed the glass and looked out at empty streets. Here and there a light would burn in an upper window. There is something mysterious about a sleeping town; like a ship abandoned by its crew, it becomes an entirely different entity when bereft of human purpose and human animation.

Then the coach would swing under an archway into the inn yard, and suddenly all would be light and bustle, the shouting of ostlers and tap-boys, the changing of horses, passengers climbing down and climbing up, voices rising and falling with jokes, curses, advice and farewells. So perverse is the human mind that within seconds of entering an inn yard I would begin to hunger for the darkness and the solitude of the countryside.

Once the horses were changed, we were on our way, mile after mile. All the inside passengers were going to Gloucester or further still to Hereford or Carmarthen. At some point in the dark hours before dawn I fell into a deep slumber, from which I was rudely awakened, along with the other passengers, when the coachman misjudged the turn into an inn yard and jarred the nearside rear wheel against the jamb of the arch.

After that I did not go back to sleep. The night slowly gave way to the long grey twilight of a winter dawn. One by one, my travelling companions woke to face the day. All the excitement of the previous evening had gone. We were unwashed, unshaven, unfed and unrested. Our bodies ached from the hardness of the seats.

We reached Gloucester before midday and were set down with our luggage at the Bell Inn in Southgate-street. Mr Carswall's carriage had already arrived. The horses were baiting and the groom was anxious to leave. We snatched a late breakfast in the coffee room. Afterwards I risked the groom's displeasure and found a barber to shave me. Curiosity moved me as much as vanity; barbers know everything.

'By the way,' I said as the man was stropping his razor, 'I believe the late Mr Wavenhoe owned property in this city.'

'Wavenhoe? Oh yes, sir. Though the old gentleman lived in London mostly. He died last month.'

I jingled the coins in my pocket. 'What was the property?'

'Oxbody-lane, sir – a pretty little inn, and also some of the neighbouring freeholds. It's all let, of course.' Head on one side like a robin, he darted a glance at me. 'If you're interested, I could give you the direction of an attorney who would be able to tell you more.'

'No,' I said abruptly. 'There is no need.'

Mr Carswall's seat, Monkshill-park, lay some ten or twelve miles south and west of Gloucester in the direction of Lydmouth. We made good time when we left the city because the first part of our journey lay along turnpike roads. The last few miles lay on smaller roads and lanes. Time dragged. Edgar fidgeted. My body ached with the undeserved weariness of the sedentary traveller.

By the time we swung off the road, the afternoon was turning to twilight. A grim-faced lodge-keeper opened the gates. We followed a winding, gradually ascending drive through parkland. Trees swayed like maenads against a gloomy sky. The wind threw drops of rain against the carriage windows.

The house burst into view, a great rectangular block with three storeys and five bays, faced with stone that gleamed coldly against the darkening landscape. We were clearly awaited, for as we drew up at the door, two footmen ran out with umbrellas and ushered us through the driving rain and up the steps into the hall. I recognised one of them as Pratt, the thin-faced sycophant whom Mr Carswall must have brought down with him from town. Charlie Frant flew to greet his friend, followed at a more sober pace by the two ladies, arm in arm.

'Edgar!' Charlie cried. 'Let me show you our room. Oh, we shall have such larks.' His mother touched his shoulder and reminded him of my presence. Blushing, he turned to me. 'Mr Shield, sir, how good of you to come.'

Mrs Frant shook my hand and gave me her gentle smile.

'My father is closeted with his agent on estate business,' Miss Carswall told me. 'But you will meet him at dinner.' She glanced at the hovering footmen. 'Pratt will show you to your room. I daresay you will want to rest after the fatigue of your journey. But not for long, I am afraid – we dine at half-past five o'clock. We keep country hours at Monkshill.'

I mounted the stairs in the wake of the footman. Far above me was an oval skylight which seemed less a means of admitting light than a way of emphasising the height of the house and the breadth of the stairwell. Monkshill was on the grand scale, a residence fit for giants. I was sensible of a stillness beneath me, as if the women in the hall below were holding their breath.

My room was large, a little shabby and very cold. I washed and changed as quickly as I could. Somewhere in the house a clock was striking five when I went in search of the drawing room. Lamps and candles lighted the landings and the stairs. But they failed to expel the darkness from the immense spaces of the mansion.

In the hall, I hesitated, wondering where the drawing room was. A figure detached itself from the shadows to my right.

'Good evening, sir.'

Startled, I swung round. 'Why, Mrs Kerridge! I trust I find you well?'

'As well as can be expected.' She nodded towards the door on my right. 'If you want the boys, they're in the drawing room.'

She left as suddenly as she had arrived, the abruptness of her manner reminding me of my ambiguous status, neither gentleman nor servant. I knocked lightly on the door and went in. The drawing room was filled with the shifting, faded yellow light of a dozen candles. Mrs Frant was sitting almost in the grate, with a book in her hand. The boys were huddled on the sofa, engaged in a whispered conversation.

'I – I beg your pardon, ma'am,' I said. 'Am I early?'

'Not at all, Mr Shield,' Mrs Frant said. 'Pray sit down. And, on the way, I wonder if you would be so kind as to ring the bell. We need more coals for the fire.'

I did as she asked and then sat opposite her. It is curious the effect that widow's weeds have on those that wear them. Some women drown in their dark folds; they become their mourning. Mrs Frant, however, belonged to the second category: the very simplicity of her plain black gown set off her beauty.

'My cousins will be here in a moment,' she said. 'You are not cold, I hope?'

'Not at all,' I lied.

'This is a cold house, I'm afraid,' she said with a faint smile. 'We have not been here long enough to warm it.'

The door opened and Miss Carswall came into the room. Her face broke into a smile.

I may have been mistaken, but I thought I heard Sophia Frant add in a whisper: 'And an unlucky house, too.'

CHAPTER THIRTY-SEVEN

FIVE OF US sat down to dinner – Mr Carswall, Miss Carswall, Mrs Frant, an elderly lady named Mrs Lee, and myself. Mrs Lee was the aunt of a local clergyman, and I understood she was paying a long visit to Monkshill-park. There was little conversation apart from that which emanated from Mr Carswall himself. He ate sparingly, but drank deeply, working his way through glass after glass of claret.

'I took it upon myself to investigate the state of Charlie's Latinity,' he announced. 'The Rector called the other morning, and I asked him to interrogate the boy on his knowledge of the *Eton Latin Grammar*. He was shocked – *shocked*, Mr Shield – when he plumbed the depths of the lad's ignorance. Why, he could not even distinguish between a gerund and a gerundive. What does Mr Bransby teach them?'

'He has not had much opportunity of teaching Charlie anything, sir. Nor has any of us. Charlie attended the school for less than a term, and for much of it he was absent.'

Mrs Frant turned her face away.

'It has not been an easy time for him,' put in Miss Carswall.

Carswall shot his daughter a glance. 'True enough, my dear,' he rumbled. 'Still, that don't alter the case. The boy wants instruction, and I daresay Edgar Allan does too. You had better stay for the rest of their holidays, Shield, and read with them in the mornings.'

I bowed.

'If the arrangement is quite convenient for Mr Shield?' Mrs Frant said, looking at me.

'Of course it is,' Carswall said. 'Mr Bransby raised no objection when I put it to him, so why should he? Neither of them will be the loser.'

'And I'm sure Mr Shield will make himself useful in other ways,' Miss Carswall said. 'He will be quite an addition to our little society. You like a game of chess in the evening, do you not, Papa, and I'm sure he can make a fourth at whist. If the weather is bad, one hardly ever sees anyone in the country, especially in winter.'

'People did not mind the weather when I was a boy,' Carswall grumbled. 'We were more sociable then.'

'Why, Papa, we are sociable still. Or we try to be. Did not the Rector ride over the other day? And in the rain!'

The meal continued to its weary end. There was some hesitation about which lady should give the signal to withdraw. In the end, Miss Carswall was the first to rise. I held open the door for them. Mrs Lee and Mrs Frant hurried past, their faces averted, but Miss Carswall smiled up at me. The cloth was removed. Carswall beckoned me back to my seat and pushed the decanter towards me.

'You will not dine with us every night,' he said.

'Yes, sir.'

'Mind you, Flora may have a point. Do you play chess or piquet? Whist?'

'Indifferently, I'm afraid.'

'No matter. You play – that is the main thing.' Carswall stared into his glass. 'We exchange few visits in this part of the country.'

We drank in silence. A clock ticked. Whereas Mr Rowsell drank wine because he enjoyed it and its effects, Mr Carswall drank it as if it were his bounden duty.

'I did not wish to alarm the ladies at dinner,' he said after a while, 'but this afternoon I received intelligence that there is a band of house-breakers in the vicinity. We must be on our guard. So it is no bad thing to have another man in the house, particularly a former soldier.'

The old man gnawed his lower lip for a moment and then bade me ring the bell. When the butler came, Mr Carswall ordered him to lock up with particular care. Then, to my relief, he gave me permission to go. I left him to his wine and his fire and went to the drawing room in search of tea. Only Miss Carswall and Mrs Lee were there, one on either side of the fire. Mrs Lee was asleep. Miss Carswall's face was uncharacteristically sad, though she looked up with a smile when I entered and patted the sofa beside her.

'Sit down and have some tea, Mr Shield. I cannot tell you how pleased Sophie and I are to see you. Papa becomes quite bearish without masculine company. I am sure you will do an admirable job of drawing his fire. Isn't that how you military men put it?'

I smiled back and said I would do my best. As I spoke, I glanced in the direction of Mrs Lee.

'You must not mind her,' Miss Carswall murmured. 'Mrs Lee is very short-sighted and rather deaf: in other words, one could not ask for a better chaperone.'

'She is a near neighbour?'

'No. In fact, I had not met her before she came here on Tuesday. She seems most amiable, though, and I will not hear a word against her. It appears that all her relations are clergymen, which constitutes her principal charm in Papa's eyes.'

I burst out laughing.

'But it is true,' she went on. 'Papa feels that neither Sophie nor I is quite the thing, albeit for different reasons. He is anxious that we should be accepted in the neighbourhood, that we should take our proper position in society. Hence Mrs Lee. She has such a store of respectability that she cannot help but shed her surplus on those around her. She is a perfect paragon in every way, and one of her nephews was acquainted with Sir George Ruispidge when they were up at Oxford.' Her eyes gleamed in the candlelight. 'Believe me, Mr Shield, there can be no higher recommendation.'

'I'm afraid I do not know of the gentleman.'

'What? How can this be? Sir George Ruispidge is our very own none-such. He lives nearby at Clearland-court. They say his rent-roll brings in six or seven thousand a year.' She looked down at her lap but I saw the smile on her face. 'And the dear man has coal mines besides, as well as a charming house in Cavendish-square and a seat in Parliament. His family have been here for generations – they know everybody, go everywhere. So you will understand that we find him a most agreeable neighbour.' She raised her head just in time to catch me with an answering smile. 'And the general opinion among the ladies is that he is a very handsome man, too.'

'And what is your view, Miss Carswall?'

Her eyelashes fluttered. 'It would not be seemly for me to disagree with an opinion held so firmly by the majority of my sex, Mr Shield. But you may soon be able to judge for yourself. We may see the Ruispidges in church on Christmas Day. Certainly my father hopes so. He has a very pressing reason for wishing it.'

'And may I ask what that is?'

For an instant the skin tightened over the bones of Miss Carswall's face. 'Why, he hopes that Sir George will make an offer for me.'

CHAPTER THIRTY-EIGHT

FLORA CARSWALL WAS her father's child in more ways than one. Their virtues and their vices went hand in hand. Both of them spoke their minds, and both lacked cant; but both could also be shockingly frank.

Carswall was almost certainly wealthier than Sir George Ruispidge but the Ruispidges were one of the first families of the county, and had been for generations. One might say that Carswall wished to purchase a form of immortality by allying his family with them. No doubt he would have had no trouble in buying a gentleman, even one with a title, a man prepared to ignore the father's mean birth and the daughter's illegitimacy for the sake of the dowry she would bring. But it is human nature to desire what one cannot easily obtain. Carswall wanted a gentleman who was not on the brink of ruin, or already deep in that bottomless abyss. He wanted a gentleman who held his head high in the world.

So much I had already inferred, not merely from my conversation with Miss Carswall on the night of my arrival at Monkshill but also from what I knew of her father. What I did not then know was that there was another reason why Sir George Ruispidge was so pre-eminently suitable for the rôle of Mr Carswall's son-in-law. Looking back, however, I realised that I received a hint of it on my very first evening.

I had left the drawing room and was climbing the stairs towards my own chamber when I heard a door close and footsteps above. At the head of the flight I met Mrs Kerridge. I presumed she had been attending Mrs Frant. I made some remark in passing about the size of this house relative to those in Margaret-street and Russell-square – a pleasantry, merely, suggesting that we had risen in the world.

'He can never rise high enough for this house,' Mrs Kerridge hissed. 'Not for Monkshill – and he knows it.'

'I beg your pardon?'

She came close to me. 'I spoke plain enough, did I not?'

'Who can never rise high enough? Mr Carswall?'

'Who else could I mean? All the other men in this house are servants.' She raised the candle she carried in her left hand and gave me a hard, considering look.

'Mrs Kerridge –'

She cut me off with a laugh. 'None of our affair, though, is it? Master Charlie's asleep, by the way – I looked in on him earlier. His friend was reading, but I made him blow out his candle.' She walked away from me, turning as she went to throw a few more words over her shoulder: 'It won't do you no good, you know, coming here. This place does no one any good. You should have stayed at that school of yours.'

CHAPTER THIRTY-NINE

THE NEXT DAY, Friday, was Christmas Eve. In the morning the two boys and I continued our long march through the *Eton Latin Grammar*. In the afternoon, we walked in the park. It was exceptionally cold that year. Everywhere the ground was hard and white with frost.

The mansion-house stood at the southern end of a ridge. The boys took me north along a path running up the ridge's spine, which commanded a prospect of the river's sinuous, shining curves beyond the turnpike road in the valley below. No expense had been spared to accentuate the picturesque nature of the spot. An obelisk surrounded by seats artfully constructed of rustic stone marked the highest point of the park and also the place where six paths intersected. We followed the widest of them, which led north-west and gently downwards to a small lake formed by damming a stream that drained down to the river. To the north and west, beyond the stretch of frozen water, lay dense woods.

Charlie pointed to the trees. 'Mr Carswall has ordered the game-keepers in the covers to shoot strangers on sight. There are poachers at work, he says, and some of them may be housebreakers too.'

Edgar stared at him. 'Surely they would not dare come here?'

'What is to stop them? We can hardly send for a constable if we see them.'

The ways of great estates were foreign to me. But before I had been twenty-four hours at Monkshill-park, I had begun to suspect that something was wrong. The domestic economy of a large establishment should run as smoothly as Mr Carswall's watch. A well-tended park should show everywhere the presiding hand of its owner. Monkshill was a splendid house, in a splendid park. There was no shortage of money. Yet it seemed to me that neither of the ladies had been entrusted with the direction of the indoor servants, and that the master did not care to interest himself in the estate.

Instead, Mr Carswall had hired people to do these things. This would not have mattered if he had ensured that those he had hired were doing their jobs. But everywhere one saw small signs of neglect: from the spots of grease on the footmen's liveries to the gate with a broken hinge in the park palings. It was possible, I thought, that Mr Carswall was not habituated to the responsibilities of such an establishment. But I knew too much of his capabilities to believe that he could not have remedied the shortcomings, had he desired to do so.

It puzzled me at first. An older man would have seen the reason directly. Mr Carswall was old; he knew that his powers were declining; and he was husbanding his energies for a purpose I did not then understand.

CHAPTER FORTY

THE CHRISTMAS EVES of my youth had left me with many happy memories. My father was a cool, grave, remote man who took no part in the festivities of the season. But my mother would take me to the house of an aunt. She had married a whitesmith and, though comfortable, the family was not in such prosperous circumstances as we believed our own to be. But on a single Christmas Eve in their house, there was more laughter than in ours the whole year round.

In my aunt's kitchen, there was always a great sprig of mistletoe, and we boys had the privilege of kissing the girls beneath it; and for each kiss, a berry was plucked from the bush. This circumstance led to much frenzied arithmetic, for when all the berries had been plucked, the privilege ceased.

I spent my last Christmas Eve in Rosington at my aunt's house. This was after my parents had died, when I was teaching at the grammar school. Fanny, the daughter of the school's new master, had paid a visit. That day I kissed her for the first time, and it was underneath my aunt's mistletoe bush. Usually the memory of her made me feel melancholy. Not this year, however – instead, the thought crossed my mind that if I had not kissed Fanny under the mistletoe five years before, I should not be at Monkshill-park today.

Not that Mr Carswall encouraged any sign that it was Christmas Eve in his house. Rustic festivities would have been out of place in this great stone block, this temple to modern taste. None of the chaste marble fireplaces was large enough to hold a Yule log, even if such a thing had been available.

That evening I was invited to dine again with the Carswalls, Mrs Lee and Mrs Frant. Mr Carswall brought the conversation round to the subject of church.

'I had a note from the Rector,' he said. 'Sir George is bringing a party over from Clearland-court.'

Miss Carswall cast her eyes up to the ceiling. 'How fortunate I purchased that new pelisse before we left town.' She glanced across the table at me, and I thought I saw amusement in her face, and an invitation to share it. 'And will Captain Jack make one of the party? And their mama?'

'I do not know,' Carswall said. 'I should think it likely.' His eyes slid from Miss Carswall to Mrs Frant, and then he turned to me. 'You and Mrs Lee will join us. We have two pews. I think it proper that you should sit behind us with the boys.'

'Yes, sir.'

'Captain Ruispidge distinguished himself in the Peninsula,' Mr Carswall said. 'Should he condescend to address you, you may wish to bear that in mind.'

'Yes, sir,' I repeated. If anything was designed to prejudice me against a man, it was the intelligence that he had distinguished himself on a field of battle.

'Sir George is patron of the living, is he not?' Mrs Frant asked.

Carswall grunted. 'He must have four or five in his gift. By rights the owner of Monkshill should have the right of presentation at Flaxern Parva. But my predecessor Mr Cranmere sold it to Sir George's father.'

The conversation lagged until at last the rich, tepid meal was over. The ladies withdrew; the cloth was removed and the wine set out with the nuts. Mr Carswall turned his chair to face the fire and waved at me, indicating that I should do the same.

'So what do you think of Monkshill, eh?' he demanded, and did not wait for an answer. 'It is a fine house, is it not? Do you know the architect? Sir John Soane himself, the very man who designed the Bank of

England. Mind you, Soane don't come cheap, and didn't come cheap even then, thirty-odd years ago. And no expense was spared in the building. Not that I had to pay for that, sir, not a brass farthing. Reap what others sow: it is a fine motto in life, young man, mark it well: and remember that the man with ready money is king. No, Mr Cranmere spent so much in tearing down the old house and building this that he could not afford to live in it. He struggled on until 1815 but in the end he had to sell in a hurry. For a fraction of its worth: it was either that or the bailiffs. The folly of mankind never ceases to amaze me.' Carswall poured himself another glass of wine and stared into the fire. 'Yes, though I say it myself, it is an establishment to be proud of, worthy of any gentleman in the county; any gentleman in the land, come to that.'

He rumbled on in this vein for twenty minutes. There I sat, an audience of one, chained to my seat. Gradually his enunciation became slurred, and the pauses between sentences grew longer, then the pauses between phrases and words. He had his feet on the fender and his shoes had fallen into the hearth. His breeches were unbuttoned and spotted with stains of wine and gravy. The last thing he said before he dropped into a doze lodged in my memory, simply because it was so out of tune with what had gone before.

'When my grandfather came to Monkshill, he touched his hat to the proprietor. Now I am the proprietor.' He glared at me with eyes half concealed behind straggling eyebrows, like a beast in a thicket, as though I had dared to contradict him. 'So who is master now, hey? Tell me that. Who is master now?'

CHAPTER FORTY-ONE

ON CHRISTMAS MORNING, there was some debate at break-fast on the subject of how our party should travel to church. There were three equipages at Monkshill: a big coach, which at a pinch would hold six; the chaise that had brought Edgar and me from Gloucester, and which would hold three at most; and finally a low pony-phaeton for the ladies, which was judged quite unsuitable for the gravity of the occasion. Mr Carswall had been of the opinion that the chaise should be harnessed as well as the coach, but Miss Carswall pointed out that they could easily accommodate six in the coach, especially in that two of them were only boys. Then, as she realised the implications of what she had said, her eyes turned towards mine in silent apology.

The arithmetic was stark: Mr Carswall, Mrs Lee, Mrs Frant, Miss Carswall and the two boys made six. There was not a seat for me. It was a perfectly clear statement of my position at Monkshill, all the clearer because I believed it unintended.

Her father said with a slight air of disappointment, 'I suppose we might make do with just the coach. But I would not like it to seem that that was all we had at our disposal.'

'Papa, I do not think that likely.'

'It is such a lovely day,' Mrs Frant said. 'I am sure the boys would like to walk.'

'Yes, indeed,' cried Miss Carswall. 'That would answer very well. I

197

daresay they would enjoy it, and we would not have to squeeze up in the coach.' Once more she turned to me. 'That is, Mr Shield, if you would be kind enough to escort them.'

I bowed my assent. 'How far is Flaxern Parva?'

'Not above a mile and a half,' she replied. 'It is nearer three if one goes by the drive and the road, but there is a path across the park, and the church is on the nearer side of the village.' She clapped her hands. 'How I envy you. The air is so refreshing.'

Later in the morning the boys and I stood on the steps outside the front door and watched the Carswalls' coach rolling round to the front of the house, rising and sinking on its long springs like a ship at sea, and glittering like a gigantic, brightly varnished child's toy. There was a coat of arms on each door. A crest glittered in silver radiance from every part of the harness where a crest could possibly be placed. The coachman wore a three-cornered hat, richly laced, and a curly wig the colour of corn. Two liveried footmen, one of them Pratt, lolled on the box behind, carrying bouquets and gold-headed canes.

Carswall came out of the house and looked with childlike glee at his toy. 'I got the machine for a hundred and fifty guineas when Cranmere sold up,' he said, beating the brass ferrule of his stick against the stone of the step. 'A bargain, hey? It was hardly a month old. He hadn't even paid for it.'

The boys and I set off across the frosty park. The sky was a dark, clear blue and the air was so cold it cut into the back of one's throat like neat spirits. Our way took us past the lake we had visited the previous day. The boys ran ahead to slide on the ice. I pretended not to notice. A church bell tolled beyond the trees on the other side of the lake.

'Come now,' I ordered, 'we must hurry. Mr Carswall will be displeased if we are late.'

They took this as an invitation to slither across to the further shore of the lake, the one nearer the trees, and I hurried along the bank after them. Charlie left the lake and plunged down the path that ran between two enclosed covers. I hoped no one was at hand to observe their behaviour: it was most unbecoming that two young gentlemen should

198

behave in such an undignified way as they walked to divine service on one of the holiest days in the church's calendar.

We hurried down a path through woodland. Charlie warned us with ghoulish relish not to venture among the trees without one of the keepers by our side for Mr Carswall had planted mantraps among the covers against the poachers.

At last the woods came to an end. To my relief, I saw the little church no more than three hundred yards away. It had a low tower, constructed of the rust-coloured local sandstone, and a sagging roof of stone tiles fissured with cracks and blotched with lichen. The churchyard was crowded with villagers in their Sunday best. The coach had not yet arrived.

The path led directly to a small gate set in the wall of the churchyard. Two grooms were walking a chaise and a curricle up and down the adjacent lane. Charlie, with a confidence I envied, made for the knot of gentlefolk standing near the church porch.

Just then Mr Carswall's coach burst into view. With a great clatter of hooves, rumbling of wheels and cracking of whips, it careered down the high road, forcing a party of villagers to press against the churchyard wall to avoid being run down. The coachman drew up outside the lych-gate. He artfully contrived to rein the horses up more tightly so they champed their bits and arched their necks as though better bred than they were.

'Damn me,' said a young gentleman standing with his back to me. 'Travelling *en prince*, eh? I must say I'd –'

A second man, a little older than his companion, had caught sight of us on the path and stopped the speaker in mid-sentence with a hand on the arm. They watched – we watched – as the footmen alighted at breakneck speed, as they opened the door and pulled down the steps, as Carswall emerged, inch by inch, like a great snail from its glistening shell, his bright little eyes darting from side to side to mark who was watching.

When the old man reached the safety of the ground, he turned, swaying, leaning heavily on his stick, and held out his arm for Mrs Lee, in a gesture which was designed to be courtly but seemed merely theatrical. The old lady stepped down, blinking in the sunlight. Next came

Sophia Frant, and I heard one of the gentlemen in front of me draw in his breath. Finally Miss Carswall appeared in the doorway of the carriage. For an instant she paused, glancing round like an actress surveying her audience, and smiling at the crowd in the churchyard with dazzling impartiality. Then she fluttered down the steps and took Mrs Frant's arm.

The bell tolled on. The villagers fell back to either side of the path as Carswall's party advanced slowly towards the porch. Beside me, the two gentlemen removed their hats and bowed. There was a marked contrast between the quiet elegance of their dress and the magnificence of Carswall's.

'Sir George!' Carswall exclaimed as they drew level with the elder of the two. 'The compliments of the season to you. And to you, my dear sir,' he added, turning in the direction of the second gentleman. 'How is Lady Ruispidge? I trust she is well?'

'Indeed,' said Sir George. 'She is already in church.'

He and the other gentleman, whom I took to be his brother, bowed again to the ladies. Carswall introduced Charlie and Edgar, and the party passed into the porch, which was thickly hung with Christmas greenery in the old-fashioned country manner. Inside the church itself, members of the little orchestra in the gallery were tuning their instruments. Miss Carswall glanced back at me and made as though to put her hands over her ears, raising her eyebrows in mock horror.

The Ruispidges occupied two pews set apart in a separate enclosure at right angles to the rest of the congregation, and facing the pulpit. Carswall had taken the two pews at the front of the nave, and on the southern side: which brought us immediately to the left of Sir George and his family.

The Ruispidge brothers joined two ladies who were already seated in the family pews. One was elderly, dressed in black and with a long, bony face resembling a horse's, as the faces of well-bred humans so often do once the bloom of youth has worn off. The other lady was much younger, and when I caught sight of her, a thrill of recognition ran through me.

It was Fanny!

An instant later, I realised that I was mistaken. Yet the lady still reminded me of the girl whom I had kissed in another time and another place under the mistletoe in my aunt's kitchen. She had the same high colouring, the same black, lustrous hair, and the same well-developed figure. She reminded me of someone else, too, a lady I had seen more recently, but for the life of me I could not remember whom or when.

At length the service began. The parson was a well-built, red-faced man, who looked as though he belonged not in the pulpit but in the saddle with a fox and a pack of hounds in full cry in front of him. I hoped from this that his sermon would be brief, bluff and to the point. Appearances proved deceptive, however, for he spoke in a thin, scholarly drone for more than fifty minutes on the subject of how we should observe the ceremonies of Christmas, and the propriety of observing the feast not merely as a day of thanksgiving but also one of rejoicing. This was straightforward enough, but he supported the correctness of his opinions with frequent and lengthy references to the work of the Fathers of the Church. We sat in unhappy silence imbibing the wisdom of Theophilus of Caesarea and St Chrysostom.

My attention wandered. The Ruispidges were still and attentive. The dark-haired lady, however, sometimes glanced to her left, into the nave where the rest of us were sitting, and once her eyes caught mine. There was a moment of welcome relief when the bass viol fell with a clatter to the floor of the balcony, no doubt because its owner had dropped into a doze. I regret to say that Mr Carswall, too, nodded off and had to be brought back to consciousness with a jab in the elbow from his daughter.

I repressed a yawn, and then another. In search of diversion, I glanced at the two mural tablets on the wall beside me. The words 'Monkshill-park' at once caught my eye. The first tablet recorded the death of the Honourable Amelia, daughter of the first Lord Vauden and wife of Henry Parker, Esquire, of Monkshill-park, in 1763. Beneath this was another tablet commemorating the manifold virtues of the Parkers' daughter, Emily Mary, who had died in 1775.

All at once I was fully awake. With a sense of foreboding creeping over me, I re-read the inscription on the second tablet.

Emily Mary, beloved wife of William Frant, Esquire, of Monkshill-park.

Had the Frants once owned Mr Carswall's house?

CHAPTER FORTY-TWO

W HEN AT LAST the service was over, the Ruispidges were the
first to file out of the church into the sunlight, with Mr
Carswall's party hard at their heels. The rest of the congregation
followed us outside, and an air of festivity and freedom filled the little
churchyard. The villagers were like children let out of school. Even
their betters acquired an air of holiday. Charlie and Edgar played a
discreet game of tag among the gravestones. I did not have the heart
to stop them.

Mr Carswall hobbled as fast as he could after the baronet and contrived
to pin him in a corner between the wall of the church and a buttress.
'Sir George,' he cried. 'Was not that an edifying sermon?'

Sir George nodded, and I noted his eyes straying away from Mr
Carswall towards Mrs Frant and Miss Carswall, who were now in conversation with his mother Lady Ruispidge and the dark-haired lady from
their pew. Captain Ruispidge hovered gracefully between the two
younger ladies.

'We should be very glad to see you at Monkshill, Sir George, you
and the Captain, and Lady Ruispidge, too, if she would not find the
drive too fatiguing.'

Sir George remarked that it was very good of Mr Carswall. Miss
Carswall had said Sir George was accounted handsome, as perhaps
baronets often are, but I thought he looked like a hungry greyhound.

He had to a nicety the art of making civil remarks which lacked warmth and substance.

'I believe you have not yet met my cousin, Mrs Frant, sir,' the old man went on. 'Pray allow me to rectify the omission.'

Sir George bowed. 'Thank you, I shall be glad to meet her.' He added, his voice and face studiously neutral, 'I was acquainted with her husband, the late Mr Frant, when we were boys.'

Mr Carswall bowed very low, as if in acknowledgement for this remarkable condescension. He led the baronet towards the knot of women. It so happened that I was standing at the side of the path, engaged partly in eavesdropping, partly in keeping an eye on the boys and partly in attempting to digest the implications of the unexpected intelligence about Henry Frant that I had recently acquired. Carswall had his head turned towards the baronet, but he was aware of my presence. With his arm he nudged me aside, off the path and on to the grass. It was carelessly done, and without malice, as one would push aside a dog that blocked the doorway of a room, or scoop a cat from a chair. He did not look at me, and he did not break off the flow of his remarks to Sir George.

I own I was angry and perhaps hurt, not least because I had been so treated in full view of the four ladies, the Ruispidge gentlemen, my two pupils and the entire population, or so it seemed, of Flaxern Parva. I felt the colour flooding into my cheeks. I watched as Carswall and Sir George joined the others, and the introductions were made. Miss Carswall had already met the Ruispidges, but none of the other party was acquainted with Mrs Frant.

'Why, Mrs Johnson,' said Miss Carswall to the dark-haired lady. 'Have you news of the gallant lieutenant? Is he still on the West Indies station?'

'Yes,' said the lady, and made as if to turn away.

'Did I not see you in town a few weeks ago?' Miss Carswall asked, in that little innocent voice she used when she was up to mischief. 'I thought I glimpsed you in Pall Mall the other week – you was going into Payne and Foss's – but there was such a crush I could not be sure, and then the carriage moved on and it was too late.'

'No,' Mrs Johnson replied. 'You must be mistaken. I have not been further than Cheltenham these six or seven months.'

At that moment, I recalled when and where I might have seen Mrs Johnson before. I was not perfectly convinced, mind you, not then.

'You must not hesitate to step out of your garden into the park, ma'am,' Carswall interrupted, addressing Mrs Johnson. 'You must treat it quite as your own. I shall tell my people so. A word of caution, though: keep away from the covers. We have had such a plague of poachers in the last few months that I have had to sow the woods with a number of surprises. I would not wish a friend to fall foul of one of them.'

Mrs Johnson bowed. A moment later, I saw her watching Mr Carswall as he turned back to Sir George and, for an instant, I surprised upon her face an expression of distaste that amounted almost to hatred.

'I say, George,' said Captain Jack, who until now had been chatting with Mrs Frant and Miss Carswall, 'I was acquainted with Mrs Frant's father. He was most kind to me when I went out to Portugal in the year nine. Colonel Marpool of the Ninety-Seventh, you know, though at the time he was seconded to the Portuguese army. A most distinguished officer – he played a great part in the recovery of Oporto, and he gave Masséna himself a drubbing at Coimbra.'

Mr Carswall beamed, as though the exploits of Mrs Frant's father were in some mysterious way his own. He pulled out his watch and showed it to the company. 'I think it very likely that Masséna had a timepiece from the same workshop that produced this. They say Napoleon himself was one of Breguet's patrons.'

'I beg your pardon, sir?' Sir George said, his forehead wrinkling. 'But who is Breguet?'

'Abraham-Louis Breguet, sir – the finest watchmaker in the world.' Mr Carswall glanced fondly at the timepiece in his palm. 'Certainly a number of Napoleon's officers are known to have had these watches, for they are accurate to a tenth of a second, proof against sudden shocks, and capable of running for eight years without being over-hauled, and without going slow. They say – and Captain Ruispidge will I'm sure correct me if I'm wrong – that many of the Emperor's victories can be attributed to his genius for timing, and it is not far-fetched to imagine that this accuracy in the matter of time depended on a Breguet watch.'

So the old man ran on, to an audience of blank faces. I was mortified on his behalf, despite the way he had slighted me, and turned aside to look for the boys. I did not see them in this part of the churchyard, so I walked back towards the porch, meaning to circumnavigate the church until I found them.

'Mr Shield,' Miss Carswall said, just behind me.

Startled, I swung round. She had broken away from the others, and stood at my elbow.

'Would you be so good as to do me a favour?'

'Of course, Miss Carswall.'

'I have foolishly left my handkerchief in the church, in the pew where we were sitting.'

'Then you must allow me to fetch it for you.'

I passed through the porch into the church and walked down the nave. A moment later, I heard the door open again behind me. I glanced over my shoulder. There was Miss Carswall, smiling.

'Mr Shield, I do so apologise. It was in my muff all the time.' She held up the wisp of embroidered silk. 'I sent you on a fool's errand.'

I retraced my steps. 'It don't signify.'

She waited on the threshold, her hand on the door. 'Oh, but it does,' she said quietly. 'Particularly as I knew the handkerchief was in my muff all the time.'

'I'm afraid I do not understand.'

'It is very simple. I wished to apologise for my father's behaviour.'

I felt myself blushing once again and turned aside.

'I know I should not say this of my father, but I cannot ignore the fact that he sometimes acts in a manner that –'

'You must not distress yourself, Miss Carswall. It is of no moment.'

She stamped her foot. 'He treats you like a servant. It is not just. I saw him pushing you out of his way. I wished the ground would open up and swallow me. Or – even better – swallow *him*.'

'I beg of you, do not be disturbed on my account.'

She turned her head, as though about to leave, but then looked back at me. 'Pray, do not take it amiss, my talking to you in this way. You must think me very forward. I should beg your pardon.'

'On the contrary, I think you most considerate of an inferior's feelings.'

'Oh?' Miss Carswall waited for me to go on. 'Is that all?'

'I honour you for it.'

'Oh!' she said, with a different inflection, and darted into the porch.

I followed her under the canopy of evergreen leaves and branches. She stopped in the middle of the porch and looked at me. Beyond the archway into the churchyard I saw the green of the grass, the grey of the gravestones and the blue of the sky. The path from the lych-gate made a right angle as it turned towards the porch. I heard the voices of other people, but I saw no one except Miss Carswall; and no one could see us.

'In the church,' I said, 'there was a tablet on the wall which –'

'Hush.'

Flora Carswall laid her hand on my arm, raised herself on tiptoe and kissed my cheek.

Shocked, I sprang back, jarring my elbow against the great iron latch on the door. Her perfume filled my nostrils, and the warmth of her lips burned like a brand on my skin. She smiled, and this time her face was full of mischief.

'This is the time and the place where such liberties are permitted, sir, or at least condoned,' she said in a voice not much louder than a whisper. 'Look.'

She pointed upwards and I saw that hanging from the vault above her head was a great bush of mistletoe studded with white berries. My heart pounded in my chest.

'You must pick off one of the berries now,' she said in the same caressing voice. 'But there are still plenty left.'

She turned away and stepped into the blinding sunshine of Christmas morning.

CHAPTER FORTY-THREE

THE FINE, COLD, clear weather continued. On the morning of St Stephen's Day, the household went to church again. On this occasion, Carswall ordered the chaise as well as the coach, and we rumbled in procession through the winding lanes to Flaxern Parva. Alas, Mr Carswall was doomed to disappointment. The Ruispidges' pews were empty.

When we returned to the mansion, the boys were in tearing spirits, partly from the holiday and partly from want of exercise. They fell in willingly enough when I proposed a walk.

'You should take Mr Shield to see our ruined abbey,' Miss Carswall suggested, looking up from her bureau; though it was Sunday, she was at work on her accounts. 'It is a vastly romantic spot, and one generally sees cowled figures flitting from pillar to pillar.'

She bent her head over her account book. She and I had not spoken in private since what had passed between us in the church porch on Christmas Day. I did not know what to think about her feelings, or indeed about my own. I was aware that we had both behaved improperly, yet somehow I contrived not to dwell on that side of the matter.

'Yes, sir,' put in Charlie, 'please let us go to the abbey. Edgar, they say the monks buried treasure there.'

Mrs Frant, who had been writing a letter at a table in the window, looked up at this. 'Don't fill Edgar's head with such nonsense, Charlie. It is only a foolish story that country people tell.'

I looked at her, sitting in the cold winter sunlight, and said, 'Are the ruins extensive, ma'am?'

'I have not seen them, Mr Shield. My cousin will tell you.'

'You must prepare to be disappointed,' Miss Carswall said. 'A few stones, that is all. It was not even a true abbey. The Rector told Papa that all the land around here was owned by the monks at Flaxern Magna, which is down by the river. He believes that our little ruins mark the site of one of the monks' outlying farms. Papa was most put out. He wanted a veritable abbey, not a tumbledown farmhouse.'

'But the monks were there. So I expect there are ghosts,' Charlie said, with the air of one dangling a further bait. 'And treasure. It's more likely they'd hide it there than in the abbey, isn't it? That's the first place people would look.'

Mrs Frant smiled at him. 'When the park was laid out, I believe a few silver pennies were found among the foundations. Perhaps that may be the origin of the story of treasure. Country people are very credulous.'

'Where were they found?'

She busied herself in folding her letter. 'I don't know, Charlie.'

'Then who told you about the silver? I can ask him if he knows where it was dug up.'

'You cannot ask him, I'm afraid. It was your papa.' She looked at her son. 'When he was a little boy he lived here – not in this house, in the old one that was here before. His grandpapa laid out the park. You can see his name on the obelisk.'

'We lived here? Monkshill was ours?'

Mrs Frant coloured. 'It was never ours, my love. Your grandpapa sold the property to Mr Cranmere many years ago.'

Charlie leaned on the back of her chair and had the wit to change the subject. 'Come out with us, Mama. You can show us where the treasure might have been found.'

'There *was* no treasure,' she said.

'But there was money,' Miss Carswall said. 'Silver coins. Is not that treasure?'

Mrs Frant laughed, and so did we all. 'I suppose it is.'

'Well then,' Charlie said. 'There may be more. We won't find it if we don't look.'

Mrs Frant glanced out of the window, at the silver expanse of the park lying beneath the hard blue dome of the sky. 'I believe it would do me good to take the air. Will you join us, Flora?'

Miss Carswall said she would prefer to sit by the fire. I tried to catch her eye but she had returned to her figures.

A quarter of an hour later, the boys were running along the path while Mrs Frant and I followed at a more sedate pace. We walked quickly, however, because of the cold. The air brought spots of colour into Mrs Frant's usually pale cheeks. We inspected the obelisk, found the inscription that recorded the virtues of Charlie's great-grandfather, and took a path leading eastward into a shallow valley. The boys scampered ahead, and were soon out of earshot. By this time, any embarrassment caused by the mention of Mr Frant had been entirely dissipated.

'I hope you do not find us too dull,' Mrs Frant said. 'You must be used to a deal of noise and bustle, I daresay. Charlie tells me that you lived in London before you entered Mr Bransby's school, and that before that you were a soldier.'

'All the more reason why I should relish the calm of the countryside.'

'Perhaps.' She darted a glance at me. 'My father served in the army too. Colonel Francis Marpool – I do not suppose you knew him?'

'No. I enlisted in the army only in 1815. As a private soldier.'

'You fought at Waterloo?'

'I was wounded there, ma'am.'

She gave me a look of admiration that filled me with shame.

I said, 'I did not fire a single shot, however. I was wounded at an early stage of the battle, and then had a horse fall beside me, which prevented me from moving. I was a most inglorious soldier.'

'I honour your frankness, Mr Shield,' she said. 'Had I been a man, and on the field of battle, I'm sure I should have been terrified.'

'To be blunt, I *was* terrified.'

She laughed as though I had said something wonderfully witty. 'That merely confirms me in my opinion that you are a man of sense. You did not run away: that is glory enough, surely?'

'I could not run away. A dead horse on top of oneself is a powerful argument against motion of any sort.'

'Then we must be thankful that Providence afforded you its protection. Even in the form of a dead horse.' She pointed to the crest of a low hill we were ascending. 'When we reach the top, we shall see the ruins below.'

The boys appeared on the skyline as they reached the brow of the declivity. Whooping like a pair of savages, they ran down the far side.

Mrs Frant and I reached the summit. The ground sloped down to a little valley, on the floor of which were the remains of several stone walls. Some way beyond these scanty signs of habitation was a line of palings, which marked part of the demesne's northern boundary. The grey roofs of a substantial cottage were visible on the other side of the fencing.

'Oh!' exclaimed Mrs Frant, pressing her hand into her side. 'They might kill themselves!'

She ran down the hill. The boys were swarming like monkeys up the tallest of the few remaining walls of the ruin, which at its highest point was no more than eight feet above the ground.

'Charlie!' she cried. 'Be careful!'

Charlie ignored her. Edgar, less accustomed to Mrs Frant's nervous disposition, paused in his climb and looked over his shoulder.

Her foot caught on a tuft of grass and she stumbled.

'Mrs Frant!' I cried.

She regained her balance, and ran on.

From the ruins came the sound of a shout. I tore my eyes away from her. Charlie was sitting astride the wall at its topmost point, bellowing with the full strength of his lungs. His words were inaudible, but his agitation was unmistakable. An instant later, I saw Edgar, a crumpled figure on the ground below.

I thundered like a cavalry charge down the slope to the ruins, passing Mrs Frant on the way. In a moment I was bending over Edgar. His eyes were closed, and he was breathing heavily. A procession of potential calamities flocked through my mind, ranging from the loss of my position to the boy's death.

Charlie landed beside me with a thud. 'Is he breathing, sir? Will he live?'

'Of course he will live,' I snapped, fear bringing anger in its train.

I took Edgar's wrist. 'There is a pulse. A strong one.'

'Thank God,' murmured Mrs Frant, so close to me that I felt her breath brush my cheek.

Edgar opened his eyes and stared up at our faces poised above him. 'What – what –?'

'You fell,' I said. 'You're quite safe.'

He struggled up to a sitting position, but at once gave a cry and fell back.

'What is it?' said Mrs Frant. 'Where does it hurt?'

'My ankle, ma'am.'

I probed the injured limb with my fingers, and moved it gently this way and that. 'I cannot feel a break. You may have twisted it as you fell, or sprained it.'

I stood up and helped Mrs Frant to her feet. She drew me a yard or two away from the boys.

'Are you sure the ankle is not broken, Mr Shield?'

'I believe not, though I cannot be certain. But I learned something of these matters while helping my father with his patients; he acted the surgeon as well as the apothecary upon occasion. Besides, if the ankle were broken, I think the boy would feel more pain.'

'So foolish of me. If I had not called out, he –'

'You must not think that. He might have fallen in any case.'

'Thank you.' Her fingers squeezed my arm and then released it. 'We must get him back to the house.'

'He should be carried.' I calculated the distance in my mind, and knew I could not comfortably bear Edgar's weight for the whole of it. 'It would be better to fetch help. He should not trust his weight to the ankle until the extent of the injury has been determined. Besides, he would be more comfortable on a hurdle.'

'Look,' Charlie said. 'Someone's coming.'

I followed his pointing finger. Beyond the ruins, near the palings, was a woman, her dark cloak flapping about her as she strode towards us. Mrs Frant turned her head to look. She expelled her breath in a sound expressing either pain or perhaps irritation.

'I believe it is Mrs Johnson,' she said in a quiet, toneless voice.

We watched in silence as she drew closer. Mrs Johnson was undeniably a fine-looking woman but there was something hawk-like in her countenance that made me wonder whether her husband was less accustomed to leading than to being led.

'Well!' said she. 'The boy took a nasty tumble, Mrs Frant. Is he able to walk if supported? We must get him to the cottage and summon help.'

I cleared my throat. 'I suggest Charlie runs back across the park.'

'Oh yes,' he cried. 'I'll go like the wind.'

'That is very kind of you, ma'am,' Mrs Frant said. 'But we cannot possibly put you to so much trouble.'

'It is no trouble whatsoever,' Mrs Johnson replied. 'It is no more than common sense.'

'Then thank you.' There was colour in Mrs Frant's cheeks, and I knew she was angry, but not why. 'Charlie, will you give Cousin Flora my compliments, explain that Edgar has hurt his ankle and that Mrs Johnson has invited us into her cottage, and desire her to send the chaise with Kerridge.'

Mrs Johnson's large, brown, slightly protuberant eyes ran down me from head to foot. Without a word, she turned back to Mrs Frant. 'Could not this – this gentleman go? Surely he would reach the house sooner than your son?'

'I think it would not answer. We shall need Mr Shield to carry Edgar.'

Mrs Johnson glanced back at her own house. 'I could send to the village for –'

'Pray do not trouble yourself, ma'am. If Mr Shield will be so obliging, we shall manage very well as we are. I would not want us to put you to more trouble than we need. By the by, I do not think you have met my son's tutor. Give me leave to introduce Mr Shield. Mr Shield, Mrs Johnson, our neighbour.'

We bowed to each other.

A moment later, Charlie ran off to fetch help. I lifted Edgar on to my back and plodded down the valley to the palings, where a gate led directly into Mrs Johnson's untidy garden. She led us to the front of the house. It was not a large establishment – indeed, it barely qualified as a gentleman's residence – and it was evident at a glance that it was in a poor state of repair.

'Welcome to Grange Cottage,' Mrs Johnson said with a hard, ironical inflection in her voice. 'This way, Mr Shield.'

She flung open the front door and led us into a low, dark hall. A portmanteau and a corded trunk stood at the foot of the stairs.

'Ruth! Ruth! I want you!'

Without waiting for a reply Mrs Johnson ushered us into a small parlour lit by a bow-window. A tiny fire burned in the grate.

'Pray put the boy down on the sofa. You will find a footstool by the bureau. Perhaps you would be so kind as to put more coals on the fire. If we wait for my maid to do it, we shall wait an age.'

Wincing and murmuring thanks, Edgar sat on the sofa. He was very pale now, the skin almost transparent. Mrs Frant knelt beside him, helped him out of his coat and chafed his hands. The servant came almost at once, despite her mistress's poor opinion of her, and Mrs Johnson ordered blankets, pillows and sal volatile drops.

'Perhaps we should send for the surgeon,' I suggested.

'The nearest is two or three miles beyond Flaxern Parva,' Mrs Johnson said. 'The best plan will be to wait until you are back at Monkshill, and then have them send a groom over.'

'I am sorry we are the cause of so much inconvenience to you,' Mrs Frant said.

Mrs Johnson did not reply. The silence extended for longer than good manners allowed. I shifted my weight from foot to foot, and a floorboard creaked beneath me. The sound seemed to act as a trigger.

'Not at all, Mrs Frant,' said Mrs Johnson smoothly. 'It is a pleasure to be of service to a neighbour. It is fortunate that you find me still here, in fact – Lady Ruispidge has asked me to stay for a week or so; her carriage will be calling for me this afternoon.'

There was another, shorter silence.

'And – and how was Lieutenant Johnson when you last had news of him?' Mrs Frant said.

'Not in the best of spirits,' Mrs Johnson said harshly. 'He does not like the West Indian station, and since the Peace there is little hope of either promotion or prize-money.'

'I understand many naval officers are now on half-pay, but he is not. So surely the Admiralty must place a high value on his services?'

'He would like to think so.' Mrs Johnson sat down. 'Any employment, he says, is better than none. But the ship is old, and is likely to be sold out of the Service or broken up. So he will have to find another captain in need of a first lieutenant.'

'I am sure his merits must win him many friends.'

'I fear your optimism may be misplaced. It is influence, not merit, that counts. Still, we should not grumble. After all, it is a harsh world, is it not, Mrs Frant?'

Mrs Frant's colour rose in her cheeks. 'There are many who are less fortunate than us, no doubt.'

'You have given up your house in town, I collect?'

'Yes.'

'It was in Russell-square, was it not? It is not a part of London I am familiar with.'

I looked sharply at Mrs Johnson. She was staring with a curious fixity of expression at Mrs Frant, almost as though daring her to disagree.

'It is very pleasant,' Mrs Frant said. 'It is quieter than in the West End, of course, and less populous.'

The ladies' words were scrupulously polite but their silences and expressions told a different story, one with darker undercurrents. Though it may sound absurd to say such a thing of them, they acted like a pair of dogs looking for an opportunity to fly at each other's throats. As so often in my acquaintance with the Carswalls and the Frants, I had the sensation that everyone else knew more than I did, a sensation that familiarity had not made any less disagreeable.

Nor was this the only mystery that concerned Mrs Johnson. As she and Mrs Frant were exchanging their barbed platitudes, I recalled Miss

Carswall's remarks outside the church on Christmas Day about seeing her in Pall Mall, and Mrs Johnson vehemently denying she had been in town during the autumn. She protested too much, just as Fanny had done.

Just as Fanny —

The thought of the girl I had once loved, and whom I was now relieved not to have won, brought another memory to mind. I recalled the dark-haired lady I had seen climbing into a hackney in Southampton-row in October when I called at Russell-square to take Charlie Frant to school. She, too, had reminded me of Fanny, as Mrs Johnson did; and the more I considered the matter, the more I thought it at least possible that the lady had in fact been Mrs Johnson herself. Southampton-row led into Russell-square. But Mrs Johnson had gone out of her way to deny all knowledge of the neighbourhood.

'Ruth is taking an age,' Mrs Johnson said after another pause in the conversation. 'How very convenient it must be to have a large number of well-trained servants at one's beck and call.'

'I am sure we are giving her a great deal of extra work.' Mrs Frant cleared her throat. 'It was very pleasant to meet Captain Jack Ruispidge yesterday. He spoke so kindly of my father.'

'Yes, my cousin Jack is nothing if not amiable.' Mrs Johnson hesitated in the way a fencer hesitates, timing his thrust to perfection. 'If he has a fault, it is that he likes to be liked, especially by the ladies.'

At that moment, the maidservant appeared with the blankets, the pillows and the smelling salts. To allow her room to approach the sofa, I stood up and retreated into the recess formed by the little bow-window. I glanced outside. A small, overgrown shrubbery had crept close to this wall of the cottage, and the dark green leaves of the laurels crowded against this side of the window.

An involuntary exclamation burst from my lips. For an instant, peering out of that tangled foliage, I glimpsed a face with staring eyes.

'Why, what is it, Mr Shield?' Mrs Frant asked.

CHAPTER FORTY-FOUR

HOW COULD I have known that Mrs Johnson, for all her poverty and her retired situation, was a person of great importance in the drama unfolding around me? True, she was one of those creatures who find it difficult to dissemble their emotions. I suspected already that she disliked Mr Carswall. After the visit to Grange Cottage with Edgar, I was convinced that she also disliked Mrs Frant to the point of hatred. But at that stage I had no idea of the reason. Indeed, I blundered through this entire affair in a state of ignorance almost from start to finish.

As soon as Mrs Kerridge and Charlie arrived in the chaise, we bade our hostess farewell with almost indecent haste. Even with the seat in the middle pulled out, the chaise could take no more than three, so Charlie and I walked home through the park. As we went, I glanced back at the cottage in its ill-kempt garden.

'What are you looking for, sir?' Charlie asked.

'I thought I saw a man in the garden while we were in the cottage,' I said, knowing I must answer frankly because Edgar would tell him what had happened. 'But Mrs Johnson was sure I was mistaken, and said there had not been a man about the place since she discharged the gardener in October. I saw only part of a face, and only for an instant. It might even have been a woman.'

'A housebreaker?' Charlie suggested. 'Wouldn't that be a lark, sir?'

'It's unlikely to be a housebreaker in broad daylight, and with company in the house.' I smiled down at him. 'More likely a beggar.'

When we reached the mansion, we found Edgar in the ladies' sitting room. He was arranged on the sofa with Mrs Lee and Mrs Frant fussing over him, while Miss Carswall sat by the fire, glancing through a news-paper. The surgeon had been sent for but Mrs Lee shared my belief that the injury to the ankle was no more than a sprain; she brought out a host of anecdotes concerning the misfortunes of her sons, brothers, nephews and cousins to support the diagnosis. Certainly the boy looked better – his colour had returned and the face he turned towards Charlie and me was almost as lively as ever.

'I wish they wouldn't fuss so,' he murmured to Charlie. 'My ankle hardly hurts at all now if I do not put any weight on it. And we had not even begun to look for the treasure.'

All day I was restless. I could not forget the face I had seen at the window of Grange Cottage. I tried to persuade myself that it had been no more than a trick of the leaves and the light. I reminded myself that I had had no more than the briefest glimpse, and that Mrs Johnson was a rational woman who had no reason to lie.

I turned over in my mind whether I should mention my suspicions, insubstantial though they were, to Mr Carswall. In London he and I had established the possibility that Henry Frant was still alive, though the corpse at Wellington-terrace had been identified as his at the inquest and was now rotting under his name in the burying ground of St George the Martyr. Even if he had survived, however, he could not afford to run risks – he was a bankrupt, an embezzler, and very possibly a murderer too. But there was not a sliver of proof that he was still alive.

No proof: merely shadows glimpsed moving out of the corner of an eye, half-heard hints, a yellowing finger in a satchel left on a tooth-puller's door. But there remained the possibility that the man at the window had been Henry Frant. I found myself pacing up and down the hall.

The library door opened a few inches. I heard the harsh tones of Mr Carswall's voice, speaking so low I could not make out the words, and a reply in a higher, lighter voice that I recognised with a thrill of interest as Mrs Frant's. I did not intend to eavesdrop and I was in the act of withdrawing, when suddenly they began to speak more loudly.

'Take your hand from me, sir,' cried Mrs Frant, and her words were followed by the sound of a sharp impact, perhaps a slap. 'I would not entertain it for a moment.'

'Then you're a damned fool, madam,' said Carswall. 'Think who bought you that dress, who puts food in your belly, who pays for your son to grow up a gentleman.'

I drew back into the recess of a doorway. I no longer had any desire to confide my suspicions to Mr Carswall. Sophia Frant emerged from the library, her face blazing with colour. She ran lightly across the hall to the stairs. At the foot of them, she paused and glanced back. She saw me standing there. I wanted to say: I was not listening on purpose, I did not mean to pry. Also, I wished I might help her, for I had overheard enough to understand the nature of the conversation.

She stared at me. Her lips were slightly parted, her hand rested on the newel post. It was a graceful pose, and curiously formal, as though her limbs had been arranged at the whim of a portrait painter. She gave a queer little sob, turned, and pattered up the stairs and out of sight.

CHAPTER FORTY-FIVE

T HE NEXT DAY, the Monday after Christmas, brought unexpected news. One of the servants rode out to collect the letter bag, returning shortly after midday. The bag was taken to Mr Carswall in the library but its arrival sent a ripple of anticipation throughout the house. A few minutes later, Mr Carswall came into the ladies' sitting room.

'I have here a letter from Mr Noak, my dear,' he said to Miss Carswall. 'He is at present taking the waters at Cheltenham Spa, on the recommendation, I understand, of Mr Allan. He proposes to travel to South Wales next week, where he has an interest in some mining machinery. He inquires whether it would be convenient for him to call as he will be passing so near.' He glanced at the two boys who were trying to make themselves as small as possible in the corner of the room. 'He promised Mrs Allan that he would send her news of Edgar if that were possible.'

'I am sure we should be delighted to see him, Papa,' Miss Carswall replied. 'If he is to dine with us, no doubt you would like to offer him a bed for the night?'

'One can hardly expect him to travel on our lanes at this time of year, and in this weather, after sunset. No, I think we should invite him to spend a few days with us. He is a very considerable man in his way, and I would not want to be backward in showing him every civility.'

He glanced at the sheet of paper in his hand and then at me. 'He writes that he is travelling with his clerk. You remember him, Mr Shield? The nigger.'

I bowed.

Mr Carswall took a turn about the room while the rest of us waited in silence. There was an element of agitation about him that I found hard to explain. At that moment, I remembered the very first occasion I had met Mr Noak, when he had arrived at the Frants' house in Russell-square and the servant had tried to deny him entry until he wrote Carswall's name on his card and sent it in to Mr Frant.

'Mama,' said Charlie suddenly. 'There are horses on the drive.'

This intelligence caused a flurry of excitement. Mr Carswall joined the boys at the window, followed almost immediately by Miss Carswall. A moment later a curricle swept into view.

'It is Sir George and Captain Ruispidge,' Miss Carswall cried. 'Heavens, I am not fit to be seen!' She broke away from the group at the window. 'My gown! And my curls need frizzing. I must find Kerridge – you do not mind if I borrow her, Sophie? – my maid is so stupid she will take an age. Do not under any circumstances let them leave.'

I opened the door for her. She smiled up at me as she passed out of the room, and I swear one of her eyelids drooped in the suggestion of a wink. She was inviting me to join her in mocking her own vanity; she had a way of making a man she wanted to please into her conspirator. And I could not help but smile back. As I did so, I saw over her shoulder that Mrs Frant had raised her head and was looking at us.

Mr Carswall was almost as excited as his daughter. Sir George had sent a servant to inquire how Edgar did after his accident, but this was the first time that he had done us the honour of calling in person at Monkshill. The condescension was all the more marked in that Captain Ruispidge had accompanied him. Mr Carswall was most put out when he recalled that a fire had not been lit in the drawing room that day, on the grounds of economy. He rang the bell.

'The fire must have been laid. We shall have it lit.'

'But it will be much more natural if we receive them here, sir,' Mrs Frant said coldly. 'They will not want us to make a fuss over them, not for a morning call from neighbours. They will feel more easy if they find us here, engaged in our ordinary occupations. Besides, it will take an age for the drawing room to warm up.'

Carswall looked sharply at her but then nodded. 'I daresay you know what you're about. Very well.'

A moment later Sir George and Captain Ruispidge were announced. First they established that the ankle, the ostensible reason for their call, was as well as could be expected; thanks to Mrs Johnson, the news of the boy's mishap had already spread to Clearland-court. Lady Ruispidge, it appeared, had interested herself in the case, and inquired most particularly after Edgar.

'She recommends the joint be fomented with vinegar, or camphorated spirits of wine,' Sir George informed Mrs Frant. 'If excessively painful, a few drops of laudanum may be added. The treatment should be frequently renewed. And of course the injured part should be kept in a state of rest.'

'How very kind of her,' Mrs Frant said. 'Pray thank her for the advice.'

Captain Jack fell to praising the park – he praised the house – he praised its appointments – he compared Clearland-court unfavourably to it – at least, with a glance at his brother, in some respects. Then, somehow, he was sitting beside Mrs Frant and engaging her in conversation. I was too far away to hear what was said but once or twice I noticed her grave face breaking into a smile.

Meanwhile, Sir George and Mr Carswall began to discuss agricultural topics. Owing to Mr Carswall's ignorance of these, they passed rapidly from the price of corn to politics. When Miss Carswall returned, however, having dressed her hair and changed her gown, Sir George's attention turned from her father to her. The couple's conversation had the stately inevitability of an old-fashioned country dance. He inquired whether she preferred the country to the town, to which she replied that they both had much to recommend them. He discovered that she played a little and painted a little. He wondered whether it would interest her to look through some of his mother's music. Later, after her delighted response to this proposal had run its course, he suggested that when the weather was warmer, it might amuse her to sketch the ruins of Flaxern Abbey down by the river. He could undertake to show her a number of particularly fine viewpoints.

Then he turned to the world of literature. I knew already that Miss Carswall enjoyed sighing over novels and the more sentimental varieties of modern poetry, and that, unlike most of her sex, she read the newspapers assiduously. It soon became apparent, though, that Sir George's tastes were altogether more serious. Fortunately he did not inquire too closely about her reading but instead described his own. Like many gentlemen, he was convinced of the importance of his own opinions and the manifold advantages that would accrue to those who heard them. He recommended several religious works of an evangelical persuasion and expatiated on the moral beauties of Cowper's poetry. Miss Carswall played her part gamely but I do not think it came easily to her.

The boys and I said little. There were no rôles for us to play in the billing and cooing between the Carswalls and the Ruispidges. I sat forgotten in my corner. Charlie and Edgar were called over to meet Captain Jack, but their conversation did not last long. Soon it became apparent that the boys were bored.

Edgar took matters into his own hands. He was a headstrong boy, unlike the pliant Charlie, and persuaded Mrs Frant to allow the three of us to withdraw on the grounds that moderate exercise would complete the cure of his ankle. Once outside, Edgar refused to take my arm but accepted a stick. We walked as far as the kitchen gardens and back. On the way, I learned that the boys had not given up their intention of searching for the monks' treasure.

'They would not hide it in the grange,' Edgar said. 'Any more than in the abbey itself. They would be the first places where King Henry's men would look.'

'They might bury it somewhere near,' Charlie suggested.

'Or find a cave. But I think it very likely they would have hidden it up at Monkshill rather than down by the Abbey. It would be far safer.'

As we were returning to the house, we heard the sound of the curricle receding down the drive. We found the rest of the party still in the small sitting room. Mr Carswall was standing by the window and rubbing his hands with pleasure.

'They are engaged to dine with us when Mr Noak will be here,' he told me, for he needed to tell someone whom he had not told before. He turned back to Miss Carswall. 'We must have game, Flora. Nothing but the best. If only Lady Ruispidge will be able to accept as well.'

He ran on in a similar vein for much of the day. There came a moment when Miss Carswall and Mrs Frant were out of the room; I was waiting for the boys to bring down their books; and Mr Carswall was enlarging upon his plans for the dinner party to Mrs Lee. Mrs Lee was his ideal interlocutor for she rarely said anything of significance but knew to perfection when to insert into the flow of someone else's words those little phrases of assent and interest that are so agreeable and encouraging to the other party.

'I have half a mind to invite Mrs Johnson, too,' Carswall said in his harsh, carrying voice. 'After all, it was she who was kind to Edgar. It would be a very proper attention, too: she is a cousin of the Ruispidges, as well as a neighbour. And it would look most odd if we did not ask her, particularly if she is still staying at Clearland.'

Mrs Lee cleared her throat loudly, an action so unusually emphatic that he stared at her in surprise. 'I do not know whether you are aware of a certain unhappy circumstance in Mrs Johnson's early life, sir,' she said in a low tone. 'It might be prudent to consider the wisdom of such an invitation very carefully.'

'What? Speak plainly, madam. I cannot understand you if you talk in riddles.'

Mrs Lee drew back in her chair, and the features of her face trembled. But her voice was perfectly steady, though even quieter than before, so quiet I had to strain to hear it: 'You must be the best judge, sir. It was merely that I wondered whether you were aware that, before Mrs Johnson's marriage, there was – or rather it was believed that there was – what they call an understanding between her and Mr Henry Frant.'

CHAPTER FORTY-SIX

MR NOAK WAS due to arrive on Monday, the 3rd January. The Ruispidges had been invited to dinner the following day. The weather continued very cold – as I have mentioned, it was an exceptionally cold winter that year.

I cannot say that we were a cheerful household. By his very nature, Mr Carswall engendered a domestic strain that affected us all, even the boys, even the servants. Now, after the exchange I had overheard in the library, I knew of another, more specific source of discord. I watched and said nothing. I noted that Mrs Frant avoided an open breach with Mr Carswall but rarely spoke to him or allowed herself to be alone with him. Once I glimpsed an expression of despair on her face when I came across her walking in the garden and believing herself unobserved. One evening I heard the sound of sobbing as I passed her door.

The boys and I were happiest outside. Sometimes we went down to the lake and skated on the ice. I had grown up in the Fens, where the combination of cold winters and an inexhaustible supply of water made skating an acquirement one picked up almost as soon as the ability to walk. The boys lacked this early training, and gave me undeserved credit for my skill on the ice.

One afternoon I saw Miss Carswall and Mrs Frant watching us from the bank. At the time I was skating slowly on the far side of the lake, with a boy attached to either hand. I released Edgar, in order to raise my hat to the ladies. His arms flailed, his body twisted to and fro, but he kept his balance. Vanity prompted me to abandon my charges, and to skate across the lake at speed, and with many graceful pirouettes, on the spurious errand of discovering whether there was anything we might do for our visitors.

'How I envy you,' Mrs Frant said with unusual animation. 'To travel so quickly, to be so free.'

'I'm sure it is capital exercise,' put in Miss Carswall. 'Look at the boys – their cheeks are as red as pippins.'

'Better than dancing, even,' Mrs Frant continued. 'It must be like gliding through another element, like flying.'

'I am sure there are more skates at the house,' Miss Carswall said. 'I wonder if we might find pairs that would fit us.'

Her cousin gave a little shudder.

'You need not look like that,' Miss Carswall said with a laugh. 'One cannot always have new things. Besides, I believe Mr Cranmere's family were all excessively well bred.'

As she spoke, she twisted her face into a painfully genteel expression. Mrs Frant and I burst out laughing.

'But how would we learn?' Mrs Frant objected. 'It must be very difficult.'

'We might have a chair brought down, if you wished,' I suggested. 'Then I could push you on it across the ice.'

'But I do not want to be pushed,' she said with a smile. 'I want to skate by myself. I'm sure my cousin does, too.'

'Then if you would permit me, I could teach you, as I have been teaching the boys.' I looked from one to the other. 'Though it is largely a matter of teaching oneself. The principal difficulty at the beginning is that of retaining one's balance. Once one has the trick of that, the rest will follow.'

As if to illustrate my point, the boys were now zigzagging across the frozen water towards us. Their progress was slow, and no one would have called it elegant, but progress it was.

Miss Carswall took a gloved hand from her muff and laid it on her cousin's sleeve. 'Oh, pray let us try it, Sophie. I am sure the boys and Mr Shield will make sure we come to no harm.'

The ladies' skating lessons began that very afternoon. Chivalry dictated that I should take them by the hand, just as I had the boys, one on my left, one on my right. There we were in the very dry, very cold air, with no sound but the hissing and scraping of the blades beneath us, the panting of our breath and the occasional bursts of laughter. Physical exertion can act as a form of intoxication, as can excitement; and sometimes it seemed to me that I was doubly drunk.

Mrs Frant fell twice, Miss Carswall five times. In order to help a lady up, I had to put my arm around her, to feel her weight. I cannot deny that I enjoyed these upsets, and I suspect that Miss Carswall fell more often than she needed. In sum, the hours we spent together on the ice were peculiarly intimate – not indecorous, but on the other hand not something that was discussed in Mr Carswall's hearing.

In the intervals of skating, the boys continued their hunt for the monks' treasure. They ranged over the park, exploring every nook and cranny they could find. They tried excavation in one of the kitchen gardens but the head gardener did not share their antiquarian enthusiasm and in any case the ground was too hard for their spades.

The treasure hunters had high hopes of a shell grotto on the shore of the lake. It was in the form of a short, barrel-vaulted tunnel ending in an apse, where stood a ghostly statue of Aphrodite. Moisture dripped through the roof and glittered on the shells that studded the interior. When one held up a lantern, it was as though one confronted a beautiful and almost naked woman in a cold cave of sparkling diamonds. The boys' hopes were dashed when Mr Carswall, overhearing their excited conversation on the subject, told them that according to the estate records the grotto had been constructed on Mr Cranmere's orders not fifteen years before.

During this period Sir George Ruispidge and his brother were frequent visitors. Usually, but not always, they rode or drove over together. They came on the slightest pretext – to inquire yet again after Edgar's ankle; to return a borrowed volume; to bring a newspaper newly arrived from London. The brothers' manner towards me did not encourage undue familiarity.

On one occasion they came down to the lake. Sir George stayed on the bank but Captain Ruispidge requested the loan of my skates and soon showed himself an able performer on the ice. He took my place beside the ladies, and I fancied he exerted himself to be agreeable, more so than mere courtesy required.

All this time, I continued to turn over in my mind the events of the last few weeks that might suggest that Henry Frant was still alive. The intelligence from Mrs Lee concerning a former understanding between him and Mrs Johnson had naturally aroused my suspicions. Mrs Johnson denied visiting London recently, but there was reason to believe that she might have done so on at least one occasion. Finally, I considered the man I had glimpsed at the window of Grange Cottage.

Puzzling and even suspicious as these circumstances were, could I deduce from them that Mrs Johnson was sheltering her former lover? The more I subjected the possibility to rational analysis, the less plausible it seemed. In the first place, a youthful attachment, however ardent, was no guarantee of a present one, as my own experience showed. In the second place, if Henry Frant were still alive, surely he would avoid Monkshill-park, where so many people who knew him intimately had gathered?

If Frant had contrived his own murder, it must have been with the intention of creating a new life for himself somewhere, under a new name. In order to do that with any security, it would be necessary for him to flee abroad. He was a man who had lived too much in the world to be safe from discovery anywhere in his native country.

One morning, when the boys were examining the ruins of the monks' grange, my eyes wandered to Mrs Johnson's cottage. The boys were absorbed in a game of make-believe so I sauntered across to the palings and through the gate. The house and garden seemed even more forlorn and unloved than on my last visit. The shutters were across the ground-floor windows. No smoke came from the chimneys. Mrs Johnson was still at Clearland-court, and even her servant had gone.

I walked round the house. At the back was a small stable and a row of outhouses. As I walked back through the yard, I noticed a footprint frozen in the patch of mud by the pump. Judging by the size, it was a man's.

I returned to the park. I knew there were a dozen perfectly innocent explanations for that footprint. Yet the sight of it was enough to feed that state of uncertainty that had become so uncomfortably familiar to me.

When I reached the ruins, the boys were no longer there. I walked up the slope, shouting for them. I had nearly reached the lake, approaching it from the east, when I heard an answering call from the edge of the wood between the water and Flaxern Parva. Mindful of the mantraps, I ran and slid across the ice to the west bank of the lake. I found the boys not among the trees but in a defile that cut into the flank of the ridge perhaps fifty yards from the lake.

The defile's mouth was angled away from the lake and faced north towards the dark mass of the woods. It was connected by a path to the track running round the shores of the lake. Both the path and the defile's entrance were partly obscured by a heap of stones, loose earth and several fallen trees, one of them a sweet chestnut of considerable size. The boys were digging like a pair of badgers into the pile of spoil around the uprooted trees. My anger evaporated.

'I do not think you will find the treasure there,' I observed mildly.

'Why not, sir?' Edgar said. 'One could hide anything here.'

'It is a most capital spot,' Charlie put in loyally.

'That may be so. But I don't think the monks would have done. The chestnut can't have been lying there for more than a month or two. Look, it still has some of its leaves.'

Edgar paused in his labours. He was as filthy as a gypsy. 'There's also that doorway, sir.' He pointed to a stone archway that closed off the far end of the defile. 'Does it not look older than the Crusades?'

'It most probably leads to an ice-house,' I said.

'Perhaps it does now,' he said. 'But who is to say what was there before?'

I scrambled over the débris towards it, with the boys frisking after me. The door within the archway was in two leaves, constructed of stout oak and strengthened with iron. Charlie took the handle and rattled it. The door hardly moved in its frame.

'Perhaps there's another entrance,' Charlie suggested.

'We'll go round the hill until we find it,' Edgar said. 'I'll race you.'

The boys cantered out of the defile and were soon out of my sight. I followed more slowly. As I rounded the spur of the ridge that concealed the mouth of the defile from the lake, I saw on the path below a man and a woman, arm in arm, walking slowly with their heads close together in the direction of the shell grotto and the obelisk. With a lurch of unhappiness, I recognised them as Captain Jack Ruispidge and Sophia Frant.

CHAPTER FORTY-SEVEN

ON MONDAY AFTERNOON, Mr Noak arrived from Cheltenham in a hired chaise. Carswall made much of him – in truth, I believe he was becoming bored in the country and welcomed the stimulus of company; he was not a man who took easily to life in a retired situation.

With Mr Noak came Salutation Harmwell; and on the same day Mrs Kerridge appeared in a new gown. Perhaps, Miss Carswall murmured to me, the two circumstances were not entirely unconnected.

The following morning, Charlie came to me after breakfast, begging that the start of our morning lessons might be deferred.

'Mrs Kerridge has an errand at the ice-house, sir, and says Edgar and I may come as well. And you too, if you wish. I am sure the Romans and the Greeks had ice-houses, so it would be most instructive. May we, sir? It would not take above twenty minutes.'

I knew the expedition would take at least forty minutes, perhaps an hour, but the morning was fine and the prospect of a walk was tempting. So the three of us met Mrs Kerridge in the side hall. We found Harmwell in attendance, carrying the basket and a lantern.

'Mr Harmwell is most interested in the construction of ice-houses and wishes to inspect ours,' Mrs Kerridge explained. 'And if he comes it will save me having to find a gardener. Besides, they speak so strangely in these parts I can scarce understand a word they say.'

Harmwell's presence solved a minor mystery: why Mrs Kerridge, a lady's maid who was fully aware of the dignity of her position, had volunteered to run an errand for the cook. The boys and I took the lead, while the other two followed more slowly, deep in conversation. We turned left at the obelisk and took the path leading to the western side of the lake. After the shell grotto we climbed the gentle slope to the defile in which the ice-house lay. The boys ran ahead and rattled the handle of the door.

'We must frighten the ghosts!' Edgar cried, and Charlie echoed him: 'Frighten the ghosts!'

Mrs Kerridge drew out a large key and inserted it in the door. Mr Harmwell crouched to light the lantern. The two leaves of the door opened outwards on squealing hinges. The boys tried to plunge into the darkness beyond like terriers down a rabbit hole. Mrs Kerridge put out an arm to bar them.

'Please, dear Mrs Kerridge, let us go first,' Charlie said. 'Edgar and I have a most particular reason for wanting it.'

'You will wait and do as you're bid,' I said. 'Or else you will go straight back to your lessons.'

Mrs Kerridge sniffed the air. 'It stinks like a charnel house.'

'It is indeed very bad,' Harmwell agreed. 'Though few ice-houses smell sweet at this time of year.'

'They say the drain is blocked.'

'So the melt-water cannot escape?' He glanced over his shoulder at the lie of the land. 'It drains down into the lake, I suppose, so the outlet may be frozen.'

'No, sir, they believe that the drain itself is blocked higher up.'

'Can they not clean it out?'

'They cannot reach it without digging.' Mrs Kerridge waved her hand at the boulders and fallen trees that cluttered the slopes of the defile. 'The storms in October caused much damage in the park, and not all of it has been made good again.'

Harmwell had the lantern alight now. At Mrs Kerridge's request, he led the way down the narrow passageway that burrowed into the side of the hill. After five or six feet, we came to another door, with two

231

leaves made of thick deal planks and edged with leather to provide an airtight seal. Beyond, there was another length of passage, ending in a great mass of barley straw.

The smell grew worse. Harmwell and I pulled aside the insulating straw, slimy with decay, and pushed it into the alcoves on either side of the passage. There at last was another two-leaved door, this one set at a slight angle to the perpendicular. It required another key to open it.

'I'm told there's a hook for the lantern inside,' Mrs Kerridge said. 'On the left.'

Harmwell pulled back the leaves. Covering my nose and mouth with a handkerchief, I edged forward so that I could look over his shoulder. Illuminated in the lantern's fitful yellow light was a dome which at its highest point was perhaps a foot above the ceiling of the corridor. As a whole the chamber resembled the interior of a gigantic egg, with its broader end at the top. It comprised a vault and a well, both faced with dressed stone glistening with moisture. A variety of bundles hung from hooks in the side of the dome. I crouched and looked down into the well itself. Some six or seven feet below was a dark mass of ice, water, straw. I made out at least a score of packages lying half submerged.

'Aye, the drain is blocked,' said Harmwell. 'Nothing is so injurious to an ice-house as want of dryness. Ice will not melt in the hottest sun so soon as in a close, damp cellar.'

'Will they ever get rid of this foul smell?' I inquired.

His teeth flashed white in the gloom. 'They should empty the chamber without delay. Then, in this weather I would leave the doors standing open to air the place. They should put down quicklime, too, for it absorbs moisture.'

'The master has a sudden fancy for venison,' Mrs Kerridge said. 'That's all we need. There should be a haunch in one of the sacks on the left. They are all labelled.'

'How long has it been there?' Harmwell asked.

'Two months or more, I believe.'

'Then I fear it will be rotting in this atmosphere, ma'am.'

'That is not our affair, Mr Harmwell. Let Cook be the judge, eh? Will those rungs bear your weight? Pray be careful.'

The black man edged into the chamber. Rungs for the feet and the hands had been set in the side of the dome, with a line of hooks above. He moved slowly across to the cluster of sacks and examined the labels at their necks, angling them so they caught the light, while Mrs Kerridge kept up a stream of admonition. At last he found the venison, unhooked the heavy sack and made his crab-like way back to us. He passed the sack to me. The stink was now overpowering. The boys retreated to the open air.

'Dear God,' I said, fighting an urge to vomit.

'What the master wants,' Mrs Kerridge muttered to Harmwell, 'the master has.'

She pursed her lips and fell silent. Mr Carswall was not popular with his servants. He was harsh and autocratic by nature and, added to this, displayed a sort of petulance, a habit of making impracticable demands upon a whim, that was perhaps a symptom of his advancing age. The unexpected desire for venison was clearly an example of this. I wondered, however, whether there might be a deeper reason for Mrs Kerridge's resentment towards him. Though Carswall paid her wages now, she had served Mrs Frant for many years. Perhaps Mrs Kerridge had acquired a knowledge of Mr Carswall's intentions with respect to her mistress.

Despite the smell, Edgar wished to pursue his researches by scrambling round the interior of the ice-house. I refused to sanction this intrepid plan but I permitted the boys to help pile the straw back against the inner door. This activity made them wet and filthy, and thus was profoundly satisfying to them.

As we were walking to the house, I learned from the boys' conversation that the subject of the monks' treasure was still in their mind. Charlie made the not unreasonable point that the ice-house was such a modern structure that it could not have been used by the monks nearly three hundred years earlier. But Edgar replied with the ingenious suggestion that the ice-house had been built in that spot because there was already some sort of cavity, bringing forward in support of this theory the observation that the stone facing on the interior of the ice-house had looked very similar to the stones used in the ruins of the monks' grange near the cottage. I had not the heart to point out to them that practically every building of any substance within a five- or ten-mile radius of Monkshill was constructed of the local sandstone, the colour of a faded claret stain, so this circumstance was not necessarily of any significance whatsoever when one came to date the construction.

The boys and I were walking at a smart pace. Harmwell and Mrs Kerridge, chaperoned by their rotting haunch of venison, lingered on the way. Glancing back as we approached the door to the kitchen gardens, I discovered that a bend in the path had put them out of sight.

A moment later, the house reared up in a great cliff of stone in front of us. We walked along the terrace towards the side door. I glanced at the window of the ladies' sitting room. Someone was standing on the other side of the glass, as shadowy as a ghost. The outline convinced me it was a woman. It could not be Mrs Lee, because she had a disease of the spine which bent her over and caused her much pain. The shape vanished, withdrawing into the gloomy interior of the room.

Miss Carswall or Mrs Frant, I wondered: that was the question. Indeed, in those days that was always the question.

CHAPTER FORTY-EIGHT

MR CARSWALL RARELY entertained in the country, and he had never been honoured by such guests as the Ruispidges. As the day of the great dinner drew near, his voice was heard all over the house, raised in expostulation. With drawn faces, the servants scurried about in their stained and frayed finery, following orders that five minutes later would be countermanded.

It suited Mr Carswall's sense of propriety that the numbers around his table should be evenly distributed between the sexes. There would be five ladies – as well as the three at Monkshill-park, both Lady Ruispidge and Mrs Johnson had accepted invitations. (After Mrs Lee's revelation concerning Mrs Johnson, Carswall had deliberated long and hard over whether to invite her; his hand was forced by the fact that Mrs Johnson was still staying with her cousins at Clearland-court.)

There were to be five gentlemen, so that each lady would have an arm to lean on when they went into dinner: Mr Carswall himself, Mr Noak, Sir George and Captain Ruispidge, and – according to the original plan – the Rector of Flaxern Parva, who providentially was a widower and so did not have a wife to unbalance the numbers. After breakfast, however, the Rector sent over a groom with a note.

'Damn him,' Carswall said to me as I was the only other person in the room. 'He's confined to bed with piles. He trusts to the mercy of

Almighty God, the application of steam to the afflicted part, and an electuary as a mild laxative. I wish Almighty God may give him inflammation of the bowels. That will serve him.' He screwed up the letter and threw it into the fire. 'You will have to sit down with us, Shield, there's no help for it. It could be worse. Mrs Frant tells me that you were intended for the Church: is that true?'

'Yes, sir.'

'And in your best coat you look a gentleman-like fellow. You need not say very much. Make yourself useful to the ladies and do not get in the way of the gentlemen.' The old man hesitated, standing there with his back to the fire in the library, raising his coat-tails so the warmth would reach him. 'Or perhaps I should have Charlie instead. He is a fine boy, one of the family, and the ladies like a lad to pet.' He scratched his thigh with a claw-like fingernail. 'No, it would not answer. If Charlie dined with us, and not Edgar, Noak might not like it – he and Allan are mighty thick, and they all have that damned Yankee pride. Besides, one can never tell with children – an excess of animal spirits is always a possibility. In this case first thoughts are best. So I will expect you in the drawing room before we go in to dinner.'

When I joined the party in the drawing room later that day, Sir George and Mr Carswall were discussing the weather while around them conversations among the other members of the party flared and spurted like damp fireworks.

'I make no apologies, ma'am,' Mr Carswall said to Lady Ruispidge as he led her into the dining room. 'I do not have fancy foreign dishes on my table.'

There is nothing like food and drink for filling up awkward silences. For the first course, we were served capons and boiled beef, a forequarter of lamb and a calf's head, oysters and mushrooms. These were followed by a fillet of veal stuffed and roasted, stewed hare, partridges in a dish, marrow-pudding, squab pigeons, and asparagus. I looked in vain for venison.

Lady Ruispidge grew quite animated as the meal proceeded, and when she tasted the partridge she burst into speech. 'This is a young bird, I fancy,' she said in a high, cracked voice. 'You are aware, sir, of the characteristics of age as it relates to the partridge? One should examine the bill and the legs. If the bill be white and the legs have a bluish cast, the bird is old. But if the bill is black, and the legs yellow, it is young. One should also look at the vent. If it be fast, then the bird is new, if it is open and green, then depend on it the bird is stale.'

'I am glad it is to your liking, ma'am,' Carswall said. 'May I help you to a little hare?'

She understood the gesture if she did not hear the words. 'Is it leveret?' she inquired. 'I prefer leveret to hare, the flavour is more delicate. To discover the true leveret, of course, you must feel near the foot on its foreleg, and if you find there a knob, or small bone, it is a leveret. But if destitute of this, it must be a hare.'

Carswall tried to rally, but the spirit had gone out of him. Lady Ruispidge had made up her mind that he was to share her interest in the preparation and consumption of food. Her deafness rendered futile his attempts to introduce other subjects of conversation. She swept them aside and told him instead of the best way to salt hams in the Yorkshire manner, and the criteria by which one should judge a turbot.

I was seated between Mrs Johnson and Mrs Lee. Neither gave me much opportunity for conversation. Mrs Lee ate steadily, as usual; she was a lady for whom food was important, and she did not care for conversation at table. When Mrs Johnson talked, she spoke chiefly to Mr Carswall, who was on her right. She looked very striking that evening in a gown of pale yellow silk, and the candlelight softened the harshness of her features and increased the lustre of her dark eyes.

Miss Carswall sat between Sir George and Mr Noak. In a lull in the general conversation, I heard Sir George say to her: 'And will you be honouring us with your presence at the assembly next week, Miss Carswall?'

'There is a ball?' She spoke so artlessly that I instantly suspected that the information did not come as a surprise.

'Indeed there is. We have them once a month during the winter months, at the Bell in Gloucester. I'm sure tickets could be arranged.'

Miss Carswall turned towards her father. 'Oh, may we go, Papa?'

The old man looked up from his plate. 'Eh?'

'They are most respectable affairs, sir,' Captain Ruispidge said. 'Ain't they, George? We go to one or two of them every year, and sometimes the Vaudens, as well. But of course Mrs Frant –'

'Pray do not concern yourselves about me,' she said. 'I would not prevent your enjoyment for the world.'

'But would it be quite proper for Papa and me to go to a public assembly?' Miss Carswall inquired of Sir George, with touching confidence in his judgement. 'Mr Wavenhoe was Papa's cousin, and he died not two months ago.'

He smiled at her. 'You need not trouble your head on that score, Miss Carswall. It would be thought perfectly proper. After all, the connection was not close, and we would never see anyone in the country if we allowed half-mourning to stop us.'

'It is a considerable way for a winter drive,' said Mr Carswall slowly. 'And at night – all the way back from Gloucester. And what if we have snow, hey? It seems to me very likely that we shall have snow.'

'Those who have far to come usually arrange to spend the night,' Sir George said.

'I daresay we should meet all sorts of interesting people,' Miss Carswall put in.

'Perhaps, perhaps.' Carswall nodded his heavy head. 'It is most kind of you to suggest it, Sir George.'

'Shall you go, ma'am?' Miss Carswall asked Mrs Johnson.

'Yes,' she said, her voice harsh and hoarse as if she had been shouting. 'Lady Ruispidge has kindly asked me to accompany her.'

'There may still be rooms you could engage at the Bell itself,' Captain Ruispidge said. 'Not that I would recommend it. Nothing could be more convenient for the ball but the establishment will be in an uproar because of it.' He turned to Mrs Frant and said in a lower voice: 'I regret that you would not be able to honour us with your presence.'

Mrs Frant inclined her head.

'Yes,' Mr Carswall said, waving his fork. 'Perhaps we should go to the ball. A little diversion would do us all good.'

'Dancing is healthy exercise, sir,' the Captain added.

'And the boys shall come, too,' Mr Carswall cried, his enthusiasm for the project growing by the second.

'I am afraid Charlie must beg to be excused, sir,' said Mrs Frant. 'For the same reason as I must.'

'Eh? Ah – yes, of course.'

'It is a pity,' said Captain Ruispidge. 'I am convinced the boys would have enjoyed it immensely. These are country affairs – we don't stand on ceremony.' He bowed to Mrs Frant. 'Charlie will come another time, I trust. And his mama.'

'Boys?' Lady Ruispidge said loudly, cupping her hand into a makeshift trumpet for her right ear. 'Boys? A sore trial, I agree.' She turned to Mr Noak, who was on her right. 'Do you have boys, sir?'

He finished chewing his mouthful and swallowed it. 'I had a son, ma'am,' he said calmly. 'But he died.'

'Dined? He has already dined?'

'Died, Mama,' said Sir George. He raised his voice: 'Died.'

'Ah,' she replied, 'yes, as I said, a sore trial. One can never tell what they will do next.'

The ball provided material for the conversation until it was time for the ladies to withdraw. I held the door for them. Miss Carswall paused as she passed me.

'Pray encourage Papa not to linger,' she murmured. 'We shall have cards – he does so enjoy cards.'

The cloth was withdrawn. Mr Carswall, who had drunk steadily throughout the meal, refilled his glass.

'Sir George,' he cried, 'a glass of wine with you, sir.'

'Thank you, sir.'

'Refill your glass first,' Carswall said. 'I can see the air in it. Let us drink proper bumpers.'

Sir George dribbled a few more drops into his glass, and the two men drank.

'I hear your keepers caught a brace of poachers the other day,' Carswall said.

'Desperate fellows indeed,' replied Sir George. 'We have increasing

239

numbers coming up before us on the bench. Since the Peace, every Tom, Dick or Harry thinks he has the right to steal my game.'

'I tell my people to shoot on sight,' Carswall said. 'Do you rely on other precautions, apart from your keepers' vigilance?'

'Traps, do you mean? Or spring guns?'

'Aye. I have seen both used to great effect in the West Indies. There, naturally, the planters have a preference for the trap – with the gun, there is a great risk of killing the poacher. A dead slave is no good to anyone, but even a maimed one may still have years of useful work in him.'

'I use both devices in my covers, and I make sure the fact is widely known. In my experience, they act as a prophylactic. A poacher may often know where your keepers are and so avoid them. But they find it harder to pin down a well-laid trap, or a cunningly concealed spring gun.'

'Very true, sir,' rumbled Mr Carswall. 'Mind you, you must move them frequently.'

'The labour is worth it. One must also bear in mind that when they catch a poacher in commission of his crime, the effect on the neighbourhood as a whole can be most salutary.'

Carswall chuckled. 'We bagged a fellow from the village a few weeks ago. Damned near took his leg off.' He raised his glass, saw that it was empty and said to Mr Noak: 'A glass of wine with you, sir.'

'With all my heart,' said Mr Noak politely. He had drunk more today than usually, and spoken less.

'Do you use traps in the United States, sir?' Sir George asked the American.

Mr Noak passed a hand across his forehead, as though wiping away unwelcome thoughts. 'They are not uncommon in the South. I am more familiar with those designed for smaller prey.'

'Are they traps on similar principles to ours?' Sir George asked. 'Spring-loaded, that is to say, and with jaws that snap shut?'

'Exactly so. There is quite an art to their use – even more, perhaps, when one is employing them to trap animals in the wild rather than humans breaking the law. Harmwell – my clerk, you know – became quite expert when he lived in Canada. We use them for marten, sable, mink, otter and beaver, principally, and also for bear.'

'I have seen a man enticed to a trap,' Mr Carswall said. 'It is a simple matter: one merely lays a bait. The nature of the lure varies with the circumstances. In this case, it was a boat on the bank of a river.'

'Similar techniques are used with lesser breeds, sir.' Mr Noak sniffed his wine. 'Though with them the hunter has a wider range of ploys at his disposal. In many cases, nothing as crude as bait is required. One relies instead upon the animal's acute sense of smell.'

'Ah,' said Sir George, looking interested. 'I have heard of fish oil being used for otter.'

'Yes, sir, fish oil is a favourite with us, too. We also use castoreum, musk, asafoetida, and oil of anise.'

'It is indeed ingenious,' said Captain Ruispidge. 'To turn a creature's strength into its weakness, its Achilles' heel.'

'A glass of wine with you, Captain,' cried Mr Carswall. 'Come, fill your glass. Shield, help the Captain to some wine.'

'So you do not use dogs?' Noak asked the table in general.

'Not in the covers, sir,' Sir George replied. 'You cannot be sure they will leave the game alone, and there is always the risk they will fall foul of the traps.'

Carswall nodded. 'We keep our dogs out of the covers as well. Mastiffs are valuable animals, one would not want them injured.'

He swallowed another glass of wine and the colour of his face darkened still further. For a moment, no one spoke. Then Noak turned back to Carswall.

'Have you visited British North America, sir?'

'Never. It is a country of many opportunities, I am sure, but I have never been north of New York.'

'But I understood you had interests in that part of the world,' Noak said gently. 'During the late war, was not Wavenhoe's Bank tolerably active there? And as a partner you must –'

'Pooh – as to that I know very little.' Carswall threw himself back in his chair so violently that the joints creaked. 'Yes, sir, I believe we did have Canadian interests, but you must understand that I was not involved in the active direction of the bank or any of its concerns. Poor George Wavenhoe was the man for that. I was only a sleeping partner, as the commercial men say.'

'But Mr Wavenhoe would not have gone to Canada himself, surely?' Noak said. 'He must have had a subordinate there, I imagine, someone to deal with the day-to-day running of the business.'

'Very likely,' Carswall agreed.

'In that case it may well have been someone I ran across,' Mr Noak observed. 'I spent a number of weeks there on family business immediately after the war.'

'I cannot call to mind who represented us. If I ever knew.' Carswall's eyes slid away from Mr Noak and glided swiftly round the table. Whether from the warmth or the wine, his face shone with perspiration. 'As I say, I left all that sort of thing to my cousin Wavenhoe. He may have found a local fellow.' Carswall beckoned me. 'Come, Mr Shield, a glass of wine with you, sir.'

I did not believe what Carswall had told Noak for a moment. He and I drank solemnly to one another and then Mr Carswall and Sir George fell into an impassioned conversation about the ingratitude of tenants.

Mr Noak looked at Captain Ruispidge. 'I wonder if you number any officers of the Forty-First among your acquaintance?'

'No, sir. I was never in North America, whereas the Forty-First spent most of their time there.'

'I see.' Noak held Captain Jack's eyes, and when he spoke next, he raised the volume of his voice a trifle. 'No matter. It is merely that it occurred to me that you might have met my son.'

'He was in the Forty-First?'

Mr Carswall broke off his remarks to Sir George in mid-sentence and stretched out his hand for the wine.

'Yes, sir.' Mr Noak picked up an orange and squeezed it gently in his hand. 'At the time of his death, he was a lieutenant.'

'Lieutenant Noak,' Captain Ruispidge said. 'If I meet any officers of the Forty-First, I will inquire after him. You may depend upon it, sir.'

'They will not have heard of Lieutenant Noak,' Mr Noak said, his voice harsher than ever. 'He was known as Saunders.'

He began to peel the orange with small, delicate fingers, working his way over the surface of every ridge and hollow. But he was looking at Carswall all the time.

'Saunders, sir? Saunders?' Carswall had abandoned the pretence that he was not listening. 'I could not help hearing – you'll not mind my asking, I hope – but – but – the circumstance was surely a trifle unusual? The son of a prominent American citizen holding the King's commission? At a time when our two countries were at war?'

It was a shockingly ill-bred thing to have said, and I doubt even Carswall would have done it had he not been drunk. Sir George contemplated the contents of his wine glass, while Captain Ruispidge drummed his fingers on the table edge.

'The explanation is quite simple,' Mr Noak replied, his eyes still fixed on Mr Carswall's face. 'My late wife's name was Saunders. In the Revolutionary War, her brother fought on the Loyalist side, and when the war was over he emigrated along with many others to Upper Canada. He and his wife had no children, and some years later they offered to adopt my son as their heir on condition that he took their name.'

'A common enough practice, I'm sure,' Sir George said. 'Without it, half the great names of England would have died out generations ago.'

I chanced to look at Mr Carswall. He was sitting back in his chair, his hand raised to his face, his ruddy complexion mottled with patches of dirty white.

'My son had a taste for soldiering,' Noak continued calmly, 'and Mr Saunders bought him a commission. Mr Saunders had served in the Forty-First as a young man. He was present at the capture of Martinique and St Lucia.'

'Did not Wellington himself serve in the Forty-First?' Captain Ruispidge asked.

Noak bowed his acknowledgement of the question, and perhaps of the Captain's tact as well. 'For a year or so, I believe, in '88 or '89. My brother-in-law was proud of the connection.'

Carswall glanced from side to side of the table. He seemed to have shrunk a little inside his clothes. He was aware, I think, somewhere in his drink-sodden mind, that his curiosity had overstepped the mark. But was there more to it? He looked to me as one who has received a blow, or at least a shock.

'Forgive me, sir,' he said slowly. 'Forgive me, that is, if my question just then was ill-judged.'

Noak turned to him and made a civil inclination of his head. 'Not at all, my dear sir.' He fed a piece of walnut into his mouth and chewed slowly.

'And now perhaps,' Carswall went on, speaking more quickly and stumbling over his words, 'now it is time for us to join the ladies. I promised them they would have cards.'

Chairs scraped back on the polished boards. Carswall swayed as he stood, and was forced to support himself on the back of his chair. I held the door for the others to pass through. Afterwards, as I walked across the hall, Captain Ruispidge lingered and fell into step with me.

'You're a wise man, Mr Shield – you listen much and say little.'

He spoke with a smile and I smiled back at him.

'Mrs Frant tells me that you were at Cambridge.'

'Yes, sir. But I did not complete my degree.'

'One cannot always finish what one begins. Do you regret it?'

'Extremely.'

'Sometimes one begins a thing without knowing how it will end. Or, to put it another way, an action, perhaps blameless in itself, may lead to an undesirable consequence.'

I stared into his bland face, floating above the white perfection of his neckcloth and the starched points of his collar. 'I'm afraid I do not understand you, sir.'

'You will not object to a word of advice, I trust?' he murmured. 'I saw you on the ice, the other day – with the young ladies. I remarked a – how shall I put it? – a certain *familiarity*, which might be liable to misconstruction. A lady's reputation is such a fragile thing.'

'Sir, I assure you that –'

'I'm sure I need say no more. *Verbum sap*, eh, *verbum sap*?'

Captain Ruispidge nodded affably and preceded me into the drawing room, where Mr Carswall was calling for coffee. Soon the place was a hive of activity, with the servants setting out the card tables and bringing coffee and tea; Mr Carswall talking loudly and wildly about nothing in particular; and the ladies full of animation, as though relieved not to be left to their own society any longer.

Miss Carswall beckoned me over. 'Thank you,' she murmured. 'You have rescued us, and rescued my father, too, I fancy.'

'I wish I could take the credit, Miss Carswall. But I did nothing.'

Her smile flashed out at me. 'You are too modest, Mr Shield. You are always too modest.'

When the tables were ready, Mr Carswall clapped his hands. 'We have time for a rubber, I hope? Now, four into ten won't go, so two of us must stand down.' He crossed the room to Mr Noak's chair and towered over the small spare American. 'You will join us, I hope, sir?'

'Thank you, no. I never touch cards.'

'No. Well – just as you please, sir. I had hoped to match you with Lady Ruispidge –'

'You must not concern yourself, Papa,' Miss Carswall said. 'Lady Ruispidge was telling me that she never plays with any other partner but Mrs Johnson if she can help it. They have a system, I fancy.'

In a few moments, the card players had been allocated to their tables: at one, Miss Carswall and Sir George would play against Lady Ruispidge and Mrs Johnson; at the other, Captain Ruispidge and Mrs Frant would play against Mr Carswall and Mrs Lee.

'I am vexed Papa did not consult you,' Miss Carswall said quietly. 'You may take my place, if you wish.'

'Not for the world.'

At that moment, Sir George came to hover over her with a fine proprietary air, ready to lead her to the card table. Mr Noak took up a book. I put a newspaper on my knee to give myself the appearance of occupation and wondered whether I should withdraw. A few minutes later, the room was almost entirely silent, apart from the crackle of the logs on the fire and the chink of china. I brooded on Captain Ruispidge's advice and wondered which lady's reputation was at risk from my undue familiarity.

By and by, Mr Noak looked up from his page, his finger marking his place, and stared into the fire. The room was well lit and it seemed to me that his eyes gleamed unusually brightly in the candlelight. I offered to help him to some more coffee. At first he did not hear me. Then he started and turned towards me.

'I beg your pardon,' he said. 'I was a thousand miles away. No – further than that.'

'May I fetch you another cup of coffee, sir?'

He thanked me and gave me his cup. He watched me as I refilled it.

'You must forgive me if I am a little melancholy this evening,' he said, when I handed him his coffee. 'Today was my son's birthday.' He studied my face. 'You have a look of him, if I may say so. I remarked the resemblance as soon as I saw you.'

He fell silent, and to fill the emptiness I ventured to suggest that it must be a consolation to know his son had died a soldier's death.

'Not even that, Mr Shield, not even that.' He shook his head slowly from side to side, as though trying to shake the pain out of it. 'I regret to say that we had been estranged for many years. He adopted the principles of his mother's family, in politics and in all else. Frank was a fine boy, but he had a sad tendency towards obstinacy.' He shrugged thin shoulders, too small for the coat. 'I do not know why I bore you with my affairs. Pray excuse me.'

'There is nothing to excuse, sir.' I thought it probable that the wine Mr Noak had taken at dinner had depressed his spirits while lessening his habitual reserve.

'I could have borne a soldier's death, even in the service of King George,' Mr Noak went on, his voice scarcely louder than a whisper. 'Or even if disease had snatched him away in the prime of his life. But not this: face-down in a Kingston gutter: they said he drowned when he was drunk.' He turned his head sharply and looked at me with eyes glistening with tears. 'That was hard to bear, Mr Shield, that was hard. To know that the world thought my son a drunken sot who died need-lessly because of his intoxication. Bad enough, you would think. Aye, but there was worse to come, much worse.' He seemed suddenly to recollect himself and broke off. 'But I must not weary you with the recital of my son's woes.'

He gave me a stiff smile and returned to his book. The tips of his ears were rosy-pink. I sipped the rest of my coffee. I had no doubt that Mr Noak's grief was genuine but I was not convinced that his frankness was as artless as it seemed.

The card players were wrapped in the wordless communion of their kind. Captain Ruispidge put down a card and drew the trick he had won towards him. He stared across the table at Mrs Frant, his partner. She looked up and smiled her acknowledgement. Despair moved within me. How intimate a connection is a partnership at cards, how private the solitude it creates. I drank my coffee to the bitter, gritty dregs and forced my mind to consider a less painful matter.

What, I wondered, had Noak meant? What could be worse for a father than the knowledge that his son had died estranged from his parent and as a result of a drunken accident of his own making? The discovery that his son had been culpably involved in a criminal undertaking?

Frank was a fine boy, but he had a sad tendency towards obstinacy.

As an epitaph it suggested Lieutenant Saunders had inherited at least one quality from his father. But it did not suggest there had been anything criminal or sinful about him. So in that case, what was worse than your son – *a fine boy* – dying as a result of a self-induced drunken accident?

Why, it could only mean that he had died for some other reason. Not disease, it appeared. So he must have been killed. But if killed lawfully, he would not have been reported as having died in an accident. So had Mr Noak's son therefore been killed unlawfully?

In other words, had Lieutenant Frank Saunders been murdered?

CHAPTER FORTY-NINE

S IR GEORGE MOST obligingly rode over on Thursday morning
with the news that a suite of apartments in a house in Westgate had
become available for the night of the assembly. Lord Vauden and his
party had taken them for several nights but the sudden illness of a near
relation from whom he had expectations had compelled him to withdraw.
Sir George had taken the liberty of bespeaking the apartments in Mr
Carswall's name, though of course this conferred no obligation upon
Mr Carswall, and it would be the work of a moment to cancel the
arrangement if it did not suit because Captain Ruispidge was engaged
to dine in Gloucester that very evening.

This was just the encouragement Mr Carswall needed. Not only was
he flattered by Sir George's kind attention but the suggestion removed
the chief practical obstacle to the scheme. Sir George added that his
mother was greatly looking forward to renewing her acquaintance with
Miss Carswall and Mrs Frant. When we were sitting in the drawing
room after dinner, Mr Carswall returned to this condescension on the
part of Lady Ruispidge.

'But Papa,' Miss Carswall said, 'you know Sophie cannot come to
the ball.'

'Of course not. But there is no reason why she should not come to
Gloucester with us, is there?' He turned to Mrs Frant who was seated
at the tea table. 'You will enjoy the shops, I daresay, eh? We have been

very cooped up here at Monkshill, and it will do us good to have a change.'

'Yes, sir,' she said.

Groaning with the effort, he leaned on the table and patted her hand with his great paw. 'You cannot mope for ever, my dear. You shall buy something pretty for yourself. And something for the boy, perhaps, too.'

Mrs Frant pulled her hand away and began to gather together the tea things.

'Sir George brought me a note from Mrs Johnson today,' Miss Carswall said brightly. 'She enclosed a receipt for eel soup from Lady Ruispidge. So obliging. I wonder how many of us will go to Gloucester, and how many beds are spoken for us. One would not like to be cramped or thrown together with people one does not care for.'

'No,' said Mrs Frant. 'I can think of nothing worse.'

The ball at the Bell Inn was on Wednesday, the 12th January. It formed the principal topic of conversation at Monkshill-park in the week before – where our party would lodge, what they should wear, whom they would encounter and whom they would like to encounter. The boys and I were to stay at Monkshill.

On Monday, two days before the ball, I came into the small sitting room to look for my pupils and found Miss Carswall with her nose in a book on the sofa by the fire. I explained my errand.

'Why not let them run wild this afternoon?' She yawned, exposing very white, very sharp teeth. 'There is nothing so fatiguing as a printed page, I find.'

'What is it you are reading?'

She held out a cloth-bound duodecimo volume. '*Domestic Cookery, and Useful Receipt Book*,' she said. 'It is a treasure house of valuable information. Here it tells you how to make a mutton-ham, which sounds a monstrous contradiction, and probably tastes like one too. And here are two and a half pages devoted solely to the laundry maid and her duties. It is so lowering. I had not realised there was so much useful knowledge in the world. It seems quite boundless, like the Pacific Ocean.'

I said something civil in reply, along the lines of being sure that a student of her ability would soon acquire all the knowledge she needed.

'The study of books does not come easily to me, Mr Shield. You must not think me a blue, far from it. But Papa believes that every woman should know domestic economy.' Her eyelids fluttered. 'He bids me model myself in that respect on Lady Ruispidge.' Her hand flew to her left eye. 'Oh!'

'What is it, Miss Carswall?'

'I believe I have something in my eye.' Miss Carswall rose unsteadily to her feet, pouting with vexation, and examined her face in the mirror above the fireplace. 'I cannot see anything in it but the light is so bad over here. It is *such* an irritation.'

'Shall I ring the bell?'

'They will take an age to come, and then they will have to find my maid. No, Mr Shield, would you be very kind and come with me over to the window and see if you can see it? Whatever it might be. It is unlikely to be a fly at this time of year. Perhaps a speck of soot or a hair. Even an errant eyelash can have such a profound and disproportionate effect on human happiness.'

I followed her to the window where she turned and held her face up to me. I came close to her and peered into her left eye. When you are near a woman, you smell her scent, not just the perfume she is wearing but the entire olfactory nature of her – a compound of perfume, the odour of her clothes, and the natural animal smell underlying all.

'Pray turn your head a little to the left,' I said. 'There – that is better.'

'Can you see anything? In the corner.'

'Which corner?'

She giggled. 'I am not thinking clearly. The inner corner.'

I brought my face a little closer so that I could see more clearly and, simultaneously, she raised herself on tiptoe and turned her face an inch or so to the right. Her lips brushed mine.

I gave a startled yelp and jumped back.

'I'm so sorry, Mr Shield,' she said with complete composure.

'I – I beg your pardon,' I muttered wildly, my heart beating like a drum.

'Not at all. At first I thought the hair had been dislodged but I think it is still there. I wonder if I might trouble you to have another look.'

She raised her face up to me again and smiled. I brought my mouth down on hers and felt her lips move and for an instant part against mine. Then her hands caught mine and she took a step back.

'Come away from the window,' she murmured, and like figures in a dance we moved a few paces together, as one creature, and then began to kiss again. She rested her hands on my shoulders and I ran my palms over her hips. Her warmth enveloped me like a flame.

Thirty seconds? A minute at most. There was a clatter on the other side of the door. We sprang apart. In an instant, I was contemplating the view across the terrace to the river far below, while Miss Carswall was seated on the sofa, turning the pages of *Domestic Cookery* with an expression of rapt concentration on her face. A plump maid with a damp red face carried a scuttle of coals into the room. She made up the fire and tidied the grate. While she was still rattling the fire irons, the boys rushed in.

'Mr Harmwell is going to show us how to trap rabbits,' Charlie said proudly. 'Ain't it famous? If we was shipwrecked, you know, like Robinson Crusoe, we could dine like kings on rabbits.'

'How very kind of Mr Harmwell,' Miss Carswall said.

'He is a very kind man,' Charlie said simply. 'Edgar says he is quite different from the niggers they have at home.'

'Why is that?' I asked.

'Most of the ones we have in Richmond are slaves, sir,' the American boy said. 'But Mr Harmwell is as free as you or I.'

The maid curtsied and left the room. The boys followed, banging the door behind them.

'And how free is that?' I said.

Miss Carswall giggled. 'Free enough in all conscience. I approve of freedom. I am a natural radical.' She rose and came to stand beside me. She glanced out of the window, and the excitement left her face. 'Look. Sophie's coming.'

We moved apart and re-arranged our limbs and our feelings. Mrs Frant passed the window as she made her way along the terrace towards the side door.

I coughed. 'Do I understand from Harmwell's continued presence that Mr Noak stays for a while longer?'

'Yes, had you not heard? At least until after the ball.' Miss Carswall laughed; she appeared wholly self-possessed. 'I had the reason from Sophie who had it from Mrs Kerridge, who had it from Harmwell himself. You recall that Kerridge and Harmwell are sweet on one another? It is touching, is it not, and especially at their time of life? Anyway, according to Harmwell, Mr Noak is contemplating the purchase of some property from my father. A warehouse in Liverpool, or some such thing. And there is talk of other investments – you know what gentlemen are like when they begin to talk of their investments. They become like girls talking of their beaux – there is the same blend of fantasy with obsession, the desire for secrecy, the lust for acquisition.'

She had moved away from me now, and sat down again on the sofa. I felt half relieved, half cheated. A moment later, Mrs Frant came into the room and held out her hands to the fire.

'Mrs Johnson is still at Clearland-court, I collect?' she said to Miss Carswall.

'I believe so. I had understood from Sir George that she was staying with them until after the ball. Why?'

'I was walking near the ruins and I saw a man in the garden of Grange Cottage.'

'Her gardener?'

'But she has no gardener now. Only the one maid of all work, Ruth, and she is not there at present. I was too far away to see him clearly but he seemed to catch sight of me, and moved away at once. Do you think we should inform Mrs Johnson?'

'It would be the neighbourly thing to do,' Miss Carswall said. 'Could you describe him?'

'Tall and well built. He wore a long brown coat and a broad-brimmed hat. I can tell you nothing about his face. He was so far away, and the collar was turned up, and the brim of the hat was –'

'I will write a note to Mrs Johnson,' Miss Carswall cut in. 'If she thinks there is something suspicious, she will consult with Sir George about what to do. I would not for the world want to worry her, but one cannot be too careful in such matters. Perhaps we should send someone to investigate before we raise the alarm.'

'If you like,' I said, 'I could walk there now.'

To tell the truth, I welcomed the chance of escaping from that snug parlour. I always found it unsettling to see Mrs Frant and Miss Carswall together, and rarely more than I did on that occasion. I was not proud of my feelings yet I could not pretend that I did not desire them both: though not entirely for the same reasons, and not in the same way.

I found my hat and stick and set out. I was surprised how soon I reached Grange Cottage. Perturbation of the mind and discomfort of the body encourage rapidity of movement. In a sense, perhaps, I was attempting to hurry away from the unholy confusion of my own feelings.

Nothing had changed since my previous visit. The building had the desolate appearance of an untenanted house – somehow reduced in importance by the absence of its owner as is a body by the absence of its animating spirit.

The shutters were still up. I tried the doors: all were locked. As I had done before, I walked round to the kitchen yard at the back. I inspected the muddy patch beside the pump, and found only a confusion of ridges and furrows, brittle with frost, where before there had been an outline of a man's footprint.

By and by, I returned through the park, walking more slowly than before. I scarcely knew the reason for my unease – whether it was what I might have left behind at Grange Cottage or what I might be walking towards at Monkshill. I skirted the lake by the longer, western route and took the opportunity to investigate both the approach to the ice-house and the shell grotto. I found nothing out of the way, and nor had I expected to do so. I was not following a rational purpose: I wanted to postpone my return, I suppose, and that part of the mind that is mysterious even to its owner was obliging enough to suggest plausible excuses for delay.

In the end, though, my powers of invention were exhausted. I took the path to the house, walking ever more slowly. Images of Mrs Frant, images of Miss Carswall, whirled through my mind. I could not think clearly, and even derived a gloomy pleasure from my plight: was I not the very pattern of a romantic hero?

As I was walking along the wall of the kitchen gardens, immersed

253

in gloomy thoughts, the boys ran whooping like redskins through a doorway. They hurled themselves into me with such force that I staggered and almost fell.

'I beg your pardon, sir,' said Edgar, glancing at Charlie.

The boys burst into giggles. I pretended to roar at them and they scampered away with cries of simulated terror. I chased them through the walled gardens and seized both of them by the scruffs of their necks.

'Juvenal tells us *maxima debetur puero reverentia*,' I said. 'Translate, Edgar.'

'The greatest reverence is due to a boy, sir.'

'But Juvenal is inaccurate on this occasion. The greatest reverence is due to a boy's master.'

I pretended to cuff them and they ran off, shrieking. Soon they would grow older and more serious. Time was running out for their boyhood. For that matter, time was running out for us all, and running faster and faster. I thought of Mr Carswall and his watch: for all his wealth the old man was time's slave, as completely in its power as any of his niggers had ever been in his. As for me, my sojourn at Monkshill was slipping away. In a few short weeks, I would take Edgar Allan back to Stoke Newington, and leave behind whatever was happening here.

Worst of all, I would leave Sophia Frant and Flora Carswall. At that moment, the prospect of losing them seemed an insupportable fate. They had become my pleasure, my pain and my necessity. They had become my meat and drink, my Alpha and Omega. I was enslaved to them, I told myself, and to what they represented: and in my addiction I was no better than an opium-eater tapping a coin on the druggist's counter as he waits for his heaven and his hell in a pill-box.

CHAPTER FIFTY

THE FOLLOWING DAY, Mr Noak sent down to say that he was unwell. He had a severe cold. Harmwell explained that his master would be obliged to keep to his bed for at least a day or two. Owing to boyhood illnesses, Mr Noak's chest was weak. The greatest care was needed if he was to avoid fever, a severe and debilitating cough and possibly pneumonia. The news spread throughout the house long before Mr Carswall announced it formally at dinner, which gave Miss Carswall ample opportunity to consult her brown duodecimo volume.

'You must not be anxious, Papa,' she said when he told us the news with a long face. 'I have already instructed Harmwell to dose Mr Noak regularly. I have prescribed a spoonful of syrup of horehound in a glass of spring water, into which he should stir ten drops of the spirit of sulphur: I am reliably informed that this is a remedy that will generally relieve the severest cold.'

'A very proper attention,' he said. 'But I was depending on him for our excursion to Gloucester.' For an instant his lips formed the pout I had seen more than once on Miss Carswall's face. 'It is so provoking.'

'I suppose the poor man cannot help his health.'

'I do not say that he can.' Mr Carswall took another sip of wine. 'But I shall miss his conversation. And Harmwell could have made himself useful when we passed through a turnpike, and in Gloucester. There are always arrangements to be made, errands to be run.'

'Surely there is at least a partial remedy immediately to hand? We should invite Mr Shield to accompany us in Mr Noak's place.'

Carswall gestured for his glass to be refilled and stared down the table at me. 'Aye, that might answer. You shall accompany us, Shield. Not to the ball itself, however – there will be no need for that. No doubt you will enjoy the change of scene. Yes, it will be quite a treat for you.'

I bowed and said nothing. Mr Carswall liked to give the impression that consulting his own comfort was merely the indirect means of doing someone else a favour. In my absence, the boys would be left in the care of Mrs Kerridge.

On the Wednesday morning, Mr Carswall plunged into a morass of indecision. He consulted his watch – he glanced at the dark, grey sky – he prophesied snow. What if we should become stuck in a snowdrift? What if a wheel should break while we were in the depths of the country? What if we had not allowed enough time for a journey at this time of year, and we were benighted on the road and froze to death? As he grew older, Mr Carswall lived in a world of terrifying possibilities, a world whose dangers increased in proportion to his own frailties.

Miss Carswall soothed him. There would be a constant stream of travellers. Most of our way would lie along the newly cut turnpike road beside the river. We would never be far from a pike-house, a farm or a village. Mr Shield, the coachman and the footmen were all able-bodied men capable of wielding a shovel or walking for assistance. Besides, it was not yet snowing, and even if it had been, there was no reason to fear that the road would be blocked.

At last Mr Carswall's anxiety subsided sufficiently for us to leave. Miss Carswall's maid and his own man had already gone on ahead to make our apartments ready, so the five of us travelled inside the great coach – the three ladies, Mr Carswall and I. Mr Carswall's splendid equipage was nothing if not luxurious. We glided along the macadamised surface of the turnpike road. The coach's big wheels and long springs combined with the perfectly flat gravelled surface to create an impression of rapid but almost effortless motion. I was in close proximity to both Mrs Frant and Miss Carswall; indeed I sometimes felt a gentle pressure from the latter's foot upon my own. There was pleasure, too, in leaving behind Monkshill-park, that elegant and spacious prison.

We came into Gloucester by the Over Causeway, a circumstance which caused Mr Carswall much agitation, for the river was rising and the masonry of the arches was already in a ruinous condition. To his relief, we crossed the Westgate Bridge and entered the city while it was still light.

Our lodgings were in Fendall House in Lower Westgate-street, not far from St Nicholas's Church with its stunted spire. Bowing and scraping, the owner of the house conducted our party up to the apartments on the first floor, formerly reserved for Lord Vauden. Nothing could have been more obliging, and nothing (I suspected) could have been more expensive.

The accommodations consisted of a large parlour with two tall windows at the front of the house, facing the south-west, and four bedrooms – one each for Mr Carswall and Mrs Lee, one for Miss Carswall and Mrs Frant, and a fourth which had been designed for Mr Noak. Having settled Mr Carswall in an elbow chair by the fire, our host handed him a letter which Sir George Ruispidge's man had delivered not half an hour earlier.

Grunting, Carswall perused it. 'Sir George asks a favour,' he said, addressing Miss Carswall. 'He has heard that Mr Noak is not come with us, and begs to inquire whether Mrs Johnson might be able to take his place. It seems that the chamber reserved for her in their lodgings in Eastgate has been damaged by fire, and there is at present no other suitable accommodation available. He adds that Mrs Johnson would be most gratified to extend her acquaintance with Mrs Frant and Miss Carswall, so the arrangement would kill two birds with one stone.'

'It is a very civil note, Papa. But what about Mr Shield?'

'I see no difficulty there.' Mr Carswall glanced up at the landlord, who was hovering in front of him. 'The boys' tutor has come in place of Mr Noak, but he will not be coming to the ball and in any case he is a plain man with simple needs easily satisfied – eh, Shield?'

I bowed.

'I'm sure you can find him a bed, hey?' Carswall said, addressing the landlord.

'Yes, sir. We have a small chamber in the upper storey, and I have taken the liberty of having it prepared.'

'Capital.' The old man waved at Miss Carswall, as if repelling an objection she had not voiced. 'You see? Shield would be perfectly happy in a hammock, I daresay. Indeed, in my experience young men prefer to rough it a little. And he will enjoy the independence, too – and not having the rest of us coming in late and disturbing him.'

The landlord murmured how very obliged he was to Mr Carswall, and how very obliged Sir George would be. He shot a sharp, sideways glance at me, which made it clear that he had assessed my position in Mr Carswall's household with tolerable accuracy.

A squat and surly hall-boy took my bag and showed me to my room. I wondered if I would ever be able to find it again. Like many buildings in this city, Fendall House was a misleading place. To the front, all was neat, new, airy and spacious. Most of the establishment, however, lay to the rear and was an elderly warren of narrow staircases, small dark rooms, winding passages, low ceilings and creaking floorboards.

The tiny bedchamber to which I was shown, though indubitably a garret nestling under the tiles, had the dignity of its own staircase at the side of the house leading to an ill-lit lobby with its own door to the street. My dormer window looked across a dark little shrubbery to a fine modern wing built of redbrick to match the frontage.

We dined together in Mr Carswall's parlour, and at an early hour because of the ball. Mrs Johnson was not yet come: she was to join our party after the ball, for Lady Ruispidge desired her attendance before-hand, and to return with the Carswalls and Mrs Lee to Fendall House afterwards.

Mr Carswall, Mrs Lee and Miss Carswall were already arrayed in their finery. Mrs Frant and I were required to admire those going to the ball, and when we had finished, those going to the ball admired each other. Mrs Frant looked wistful and said little. Around us, the house was in even more of a bustle than before, for other, lesser apartments had been let, and their occupants were also going to the ball. Though the parlour door was closed, we were constantly aware of hurrying footsteps, of slamming doors, shouted greetings and instructions.

When we had finished dinner, the time dragged. The only person who seemed content was Mrs Lee: she sat staring at the fire, her hands idle in her lap, an unopened book on the table beside her; she was well used to waiting upon the convenience of others. Mrs Frant sat sewing on the sofa, rarely speaking unless one of the Carswalls addressed her. I sat at the table with a copy of the previous week's *Gloucester Journal* spread out before me.

Miss Carswall was never still for long – sometimes she would rush to the window to look down at the street; sometimes she would dart to the mirror; sometimes she would fly to Mrs Frant to hold a whispered conversation. There was a vitality about her that I had rarely seen at Monkshill-park. Society was meat and drink to her, and she fairly glowed with the prospect of nourishment. I could not suppress a pang at the knowledge that I was excluded.

There was a quality of happy anticipation about Miss Carswall's fidgets. But Mr Carswall could not settle, either, and his restlessness was a darker matter. At first he tried with little success to engage Mrs Frant in conversation. There was a strain of gallantry in much of what he said, which could not but be offensive to the recipient. Then, still talking, he took out his watch and looked at the time. Ten minutes later he repeated the action. As the evening crept towards the hour of the ball, he fell silent; the level in the decanter sank and he consulted his watch with increasing frequency. Finally, he left the timepiece open in the palm of his hand all the time and stared at the dial with a look of strained fascination upon his face.

The arrival of the tea things at seven o'clock brought a moment's relief. Here at last was something to do. With the best will in the world, though, we could not take tea for ever. Soon that uncomfortable silence descended upon the room once more, punctuated by brief spurts of speech. Even Miss Carswall fell silent.

'Half-past eight o'clock,' said Mr Carswall, reverting to a subject that had been touched upon many times that evening. 'That would not be unreasonably early, I believe.'

'Papa,' cried Miss Carswall, 'no one you would want to speak to would be there so early.'

'But should we not send for the coach? That will take a little time. We should want a place by the fire, after all.'

'The only people there would be tradesmen and their families,' his daughter replied tartly, for her upbringing had given her a finer notion of gentility than her sire. 'They will still be tuning the fiddles! You may depend upon it, everyone else will dine much later and therefore come later.'

Carswall grumbled, Miss Carswall protested; but I knew from the way Miss Carswall's feet were tapping on the carpet that secretly she longed to be in the Assembly Rooms. In the end she and her father compromised on nine o'clock and they sent for the coach.

The hands of Mr Carswall's watch crept around the dial until the noises inside the house and in the street made it clear that the Carswalls would not suffer the ignominy of being the first people at the ball. A few minutes before the hour, Mrs Frant's dress rustled as she rose to her feet. I pushed back my chair.

'Pray do not disturb yourself, Mr Shield.' She raised her voice, addressing the Carswalls and Mrs Lee: 'I – that is, I find the excitement of the day has tired me out. You will forgive me if I retire?'

I held the door for her. As she passed me, no more than a few inches away, I felt the familiar pull, as iron filings to a powerful magnet. She looked up, and for an instant I thought – I hoped – that she had felt it too. Then she smiled up at me, wished me a quiet goodnight and slipped away.

'Poor Sophie,' Miss Carswall said, moving to the window, drawn by the sound of carriages arriving. 'So mortifying not to be able to enjoy oneself – and the poor love will be in mourning for months and months.' She parted the folds of heavy curtains and peered into the street. 'Oh!'

'What is it?' Carswall asked.

'It is snowing. Look – great big flakes like saucers.'

'There! What did I tell you? We should never have come.'

'You must not let it prey on your mind, Papa. Ten to one the snow won't settle. Everyone says it is milder today. Besides, here we have

260

warmth, food, society and comfortable beds. If the worst should come to the worst and we are snowed in, not that we shall be, it would at least be in agreeable circumstances.' She glanced outside again. 'Look at the press of carriages! Oh – there is ours pulling up at the door! Would it not be heaven if we reached the Bell just after the Ruispidges? Then we might encounter them in the passage, and enter with them. It would look very well, would it not? It would seem as if we were come together.'

Mrs Lee suddenly emerged from her torpor. 'My dear, you must wear your wrap when we go out in the passage at the Bell. The draughts are most dangerous. Oh, I do hope they have swept the floor properly this time – after the last ball, the hem of my dress was quite black with dust. And it was the passage to blame, I am sure of it.'

Miss Carswall stood on tiptoe and twirled, admiring herself in the mirror between the windows. 'Thank heavens I bought this wrap. It sets off the colour of the dress to perfection.' In the brackets flanking the mirror the candle flames seemed to nod in agreement.

I murmured, 'It matches your eyes, too, Miss Carswall, if I may say so.'

She looked at me, her face grave as a nun's but her eyes sparkling. 'You are too kind, sir,' she said softly.

'My gloves, my gloves,' cried Mr Carswall. 'Who has taken them?'

'I believe I see them on the arm of your chair, sir,' I said.

'I hope there will still be a place by the fire,' croaked Mrs Lee. 'If only we had not waited so long.'

At last the three of them were gone and I was alone. I listened to their voices and footsteps fading on the stairs and in the hall. The front door closed. Silence flowed into the parlour. I sat down at the table again and turned a page of the newspaper.

I tried to read. But the newspaper bored me. I was aware of noises outside the room – the hurrying of servants' feet, the ebb and flow of carriages in the street below, raised voices, and distant snatches of music. Miss Carswall was right. There is nothing so sad as sitting alone and listening to the sounds of others enjoying themselves in society.

I was not sleepy. I could have gone out and settled in the corner of a taproom or a coffee house but I was not in the mood for company.

Instead, I fetched pen and paper and settled down to write overdue letters to Edward Dansey and Mr Rowsell.

I must have written for well over an hour. I could be entirely frank, of course, with neither man, though for different reasons. But there was plenty of matter for my pen in describing the splendours of Monkshill-park and the characters of its principal inhabitants. I was nearing the end of the second letter when there came a tap on the door. I looked up, expecting a maidservant. Instead it was Sophia Frant, still in the dress she had worn at dinner.

'I beg your pardon, Mr Shield,' she said hurriedly in a voice that was not altogether steady. 'I hope I do not disturb you.'

'I am entirely at your service, ma'am.'

'I wish to consult with you on a matter of – of some delicacy.'

I drew up a chair to the fire. 'Pray sit down.'

'A moment ago, I happened to go to one of the windows in our chamber,' she began in a low voice. 'The sashes were rattling, and I wished to wedge them. The window on that side overlooks the lane running up to Westgate-street. I looked down, and I saw a woman.' She hesitated. 'I – I must request you to treat this as a confidence, Mr Shield.'

'Of course, ma'am.'

'I knew I might rely on you.' She was calmer now, fully in control of herself. 'The fact of the matter is this: a shaft of light fell across the lane from a doorway of a tavern, and it showed the face of the woman. It was Mrs Johnson.'

'But I thought she was with the Ruispidges, at the assembly.'

'So did I. But wait, there is more. Mrs Johnson was wearing a cloak with a hood. But the hood had fallen backwards from her head. She did not have a cap, and her hair was quite loose, falling in disarray to her shoulders. I – I watched her walking up to Westgate-street. She swayed from side to side, and once she slipped and nearly fell. A man came out of the tavern and put his hand on her arm and she pushed him away. Then she turned the corner and I saw her no more. And the man followed her.'

'She is indisposed?' It was my turn to pause. 'Or –?'

'Or something worse,' Mrs Frant finished for me. 'It is possible that she entered the house once I lost sight of her. I went to the chamber set aside for her – it is just along the passage from ours. Her luggage is come but there was no sign of her. Not that I thought it likely, because we would have heard her knocking on the door.'

'Might she be below-stairs?'

'No, she is not – I rang for the maid and asked if she had seen Mrs Johnson this evening. I pretended I had a message for her – I did not like to say the truth. I do not know whether the people here are trust-worthy. And if Mrs Johnson is not herself . . . ' Her voice died away.

'No,' I said. 'I understand your drift, ma'am. May I suggest that I go in search of Mrs Johnson? It will not take me a moment to fetch my hat and greatcoat. The part of the building where I am lodged has a separate flight of stairs that runs down to a side entrance. I am sure I could slip out without attracting attention.'

'Let us hope so.' Mrs Frant stood up. 'I am infinitely obliged to you, Mr Shield. If you allow me two minutes.'

'Madam – you cannot accompany me.'

'Why not?'

'It would not be fitting. If you were seen –'

She was already at the door. 'I shall not be seen.'

'It is still snowing, ma'am.'

'A little snow will not harm me. I too have a cloak with a hood. You must be sensible of Mrs Johnson's feelings if she were to suspect that a man were pursuing her at this time of night. Especially if her wits are at all disordered.'

'But she knows me.'

'She does not know you well. No, Mr Shield, my mind is quite made up. I shall be perfectly safe under your protection. And if we find – when we find – Mrs Johnson, she need feel no uneasiness at being accosted by a lady.'

CHAPTER FIFTY-ONE

A S TO TIME, Mrs Frant was as good as her word. Hooded and cloaked, with a pair of pattens in her hand, she met me in the passage. We passed no one as we threaded our way across the upper floors of the house to the flight of stairs that descended to the lobby and side door. Impatient to be gone, she led the way down to the dingy hall, which was lit by a solitary lamp.

The door was bolted, not locked. It opened on to a narrow alley on the other side of the house from the lane with the tavern. Mrs Frant slipped on her pattens and took my arm. We picked our way through the gloom to the lights of Westgate-street.

People were still abroad. The paved footways on either side were covered with a feathery layer of snow; the cobbles of the pitching were coated with rutted, partly frozen slush. We saw no one resembling Mrs Johnson in either direction.

'Let us walk up towards the crossroads,' Mrs Frant suggested. 'If she did not call in at the house, we must assume she went in that direction.'

So we set off, looking into the dark mouths of doorways and alleys, glancing into brightly lit taprooms, examining every passer-by. We did not speak. The hood of Mrs Frant's cloak was across her face, so nothing was visible of her except a pair of eyes. I feared she might fall, for there were patches of black ice concealed beneath the powdering of snow. I listened anxiously to the sound of her pattens clinking and scraping on the pavement, ready to hold her more tightly if she should slip.

We passed St Nicholas's Church. A few yards beyond was another of the city's principal inns, the King's Head on the corner of Three Cocks-lane. Two servants loitered in the doorway, no doubt waiting to light their masters home. They were smoking and, despite the cold, had the air of men who were at their leisure. I asked if they had seen a lady in the last quarter of an hour, not in the best of health, perhaps, and wearing a long cloak.

'Hear that, Joe? The gent here's looking for a lady.' He poked the stem of his pipe towards Mrs Frant, waiting some yards away with her back to us. 'Another lady.'

Joe chuckled. 'Ain't we all? Could be in luck. Plenty of ladies tonight. If you ain't too particular.'

I felt in my pocket and produced a shilling. 'A lady in a cloak. She came up from the lane beyond Fendall House. You know where I mean?' The shilling was on the palm of my hand and I let the light fall on it from the lantern beside the door. 'She is not well – we are looking for her.'

Joe scooped the shilling from my hand. 'Aye, sir. There was a skirt come up from there – ill, you say? I'd say she was lushy. Slipped on some ice, fell on her arse in the gutter, and let fly like a trooper.'

'Which way did she go?'

'They went up Westgate.'

'*They*?' said Mrs Frant just behind me. 'She was not alone?'

'No, ma'am.' Joe studied her and would have come closer if I had not taken a step forward to prevent him. 'A gent come running up from behind when she fell down, and he helped her up and gave her his arm.'

'What did he look like?'

'I don't know. Big fellow. Well set-up. I expect you'd know him, sir, eh? I expect he's one of her friends as well.'

There was no mistaking the impudence, though it was phrased in such a way that there was no objecting to it either. The shilling had not been enough to buy respect as well as information.

Mrs Frant took my arm again and we hurried down the street which

265

sloped gently upwards to the ancient crossroads at the centre of the city. A burst of ribald laughter followed us.

'Loathsome men,' she murmured.

'Not loathsome,' I said. 'Merely ordinary.'

I felt her hand tighten on my arm but she said no more. I knew she was upset. Joe and his fellow servants might indeed be ordinary men, but they were not ordinary men of the type with which she was familiar. It shocked her to discover that Mrs Johnson had sunk to become a figure of fun, a drunken woman to be ridiculed when she fell on the street rather than helped to her feet; a woman whose morals were perhaps suspect in all matters – at least in the opinion of those ordinary men.

The snowflakes still floated silently down from the great darkness of the sky, though less urgently than before. It was as cold as charity. We hurried onwards as fast as we dared. We reached the crossroads, and lingered for a moment on the corner by the Tolsey, the building where the city's business was transacted.

'What shall we do?' Mrs Frant said. 'She might be anywhere. Should we go on?'

'But in which direction?'

'I fear for her safety.'

'At least she is not alone.'

'Some companions may prove worse than solitude.'

'I think we should retrace our steps,' I said. 'Is it not more likely that they turned into one of the alleys we passed? Or went into one of the inns or alehouses?'

Mrs Frant shivered. 'We cannot abandon her. We must try something. Anything might have happened to her. Should we not find a constable?'

'If we cannot find her, then we must.'

'I shudder to think of the scandal.'

'Listen,' I said.

Someone close at hand was crying quietly. Mrs Frant's hand tightened its grip on my arm. Suddenly, a man burst out of a doorway on the other side of Westgate-street. He ran across the road, slipping on the cobbles, and into a lane below the Fleece. The sobbing continued.

Mrs Frant tugged her arm, trying to free it from my grasp, but I would not let her.

'Wait,' I said. 'Let me investigate first.'

'We shall go together,' she said, and I knew that nothing short of brute force would change her mind.

We moved cautiously across the road. The sobbing came from outside an old house used as a bank. We drew nearer. The storeys above projected into the street, and there was enough light to read below the first-floor windows the words

COUNTY FIRE OFFICE
PROVIDENT LIFE OFFICE

'Is anyone there?' Mrs Frant said.

The crying stopped. My eyes made out a patch of deeper darkness among the shadows along the base of the bank's frontage. I heard a whimper.

'Mrs Johnson?' I said. 'Is that you, ma'am?'

'Let me alone, damn you.' Mrs Johnson's voice was so thick and weary that it was barely recognisable. 'Let me die.'

Mrs Frant tore her arm away from mine and knelt beside the unfortunate woman, who lay curled on her side in the bank's doorway, with flecks of snow on her mantle. 'Mrs Johnson, we are come to find you.'

'I do not wish to be found. I wish to stay here.'

'Indeed you shall not. You will catch your death of cold. Are you hurt?'

Mrs Johnson did not answer.

'Come, ma'am, Mr Shield is here too, and you may lean on my arm on one side and his on the other.'

'Let me alone,' Mrs Johnson murmured, but this time there was more habit than conviction in her tone.

'No, of course we shall not,' said Mrs Frant briskly, as though Mrs Johnson were a sick and foolish child. 'Lady Ruispidge would worry, so would we all, and that would never do. Let me help you up.'

Between us, Mrs Frant and I raised Mrs Johnson and propped her against the door. Her head lolled against my arm and she muttered something I could not distinguish. Mingling with the unpleasant odours of the street was the sharp tang of brandy.

'Who was the man who ran away?' Mrs Frant said.

'I don't know,' Mrs Johnson said. 'What man?' She jabbed her elbow in my side with unexpected force. 'This man? Who are you?'

'My name is Shield, ma'am. I –'

'Oh, yes – the damned tutor.' The voice was slurred but the malignancy as clear as a curse. 'You're no good. No, no, no.'

'You will be more comfortable directly,' Mrs Frant said, ignoring this. 'In any case, I did not mean Mr Shield. I meant the man who ran away as we came up to you. Who was he?'

Mrs Johnson did not reply for a moment. Then: 'What man? There was no man. No, no, you must be mistaken. Oh, dear God, I feel so ill. So terribly ill.'

She began to weep all the harder. A moment later, she turned to retching, then gave a great groan and vomited. I sprang back just in time to prevent her fouling my greatcoat.

'We must get her to Fendall House,' I said. 'A pair of men might carry her upon a door, if we cannot find a cart or a sedan chair.'

'No,' Mrs Frant said. 'That would not do. She – she is too ill to be seen like this. Besides, moderate exercise might be beneficial. I believe that if we supported her –'

'Murder,' said Mrs Johnson quietly. 'No, no.'

'What is it, ma'am?' Mrs Frant cried. 'What do you mean?'

'What – was I dreaming?' Mrs Johnson tried to stand up. 'Oh, pray take me home, Mrs Frant. I do not feel at all the thing.'

Mrs Frant pulled and I lifted; and between us we brought Mrs Johnson to her feet. For a moment she swayed to and fro. But her knees held out and she remained upright, clinging to our arms.

'You felt faint,' Mrs Frant said firmly. 'That is what we shall say if we encounter anyone on our way back. You felt faint, and no doubt that is why you are not at the ball. I suggested to you that fresh air might be the best medicine, and Mr Shield was obliging enough to escort us while we took a turn up and down the street.

Your stomach is upset, and there is the possibility of an inflammation of the bowels.'

Mrs Johnson groaned.

'Do you understand?' Mrs Frant said. 'If we meet anyone, pray remain silent. Mr Shield or I will say whatever needs to be said.'

I own that Mrs Frant's behaviour both surprised and impressed me. I had not anticipated such firmness of character, such presence of mind in a crisis. We made our way slowly, painfully, back to Fendall House. Mrs Johnson leaned heavily on our arms but did not fall. Gradually the fresh air and the motion revived her slightly, and she took more of her weight herself. I glanced down at her as we came into a circle of lamp-light, and saw her haggard face, her disordered hair, and, beneath the stained cloak, a bedraggled ball dress. But she had not changed her shoes: in other words, she had never reached the assembly rooms at the Bell: which suggested that she had intended to go to the ball but something, or someone, had diverted her from her purpose.

We walked, or rather staggered, in silence for most of the way, our feet slithering on cobbles made triply treacherous by their covering of snow and by patches of ice. Fortunately the servants were no longer idling outside the King's Head so we were spared their catcalls. The only people abroad seemed as drunk as Mrs Johnson. They avoided us, and we avoided them. The snowflakes fell even more thickly than before, which was a blessing because the passers-by kept their faces sheltered from the weather.

At Fendall House, we faced another difficulty, that of avoiding servants. We guided our unstable burden into the tunnel-like alley. The little door was still unbolted. The lobby was empty, though there were voices somewhere in the back of the house. On the stairs, Mrs Frant pulled, I pushed, and Mrs Johnson showed an inclination to collapse.

'You must not,' Mrs Frant hissed. 'Come, ma'am, it is only a few steps more.'

'Why must I not?' wailed Mrs Johnson. 'What does it matter?'

'You must go on because otherwise I will pinch you until you shriek,' Mrs Frant replied with such resolution in her voice that Mrs Johnson gathered up her skirts and fairly cantered up the remaining stairs.

The burst of energy did not last. She clung to us as we steered her through the labyrinth of passages to the front of the inn, where the Carswalls' apartments were situated. She moaned almost continuously, a low, mournful drone strangely wearing on the nerves. At one point she muttered, 'I wish I was dead. I wish I was dead.'

'We will all be dead soon enough,' Mrs Frant told her.

'Cold, unfeeling woman!' whispered Mrs Johnson. 'No wonder –'

'In the meantime, however,' Mrs Frant interrupted, 'I am persuaded you will feel much better in the morning.'

We were fortunate to meet no one. At last we attained our own part of the house. Lamps burned in the passage, but when we opened the door of the chamber where Mrs Johnson was to sleep, we found the room beyond lit only by a sullen orange glow from the fire. I helped Mrs Frant lower Mrs Johnson on to the bed and went in search of candles. When I returned a moment later, I found Mrs Johnson lying flat on her back, snoring quietly, still in her sodden ballroom finery.

'Would you be so good as to attend to the fire, Mr Shield?' Mrs Frant said. 'Mrs Johnson is very cold.'

So indeed was I. I jabbed the fire with a poker, added a few more coals, and soon there was a respectable blaze in the grate. A moment later, Mrs Frant joined me, and we stood there by the fire, warming our hands. A few yards away behind us, the air pumped noisily in and out of Mrs Johnson's lungs. I glanced at Mrs Frant, whose cheeks looked flushed in the firelight.

'Should you like me to fetch a doctor, ma'am?'

'I think not.' She turned and looked at me. 'Her clothes must be changed, but then the best medicine for her condition is rest and warmth. I know I need not ask you to be discreet.'

I inclined my head.

'We were fortunate not to encounter anyone.' She sat down on the chair by the fire and passed her hand across her forehead. 'But we are not safe yet.'

'Has Lady Ruispidge sent a maid for her?'

'I doubt it. If only Kerridge were here.'

'Then we must ring for Miss Carswall's maid.'

'There is a risk of scandal –' Mrs Frant began.

'There will be a worse risk of scandal if she is not made comfortable. We have to trust someone on Mrs Johnson's behalf, do we not? She cannot be found like this, ma'am, and you cannot shut yourself up here with her without arousing comment. We should tell the maid that Mrs Johnson is indisposed, and leave it at that.'

'You are in the right of it. I – I might mention to her – the maid, that is – that earlier in the evening Mrs Johnson attempted to revive herself with a glass of brandy.'

'That will be wise.'

Our eyes met. A spark of amusement leapt between us.

'Let us say you went for a stroll,' she continued, 'and you chanced to meet her at the Bell, and offered to escort her back. She felt faint, and needed air. You brought her back and came in with her by the side door, to avoid troubling the servants.'

'It will serve, ma'am. And the Ruispidges?'

'I shall write to Lady Ruispidge directly.'

'If you wish, I will deliver your note to their lodgings myself. They will naturally be anxious.'

I knew we understood each other perfectly. Leaving Mrs Frant to minister to the invalid, I returned to the parlour and rang for the maid. In one respect, I was not entirely surprised by the turn the evening's events had taken. Even in the smallest village, one sees the effect that an unhealthy dependence on liquor has on women as well as men. If a woman might drink in the purlieus of the Strand or in Seven Dials, so too might her more affluent sister in Belgrave-square or indeed Clearland-court. I had noted Mrs Johnson's high colour from the first, and marked a slurring in her speech; and she was irritable with servants for no good reason.

But there remained much that was puzzling. Why had Mrs Johnson left the Ruispidges so early, though by her dress she had clearly intended to accompany them to the ball? Why had she found it necessary to drink a great deal in a very short time? Why had she left the warmth and safety of the Bell or the Ruispidges' lodgings? Above all, was her extraordinary behaviour connected with the man who had run away as Mrs

Frant and I approached the corner where she lay? If so, who was the stranger?

At last the maid came, her cap awry, her pert face flushed and liquor on her breath. I told her that Mrs Johnson was unwell, that Mrs Frant was at present with her and that she was to take her place and settle Mrs Johnson for the night. I sweetened this intelligence with half a crown I could ill afford, after which the woman's expression softened.

I led her into the passage, where I tapped on Mrs Johnson's door. As the maid slipped inside, Mrs Frant handed me a pencilled note for Lady Ruispidge. A moment later I left the house by the side door and walked briskly up Westgate-street to the Cross. The music from the Bell was loud and clear in the night air, and there was a press of people and carriages outside the inn.

The Ruispidges' lodgings were in a fine, ashlar-fronted mansion at the far end of Eastgate-street. I explained my errand and asked for Lady Ruispidge's maid. She positively ran into the hall.

'Thank God you're come, sir,' she said in a rush, her face as shiny as a polished apple. 'Is Mrs Johnson safe? I've been fretting about her, not knowing what to do for the best.'

Relief made the woman garrulous, and she needed little encouragement to tell her story. Mrs Johnson's lack of consideration gave her narrative the spice of malice. A boy had brought a letter for Mrs Johnson soon after the party's arrival in Gloucester, and its contents had depressed her spirits. The maid hinted that it had probably been a bill, and also that such occurrences were not uncommon in Mrs Johnson's life. She had dashed off a reply, which the boy had taken, and had been in the sullens thereafter.

The party from Clearland-court had dined together before the ball. Mrs Johnson complained of tiredness and the headache and decided to rest on the sofa, which did not please the servants, who had hoped for a few hours to themselves. The Ruispidges had gone to the Bell without her, on the understanding that Mrs Johnson would join them later. Her luggage had already been sent down to Fendall House.

An hour later, a servant of the house had gone to make up the fire and found her gone. He had not thought to mention the circumstance, assuming she had followed the others to the Bell. Lady Ruispidge's maid had not discovered Mrs Johnson's disappearance until twenty minutes before my arrival.

'I didn't rightly know what to do, sir. She might have gone to the Bell. But I couldn't be sure one way or the other. The servants are coming and going tonight so I couldn't ask them all if they'd taken her, or called a chair for her. And I knew her ladyship wouldn't be best pleased if I raised the alarm for nothing.'

I would have liked to question the woman further, but I dared not run the risk of arousing her suspicions; she was already willing to think the worst of Mrs Johnson. I said goodnight and walked back to Fendall House.

I will not conceal the fact that I was now greatly agitated. At our lodgings, I considered knocking on the bedroom door again, and asking Mrs Frant to discover whether Mrs Johnson still had the letter on her person. For a moment or two, I paced up and down the passage in an agony of indecision. At length, I went back to the parlour.

I cared little or nothing for Mrs Johnson and her plight: if I am to be completely honest, I would admit that my motives for helping her were entirely self-interested: on the one hand I wished to ingratiate myself with Mrs Frant, and on the other I wished to guard against the possibility of open scandal because I strongly suspected that if Mr Carswall required a scapegoat, he would have no hesitation in selecting me for the rôle. No, as far as I was concerned, Mrs Johnson could go hang.

Unfortunately it was no longer a simple matter of concealing an episode of drunkenness and protecting a lady's reputation. What worried me most was the possible implication of the evening's events for Mrs Frant. I tried to convince myself that Mrs Johnson's letter had been no more than a bill, and the man who had followed her was simply a drunkard.

But what if this were not the case? What if the letter and the man were connected? What if Mrs Frant found the letter and recognised the handwriting as her husband's?

Well, what then?

CHAPTER FIFTY-TWO

'BUT I AM quite accustomed to drunken women,' Mrs Frant said as we sat opposite each other by the parlour fire half an hour later. 'When liquor is taken to excess, a woman is no different from a man. If a person is intoxicated, a sudden elevation of the spirits, or a sudden depression of them, may have a disproportionate effect. The emotions bolt like a horse.'

'Having first reared and thrown off their rider?' I inquired.

'What?'

'I beg your pardon – I ventured to extend your metaphor. If the emotions are a horse, then we may at least hope that Reason is their rider.'

'Ah. I understand you. We have made a pretty conceit between us, have we not?' After a pause, Mrs Frant went on: 'You must not wonder at my knowledge. I have lived in the world and am used to its ways. When I was a child, my father could not bear to part with me, especially after my mother's death, so I followed him from place to place.'

She was about to continue but there were footsteps in the passage and she fell silent. A moment later came a knock at the door. Miss Carswall's maid entered.

'If you please, ma'am, Mrs Johnson's sleeping like a baby.'

'If I have retired by the time your mistress comes in, be sure to tell her that Mrs Johnson is unwell. You may add that there seems no cause for alarm.'

'Yes, ma'am.'

The woman left us alone. One of the candles guttered, and we stared at its swaying flame until it died and the room became suddenly darker.

Mrs Frant murmured, 'What concerns me is whether there is more to this than brandy.'

'Something that drove her to run such risks?'

'Precisely. Though we shall never know what it is unless she chooses to make confidants of us, and that is unlikely enough. You do not think she may be – that her mind may be deranged?'

'It is possible.' I was happy to encourage this line of thought, though I believed Mrs Johnson to be as sane as Mrs Frant. I was relieved, too – I did not think Mrs Frant would talk so coolly if she had discovered a letter in her husband's handwriting on Mrs Johnson's person.

Then she took me by surprise, as so often: 'I hope I may not be a cause of her behaviour.'

'But how could that be?'

'She dislikes me, I am afraid.' Mrs Frant raised a hand to prevent my interrupting. 'You must have remarked it. At Grange Cottage, for example.'

'Yes,' I said. 'There was indeed a coldness.'

'More than that.' She turned her face away. 'In fact she hates me. There is no reason why you should not know the truth – you deserve to hear it after tonight. Long before my marriage to Mr Frant, or Mrs Johnson's to her husband, there was an understanding between them.'

'While Mr Frant was living at Monkshill?'

'No – the family left Monkshill when Mr Frant was no older than Charlie. After that he lived chiefly in Ireland when he was not at school, until he started at Wavenhoe's. But his mother was connected by marriage to the Ruispidges, and during his vacations he would sometimes stay at Clearland-court. Mrs Johnson grew up at Clearland, quite as one of the family. So they were thrown together a good deal.' She hesitated. 'Neither she nor Mr Frant had a penny to their name. Otherwise they would certainly have married.' She paused again and then added sadly, 'I – I have no reason to doubt my informant on that score.'

I looked at her, and her large eyes shone with unshed tears. I suspected then that it had been Mr Frant himself who had told her, that he had taunted her with his prior attachment.

'Who knows?' she murmured. 'She may even hold me responsible for what happened to Mr Frant.'

'But that would be nonsense, ma'am.'

'One does not think clearly when one's mind is in turmoil.' Her voice trembled. 'His murder might well have shaken her reason. God knows, it was frightful enough in all conscience – and the uncertainty makes it worse, that and the fear that something even more terrible may yet – I myself have felt that –' She broke off and again turned her head away from me. In a moment she resumed in a calmer tone, 'Tell me, did you ever feel that you were not entirely in possession of your senses?'

'Yes.'

A glowing coal fell from the grate to the hearth, sending up a shower of sparks. I bent to retrieve it with the tongs. Her question had thrown me into confusion. She and I were the same people we had been at the start of the evening. But something had changed, something invisible and profound, and I could only guess at its nature and its implications.

I raised my head. 'When I was wounded, it seemed to me I was wounded in mind as well as in body.'

She nodded. 'My father once remarked that in war a man sees such terrible sights that he may see them for ever.' We sat in silence for a moment. Then: 'What happened?'

'My body healed more quickly than my mind. For many months, nothing truly mattered very much, and I was angry. I was angry that I had been wounded, and that all those men had died, and that I had done nothing and yet I was still alive. I despised myself.' I hesitated and then added: 'And there were dreams, every night there were dreams. Now I believe I was as much afraid as angry. Or perhaps anger and fear are different aspects of the same thing.' I thought briefly of Dansey with his Janus face. 'But I must not weary you.'

'When I first saw you, you looked ill. No, that is not quite the word: you looked as though there were a sheet of glass between you and the rest of the world. And if the glass broke, then so should you.'

I said, picking my words one by one from the silence, 'I fell so far

276

into despair that one day I lost my senses. Only for a moment but it was enough. I threw a medal at an officer in the Park. His horse reared, and he fell. They arrested me. I was afraid they would shut me up for ever, or transport me. But I was fortunate: I came up before a humane magistrate, who decided that I was but a temporary lunatic whose madness would yield to a course of treatment.'

'I am very often afraid,' Mrs Frant remarked. 'If a woman has a child she must be afraid for him, if not for herself. And at present there is so very much to be afraid of.' She was quiet for a moment. Then she raised her head and went on in a sudden rush of words: 'Why did you join the army, Mr Shield?'

I looked down the years at my younger self and marvelled at its folly. 'A girl jilted me, ma'am. I drowned my sorrows, and when I was drunk, I spoke intemperately to the girl's father, who was also the master at the school where I was teaching. As a result, I lost my position. To show the world how little I cared, I took the King's shilling – and regretted it as soon as I was sober again.'

'I beg your pardon. You must think me impertinent. I should not have asked.'

'It is of no consequence.'

'Oh, but it is.'

Her eyes stared into mine. I was alarmed by what she might see – such a degree of longing, such overwhelming desire. Simultaneously, I realised I was holding my breath, as if by not breathing I might prolong the moment indefinitely, as if I might stop time itself.

Then came a great knocking on the street door, and the sound of voices and laughter outside. I let myself breathe once more, and went to sit at the table, returning to the newspaper I had abandoned, it seemed in another life. Mrs Frant did not speak.

In a moment we heard footsteps in the passage and the sound of Mr Carswall's voice raised in triumph: 'And he did not know I had the last heart, the poor fool, he thought Lady Ruispidge had it. No, it was neatly done, by God, and after that trick, the rubber was ours.'

The door flew open, colliding with the back of a chair. In an instant the quiet parlour had filled to overflowing with lights, noise, people. As well as Mr Carswall, there was Miss Carswall, Mrs Lee, Sir George and the Captain. Lady Ruispidge had retired for the night but her sons had insisted on escorting Mr Carswall's party back to Fendall House.

Mr Carswall was not drunk, merely boisterous. In Mrs Johnson's absence, Lady Ruispidge had condescended to partner him and I believe he felt he had acquitted himself well, both at whist and in society in general. Mrs Lee and a clergyman had opposed them in the card room, and Mrs Lee did her best to appear complacent about the losses she had sustained.

Miss Carswall, we soon learned, had danced almost every dance, many of them with Sir George, two with the Captain, and several with officers from the local militia. She looked very handsome, with her colour high and the excitement running through her like electricity. Sir George had taken her down to supper, and everyone had been most attentive.

Sir George was quieter, but almost equally pleased with himself. His brother, on the other hand, was at pains to give the impression that he had been miserable for most of the time: first, contemplating how Mrs Frant was faring on her own, and later, when the news of Mrs Johnson's indisposition had reached him, being sensible of Mrs Frant's kindness to his unfortunate cousin. Indeed, to hear him speak, one would think that Mrs Frant, but for an accident of faith, were a prime candidate for canonisation. No one seemed unduly concerned about Mrs Johnson – Sir George remarked that hers was one of those unequal constitutions that alternate between spells of intense activity and periods of low spirits and general debility. He trusted that his cousin's indisposition would not inconvenience us in any way. A good night's sleep would soon set her right.

'She certainly sleeps soundly,' cried Mr Carswall. 'Why, I heard her snoring as we passed her door.'

The hour was late – after one o'clock in the morning – and, having escorted the Carswalls back to their apartment and made civil inquiries after the well-being of Mrs Frant and Mrs Johnson, the Ruispidge brothers had no further excuse for remaining. Almost immediately after their departure, there occurred an ugly little scene which made me wonder whether Carswall were drunker than he appeared.

278

Mrs Frant rose, saying she was fatigued and would retire. I was about to open the door for her when Carswall plunged across the room and forestalled me. As she passed him in the doorway, he laid a hand like a great paw on her arm and begged the favour of a goodnight kiss.

'After all,' said he, 'are we not cousins? Should not cousins love each other?' The intonation he gave the words made it quite clear what sort of love he had in mind.

'Oh, Papa,' cried Miss Carswall. 'Pray let Sophie pass; she is quite fagged.'

The sound of his daughter's voice rather than the words distracted him for an instant. Mrs Frant slipped into the passage. I heard her talking to Miss Carswall's maid. Then came the sound of a door opening and closing.

'Eh?' Mr Carswall said to no one in particular. 'Fagged? Aye, no wonder – look at the time.' He thrust his fingers into his waistcoat pocket and in a moment was matching his actions to his words. Then he turned his back to us and went to stand at the window. 'God damn it, it is still snowing.'

He wished us a curt goodnight and stamped out of the room, jingling the change in his pocket. The rest of us followed almost at once. Miss Carswall lingered in the passage, however, adjusting the wick of her candle. Mrs Lee went on ahead and into her own chamber. Miss Carswall turned back to me.

'I am sorry you was not at the ball,' she said. 'It was but a country assembly, of course, full of tradesmen and farmers' wives, but it was most agreeable for all that.' She lowered her voice. 'And it would have been more agreeable, had you been there.'

I bowed, looking at her; and I could not help admiring what I saw.

Miss Carswall studied my face for an instant. Then she took up her candle and turned as if about to retire. But she checked herself. 'Would you do something for me, sir?'

'Of course.'

'I have a mind to perform an experiment. When you go to your room, will you stand at the window for a moment or two, and look out?'

'If you wish. May I ask why?'

'No, sir, you may not.' She devastated me with a smile. 'That would be quite unscientific – it would ruin my experiment. We natural philosophers would pay any price to avoid that.'

A moment later I was alone. I threaded my way through passages and up and down the stairs until I reached my room. The old building was full of noises, and I encountered several servants going about their business.

At length I climbed the last flight of stairs to my door. My room felt almost as cold as the ice-house at Monkshill-park. My body was tired but my mind was restless, stirred by the events of the evening. I threw on my greatcoat and felt in my valise for a paper of cigars. I forced open one half of the casement window which had been wedged with newspaper. A moment later I was leaning on the sill and filling my lungs with sweet, soothing smoke.

The roofs of the city were silver and white. Somewhere a church clock sounded the half-hour and was answered by others across the city, their bells muted by the covering of snow. My mind filled with a parade of images, its constituent parts as random as the flakes still falling from the sky.

I saw Miss Carswall, of course, with that smile that promised so much, and Mrs Frant's gravely beautiful face lit by a guttering candle flame and the glow of the parlour fire. I saw Mrs Johnson huddled on the pavement, and a man running across the road from her. I looked further back, to the man glimpsed at the window of Grange Cottage, to the dried, yellowing finger I had found in the satchel, to the mutilated corpse on the trestle at Wellington-terrace.

Dansey, too, and Rowsell joined the parade, and I wondered idly at the reasons for the kindnesses they showed me. (One of the oddest things about affection is surely that in many cases its object so little deserves it.) I thought of the boys, Charlie and Edgar, so like each other in appearance with their high foreheads, their air of refinement, their vulnerability, but so different in their temperaments. I had met the American boy on my first visit to Stoke Newington, the day I had first seen Sophia Frant, and he seemed, albeit unconsciously, to have acted as the proximate cause of much that had happened. He had brought

David Poe into my life, and without David Poe I would not have become entangled with the Carswalls and the Frants.

I was also aware of an underlying layer of anxiety in my mind, which reminded me of something. After another half-inch of the cigar, I had fixed the memory like a butterfly with a pin: I had felt this way in the days before Waterloo: then, as now, there had been a sense of foreboding, of disaster drawing ineluctably closer. The difference was this: then I had known the nature of the impending catastrophe; now I did not.

Ayez peur, I thought. *Ayez peur*. Perhaps the quack's parrot was wiser than it knew.

All at once, my mind was jolted away from these aimless but gloomy reflections. A long narrow triangle of yellow light appeared in the wall of the house's modern wing beyond the shrubbery, almost opposite my window but several feet lower. The heavy curtains were moving. The triangle of light widened still further and a figure carrying a candle slipped through the gap into the narrow space between curtains and glass. The left hand cupped the flame and concealed its owner's identity. All of a sudden, the window embrasure was neither one thing nor the other, as equivocal as a proscenium. It seemed to me as though I were in a box overlooking the pit of a darkened theatre.

The curtains swung back behind the figure; the hand lifted, and I saw a woman standing there, as unfamiliar and as vividly unreal as an actress on a stage. She wore a dressing gown of patterned silk, and red-gold hair flowed to her shoulders. She set down the candle on the sill and took something made of silver from the pocket of the gown. She stood there, facing the window and staring straight at me, and began to brush her hair. Her movements were languorous as though she were stroking herself. The front of the gown fell open, and I saw the night-dress beneath, with its low-cut neck.

I doubted that Miss Carswall could see me but I knew that the performance was for me, just as I knew that Mrs Frant, waking or sleeping, was in the room on the other side of the curtains. My mind filled with unchaste thoughts. They say that redheads are lubricious. Here, it seemed, was ample confirmation: Miss Carswall was revealing herself to me, and deriving pleasure from the knowledge that I was watching, and perhaps also from the fact that Sophie was a few yards away from her.

The snow continued to drift down into the yard. My mouth was dry, my breathing shallow. I hardly noticed how cold I was becoming, or that my cigar had gone out. At last, Miss Carswall slipped the brush back into the pocket and stood for a moment, gazing out. Slowly she shook her head, and the movement made her hair ripple and sway above her shoulders. Her lips parted. She smoothed her nightdress against her body, against the swell of her bosom.

She dropped me the ghost of a curtsey, picked up the candle and slipped through the gap in the curtains to the room beyond.

CHAPTER FIFTY-THREE

THE SNOW HAD stopped by morning, and the sky was a hard, brilliant blue. Though the main thoroughfares of the city soon turned to chilly brown slush, most of the snow remained a pristine white, so bright it seemed to possess its own inner illumination. For an hour or two the world lost its familiarity.

We ate our breakfast in the private parlour. There was, Mr Carswall announced, no question of returning to Monkshill-park today. John coachman believed the road would be perfectly safe, but John coachman was a fool. Miss Carswall was in complete agreement with her father, not least because she wished to make a number of purchases.

'I daresay Sir George and the Captain will come and see how Mrs Johnson does,' she added with a little laugh. 'And perhaps, if there is time, I might see the property Uncle Wavenhoe left me.'

'Aye, why not?' said her father. 'There is the inn, of course, and a small brewery adjacent, together with a row of cottages.'

When Miss Carswall talked so blithely of her inheritance, I noticed that Mrs Frant stared at her plate, and her lips were compressed. It was unfeeling in her cousin to talk so: had it not been for that strange scene at Mr Wavenhoe's deathbed, the legacy would have been Mrs Frant's; though perhaps it might have been hers only to vanish in the collapse of Mr Frant's fortunes.

They had hardly cleared the table when there came a tap on the door and Sir George and Captain Ruispidge were announced. They asked after their cousin.

'She is still asleep,' said Miss Carswall. 'My maid is watching over her. I looked in a moment ago. She woke in the night and was restless, and we gave her a dose of laudanum shortly before dawn.'

'I shouldn't wonder if she was afflicted with an inflammation of the brain,' Mr Carswall said. 'It can strike with great suddenness.'

The Ruispidge brothers said everything that was fitting about Mrs Frant's and Miss Carswall's kindness to their unfortunate cousin. Then they and the Carswalls were free to discuss the ball, and to agree how delightful it had been. Mr Carswall described several games of whist in perhaps excessive detail to an audience that dwindled to Mrs Lee dozing by the fire. Captain Ruispidge sat by Mrs Frant, and talked with her in a low voice. Sir George and Miss Carswall moved away from the group at the fire and sat beside a window. I overheard fragments of their conversation, which suggested that he was outlining to her his plans to endow a village school, to be run on strict religious principles. Miss Carswall listened to him with every appearance of delighted attention; she was not a woman who did things by halves.

A little later, Mr Carswall was shocked to discover that Lady Ruispidge intended to drive back to Clearland-court with Mrs Johnson later in the day. 'Quite apart from the inclement weather, my dear sir, what of Mrs Johnson's health?'

'She will be far better off at Clearland,' Sir George said. 'Besides, we have trespassed on your kindness long enough.'

Miss Carswall clasped her hands. 'Will you and Captain Ruispidge return with her?'

Sir George's long, bony face re-arranged itself into a smile. 'I think not. Indeed, my brother and I were hoping we might prevail on you and Mr Carswall – and Mrs Frant, of course, and Mrs Lee – to dine with us.'

'We will be just ourselves, a family party,' the Captain put in, smiling winningly at Mrs Frant. 'If you do us the honour of accepting, you need have no scruples about the propriety of it.'

Dinner was soon understood to be a remarkably elastic term: it stretched to include a shopping expedition and the inspection of Miss Carswall's property in Oxbody-lane. But none of these activities required my presence. After breakfast, Mr Carswall went to sleep and I was left without employment.

I gave myself a holiday and passed an hour or two in exploring the city. After visiting the cathedral close and the cathedral itself, I retraced our route to the Tolsey the previous evening, to the doorway of the bank where Mrs Johnson had lain; and, on the other side of the road, to the alley which had swallowed up the running man. I allowed myself to drift with the crowds, who washed me down to the forbidding walls of the County Gaol, to the workhouse, and then to the quayside, where the spars and rigging formed a tangle of black scratches on the louring winter sky.

Growing weary, in mind as well as body, I returned to Fendall House. I longed for certainty. At times it seemed to me that I could rely on nothing and no one, except perhaps on the affection of Rowsell and Dansey; and even their goodwill might evaporate if I examined it too closely or relied overmuch upon their benevolence.

I went upstairs to my room. Though there was no fire, I preferred its solitude to the warmth of the parlour and the probability of company. I had still to finish my letter to Rowsell. The windowsill had a broad ledge which I used as my desk. I had been writing for no more than five minutes when I heard a tap at the door.

'Come in,' I called.

I turned in my chair as the door opened. Mrs Frant stood hesitating on the threshold. I leapt up, upsetting the ink in my agitation and sending a spatter of black drops across the page. We looked at each other in silence. At last, and at the same moment, we burst into speech.

'I beg your pardon, Mr Shield, I –'

'Pray sit down. I'm afraid –'

We stopped. Usually in such situations, one smiles at the other person, for the simultaneous speech removes the embarrassment by giving one something to share with the other. But neither of us smiled.

It was such an unbearably squalid little room, an unworthy setting for a lady. I was aware of the unmade bed, and the stuffy atmosphere, the faint hint of cigar smoke remaining from the previous evening. Yet because of the setting, Mrs Frant's beauty blazed all the more. She was like the sun on the snow: so brilliant she seemed to illuminate herself from within; so beautiful that my eyes could hardly believe what they saw.

In a whirlwind of activity, I pushed my writing materials aside and covered them with a handkerchief. I turned the single chair and begged Mrs Frant to sit down. I remained standing. The room was so tiny, like a cabin on a ship, that I could have stretched out my arm and touched her. She looked down at her hands and then out of the window. From her chair she must have seen the window of her own room, the setting of her cousin's private performance the previous night. At the memory, I felt simultaneously ashamed and excited.

Mrs Frant turned back to me and said, 'Miss Carswall asked me to accompany them to Oxbody-lane, and so did Sir George and Captain Ruispidge.' She spoke as though answering a question, as though we had been in the middle of conversation. 'But I felt it wiser to decline.'

'I see.'

'I noticed your expression when she proposed the expedition at break-fast. Miss Carswall does not mean to be vexing, you know. She is like a child when in high spirits. She cannot see beyond her own excitement.'

'Surely it would pain you to see the inheritance Mr Wavenhoe left her, that should have been yours?'

She inclined her head. 'I am ashamed to admit it. It is merely that – oh, what is the use of complaining?'

'I should never have witnessed that codicil,' I said. 'I regret it extremely.'

'Truly, it does not signify. If it had not been you, Mr Carswall would have found someone else.'

'He is a monster!' I burst out. 'And Miss Carswall is –'

'Believe me, Miss Carswall has hardships of her own,' Mrs Frant said. 'She has suffered. I cannot condemn her.'

The silence returned. For the moment I brushed aside this new mystery concerning Miss Carswall in favour of an infinitely more urgent matter. Mrs Frant's presence in this room was quite improper, so much so that I could hardly believe the evidence of my senses. If we were discovered, the scandal would ruin us both. I should advise her to leave immediately. Yet I did not. I knew, in that part of me that was still capable of rational thought, that the very fact that she was here must mean that she needed me for a reason so overwhelming that in comparison nothing else truly mattered.

She stood up. 'I beg your pardon,' she said again, in a rush. 'I have no right –' She broke off and stared at the windowsill, at the spots of ink and the grubby handkerchief. 'I – I have caused such confusion.'

'You should not beg my pardon,' I said. 'I am glad you are come.'

She looked directly at me then. I had no words left to say. Still with her eyes on mine, she held out her hand, palm downwards, the fingers slightly curled, for all the world as though she were a great lady receiving me, and extending her hand for me to kiss.

Into my mind flooded the realisation that I had arrived at last at my Rubicon: like Caesar at his river, I could go back or I could go forwards. If I retreated, then nothing need change. If I went forward, I would move into the unknown, and all I would know for certain was that nothing would ever be the same again.

Slowly I stretched out my own hand and wrapped my fingers around hers. It was a cold day, and a cold room, but by some miracle her skin was warm. I looked at her slender fingers, not her face. I encircled her hand in both of mine. She whispered something I did not catch. I took a step forward and bowed my head.

CHAPTER FIFTY-FOUR

I T IS OF no concern to the reader why, since that day, I have kept and shall always keep the 13th of January as a private anniversary. No lips shall breathe the secret of what happened that afternoon in the cramped, whitewashed garret of the house in Westgate-street. Even the cracks in the windowpanes, the splashes of ink and the swirling brown damp stains on the ceiling shared in its perfection. It resolved nothing: it was merely perfect, merely itself.

Later that day, the rest of the party dined with the Ruispidge brothers in a private room at the Bell. They returned late, by which time I had retired, and the following morning Mr Carswall pronounced the roads safe enough for travel.

We left Gloucester under convoy of the Ruispidges in their chaise; the brothers had obligingly delayed their departure until we were ready to leave. We drove together along the toll road as far as the turning to Monkshill-park, a circumstance that greatly contributed to Mr Carswall's peace of mind.

The Ruispidges left us a mile or two from Monkshill. Mr Carswall's coach crawled up the long, curving lane running along the northern boundary of the park to Flaxern Parva. As we passed Grange Cottage, I noticed that the shutters were open, and that smoke was emerging from two of the chimneys.

'Mrs Johnson must be coming home soon,' Miss Carswall said. 'She may be back already.'

Sophie glanced at me. 'She has made a swift recovery.'

'Yes – Lady Ruispidge will be so relieved, I'm sure. And Sir George, of course.'

At last the coach entered the drive of Monkshill-park. Carswall drew out his watch and studied the dial, whistling tunelessly and noiselessly as he did so. He announced with grim satisfaction that our speed from Gloucester had been, on average, four and three-quarter miles per hour, a commendable achievement given the inclement weather.

We drew up outside the house. The boys ran to greet us. I saw with a pang of jealousy how Sophie – as I now allowed myself to think of her – seized upon Charlie as if she were starving and he a loaf of newly baked bread. Mrs Kerridge and Harmwell came out, and Sophie at once inquired after Mr Noak.

'He is much improved, ma'am, thank you,' Salutation Harmwell said in his sonorous voice.

'What are these boys doing?' cried Carswall. 'Have they run mad in our absence?'

'Oh, Papa,' said Miss Carswall. 'It is only that they are pleased to see us. Look, the dogs are acting in just the same way.'

'I cannot abide children under my feet. Besides, it is clear they want instruction in manners as well as their schoolbook. Take them away, Shield, and make them learn something. And if they will not apply themselves, use the strap.'

I said nothing. I was still in my greatcoat, and I was hungry and thirsty and cold.

'Get along, man,' roared Carswall. 'I do not pay you to stand there gawping at your boots.'

For a moment there was the sort of silence that precedes a scream, as if everyone in the hall were holding his breath. Carswall had never before spoken so rudely to me: and this was in public, in front of the boys, the servants and the ladies. In Gloucester he had spent most of his waking hours on his best behaviour, and now at last, I suppose, he could be comfortable after his own fashion: he was like a man who, when the company has gone, spits in the fireplace and breaks wind in the drawing room.

289

I would like to say that I made some grand romantic gesture: that I dashed my glove across the old tyrant's face and demanded satisfaction, or at the very least stormed out of his house, vowing I would never darken his doors again. Instead, mindful of Sophie, mindful of my precarious place in Mr Carswall's scheme of things and at Mr Bransby's school, I kept silent. I walked up the stairs. I heard the boys pounding after me.

'Come, come,' Carswall said below me. 'Why are we standing here? Pratt! Is there a fire in the library?'

I do not know whether the boys sensed my shame or my anger, but they were remarkably obliging for the rest of the afternoon. They did not whisper to each other; they construed and translated as though their lives depended on it. While they were working, I could not help thinking of Sophie, and at times I looked at Charlie and tried to trace her dear features in his face.

A little before five o'clock, I tired of this unnatural diligence, not least because I disliked the knowledge that I was the object of the boys' fear or their pity, or possibly both. I asked them what they had been doing while we had been away and the flow of their conversation soon swept away the barriers of reserve between us.

'It was like a holiday, sir,' Edgar said. 'Mr Noak kept to his bed the whole time, and there were only the servants.'

'So you ran wild?'

'Oh, no, sir,' cried Charlie. 'Well, not very often. Kerridge would not let us.'

'So she kept an eye on you?'

'She and Mr Harmwell. Did you know, he has an immense fund of stories. Ghost stories that chill the blood.'

The boys looked anything but chilled. They needed little encouragement to launch into one of Mr Harmwell's stories, a garbled tale about a pirate's treasure situated on an island off South Carolina and involving a one-legged ghost armed to the teeth with cutlass and pistols. When a ship foundered nearby, and a poor boy was cast away on the island, this amiable ghost encouraged him to find instructions written in cipher to the treasure's location. Clearly an enterprising youth, the intrepid hero

290

deciphered the code and found the treasure, which necessitated excavating a pile of skulls and digging until he discovered first the headless skeletons of a number of pirates and then the iron-bound chest containing the treasure itself.

'Guineas, doubloons, louis d'ors,' said Charlie.

'Chalices and crucifixes and watches,' said Edgar.

'And what did the boy do with all this?' I inquired.

'Why, sir,' Charlie said, 'Harmwell told us that he bought a great estate and married a wife and had many children and lived happily ever after.'

'He only said it to please Mrs Kerridge,' Edgar explained.

'So she was there too?'

'She was nearly always there when Mr Harmwell was.' Charlie paused before adding in a matter-of-fact voice, as though it was so obvious it hardly needed saying, 'I believe they are courting.'

Edgar said, 'You can always tell when people are spoony upon each other.'

'Yes,' Charlie agreed. 'You can.'

I glanced at the boys and wondered if there was more to this remark than there seemed.

'Oh,' Charlie went on. 'How I wish I was rich like the boy in the story.'

I wished I were rich, too. As the evening continued, I wished it more and more. I went down to dinner and found that Mr Noak was still not well enough to leave his room, which was perhaps the reason I had been summoned to dine with the family. The meal was a quiet, sad affair, with the five of us occupied with our thoughts. Afterwards, in the drawing room, I tried very hard to get Sophie to talk to me. But she slipped away from me and a moment later announced to everyone that she had a headache and would retire early.

Perhaps the sight of Charlie had reminded her what was important, and what was not. In any event, I thought I read in her silent, unsmiling face the blunt and unwanted truth that she now regretted what had occurred, and disliked me for the part I had played.

CHAPTER FIFTY-FIVE

THE FOLLOWING DAY, Saturday the 15th January, was very cold, but there was no more snow. After lessons, I took the boys for a long walk in the park. They wished to visit the ruins again, for Harmwell's story had given them the notion that they might find the monastic treasure if they succeeded in enlisting the assistance of a benevolent ghost.

'If a monk was burnt at the stake,' Edgar said with the callousness of youth, 'he would naturally linger upon the earth, chained to the scene of his torment.'

'But why should he tell you where the treasure is?' I asked. 'If there is any treasure.'

'Because we shall treat him with benevolence,' Edgar explained. 'Even though he is a Papist. After all, it was not his fault, not in those days.'

'He will be so gratified by our kindness, after hundreds of years of solitude and persecution, that he will wish to do anything in his power to help us,' Charlie said. 'And he will not mind us having the treasure. Why should he? What use is it to him now?'

That at least was unanswerable. While the boys searched the ruins yet again, I walked to and fro, staring down at the roofs of Grange Cottage. A man on a skinny skewbald mare was picking his way up the lane from the turnpike road.

'If he didn't put the treasure here,' Edgar said, 'he must have put it where the ice-house is. That was probably the site of the crypt or hermitage or –'

'You must not search in there,' I said. 'The ice-house is dangerous and unhealthy.'

'Besides,' Charlie pointed out in the smug voice of reason, 'we can't. It's locked.'

When at last we returned to the house, we discovered that Sir George Ruispidge had called. He was closeted with Mr Carswall. The boys and I joined the three ladies in the small sitting room. Miss Carswall was unusually quiet. She applied herself to her account book, in which she was entering her purchases at Gloucester.

'Sir George has brought a letter from Mrs Johnson,' Mrs Lee said to no one in particular. 'He and his brother are so attentive to their unfortunate cousin. He called on her earlier today – did you know she is back at Grange Cottage? – and I'm sure she wished to write in order to express her gratitude for the way Mrs Frant and Miss Carswall nursed her so devotedly during her illness.'

Sophie got up and left the room.

Mrs Lee continued speaking in a loud whisper, directing her conversation to Miss Carswall: 'Poor Mrs Johnson! She was never quite the same after a certain gentleman went away. She used to be so high-spirited. Wilful, almost. I remember Lady Ruispidge telling me that Mrs Johnson was more headstrong than her sons.'

'I cannot think Sir George was ever headstrong, ma'am,' Miss Carswall said. 'Was not he too good?'

'What? Sir George is good? Oh, indeed. Even as a boy, his thoughts were often on higher things. I'm sure he was beaten less than his brother.'

Pratt came into the room, and Miss Carswall jerked like a fish on the end of a line. Mr Carswall asked if it would be convenient for her to join them in the library. She leapt up, and flew to the mirror where she peered anxiously into her eyes and patted her curls. She glanced round the room, at me, Mrs Lee, the boys, though I doubt if she saw any of us. Then she was gone.

A moment later, Mr Carswall himself came in. He glared impartially at us, as if to ask us what we did there, and began to pace up and down, humming discordantly. No one dared to speak to him. I murmured to the boys that we should return upstairs to our books, and they followed me with remarkable willingness. I do not think Mr Carswall noticed our departure.

Upstairs, Charlie burst out: 'So what is afoot?'

'I know what I think,' Edgar said slowly.

The boys exchanged smiles.

'That is enough,' I said. 'We will return to Euclid, and you may keep your thoughts to yourselves.'

And return we did, though without much profit to any of us. After a while we heard a horse on the drive. I strolled over to the window and looked out. There was Sir George riding away.

Soon afterwards, when we gathered in the drawing room before going into dinner, Miss Carswall's face made all as plain as day. It was as if she had lit a candle inside her. Carswall himself was, in his own way, equally elated.

The news would not keep. 'You must give me joy, Cousin,' Miss Carswall burst out, rushing up to Sophie. 'I am to be married.'

'Sir George has offered?'

'Yes, my love, and everything has been done as it should. He talked to Papa first, and asked if he might pay his addresses. And then Papa called me in, and he left us alone.'

It is at this point in novels that young ladies blush. Miss Carswall did not blush. She looked like the cat who has licked the cream.

Sophie embraced her. 'Oh, my dear, I do indeed give you joy. I hope you will be very happy.'

'He would not dine with us,' Mr Carswall put in. 'He would have liked to, of course, but he felt obliged to ride back to Clearland and inform Lady Ruispidge of what had passed. Very proper, I'm sure; I should expect no less of him.'

We went into dinner, where the presence of servants inhibited conversation. The engagement was not to be announced until Lady Ruispidge had been told. No doubt the servants knew, because servants always do, but neither we nor they could admit it. This left Miss Carswall and her father in a sort of purgatory because they so desperately wanted to talk about the subject. When the ladies had left, and the cloth had been withdrawn, Mr Carswall crooked his finger at me. Mr Noak had not come down to dinner and the servants were gone, so only the two of us were in the room.

'Stay and take a glass of wine with me, Shield.'

I returned slowly to my chair, hardly caring whether my reluctance showed.

'Now the servants with their long ears are out of the way we shall drink a toast,' he said, seemingly oblivious to my distaste for him. 'A bumper, mind, I'll have no damned heeltaps tonight. To my little Flora, God bless her: to the future Lady Ruispidge.'

I drank the toast and then we drank another to Sir George.

'Carswall Ruispidge,' the old man murmured. 'Sir Carswall Ruispidge, Baronet. It has a fine sound, does it not? Sir George assures me that if the union is blessed – and why should it not be, for both parties come of sound English stock? – *when* the union is blessed, I say, their eldest boy shall be called Carswall. That is handsome, eh? It is a pleasure to deal with a gentleman, Shield. I tell you plainly: I shall have no more to do with scrubs. I give you another toast: to Carswall Ruispidge, may God bless him. Come, recharge your glass.'

Whatever mood possessed him, Carswall lived it to the full. There were more toasts, more bumpers. I fancy he was already more than a little cut before we sat down to table. In under an hour, he was slumped in his chair, his eyes glistening with moisture and his waistcoat spotted with wine. I confess I was a trifle the worse for wear myself, for Carswall had urged me to drink glass for glass with him, and a dark, despairing mood had possessed me since I had been alone with him. I drank in the hope of forgetting all that I desired and would never have.

'When will the marriage take place, sir?' I inquired.

'Sir George and I have settled on June. That will give the lawyers time to tie up everything as tight as need be. Then I shall give away my little Flora.' He grunted and stared at the fire. 'Ready money, my boy, that's the secret. As I told you before, the man with ready money is king. He may purchase anything he wishes.'

I understood his meaning, though he would never put it into words, perhaps even to himself. His money had wiped away the stain of his daughter's bastardy. It had made a titled gentleman overlook Mr Carswall's lack of gentility. And, best of all, it had bought him the prospect of a vicarious immortality in the persons of his unborn grandson and all the little Carswall Ruispidges that might descend from him and lord it over all and sundry.

The old man took out his watch but did not open it. He pressed the button and the repeater emitted its tiny chime.

'Has one of the servants blabbed about my grandfather?' he said. 'Before he went to London, he was clerk to the steward of Monkshill when old Mr Frant had the estate. I came here once as a boy, and watched the fine gentry through the trees by the lake.' Carswall tapped the watch's case, yawned and added in a gloating, childish whisper: 'But who is master now, eh? Tell me that: who is master now?'

CHAPTER FIFTY-SIX

SOPHIE WAS BY herself in the drawing room, her face golden in the light of the candles. I looked away, wishing I were a little less elevated.

'Will you take tea?' she said. 'And shall I set a cup for Mr Carswall?'

'I do not think he will be joining us.' My voice emerged more loudly than I had anticipated, and I enunciated my next words with particular care. 'Have Mrs Lee and Miss Carswall retired?'

'They are in the library. Mrs Lee recollected seeing a volume containing views of Clearland-court. They have been longer at it than I expected.'

I said that it was not to be wondered at that Miss Carswall wished to dwell upon the scenes of her future felicity. I took my cup of tea and sat on the sofa to drink it. The room was huge and chilly, built for show not comfort. The brief excitement of the wine receded, leaving me still in low spirits, yet still a long way from sobriety. Sophie's silence unnerved me. There were no forms, no rules of conduct, to guide us in our present position. Dear God, how I would have liked to kneel by her and lay my aching head on her lap. The cup and saucer rattled as I set them down.

'Sophie.'

She stared at me, her face stern, even shocked, as if what had happened yesterday meant nothing, or was merely a figment of my imagination.

'I have to know,' I said. 'What happened means everything to me.'

'You are not yourself, sir.'

'I wish to marry you.'

She shook her head and said in a voice so low I had to strain to hear: 'It is not possible, Mr Shield. I have to think of Charlie. What is past is past. I regret it immensely, but I am afraid I must ask you never to raise this subject again.'

Miss Carswall's voice was audible in the hall, addressing Mrs Lee. 'The west wing is altogether too mean for a house like Clearland. It will have to be rebuilt. I shall talk to Sir George, by and by.'

So, as the ladies drank tea and chattered about Clearland-court, I knew I was justly repaid for both my presumption and my mendacity. First the presumption: it was one thing for a lady like Sophia Frant to forget herself for an hour or two on a winter afternoon, and quite another for her to marry an apothecary's son who eked out a living at a private school. Nor was this the end of my bitter reflections on this head. Sophie's richly deserved refusal of my offer had re-awoken my jealousy of Captain Ruispidge, and granted it a double force.

Then the mendacity: I had not been honest with her about so many things, not least my suspicion that Mr Henry Frant might still be in the land of the living; that he was a murderer as well as an embezzler; and that for all we knew to the contrary he was within a few miles of us. So great was my desire for her that I had urged the innocent Sophie unwittingly to run the risk of committing bigamy, a crime in the eyes of both God and man.

Oh yes, I was justly served. Even I realised that.

The following day was Sunday, and we drove to Flaxern Parva for divine service. Mr Noak and Mr Carswall did not feel equal to the journey and kept each other company by the library fire. The Ruispidge brothers were in church, but not the ladies. Though we sat in separate pews, afterwards I had ample opportunity to watch Miss Carswall and Sir George, Sophie and the Captain, billing and cooing again.

In the coach on the way back, Miss Carswall said, 'Poor Mrs Johnson!'

'She is unwell, I collect?' Sophie said.

'Sir George says she has quinsy. Her throat is so swollen she can hardly speak. She had hoped to be well enough to call upon us within a day or two, Sir George said, but must beg to be excused until she is better. The servant has orders to admit no one.'

The coach rumbled on, the horses slipping and the machine swaying dangerously as we bounced in and out of the ice-caked ruts of the road. Miss Carswall said, 'Thank heavens Papa is not with us. Can you imagine?' No one replied, and no one spoke for the remainder of the journey.

All that day, Sophie avoided my company. When circumstances threw us together, she would not meet my eyes. I snapped at the boys and was surly with the servants. It is all very well to say one should bear misfortune with philosophy, but in my experience when misfortune comes in by one door, philosophy leaves by the other.

CHAPTER FIFTY-SEVEN

THE WEATHER WAS still fine on Monday morning. After lessons, the boys begged me to take them down to the lake with their skates. On our way, we met Mr Harmwell and Mrs Kerridge returning to the house.

'Skating?' Mrs Kerridge said. 'Enjoy it while you can.'

'Why?' Charlie asked. 'Is there to be a thaw?'

'It's not that. The men are cleaning out the ice-house. Once they start filling it, there'll be no more skating for a while.'

'To my mind,' Harmwell said, 'it is a most insanitary arrangement.'

Mrs Kerridge turned to him. 'Why ever so, sir?'

'The problem here derives from the fact that the lake serves many purposes – it is not only ornamental, but a source of fish, and used for skating in winter and boating and swimming in summer. I understand from the head gardener that it is nigh on eighteen feet deep near the centre. This makes the ice hard to extract, and indeed dangerous for those charged with the task. And the quality of the ice is inevitably poor, bearing in mind the culinary uses it is intended for. It often contains rotting vegetation, for example, and the corpses of small animals. No, I believe the Dutch method –'

'Lord, Mr Harmwell,' Mrs Kerridge broke in. 'You talk just like a book.'

'What about the ice?' I asked. 'Will they start cutting it today?'

'I believe not,' he said. 'So I cannot see that there will be any objection to your skating. While you can.' He raised his stick and pointed towards the south-western quarter of the sky, where clouds were massing. 'There may be snow on the way.'

We parted. The boys raced ahead. When I reached the lake, they were not in sight. I took the path round the bank to the defile leading to the ice-house. Edgar and Charlie were perched on the trunk of a fallen tree. Half a dozen men were engaged in emptying and cleaning the building. For a few moments we watched them carrying buckets of ice and muddy straw down the path to a hollow where they discharged their noisome burdens.

The foreman touched his hat and asked if we would like to see the scene of their operations. I followed him down the passage, with the boys behind me. The chamber was illuminated by half a dozen lanterns strung round the dome. Two men were working in the pit itself, shovelling the slush into buckets. As we watched, one neatly decapitated a rat with the blade of the shovel.

'It stinks worse than usual, sir,' the foreman said. 'The drain was blocked.'

I looked over the edge. 'It looks clear now.'

'We rodded it, and it's draining slowly. But not like it should. If we can't clear it properly from this side, we may have to wait till spring.'

'How so?'

He jerked his thumb outside. 'The water runs into a sump and then flows through a drain to the lake. But it blocks easy on account of the grids that keep the rats out. There's a shaft down to the drain so you can clear it. Big drain, look, you can crawl right up to the sump chamber. But we had a terrible storm in the autumn, and them trees came down, and half the bank besides. We'll need to dig out the head of the shaft all over again.'

'The ground's too hard at present?'

'Aye. Like iron.' He spat, narrowly missing one of his men, and squinted up at me. 'We should have dug it out earlier.'

I returned outside and filled my lungs with fresh air. The boys were talking with another of the workmen and jigging up and down with cold and excitement. As I approached, they fell silent. These signs should have made me wary; but I was too taken up with my own thoughts to pay them the attention they deserved. A moment later, we walked back to the lake, where the boys skated slowly up and down, conferring privately together.

That afternoon, my spirits were at a low ebb, and I came close to despair. I reasoned with myself, saying that it was the height of folly that I should entertain any hopes with regard to Sophie; reminding myself that what had happened in Gloucester was exceptional, something that would never occur again; and advising myself to put it and her completely out of my mind.

Mr Carswall called me down to the library to take dictation and make copies. He was writing yet another letter to one of his lawyers, this time concerning the negotiations over the possible sale of his Liverpool warehouses to Mr Noak. I understood from the tenor of the correspondence that Mr Noak's London lawyer had raised a number of questions with Mr Carswall's man. The work was mechanical, leaving my mind prey to a succession of gloomy thoughts.

Yet, looking back on those few hours on Monday afternoon, as the sky grew steadily darker in the south-west, I now see the time for what it truly was: the calm before the storm that was about to break over our heads. With hindsight, I can fix the exact moment when I saw the storm's harbinger approaching.

There had come a pause in the harsh, stumbling torrent of Mr Carswall's words, and I was staring out of the library window. A movement caught my eye in the gathering twilight. Riding up the drive was a solitary horseman.

CHAPTER FIFTY-EIGHT

CAPTAIN RUISPIDGE WAS shown into the library, not into the small sitting room where the ladies were. I stood silently by the window while he and Mr Carswall exchanged greetings. When they had established that their families were well, and that further falls of snow were likely, the Captain begged the favour of a few words in private.

Carswall opened his eyes very wide. 'You may leave us, Shield,' he said without looking at me. 'Do not go far; I may want you again. Wait in the hall.'

So I kicked my heels by the fire in the hall, watched with barely concealed insolence by the thin-faced footman. Few sounds penetrated the heavy door of the library. Occasionally there was an indistinct murmur of voices, and once the bray of Carswall's laugh.

In about ten minutes, Captain Ruispidge emerged, and the upper rims of his ears were pink. He did not wait to pay his respects to the ladies, but called at once for his horse. His eyes settled on me.

'Why are you standing there?' he demanded. 'What are you staring at?'

'Mr Carswall told me to wait.'

His lip curled. All his affability had vanished. Without another word, he pulled on his greatcoat and, despite the cold, went outside to wait for his horse to be brought round.

Carswall called me back into the library. He did not mention his recent interview, and we continued with the letter. As I wrote, it grew darker and darker, and at last Carswall called for candles. Since Captain Ruispidge's visit, he had been restless, finding it hard to settle either to the letter or in his chair. In the intervals between spates of dictation, I sometimes saw his lips moving, as though he were talking silently to another, or to himself.

When the first flakes of snow began to fall, Carswall said we had done enough for the day and told me to ring the bell for the footman. As I was gathering together my writing materials, I heard him ordering Pratt to close the shutters and then to step across to the ladies' sitting room and desire Mrs Frant to wait upon him. I had no wish to see Sophie unnecessarily – it would only distress her, and add to my humiliation – so I hurried away.

Later that day, when I came down to dinner, I found the drawing room empty apart from Miss Carswall, who was sitting at a table and leafing through *Domestic Cookery*. She looked up as I entered and gave me the full force of her smile.

'Mr Shield – I am so glad you are come. I was beginning to feel I had been abandoned on a desert island and would never again hear the sound of another human voice.'

I looked at the clock on the mantel. 'I am surprised that no one else is down.'

'Papa has put back the time of dinner by a quarter of an hour. It appears that we are the last to hear.' The smile flashed out again. 'Still, we must keep each other company. You will not mind?'

'On the contrary.' I returned the smile, for it was hard to resist Miss Carswall in this mood. 'It will be no hardship, at least for me.'

'You are too kind, sir. Pray sit down and amuse me. I am afraid we shall be very dull this evening.'

I sat down. 'Why so?'

She leaned close to me, so I smelled her perfume and sensed her warmth. 'You have not heard? Captain Ruispidge came to call on Papa. I thought the whole house knew.'

'I was aware that the Captain was here. I was with Mr Carswall in the library when he was announced.'

'Ah – but do you know why he came?'

I shook my head.

Miss Carswall brought her head a little closer still and lowered her voice. 'If I do not tell you, someone else will. He wanted to ask Sophie's hand in marriage.'

A chill stole over me. I moved away from Miss Carswall and stared at her.

'Surely you expected it?' she said. 'I know I did. You must have seen what was in the wind. He was making up to her while Sir George – oh, it is so provoking. I would have liked Sophie as my sister above anything. It would have been such a suitable match for them both.'

'So Mrs Frant did not accept him?'

'She never had the opportunity.'

'I do not quite understand.'

'In the event he did not offer for her.'

I tried to smile, and nodded.

'He is much taken with Sophie,' Miss Carswall continued, with her soft brown eyes fixed on my face, 'as who could not be, but he is a younger son and he cannot afford a penniless wife, particularly one already encumbered with a son. And, though Sophie's family is perfectly respectable, there is the delicate matter of the late Mr Frant. Even if she remarried, Sophie would not necessarily be received everywhere.'

So now the Captain's behaviour in the hall was explained. It had been the petulance of a disappointed man.

'But if he truly loved her, would that matter?'

'I find you are a romantic at heart.' She smiled at me. 'I suppose Captain Jack felt he deserved something in return for his sacrifice. Love in a cottage is all very well, Mr Shield, but it don't pay the bills.'

'I suppose Captain Ruispidge had hoped that Mr Carswall would settle something on her?'

'I believe so. But Papa declined, though of course with great regret. Poor Sophie. I have been quite cast down since she told me, and of course her spirits are even lower.'

I said, 'Though Mr Carswall has given Mrs Frant the shelter of his roof, he is not obliged to provide for her.'

305

'No: but it is not merely a matter of money. When Sir George and I are married, Papa will need someone to keep him company in the evenings. He abhors solitude. If Sophie went as well, he would be quite alone.'

Miss Carswall gave me a cool, intelligent stare. There was nothing flirtatious about her now. She was about to say more when we heard footsteps in the hall and the door opened. Monkshill-park was a place of interrupted conversations, a place where nothing could ever be satisfactorily concluded.

CHAPTER FIFTY-NINE

THERE WERE SIX of us at table that day, for Mr Noak came down to dinner. He was mending fast, he said, and hoped to trespass on Mr Carswall's hospitality no further than the end of the week. In return, his host huffed and puffed and protested that he would be delighted if Mr Noak would stay for ever.

It was a dreary meal. Noak was not a man who habitually volunteered conversation. Carswall appeared anxious and unwontedly humble, which made me wonder whether the negotiations over the sale of the Liverpool property were not going as smoothly as he had hoped. I knew from the correspondence I had copied that something was afoot, but it was difficult to ascertain precisely what.

Miss Carswall picked at her food and complained of the headache. Mrs Lee said little but ate much. Sophie stared at her plate and seldom opened her mouth. The loss of her suitor must have hit her very hard. I had suspected that she had a tenderness for Captain Ruispidge but I had not known that her affections were so deeply engaged. It was a bitter pill for me to swallow.

As dinner went on, Carswall drank more and talked less, until by the time the ladies left us, he had lapsed into a surly silence. However, when the three of us who remained had drawn our chairs closer to the fire, he turned to Mr Noak and made a palpable effort to be civil. I soon realised that there was a purpose to this. Mr Carswall hoped to complete his Liverpool transaction before Mr Noak's departure. He talked about the advantages that derived from doing business face to face, rather than at a remove, and through intermediaries. He hinted at a willingness to lower his price a trifle in return for a speedy completion. It was a fine thing for Miss Carswall to marry a baronet with a splendid rent-roll, as well as considerable income from his coal mines, but the matrimonial alliance of two fortunes always entailed a great deal of business. The matter of settlements was on his mind.

Noak listened to all this, nodding occasionally, and taking very small sips of wine. Carswall encouraged him to drink toast after toast, but Noak pleaded his health and said that a mouthful of wine must stand for a bumper. Indeed, he did not look well. Though Mr Carswall's vein of persuasion showed no sign of nearing exhaustion, Mr Noak begged to be excused and said he required an early night.

All this conversation between them, much of it tolerably private in nature, was carried on without the slightest notice being taken of me. To Mr Carswall, I was a man whose services he had hired, and therefore no more expected to be the possessor of feelings than the horses who drew his chaise or the chair he sat upon or the kitchen maid who peeled his vegetables. While they talked, I was alone with my own thoughts, which followed an uneasy, even guilty course.

After Mr Noak's departure, Mr Carswall and I joined the ladies in the Arctic waste of the drawing room. Sophie was reading in a corner a little apart from the rest. Mrs Lee poured our tea. Miss Carswall asked me to play backgammon. We drew up a table, set the board and played two games in a companionable silence. I was grateful for the diversion.

Mrs Lee began to snore in her chair by the fire.

Halfway through the third game, Sophie retired. With unusual gallantry, Mr Carswall stood up and opened the door for her. He followed her from the room.

'Your turn,' Miss Carswall said.

The dice rattled on the board. I raised my hand, ready to move a piece that would take one of Miss Carswall's, knowing that the game was now as good as mine. I looked up at her and found her looking at me while her hand played with an auburn ringlet. The tip of her tongue appeared for an instant between her lips and was then withdrawn. She teased the lock of hair between her fingers and my mind filled with the shameful recollection of her brushing her red hair in her nightgown; and I knew she wanted to remind me of how she had played the wanton as she stood by the window in Fendall House.

At that moment, there came a scream.

All trace of flirtation fled from Miss Carswall's face, and I saw mirrored in her expression the shock I myself was feeling. I pushed back the gilt chair with such force that it fell over. Mrs Lee stirred; her snoring faltered and then resumed its placid rhythm. I ran to the door and wrenched it open.

In the hall, Stephen Carswall loomed like a dishevelled bear over Sophie. His arm was around her waist and his head bent towards hers.

'Just one,' Carswall said in a slurred voice. 'Just one for now, my pretty.'

Sophie saw me and her face changed. Even as he spoke, Carswall was turning away from her. I bounded towards him and seized his collar and his arm. I wrenched at him, but he would not loose his hold. His face darkened, becoming so deep a purple it seemed almost black.

'You damned blackguard,' he roared at me. 'Can you not see what I was doing? Mrs Frant had a coughing fit, and would have choked if I had not slapped her back.'

His words were so preposterous that they reduced me momentarily to silence. My hands fell away from him. He released Sophie, who opened her mouth as if to say something – her colour was high, and she was breathing fast. Carswall swung back to her.

'Ain't that true, my dear? Now I mustn't prevent you from saying goodnight to Charlie. Dear little Charlie, eh? He will be waiting.'

The implied threat was unmistakable. Sophie's eyes widened. Without a word, she turned and ran up the stairs.

'I beg your pardon, sir,' I said quickly. 'I heard a cry and thought – I thought you might be unwell.'

Breathing heavily, he glared at me. 'And now, Mr Tutor, you and I have something to discuss.'

Over his shoulder I glimpsed Miss Carswall closing the drawing-room door. How much had she seen or heard? I followed Mr Carswall into the library, where he flung himself into the armchair by the fire. He was as drunk as ever but now his lust had been replaced by a cold, calculated anger. He waved me to stand before him like a miscreant before a judge.

'I'll not have my servants placing their grubby little hands on me,' he said. 'You overreach yourself. I am your master. Do you hear? Your *master*.'

I abandoned all thought of preserving the decencies with a placatory lie. 'You were not acting as a gentleman should.'

'You presume to teach me my duty?' Carswall said. 'I will not have it, sir, do you hear?' He glared at me, chewing his lips. 'If it were not for the scandal, I would bring an action for assault against you. Unfortunately, such a course would distress the ladies still further, and you have distressed them quite enough this evening. But you will leave this house tomorrow morning, Shield, is that clear?'

'With Edgar?'

'No!' he roared. 'Do you think I would trust Mr Allan's son to you after this? When I write to Mr Bransby, I shall tell him how much your general conduct at Monkshill has left to be desired. I have been concerned about this for some time.'

I said nothing. What can one say to a tyrant?

'A groom will take you to Gloucester. I shall give orders that you are not to be admitted again to any house of mine. If you attempt it, I shall have them set the dogs on you.'

I walked slowly to the door.

'Stay – I have not given you leave to go.'

I turned back to him. I was shaking with rage, but I knew I must not allow myself to lash out, for Sophie's sake as well as my own. I had seen the results of a hasty blow or a hasty word too often before: I remembered the recruiting sergeant, with the bumper of brandy in one hand and the King's shilling in the other; I saw the Waterloo Medal gleaming and twisting in the air just before it hit the cheek of the officer in the Park. Perhaps I had learned something after all.

'If I am no longer in your employ, sir, I do not have to wait for you to give me leave.' I bowed. 'I wish you goodnight.'

CHAPTER SIXTY

AS I PACKED my few belongings that evening, the reflections that filled my mind were bitter indeed. I could not for the life of me see how else I could have acted. How could I have stood by while Carswall mauled Sophie? But what had I achieved by my intervention?

There was a tap on the door. Pratt poked his sharp little face into the room and told me that a groom would be waiting with the dog-cart at eight o'clock sharp in the morning. The footman's expression was a mixture of sly excitement and glee, and I knew at once that he had heard the news of my disgrace. You cannot keep secrets for long in a house like Monkshill-park.

When Pratt had gone, I flung open my window. Snowflakes drifted out of the darkness. I had been expelled from Monkshill; I had almost certainly lost my position at Mr Bransby's; and once Miss Carswall was married, Sophie would be at Mr Carswall's mercy – I knew all these things but my emotions were too numb to feel them. I draped a blanket over my shoulders, lit a cigar and leaned on the sill to smoke it. Hardly a moment had passed before I heard another tap on my door. Cigar in hand, I opened it and to my consternation saw Sophie herself outside. I retreated in confusion.

'Sophie,' I said, flinging the smouldering butt from the window. 'Sophie, my dear, you should not –'

She cut me off with a wave of her hand. Her face was very pale, and her eyes were huge. She wore a cloak which covered her from neck to ankles. 'The boys,' she said in an urgent whisper. 'Have you seen them?'

'Surely they're in bed?'

'They were. But I looked in a few minutes ago and found them gone. Kerridge and Harmwell are searching the house, but I think they must be outside, for they have taken their coats and hats, as well as their boots.' She pressed her hand against her bosom, as if to calm the beating of her heart. 'The dogs are out.'

'The mastiffs are well acquainted with them – Charlie has made pets of them – they will not harm the boys, I'll take my oath on it. Who else knows they are gone?'

'Most of the servants are already in bed. I tried to tell Mr Carswall but he is – he is asleep in the library. Kerridge was in my room waiting to undress me, and fortunately she knew that Mr Harmwell was still reading in the servants' hall.'

I nodded. 'Depend upon it, the boys are engaged on some prank or other. I am sure they are safe.'

'You are not their mother, Tom.' She turned her face away from me. 'Oh, where can they be?'

'Stay – if they're not in the house, I have an idea where they might have gone.'

She looked up at me, her face alive with hope.

'You have heard about the monk and the treasure?'

'What?'

'The boys have woven a story around the ruins. They pretend that when the abbey was dissolved, one of the Flaxern monks buried the monastery's treasure in the park. They have been searching for it.'

'But that is just a childish game.'

'Of course it is. But both boys have a lively fancy and I believe the game has become almost real to them. Indeed, they may sometimes forget the distinction between fiction and truth. Part of their story is that the monk who hid the treasure is now a ghost, and if you find him and talk to him the right way, he will show you where the treasure is.'

'It is quite absurd.'

'Not to them.'

'But they cannot have gone down to the ruins on a night like this,' she protested, clinging to the door for support. 'It is as black as pitch and still snowing.'

'That would not necessarily deter two high-spirited boys. If they are not in the house, then the next place to look would be the ruins and the ice-house.'

'The ice-house? Where is that?'

'Tucked into the side of the hill near the lake. The boys think it a highly suitable location for treasure. I will visit it directly, and if they're not there go on down to the ruins.'

'Harmwell shall go with you.'

'Very well. I will meet him by the door to the terrace.'

'Kerridge and I will accompany you.'

'It will be better if you stay at the house,' I said quickly. 'They may still be here. Or they may return by a different path.'

Sophie slipped away to make the necessary arrangements. It did not take me long to find my outdoor clothes and go downstairs. Mrs Kerridge and Sophie arrived, followed in a moment by Harmwell, who was carrying two lanterns. Sophie pressed a flask of brandy into my hand, and Mrs Kerridge had brought a spare cloak.

'If I know boys,' she said, 'one or both of them will have found a way of getting theirselves wet.'

Harmwell and I slipped out on to the terrace. It was still snowing, though not as heavily as before. Nevertheless there were two or three inches on the ground, and more where the wind had blown it up into drifts: virgin snow, white and crisp, the very devil to walk through when you were in a hurry.

Not only was it dark, but the snow had covered the path and obliterated many familiar landmarks. We made our way round the corner of the house to the path leading to the lake. Harmwell discovered what might have been small footprints; but they had been blurred to the point of ambiguity by subsequent falls of snow.

In silence, we plodded along in the shelter of the wall of the kitchen gardens. It was not long before we stumbled, quite literally, on our first unwelcome discovery. There, lying near the doorway where Edgar and Charlie had prepared their ambuscade for me on a cold, clear afternoon, was a shadow, black against the snow.

Harmwell swore. We stooped over what proved to be the body of one of the mastiffs. I bent down to examine him as well as I could, for the great dog was so heavy that it was impossible to move him. I ascertained only that he was dead and that there was no obvious mark on him, only dribbles of what looked like foam or vomit around his mouth and on the snow where he lay.

My companion grunted. 'Poison?'

The discovery put a new complexion on the night's adventure. We hurried on as fast as we could. We found no trace of the other mastiff, alive or dead. Every now and then, we called the boys' names. At least we knew we were on the right track for we found clearer traces of their footsteps. The going was hard enough for two grown men: what must it be like for the boys? My mind ran ahead: if we could not find them, we would have to rouse the household and organise a party to search the park. Without shelter, they might well freeze to death.

We reached the obelisk, the hub of the paths in the northern part of the park. A little beyond it, the spreading branches of a Spanish chestnut had protected the ground beneath it from much of the snow. Lantern in hand, Harmwell crouched and took a few lurching steps sideways like an ungainly crab.

'What the devil are you doing?' I said between chattering teeth.

'Look –' He angled the beam so it fell on a particular spot on the ground. 'You see?'

I squatted beside him. In the light covering of snow was a perfectly formed small footprint. Harmwell moved the lantern a fraction and the beam shifted to reveal another.

'How should we interpret them?' I asked. 'The lake or the ruins?'

'The lake, I think. They were going west, not east.'

'To the ice-house?'

'Perhaps.' He began to walk on. 'It was an evil day I mentioned the word treasure.'

'There is nothing to reproach yourself for, Mr Harmwell. They started on about treasure as soon as they saw the monastery ruins, and that was long before you and Mr Noak arrived.'

'I made it worse.'

'Nonsense. You cannot prevent boys from being boys.'

We walked in silence until we came to the shores of the lake. Here Harmwell crouched again and began his crab-like examination of the ground.

'Yes – I have them.'

'Coming or going?'

He straightened up. 'I cannot be sure. But I do not think they have returned. If we are lucky we will not be far behind.'

We had not gone further than a few yards along the path when a strange sound came out of the darkness. Though deadened by the snow, it was unmistakably metallic in nature. I judged its source to be perhaps a quarter of a mile away from us. Such was the silence, however, that it was perfectly audible.

'The door of the ice-house?' I said to my companion. 'Or perhaps a spade or a pickaxe?'

'I think not, Mr Shield.' Harmwell's face was invisible, and his deep voice came at me out of the darkness and appeared to be part of it. 'I believe it may have been the sound the jaws of a mantrap make when they meet.'

'My God! The boys!'

'I doubt it. Why should they have gone into the woods?'

'But we cannot be sure they did not.'

Harmwell said matter-of-factly, 'They had no reason to. Besides, if a living creature had been caught in a mantrap, man or beast, we should almost certainly have heard the screams.'

He strode tirelessly forward with long gliding steps, his legs slightly bent at the knee. I staggered after him, thinking of reasons why a boy in a mantrap might not scream: he had fainted from the pain, he had lost his voice, he was dead. The image of the mantrap filled my mind until it became an emblem of all that was cold, ruthless and inhumane, all that preyed on the weak, the poor and the unfortunate. The snow slackened and at last dwindled to the occasional flake. To the east a few stars appeared over the lake, though most of the sky remained cloudy.

'How did you know it was a mantrap?' I asked in a trembling voice.

'When one is habituated to it, the clang it produces is quite distinctive.'

'You speak with the experience of the hunter?'

He left a pause before he replied, 'And of the hunted.'

We came at length to the mouth of the defile leading to the ice-house. Our progress became slower and slower. The ground was strewn with the consequences of the autumn gales, pieces of rock, uprooted trees, and branches, all disguised by the snow and blanketed further by the darkness. Nor was there as much shelter here as I had expected, for the wind had changed direction during the evening and was now blowing across the lake and up towards the ice-house. With the wind had come the snow.

A few paces ahead of me, Harmwell crouched and again examined the ground. 'Someone else has been here recently,' he said over his shoulder. 'Perhaps more than one.'

I brought my mouth so close to his ear I felt the coldness of his skin. 'You do not mean the boys?'

'Grown men, I think. But I cannot be sure, not in this light – the tracks are confused.'

We hurried up the path until at last we came to the ice-house. The double doors stood wide.

'They are here!' I cried.

'It does not follow,' Harmwell said. 'The place was left open. The workmen desired to air the place overnight.'

'But someone has been here,' I said. 'Look at the snow in the doorway.'

As I spoke, we stepped into the passage. The familiar stench of decay, less powerful than before, swept out to meet us. Harmwell pushed roughly past and, holding his lantern high, preceded me towards the chamber. I pulled my muffler over my nose and mouth and followed.

The inner doors were open. We looked into the black depths of the pit. The light from the lanterns, feeble though it was, flowed like water into the darkness below.

'Oh God,' I murmured. 'Oh dear God.'

Harmwell clicked his tongue against the roof of his mouth. 'Who is it?' he said.

I did not answer. Lying on the floor of the pit was the body of a man, face-down, his head obscured by a hat. He wore a long dark coat with a high collar. His arms were outstretched, and his body was embedded in the thin layer of dirty straw and slush.

'Who is it?' said Harmwell again, and there was a thrill of urgency in his voice. 'For Christ's sake, man, who is it?'

CHAPTER SIXTY-ONE

THERE ARE MEMORIES that haunt the mind like ghosts: some benign, some not, but in either case one cannot avoid them, one cannot pretend they do not exist. So, though I do not care to dwell on what happened next, I shall set it down here, in its proper place.

First, the light. The only source of illumination, of course, was from our lanterns. A faint, murky radiance filled the chamber, as unsettling as marsh gas, making the very air seem solid and unwholesome. The stones, the brickwork, the slush on the floor, the thing that lay in the bottom of the pit – everything glistened with drops of moisture that reflected back what little light there was.

I glanced at Harmwell, who was holding the jamb of the door with one hand and staring down at the body. I fancied there was a clammy sheen on his black cheek. He was muttering something under his breath, a continuous mumble, perhaps a prayer.

'Who is it?' he repeated, speaking low, but his rich, deep voice rolled round the ice-house and bounced back at us like the light of the lanterns.

'I don't know.'

But I did know. That was what made it infinitely worse. I grasped the bracket on the wall, set the lantern on the threshold of the doorway, and swung my weight into the void. My foot lodged on a rung of the iron ladder. Step by step I descended, climbing slowly because of the damp flapping skirts of my topcoat. The foetid smell rose up to greet me, growing stronger and thicker with every step I took.

'Shall I lower the lantern?' Harmwell called down.

The cold was intense: it seemed to creep into my bones and take up residence there.

'Mr Shield? Mr Shield?'

I looked upward and saw Harmwell's face, the whites of the eyes shockingly vivid, poised over the pit. I gave a little shake of the head; I was reluctant to speak for that would mean opening my mouth and allowing in more of that foul air. I lowered my foot on to the next rung. No need for a lantern because I knew what I would find on the floor: a nightmare which would poison all our lives, that would fill every crack and cranny of our existence like the air itself.

My right boot splashed into the mess of straw and icy water that carpeted the floor. The body, a black, wet bundle, lay with its head near the foot of the ladder, and its feet towards the centre of the chamber. Propped against the wall was a cartwheel. I stared at it stupidly, trying to imagine what it was doing here, where no wagon would ever come. I stripped off my right glove and extended my arm towards the wheel. Where my fingers expected wood, they found the cold, abrasive surface of rusting cast-iron.

'Mr Shield?' Harmwell called, and there was a curious intensity, almost excitement, in his tone. 'Mr Shield, what have you found?'

'It looks like – like a cartwheel.'

'It will serve as the grating for the drain,' Harmwell said.

My eyes ran down the length of the body to the circular vacancy, about a yard in diameter, in the middle of the floor. One of the body's feet dangled over it. I bent and touched the long, black coat with the tip of a finger. The man still wore a flat-crowned, broad-brimmed hat, held to his head by a scarf tied round the chin and now tilted to one side by the impact of the fall.

From the first, I had had a powerful conviction that the man in the pit was dead. Now I saw that he could hardly be anything else: his mouth and nostrils were submerged beneath the watery slush on the floor. As Mr Noak had learnt from the example of his unhappy son, a man may drown in a puddle – that is, if he is not already dead before he goes into it. I moved my hand to the fold of bare skin above the neckcloth. It was like touching a dead, damp, plucked pheasant.

'Is he still breathing?' Harmwell said, his voice now an urgent whisper. 'Wait, I'll bring down the lantern.'

Nausea burned in my throat. 'God damn it, of course he's not breathing.'

Hobnails scraped on the iron rungs. The light swung to and fro: and for an instant my mind was adrift from its moorings, as it had been in the days when they quietened me with laudanum, and I thought that the pit itself was swaying, not the lantern, that this entire chamber was like a cold bird's cage covered with a blanket and swinging from side to side over a dark void. The black shape of the body receded into shadow, and then burst into view again.

Ayez peur, the bird said in Seven Dials. *Ayez peur*.

I was full of fear for all of us now, and most especially for Sophie.

'Poor fellow.' Harmwell held the lantern over the upper part of the body. 'We must turn him over.'

We bent over the corpse. I took hold of its left shoulder and upper arm, and Harmwell clasped a massive hand round its hip and thigh. We pulled. It did not move. The wet, inert body seemed an immense weight. We pulled harder and at last the slush sucked and heaved as it gave up its burden. The body fell with a splash on to its back. Harmwell and I sprang up. There was a moment's silence, apart from the slapping and rustling of the disturbed water. The light from the lanterns fell on the face.

'No,' I said. 'No, no, no.'

'No what?' Harmwell rasped in my ear.

No, it was not Henry Frant lying there. Instead it was the woman who had loved him.

CHAPTER SIXTY-TWO

'IT IS IMPERATIVE that we find the boys,' I said as I followed Harmwell up the ladder.

He was standing by the inner door into the passage. 'You know their haunts better than I. If you wish, I will stay here to guard the corpse.'

'We shall find the boys more quickly if we both look. And when we find them, they may need help.'

'True.' Harmwell's face was in shadow. 'On the other hand, we can hardly leave Mrs Johnson unguarded. It would not be fitting.'

'She will not mind, sir, not now. The boys are more important. We must search by the ruins.'

His persistence in the matter puzzled me, even with the boys' safety weighing on my mind. I remembered what the foreman had told me the previous morning about the blocked drain of the ice-house, and all of a sudden it occurred to me that this was one of the few nights of the year when the building would not only be unlocked but empty – in other words, with its floor and the sump below easily accessible. Was it possible that the same thought had occurred to my companion?

I pushed past him and walked down the passage to the outer doorway. The events of this terrible night were not over. The poisoned mastiff and the clang of the mantrap were fresh in my memory. Harmwell followed me into the open air.

'The poor lady has gone beyond all mortal harm,' he observed in his deep preacher's voice. 'You are in the right of it – we must look to the living.'

We picked our way slowly down the defile and reached the path along the bank of the lake. Here we made better speed. Every few paces one of us would call the boys' names, Harmwell's great booming bass mingling with my baritone. At last we attained the crest of the ridge that sloped down towards the ruins and Grange Cottage beyond. The smothering weight of the darkness lay heavily on the sleeping land. To our left was the dense shadow of East Cover.

'Stay,' Harmwell said. 'Did you hear? Call again.'

A moment later, I heard it too – a high, faint response to our shouts, coming from somewhere below. Careless of danger, we stumbled and slithered down the snowy slope. As I plunged into the dark, I remembered the bright, cold afternoon of St Stephen's Day when Sophie and I had run together towards the boys.

A single voice called repeatedly: 'Here, sir! Here!'

We found the boys huddled in the lee of the tallest part of the ruins. They had found shelter in a recess made by a blocked doorway. Snow had drifted over their lower legs. Charlie was slumped at the back of the niche, and Edgar held him in his arms.

'Oh, sir,' said the little American through chattering teeth, 'I am so glad – Charlie was so distressed – and then he fell asleep – and I thought I should fetch help, but I did not like to leave him and I did not know which way to go.'

'You did quite right. Mr Harmwell, I suggest we wrap them like a pair of parcels, and carry them home.'

Charlie stirred as we moved him and began to whimper. We covered him with the spare cloak. I took off my coat and draped it round Edgar. We gave both the boys a drop of brandy and then swallowed rather more ourselves. Then, groaning with the effort, I lifted Edgar on to my back; Harmwell lifted Charlie; and we began the slow, infinitely laborious climb up the slope.

I knew that our troubles were not over. Our best course was to aim for the mansion-house, for who knew what we might find at Grange Cottage? But it would not be easy to carry the boys for the better part of a mile, especially in this weather. As we were encumbered with our burdens, we could not use the lanterns to their best advantage. I was worried about the boys, too, in particular Charlie, who seemed barely conscious of what was happening, and the thought of frostbite was never very far from my mind.

As we reached the brow of the ridge, however, I heard the sound of hallooing voices by the lake, and saw in the distance the swaying lights of a dozen lanterns and torches. I turned back to Harmwell, to share my relief, and discovered him facing the way we had come with a hand cupped over his ear.

'Listen, Mr Shield. Listen.'

A moment later, I heard it too. Somewhere below us, perhaps on the lane by Grange Cottage, came the sound of hooves, muffled by the snow and moving very slowly.

'Come,' I said. 'The boys are growing colder.'

Without further words, we staggered on towards our rescuers. Charlie lay inert and silent on Harmwell's shoulder as we plodded towards the lights dancing in the darkness.

'The monk ran away from us, sir,' Edgar whispered. 'We did not see him but we heard him.'

'What?' said Harmwell. 'What was that?'

'Hush now,' I replied, thinking of those hoof-beats. 'We must save our breath.'

After what seemed like hours, our rescuers reached us, and willing hands received our burdens. We had men enough to spare – Sophie and Mrs Kerridge had woken Miss Carswall, and together they had roused the household and the stables. At the lake we divided into two parties. One took the boys back to the mansion. Harmwell and I led the remaining five men up the defile to the ice-house. The sight of Mrs Johnson in trousers seemed to shock some of them more than the fact of her death. We brought her up from the pit of the chamber – it was no easy task, and it needed all of us to do it. We laid her on a leaf of the ice-house's inner doors, covered her face with her cloak for decency's sake and bore her away on her makeshift bier.

When we reached the mansion, which was ablaze with lights, the footmen were carrying the boys up to bed, with Miss Carswall, Sophie and Mrs Kerridge fluttering about them on the stairs. But Sophie ran back to the hall for a moment, and pressed Harmwell's hand and then mine.

'Tell them to bring you whatever you wish, Mr Harmwell, Mr Shield – you must be chilled to the bone. I shall go to the boys.'

'Let them grow warm gently,' I said, for my father had been used to dealing with frostbite in the Fen winters. 'Wrap them in blankets. Sudden heat is harmful.'

Carswall appeared, stamping into the hall in his dressing gown, ready to rant and roar. But Mrs Johnson under her black cloak brought him up short. Sophie left us and ran upstairs without another word.

'Uncover her,' he said to Pratt, who had just returned from carrying Edgar upstairs.

Carswall studied Mrs Johnson for a moment, as she lay there on her back, her skin grey and waxen, her big body ungainly in that unseemly attire, the hat tied under her jaw, as though she had laid herself out for death and did not want to be found with her mouth open. He looked up, saw me standing there at the foot of the stairs and at once looked past me to Harmwell.

'Was she dressed like that when you found her?' he asked.

'Yes, sir.'

'What the devil possessed her?'

Harmwell shrugged.

Carswall told Pratt to cover her face again. 'Take her up to the Blue Room, and lay her on the bed. Find Kerridge to go with you and do it decently. Then lock the door and bring me the key.' He turned on his heel and went into the library, calling over his shoulder for someone to make up the fire.

A maid approached me, and said that soup, wine, sandwiches and a good fire were waiting for us in the little sitting room. We ate and drank in silence, facing each other across the fire. Miss Carswall came in as we were finishing.

'No, do not get up. I came to tell you that Charlie and Edgar do very well and are now sleeping the sleep of the unjust. Are you yourselves recovered from the ordeal? Have they brought you all you wish for?' She was kindness itself, yet it was not long before her curiosity peeped through. 'Poor Mrs Johnson! I'm sure none of us will sleep a wink for thinking of the horror of it. Tell me, was there no clue as to why she was there, and how she happened to fall?'

We assured her there was none.

'Sir George must be told as soon as possible – quite apart from the tie of blood, he is the nearest magistrate. Mr Carswall has ordered a groom to ride over to Clearland at first light.'

She wished us goodnight, and Harmwell withdrew at the same time, leaving me to my wine and my reflections, which were not happy. The clock on the mantel was striking three in the morning when I stood up to leave. In the hall, I picked up my candle from the table. Pratt was waiting there, and he coughed as I approached.

'Mr Carswall's compliments, sir, and it will not be convenient for you to leave tomorrow after all.'

That night I hardly slept, and when I did my sleep was uneasy, crowded with memories and fears which mingled with one another and masqueraded as dreams. In one of them all was dark, and I heard again the clang of the mantrap closing its jaws; but this time the sound was immediately followed by two others, first a high scream, rising rapidly in pitch and volume, and then the sound of hooves on the lane by Grange Cottage.

What lawful business would take a man and horse abroad on a night like this?

CHAPTER SIXTY-THREE

EARLY IN THE morning, the sound of the groom's horse on the drive brought me back to consciousness in a rush, yet seemed also an echo of the hoof-beats in my dream. In a flash, the events of the previous night lost their fantastic forms and paraded through my mind as black and sober as a funeral procession.

I spent that day in limbo. I had no duties. But I could not leave. Mrs Frant sent word that she would stay with the boys, and that Charlie, though recovering rapidly from his ordeal, would spend at least the morning in bed.

There was little to keep me within-doors. The silent presence in the Blue Room cast its shadow over the house. But the morning was fine and the temperature had risen a few degrees. After breakfast, I decided that as I had nothing better to do I might as well indulge my curiosity. I took the path to the lake, retracing the route we had taken the previous evening. A knot of men was standing by the door to the kitchen gardens. As I drew nearer, I recognised two under-gardeners and one of the gamekeepers.

My approach stirred them into activity. Each of them bent and seized a leg of the dead mastiff. The door to the garden was open. Immediately inside stood a sledge. Muttering curses, they hoisted the unfortunate animal on to it.

'Have you found his fellow?' I asked.

The gamekeeper turned and civilly touched his hat, which told me that news of my disgrace had not yet reached him. 'Yes, sir. In the shell grotto. As dead as his brother here.'

'And for the same reason?'

'Poison,' he said flatly.

'Are you sure?'

'He had a mutton bone in there with a few grains of powder still on it. Rat poison, I'd say.'

I beckoned him aside. 'Mr Harmwell and I were out last night.'

'I know, sir.' He watched the other men hauling the sledge along the path, their heavy boots slipping and sliding on the layers of snow.

'We found the dog. There was something else. As we were passing the lake, we heard a noise in the distance. Mr Harmwell thought it was a mantrap snapping shut.'

The man rubbed his unshaven chin. 'He were right. One of the big ones in East Cover was sprung last night.'

'The wood beyond the lake?'

'Aye.' He spat. 'That thieving bugger had the luck of the devil. The teeth caught his coat, look, tore off a piece. A few inches to the left and we'd have had his leg.'

'A poacher? And a poacher could have been responsible for poisoning the dogs?'

He looked beyond me at the little procession moving down the central path of the garden, the men's panting breath loud in the surrounding silence and the sledge's runners slithering on the icy ground. 'Who else would it be, sir?'

'Where precisely was the mantrap set?' I asked.

He looked askance. 'I told you, sir – East Cover. We got several in there, Master had them put down in the autumn, but this one was near a place we call Five Ways, where five paths meet. We move them around, though. It's no good leaving them in the same place, is it? You'd never catch anyone that way, even those chuckle-headed numskulls from Flaxern Magna.'

I left him and walked on. East Cover, the larger of the two enclosures near the lake, lay on the right of the broad path leading to Flaxern Parva and the church. On the other side of the wood was the undulating open parkland that sloped down to the monastic ruins, with Grange Cottage on the far side. If Mrs Johnson had wanted to go by the shortest way from Grange Cottage to the mouth of the defile which led to the ice-house, then passing through the middle of East Cover might have been the best way for her to do it, assuming that she was not troubled by the thought of mantraps and armed gamekeepers. I would have liked to examine the paths in the wood and the mantrap itself, but I did not feel sufficiently intrepid to do so without a gamekeeper to guide me; and I dared not make my interest too obvious, in case Mr Carswall heard of it.

Yet there was something not quite right with this: we had been approaching the lake when we heard the clang of the mantrap closing its jaws. If the trap had been sprung by Mrs Johnson, I did not think she would have had time to come through the cover, work round the northern bank of the lake, negotiate the defile and fall to her death in the chamber of the ice-house. Had she done so, we must have heard her movements, particularly as she went up the awkward broken terrain of the defile. Moreover, we should have found traces in the snow of such a recent passage. And her body would still have been warm to the touch.

The conclusion followed inescapably: someone else had sprung the trap. I remembered the sound of hooves I had heard last night, after we had found the boys, the sound that had worked its way into my dreams. Who would be out on horseback at such a late time? The night had been moonless, the ground treacherous with snow and ice.

I approached the ice-house warily, alert to the possibility that Mr Carswall might have placed a guard on it. But there was no one in sight, and the doors stood wide open. Fumbling in the pocket of my greatcoat for the stump of my bedroom candle, I entered the passage. At once I heard the sound of stealthy movement in the chamber beyond. I tiptoed forward and looked down. The light of a lantern flickered on the domed ceiling. Harmwell stood in the pit below, lantern in hand. He must have heard something because he was looking directly at me, the whites of his eyes very bright.

'Why, Mr Shield. What brings you here?'

'A very good day to you, Mr Harmwell. I might ask you the same question.'

He waved his arm. 'As you are aware, I have made a study of the construction of ice-houses. I am particularly interested in the commercial applications. Crystal-clear block ice, that is what the modern world requires –' he pointed down at the slush on the floor '– not this poor, polluted substitute dragged here from any frozen ditch, however dirty. No society can call itself truly civilised that allows ice of such degraded quality on its table.'

While he was talking, I swung myself on to the ladder and climbed down to the floor of the ice chamber. 'You are a persuasive advocate, sir. But I confess I still do not understand why you are here.'

Harmwell backed away from me and leaned against the wall, affecting a nonchalance I did not think he felt. 'The explanation is perfectly simple: it lies there.' He pointed at the great circular drain in the middle of the chamber. The cartwheel which served as the drain's grid was still propped up against the chamber wall and the opening to the sump was a great black disc.

'I do not follow, sir.'

'The ice-house at Monkshill is particularly well drained – or at least it should be. The man who designed it knew what he was about.' He squatted and held the lantern over the sump. 'See – this will take a crouching man with ease. And the drain that leads from it is remarkably broad. It will have several other grills, I fancy, rather finer than this wheel, to keep out rats and other undesirable invaders. You can see the first of them below, like an iron gate dividing the sump from the drain proper. As straw and other débris descend into the sump, the grills become blocked, and the melt-water backs up into the chamber itself. Hence the foulness of the air.'

'I think I recall Mrs Kerridge mentioning a shaft?'

He straightened up to his full height, and his shadow ballooned out into most of the chamber. 'You are perfectly correct – a shaft, allowing access to the drain from the outside world and no doubt also serving as a vent. I understand that it is now unfortunately blocked, but the principle is sound: it permits both the drain and the sump to be periodically

329

cleaned out, even when the ice-house is full. Such a refinement is most unusual.'

'So this should be a veritable nonpareil among ice-houses?'

'Exactly so. I had hoped to have a sight of the original plans, but Mr Noak tells me that Mr Carswall is not able to lay his hands on them.'

'I confess I had no idea there was so much to learn about the subject.'

'I hope I have not prosed on at tedious length, sir. You must forgive me – it is something of a hobbyhorse, I confess – and one day, perhaps, it may be something more: there are fortunes to be made from the manufacture and trade of ice, I believe, particularly in America.'

I crouched beside the sump. Mr Harmwell obligingly held out the lantern so its rays shone into the depths. I had no doubt whatsoever that his interest in the manufacture of ice was genuine – there was no mistaking the enthusiasm in his voice – but, as I had once observed to Mr Carswall, a man may have more than one motive for his actions. Harmwell had wished to linger in the ice-house last night, and now he had taken the first opportunity to come to it when there was nobody else there. Last night, I had assumed he wanted to search the body of Mrs Johnson: now I wondered whether his real aim had been to search the ice-house itself.

'Look,' I said. 'Is not that a little recess – there, on the left?'

The effect of my words surprised me. I had spoken almost at random, to keep the conversation going, to avoid the awkwardness of a silence. Yet Harmwell immediately swung himself down into the sump. The drop was about four and a half feet. He shone the lantern at the small rectangle of shadow I indicated with my finger.

'How curious,' he said. 'I had not noticed. It looks as if two of the bricks have worked loose.' He put his hand into the recess and sucked in his breath.

'What is it?'

'Yes – how – how *very* curious.' He withdrew the hand and brought out a small object which he proceeded to rub against his coat and then to examine in the light of the lantern. He looked up at me and once again the whites of his eyes gleamed. 'Do you know, I believe it might be a ring. See for yourself.'

While Harmwell was hauling himself out of the sump, I examined the ring. I cleaned it with my handkerchief and discerned first the glitter of gold and then the sparkle of a diamond. Was it possible that the discovery had been made too easily? Had the ring been put there only a few minutes before Harmwell had pretended to find it?

My companion cleared his throat. 'Perhaps Mrs Johnson dropped it?'

'Perhaps.' I knew as well as he did that this suggestion was absurd: why should Mrs Johnson drop a ring into the sump in the first place, and why should the ring bounce, fly neatly into the back of a recess, and cover itself with sludge, all in defiance of the principles of physics? 'We should take it to Mr Carswall.'

'Oh yes.' Mr Harmwell bowed, as if in acknowledgement of my wisdom. 'After you, sir.'

So we left the ice-house and walked briskly back towards the mansion. As we were approaching the side door, Miss Carswall came round from the front of the house.

'Mr Shield – Mr Harmwell. I trust – why, Mr Harmwell! – you are soaking!'

'It is nothing, miss. A trifling mishap.'

'We have been down to the ice-house,' I said, choosing to gloss over the fact that we had returned together but met by chance. 'We made a discovery in the drain in the floor of the chamber.'

I thought it wise to share the discovery with as many people as possible. I felt in my pocket, found the ring and handed it to Miss Carswall. For the first time we saw it clearly in the broad daylight. It lay in the palm of her gloved hand, the great stone winking at us in the sunshine. Though the ring itself was of gold, the outer edge was enamelled white and delicately wrought so that it resembled a ring made of twists of ribbon rather than gold.

'It is a mourning ring,' Miss Carswall said suddenly. 'See, there is writing: and look, under the stone, there is a length of hair.'

She held the ring against the light so we might see it. Beneath the diamond I glimpsed a rectangle of coarse brown hair.

'What does it say around the edge?' Harmwell asked.

Miss Carswall held it closer to her eyes and read out in a halting voice: '*Amelia Jane Parker ob: 17 April 1763.*'

'I know the name,' I said.

Miss Carswall looked up through her lashes at me and smiled. 'Is she not buried in the church at Flaxern Parva? The Parkers had Monkshill before the Frants, I believe – she must have been one of Charlie's forebears.'

CHAPTER SIXTY-FOUR

MISS CARSWALL CARRIED us with her into the house and took us not into the library where Mr Carswall sat but into the parlour. Mrs Lee was dozing by the fire and Sophie was reading to the boys, who were spending the day unwillingly in the rôle of invalids.

'Such excitement, my love!' Miss Carswall cried. 'Mr Harmwell and Mr Shield have found a ring in the ice-house. It is a mourning ring for Amelia Parker. We believe she must have been one of Henry's ancestors.'

For a moment the only sound was the ticking of the clock on the mantel. The colour fled from Sophie's cheek, and her bosom rose and fell.

'Treasure!' Edgar burst out in a piercing whisper to Charlie. 'There – what did I say?'

Miss Carswall thrust the ring at Sophie. 'So pretty,' she went on, seemingly unaware of the awkwardness she had caused, 'but so morbid, too, and the diamond is cut in that dull, antique way, and the setting is dreadfully old-fashioned. Have you seen it before?'

Sophie looked up, her face pale but composed. 'No. But I know who Amelia Parker was. Her daughter married Charlie's grandpapa, which was how Monkshill came to the Frants.'

Charlie leaned on the arm of his mother's chair and she allowed him to take the ring. 'Mama? Will it be ours?'

'I doubt it, dearest – mourning rings are often made for a person's family and friends – sometimes a dozen or more. There's no reason why we should have a right to this one.'

He dropped it on the palm of his mother's hand. 'But she was my family.'

'What a pity Sir George and the Captain are not still here,' Miss Carswall said. 'We might have asked them if they had seen it before. Still, I am sure they will be back after they have inspected Grange Cottage.'

'In the meantime, should we give it to Mr Carswall?' I said.

Miss Carswall glanced at me. 'Indeed, you are right, Mr Shield. I wonder if poor Mrs Johnson dropped it in her last moments. But that is by the by. In itself, it must be a ring of some considerable value, for the stone alone, and Papa should see it. But first I shall make a note of the inscription – I am sure Sir George will be interested.' She sat at the table, took pencil and paper and began to make a copy of the words. The point of her pencil broke. 'Oh! How vexing!'

'Allow me to sharpen it for you,' I said.

She watched with flattering interest as I trimmed the point with my penknife. Afterwards, she asked me to check the accuracy of what she had written. Having thanked me prettily, she fluttered out of the room.

'Sir George and Captain Ruispidge have conferred with Mr Carswall,' Sophie said quietly. 'They have also seen their unfortunate cousin. Now they have ridden to Flaxern.'

'They mean to return today?'

'After they have called at Grange Cottage, they will come back through the park.'

A moment later Miss Carswall reappeared and said that her father wished to see Mr Harmwell. The boys scampered out of the room in his wake, leaving me alone with the three ladies.

'Such a pretty stone,' Miss Carswall said. 'One could always have it re-cut and re-set. By the by, Mr Shield, I find that you have fallen out of favour with my father.'

I bowed. 'I regret to say that I have unintentionally offended him.'

'Oh.' She waited for me to continue, though she must have known how I had offended him and how delicate the matter was. When I remained silent, she glanced from me to Sophie and then back again. 'Should you like me to speak to him?'

'You are very good, Miss Carswall, but I do not think it would answer. Besides, perhaps Mr Carswall is in the right of it: it is better that I leave.'

Sophie looked up. 'When are you going?'

'I was to leave this morning but the death of Mrs Johnson has made it necessary to postpone my departure.'

'I wish –' she began; but I was never to know what she wished because at that moment the door opened and there was Mr Carswall himself.

'Shield,' he said. 'A word with you.' He beckoned me into the hall and then into the library. 'Close the door. Harmwell tells me it was he who actually put his hand on the ring, but it was you who saw the hiding place beforehand?'

'Yes, sir.'

'He said you chanced to meet in the ice-house, and that he is interested in the construction of such buildings, and that was why he was there: is that correct?'

'That is what he told me. I cannot express an opinion as to the truth of what he said.'

Carswall grunted. 'Sir George may need to see you: you must stay within-doors for the rest of the day. You will not dine with us, by the by. You may go.'

I opened the door to pass out of the room. But he called me back.

He lowered his head and glared at me through tangled eyebrows. 'I hold you directly responsible for the boys' imprudent escapade last night. It might have led to serious injury, if not worse. I shall inform Mr Bransby so.'

What he said was clearly audible to everyone in the hall, to Harmwell and both the footmen. I did not attempt to rebut so unfair a charge because I knew it would serve no purpose. Instead, I bowed again and closed the door on that cruel, fleshy face.

I avoided meeting Harmwell's eyes. I went up to the schoolroom. On the way I caught the boys kneeling beside the door of the Blue Room, with Charlie peering through the keyhole while Edgar kept up a running commentary.

'No, you great booby, look to the left and you can see the corner of the bed, and there's a bit of black cloth, which I think might be her –'

He broke off, turned his head and saw me. Both boys leapt to their feet.

'Are we – are we to have lessons today?' Charlie inquired.

'No, I believe not.' I realised that no one had thought to tell them that they would never have lessons in this house from me again. 'In fact, I shall soon be leaving you.'

'You return to Mr Bransby's, sir?' asked Edgar.

'Probably.' Though for how long, I dared not guess. 'You are to remain here, Edgar, at least for the time being – Mr Carswall will write Mr Allan. So, unless Mr Carswall finds you another tutor, you will have to run wild for the next fortnight.'

Boys are strange creatures. They stared up at me in silence for a moment, their faces curiously similar, in expression as well as feature. Then, without a word, they turned and ran along the landing.

Dusk came earlier than usual that afternoon, the colours and shapes fading steadily as though a shadowy mist were creeping through the house in search of someone or something. More than once I found myself wondering whether they had lit a lamp in the room where Mrs Johnson lay.

I spent the rest of the day beside a small fire in the schoolroom. By now, news of my disgrace had spread far and wide. I had half expected the servants to rejoice in my downfall but to my surprise they seemed almost sorry at the prospect of losing me. The housekeeper arranged for my spare shirt to be washed and ironed. The little maid who saw to the schoolroom offered to brush and sponge my outdoor clothes, which had suffered from the adventures of the morning and the previous night.

During the afternoon I heard the bustle of arrivals below. Sir George and Captain Ruispidge had returned. The girl who took my clothes told me that the brothers were to dine at Monkshill and spend the night. She also had a message for me from Pratt the footman, now grown too grand to run errands to a mere tutor himself: a groom would take me into Gloucester in the morning; the gig used by the servants was ordered for eight o'clock. From this I deduced that Sir George, in his capacity as a magistrate, saw no legal reason why I should be detained any longer.

I dined early with Mr Harmwell. He was reluctant to talk about recent events and spent most of the meal sunk in thought. Afterwards he shook hands with me and said that he and his master would soon be leaving Monkshill themselves.

'Do you go to South Wales?' I asked.

'I believe Mr Noak has changed his plans. We shall probably travel back to London.' He gave me an unexpected smile. 'How I long to return to America.'

We bade each other Godspeed. I returned to the schoolroom and tried to read. In a short while, the maid brought up my clean shirt.

'Please, sir,' she said, stumbling over her words and blushing, 'but Mr Pratt says he saw your penknife in the parlour.'

The girl was not allowed to enter the parlour herself, but I wished Pratt had had the kindness to give her the knife so that she could return it to me. I had left it on the table after sharpening Miss Carswall's pencil.

I waited until the family had gone into dinner and went downstairs again. I slipped into the familiar room feeling almost like a thief. Though it was empty, a fire burned brightly in the grate, and candles were alight in the wall sconces.

I found my knife and was about to go when I noticed on the table beside it, lying in a little enamelled dish, the mourning ring we had discovered earlier in the day. I was surprised at Carswall's carelessness. I picked it up for a moment and held it to the flame of the nearest candle. The lock of Amelia Parker's hair was a black smudge behind the diamond. I had no taste for the preservation of mementoes of the dead. But I could not help wondering about Henry Frant's grandmother who had lived at Monkshill sixty years before.

I returned the ring to the dish. As I crossed the hall to the stairs, I heard the bray of Carswall's laughter from the dining room. The boys, jigging from foot to foot in their excitement, were waiting for me in the schoolroom. They burst into speech as soon as they saw me.

'We regret that you are leaving us, sir –' Charlie began.

'– and we would be grateful if you would do us the honour –' Edgar interrupted.

'– of accepting this small keepsake, as a token of our esteem –'

'– and gratitude.'

Charlie held out a large red handkerchief with white spots. It had been washed, ironed and folded into a neat square.

'I hope you do not mind our giving you something, sir,' he said. 'We were concerned in case it was not quite the thing. But Mama said it would be perfectly proper.'

I bowed. 'Then I am quite sure it is.'

The gift unexpectedly stirred my emotions. The boys explained that such a handkerchief had many purposes. Worn round the neck, Edgar told me, it would give me the appearance of being a bang-up sporting cove, even a coachman. Alternatively, Charlie pointed out, I might wrap my bread and cheese in it, or use it as a napkin at table, or perhaps blow my nose on it. Suddenly embarrassed, they made the implausible excuse that it was bedtime, and left me in an undignified hurry.

I sat on. My belongings were already packed. I passed the time by drawing up a memorandum of the events that had taken place during my stay at Monkshill-park, and in particular those of the last few days. I wrote in my pocketbook for nearly an hour, interrupted only by the maid bringing back my brushed clothes. I was thus engaged, sitting at a small table drawn almost on top of the fire and writing by the light of a single candle, when there came a tap on the door.

Miss Carswall entered, wearing a black gown out of courtesy for Mrs Johnson, or rather for Sir George whose cousin she had been, and with a grey cashmere shawl draped becomingly over her shoulders. I sprang to my feet. Her boldness astonished me.

'My father says you leave us early in the morning,' she said. 'I hope I do not disturb you, but I wished to say goodbye.'

I set a chair for her by the fire and she sat down with a rustle, the movement sending a waft of her perfume to my nostrils. I wondered if she had learned the reason for my dismissal.

'The gentlemen are still at their wine,' she said. 'We have been talking all evening about this sad affair with Mrs Johnson. I wish you had not been obliged to discover her last night. It must have been truly frightful.'

I acknowledged her consideration with a bow.

'Pray sit down, Mr Shield.' Miss Carswall indicated the chair I had just vacated. 'Yes, a terrible accident. Sir George says she may have been drunk, too.' She broke off, her hand flying to her mouth, and her eyes fixed on my face. 'Oh, I should not have said that, I'm sure. Sometimes I have only to open my mouth for the most wildly indiscreet things to fly out.'

'I had heard something of the sort before, so you have not betrayed a confidence.'

'You had heard it?' She sounded disappointed. 'It is common knowledge?'

'That I cannot tell you, Miss Carswall.'

'They say she drank too much because she was unhappy. By all accounts Lieutenant Johnson is a poor fish.'

I nodded, and Miss Carswall smiled. Our chairs were scarcely two feet apart. The room was lit only by the feeble glow of the fire and the single candle on the table. The circumstances created the illusion of privacy that perhaps encouraged her to regale me with servants' gossip. It is true that there was a streak of vulgarity in her a yard wide but it was part of her charm: she would not trouble to affect a sensibility she did not feel.

'There was a brandy flask in the pocket of her coat. Did you know she was wearing her husband's clothes? No doubt it was eminently practical on so cold a night, but so shockingly immodest! I cannot understand how she could have borne to do it.' Miss Carswall's eyes sparkled with reflected fire from the candle. 'A most unusual sensation, I should imagine,' she added in a low voice. 'Still, we may depend on it, the Coroner will not make too much of it. Sir George will see to that.'

'So what will the verdict be?'

'That the unfortunate lady died by accident. What other verdict can there be? She was ill – quite possibly feverish – her mind unsettled by her husband's long absence – and no doubt lonely, too, in the cottage because her servant was not there. So she took advantage of Papa's kind invitation to walk in the park, but dusk fell early and caught her unawares; and then the snow began, and she took shelter in the ice-house, which was standing open after the men had left. Alas, she blundered in, not

339

knowing her way, and plunged straight into the empty pit of the chamber. How terrible! And then, by the most unfortunate chance, the side of her head struck that great iron grating. Sir George says that was the blow that killed her. Or so Mr Yatton told him – he is the surgeon from Flaxern.'

'And the mastiffs, Miss Carswall?'

She opened her eyes very wide. 'Hush! Papa has given out that it was poachers from the village. That's all my eye, as the servants say. You must not tell a living soul but Sir George and Captain Ruispidge found a great quantity of arsenic in the larder at Grange Cottage.'

'They believe Mrs Johnson poisoned the dogs?'

'I know it is hard to credit, but who else could it have been?'

'Why should she do such a thing?'

'Because she wished to walk in the park at night when the dogs were loose, and they would not let her. It is agreed that the circumstance will not be mentioned at the inquest, it would be too unkind. Sir George believes that she nursed an inveterate and wholly irrational hatred for my father. She – she held him to some degree responsible for the ruin of Mr Frant.' She hesitated. 'You are familiar with that aspect of the matter?'

I nodded. 'I understand Mrs Johnson and Mr Frant had been childhood sweethearts.'

Her voice had been becoming quieter and quieter, but now she had dropped it to a thrilling whisper. 'It was the ruling passion of her life. Mrs Lee says she never got over him. The ring confirms it, of course. Mr Frant must have given it to her when they were young, as a love token. Sophie had never seen it.'

'I still do not understand why she found it necessary to go into the park.'

'Who can tell what disordered fancies filled the poor woman's brain? For all we know, she meant to murder us all in our beds. Sir George is in the right of it, do you not think? It is the kindest thing for everyone, including Mrs Johnson and indeed the poor Lieutenant, to say that her death was nothing more than a dreadful accident. Which of course is all it was, leaving aside the question of her motives for being there.'

She looked at me and smiled brightly – and she had a smile that would charm the Grand Inquisitor himself. I thought I knew what she was at. Mrs Johnson's death at Monkshill-park was bad enough, and could not be concealed, but Miss Carswall did not want any more scandal to cast a blight upon her forthcoming nuptials. This evening she had set out to ensure I understood her position: and that was the purpose of her visit. For all her appearance of candour, she had told me very little I did not already know or guess.

Miss Carswall stood up. 'And now I must leave you. In a moment, the gentlemen will be wanting their coffee.' She took something from a reticule she carried over her arm. 'I beg of you, Mr Shield, do not be offended, but I think my father has his head so full of other matters that he may not have considered your expenses.'

'Miss Carswall, I –'

She waved aside my attempts at protest. 'Pray consider it a loan. I would like to think of you travelling back to town in some comfort. It is such an inhospitable time of year for a journey.'

She held out a five-pound note and would not allow me to refuse it. I did not protest so very much, because I had scarcely any ready money at Monkshill. But it felt like a bribe or a payment, a transaction to be entered in her account book.

'Well, goodbye, Mr Shield. I hope we shall meet again.'

As I took her hand, she came a step closer, raised herself on tiptoe and kissed my cheek.

'There,' she said, smiling at my confusion. 'Consider that a payment of interest on my loan.'

Miss Carswall turned and waited for me to open the door. I stood in the doorway and watched her walking along the landing to the head of the stairs. Her hips swung as she moved, a fluid, graceful motion that reminded me of a snake I had seen at a fair, swaying to the flute of his Hindoo master.

But we were not alone. Sophie was at the other end of the landing, in the doorway of the room the boys shared, and her eyes were fixed on my face.

CHAPTER SIXTY-FIVE

THE FOLLOWING MORNING, Wednesday, I knew that the temperature had risen for the contents of my pot had not frozen over and the ice was less thick on the windowpane. At eight o'clock, they directed me to the stableyard, where I found a groom waiting impatiently with the gig.

Soon we were jingling down the back drive, our progress impeded by the snow and ice. A fine, persistent rain began to fall, lent periodic venom by gusts of wind. I craned my head to have a last view of the blank windows of Monkshill-park. Our speed improved a little once we reached the high road, but there was no other reason to rejoice. Cowering beneath our waterproofs, we had a wet and miserable journey. The groom hardly said one word, replying with monosyllables and hisses to my attempts at conversation. His salient feature was his neck, a broad trunk ending in a head of much the same diameter, which gave him a hybrid appearance: from shoulders downwards he was a man; but the rest of him was closer to a reptile.

At last the spires and towers of Gloucester came in sight, the snow-covered roofs of its buildings gleaming brightly even in the dreary light of this January day: the celestial city itself could hardly have been more welcome to me. On Westgate-street, we passed Fendall House, its prim modern frontage concealing the little room where the most joyful scene of my life had been enacted. Further on, I saw the doorway of the bank where Sophie and I had discovered Mrs Johnson in a drunken stupor on the night of the ball.

The street grew increasingly congested as we neared the Cross, and the groom muttered continuously under his breath as we waited to turn into Southgate-street. At length, we drew up in the yard of the Bell. The man waited, reins in hands, staring fixedly at his horse's head, leaving me to summon a servant myself or to carry my luggage unaided. I beckoned a boy, who ran forward and lifted down my bags. Next to them was a large leather satchel.

'Leave that,' the groom snapped at the lad. 'It's mine.'

Having no desire to stay at the Bell, where Carswall and his people usually put up, I walked down to the Black Dog in Lower Northgate-street, with my little porter staggering behind me. A few minutes later I had bespoken a room and was steaming gently by a fire. I felt better after I had dined. It is much easier to contemplate an uncertain future on a full stomach than on an empty one.

Afterwards, I discovered that I had left a parcel containing my clean shirt in the gig. I walked rapidly to the Bell, hoping that the groom had not yet returned to Monkshill, and nursing a suspicion that he had intentionally allowed me to leave without it. But I had wronged him. The gig had been backed into a corner of the big coach house at the Bell, and my parcel was where I had left it, tucked under the seat to keep off the rain. The groom himself had gone.

'Hired a horse and off he went,' an ostler told me. 'He'll have a wet ride.' He spat and grinned up at me. 'Can't look much sourer than he already does, can he? That face would turn milk.'

Later that afternoon I went to the coach office at the Booth-Hall Inn. I was fortunate enough to get an inside seat on the *Regulator*, the London day coach, leaving the following morning at a quarter before six, and reaching Fleet-street by eight in the evening. I went early to bed, leaving orders that I be called at five o'clock in the morning. I dropped into a deep, dreamless sleep from which I was only awakened by repeated knockings on my chamber door.

The *Regulator* was a light post-coach, hence both its speed and the fact that it carried only four passengers inside. I was lucky in that my companions were as disinclined for conversation as I was – a stout farmer going as far as Northleach, a clergyman returning to his Oxford college and an elderly woman with a prim mouth and a pair of knitting needles that were never still. The other passengers came and went, but the knitting lady and I were both going all the way to London. I spent the journey reading, dozing and staring out of the window.

The recent events at Monkshill unfolded again in the theatre of my mind as the coach rolled through the bleak winter landscape. I felt a profound and paralysing sense of loss. For the first time, I allowed myself to look long and hard into the future and what I saw there was desolate. But there was no help for it. At least I had employment, I told myself, a roof over my head and the prospect of food in my belly.

The last of the daylight had long gone by the time we reached London. The familiar stench and taste of the metropolis oozed into the coach. The glare of the gaslights in the West End loomed out of the fog. We set down the knitting lady in Piccadilly. I let the *Regulator* carry me a mile or so eastwards to the Bolt-in-Tun, its terminus in Fleet-street.

In the yard of the inn, they were bringing down my luggage from the roof when I felt a tap upon my arm. Turning, I recognised with surprise the face of Edward Dansey.

'How very glad I am to see you,' I said. 'How do you do?'

'Very well, thank you. Is this all your luggage?'

'Yes.' By now I was puzzled, for the strangeness of the situation had become apparent to me. 'How did you know that I was travelling on this coach?'

'I wasn't sure you were,' he said. 'It was a probability, no more than that.'

'I – I do not understand.'

Dansey presented me with the grimmer, graver aspect of his Janus face. 'We must talk, Tom. But we cannot do so here.'

I left the luggage to be collected at the coach office and followed Dansey out into the murky bustle of the evening. He took my arm and guided me through the fog to a chophouse filled with lawyers' clerks in one of the streets running into Chancery-lane. I did not see him clearly until we were sitting in a booth and waiting to be served. It struck me immediately how pale and drawn his face had become. The two vertical lines scored in his forehead were deeper than I remembered.

We were quite private in the booth, and the buzz of conversation insulated us from the rest of the world. Despite my curiosity, I wasted no time in ordering steaks and porter. I had dined on the road not long after midday but my stomach still obeyed Mr Carswall's domestic time-table.

'And now,' said I, 'how did you come to meet me? Not that I regret it – far from it – nothing can be more pleasant than the sight of a friendly face at the end of a journey.'

Dansey stared glumly across the table. 'I am afraid there will be little pleasure about this meeting.'

'I do not understand you.'

'Mr Bransby received a letter early this morning. It was brought by one of Mr Carswall's servants riding post.'

'From Monkshill?'

He nodded. 'Where else? The man had travelled overnight. He could hardly stand by the time he reached Stoke Newington. It was he who told us you were travelling up from Gloucester, by the way, and which coach you were likely to be on. But the –'

He fell silent as our drinks arrived.

When we were alone again, I said, 'Was Carswall's man a groom? A bandy-legged fellow with a tiny head on a thick neck?'

'Yes. You know him?'

'It must be the same man who drove me into Gloucester yesterday morning.'

'Very probably.' Dansey pushed back his wig and scratched his scalp. 'Tom – there is no easy way to say this. When Mr Bransby read the letter, he flew into a great passion, and began shouting so loud I could hear him on the other side of the school. At length he sent for me: and he gave me the letter.'

I sat very still, watching him. I did not speak, for there was nothing to say.

'He – that is to say, Mr Carswall – accuses you of habitual neglect of your duties, and says that when you were with the boys, you rarely taught them but joined in their sports and played the fool and encouraged them to do likewise.' He held up his hand, to prevent my interrupting. 'He alleges you were often the worse for drink.'

'My dear Ned –'

'There is more, and worse: he says you made improper advances to the ladies, to both Miss Carswall and Mrs Frant.'

'That is quite untrue,' I snapped. But my voice sounded false even to myself, and I felt my cheeks grow warm.

Dansey regarded me coolly for a moment and then went on: 'I leave the very worst till last, Tom. Mr Carswall says that shortly after your departure, he discovered that a valuable ring was missing, an heirloom.'

'There certainly was such a ring,' I said. 'A mourning ring commemorating a lady named Amelia Parker, the grandmother of Henry Frant. Together with Mr Noak's clerk, I was instrumental in finding it on the day before I left. The circumstances of its discovery were –'

'How it was found is beside the point,' Dansey cut in. 'We are concerned with how it was subsequently lost. When did you last see it?'

'On the evening of the same day. In the small sitting room at Monkshill.'

'Mr Carswall alleges that while he and the others were at dinner, you slipped into the room where the ring was and stole it.' He paused and licked his lips. 'It was a room you had no right to be in, either, he said, but you were seen coming out of it by one of the servants, and no one saw the ring after that.'

I shook my head. 'The groom who brought you the letter drove me into Gloucester: in other words, Mr Carswall cannot have discovered the ring's loss after my departure. If his tale is true the theft must have come to light beforehand. And if we admit that circumstance, the whole tale becomes suspect.'

Something like hope leapt and died in Dansey's face. 'You are assuming it is the same groom. But even if it were the same man, there are obvious reasons why Mr Carswall did not charge you at once with the crime. Is it not probable that he would wish to spare the ladies from scandal? And there was Mr Bransby to think of, not to mention the boys and Mr and Mrs Allan. No, the more I think of it, the more his conduct shows a very proper delicacy.'

'Then it is evident that you do not know Mr Carswall.'

'That is unnecessary, Tom. And unkind.'

'But it is true.'

Dansey's lips tightened. His face wore the expression it had when he was about to beat a boy. He said quietly, 'There is one further particular. According to the letter, when he discovered the loss, Mr Carswall immediately made inquiries; and a footman said he had come across you mending your coat, your topcoat, with a needle and thread during the evening, a circumstance which struck him as unusual: in the ordinary course of things, he thought, a man in your position would have asked one of the maids. Moreover, the servant claimed, you appeared embarrassed to be caught with the needle in your hand and thrust the mending away from you.'

I smacked the palm of my hand against the surface of the table. 'It is a fabrication concocted by that villain Carswall with the aid of an equally villainous footman. I wondered at the time at the servants' kindness to me on my last evening.'

'The coat, Tom,' Dansey said quietly.

'What of it? It is hanging over there.'

'Bring it here.'

I stared at him in silence, while thoughts rushed in an angry torrent through my mind. After a moment, I fetched the coat from its hook and, still without a word, laid it on the table between us. Dansey explored the pockets, and methodically felt the lining. His fingers paused when he reached a place at the bottom of the coat, close to a spot where a seam ran down from the waist to the hem. Slowly he raised his head and looked at me.

'There is something here.'

'That may be so. But that is not to say I put it there.' They were the wrong words: they made me sound defensive, like a rogue squirming in the dock. I went on quickly, 'Here – take my penknife, see what it is.'

Dansey opened the knife and sliced through the stitches of the seam

347

with the tip of the blade. The thread was black but some of the stitches were darker, as if recently renewed. He worked his fingers into the gap and folded back the lining.

'It is tucked into the hem itself, I fancy,' he said. 'A few of the stitches are cut so it forms a little pocket.'

He drew out a paper that had been folded into a compact square. He laid this on the table and opened it. I saw a scrap of writing on the paper, my own writing, and there at last was the ring in all its glory. I pushed my hand across the table and picked it up. Dansey made no move to prevent me. My head was swimming.

'Yes, Ned: it is the very ring that Mr Carswall describes. Underneath the stone is a scrap of Mrs Parker's hair. You see?' I dropped it on the table.

He let it lie. 'It is your handwriting on the paper, is it not?'

'Indeed it is.' I took up the paper and examined it under the lamp. *Caesar commanded the legions to march to their winter quarters.* 'Yes, it is part of a translation I set Charlie and Edgar, one of the last tasks I gave them. Look – the paper is crumpled. When they finished they must have thrown it away.'

'You suggest that someone found it and used it to wrap the ring, knowing that it would implicate you further?'

'I cannot think of any other explanation.'

The waiter was approaching. Dansey dropped his glove on top of the ring. Neither of us spoke again until the dishes had been laid on the table, and the man was gone.

'Mr Carswall begged Mr Bransby to examine your coat when you arrived back at the school,' Dansey said. 'If the ring were found, he wrote, he regretted that he might be obliged to press charges. He added something to the effect that he would see that neither Mr Bransby nor the school should suffer.'

The food grew cold on our plates. Around us the noise rose and fell like waves breaking on a beach. Carswall had manufactured a neat little plot. Involving Mr Bransby as his agent was particularly astute. Who would doubt the word of a clergyman, and one who had so benevolently offered me a position as a favour to an old servant, my aunt? And if public scandal resulted, it would do so from Stoke Newington, not Monkshill-park.

'Carswall is a tyrant and a lecher in his own house,' I said. 'Particularly when drunk. The other evening, I restrained him from paying unwanted attentions to Mrs Frant.'

Dansey cut into his meat. 'Were there witnesses?'

'None that I know of, apart from Mrs Frant. It is possible that Miss Carswall and some of the servants heard our altercation, but that would not answer.'

'Would Mrs Frant testify to that effect?'

'I would not ask her to do so. I could not ask it of her, Ned, you must see that. Besides, she and Charlie are dependent on Carswall for the clothes on their backs and the roof over their heads.'

'I see.'

I picked up my knife. For a few minutes we ate in silence. If the case came to court, and if it went badly for me, I might find myself facing transportation, or even the gallows. My fate hinged on Edward Dansey.

'What do you intend to do?' I asked.

He continued chewing, slowly, very deliberately. He was a fastidious fellow, Dansey. I could not hurry him and I could not persuade him. There, on the other side of the table, sat my judge and jury: and all I could do was wait to hear the verdict and the sentence.

'I tell you fairly, Tom, it looks black.'

'I am not a thief.'

The Janus face saw both ways. 'Mr Carswall is a respectable citizen, a man with a considerable position in the world,' Dansey said. 'And Mr Bransby is both a man of the cloth and our employer.'

'Mr Bransby is anxious to oblige Mr Carswall.'

Dansey did not reply. All of a sudden, I knew I might have added *And you in turn are anxious to oblige Mr Bransby*. There at last was the nub of the matter: Dansey did not want to imperil his position; on the other hand, his conscience was a tender organ and, despite the ring now lying under his glove, he could not be sure that I was not speaking the truth. Indeed, I think he wanted to believe me.

'Mr Bransby does not know you are here?'

He gave a little shake of the head.

'If Mr Carswall were to lay charges against me, everything would depend on the ring,' I said. 'Without the ring, there would be no case to answer.'

'Very probably.' Dansey pushed aside his plate. 'Believe me, Tom, I do not know what to think.'

'You mean whom to believe.'

He darted an imploring glance at me. 'If I did, it would be so much easier.'

'Then you must do as you think right.'

He took out his purse and laid a few coins on the table. He picked up his gloves and slid along the bench and out of the booth. He did not once look at me, but I watched him. He put on his coat and hat and wound his muffler round his neck. At last he pulled on his gloves, nodded to the waiter and left.

My eyes were hot, and I could have wept for the injustice of it all. Instead, I cupped my hand over the ring and drew it towards me.

CHAPTER SIXTY-SIX

I SLEPT – or rather lay – that night in a lodging house in an alley off Fetter-lane. It was a daedal maze of chambers like evil-smelling cupboards; but I paid to have a room to myself and wedged the palliasse against the door. The only intruders were rats and insects, though the house around me was never still, never quiet.

My mind was equally restless. Even if I disposed of the ring, I did not think it would be wise for me to return to Stoke Newington. Mr Bransby was not a corrupt man but he was zealous in attending to the wishes of wealthy parents and guardians. I had little doubt he would dismiss me from his employment; leaving aside the accusation of theft, either of the other accusations was sufficiently grave to justify him in dispensing with my services.

Dansey's conduct saddened me, though by warning me of what was afoot, he had saved me from almost certain arrest. I was grateful for his kindness, but I own that his unwillingness to trust me rankled. I had not expected that of him. For all his kindness, there seemed something mean-spirited about his behaviour.

Now, as perhaps never before, I needed the advice of a disinterested friend. As the night wore on, the conviction grew that my best course was to find Mr Rowsell as soon as possible and lay the whole matter before him – or almost the whole, for I did not wish to elaborate on what had passed between Sophie and myself, or even between myself and Miss Carswall. As a lawyer, he would be well placed to advise me, and as a friend he had always treated me with kindness.

On Friday morning, therefore, I washed as well as I could and put on fresh linen. I left the lodging house, breakfasted at a stall and went to a barber's to be shaved. Fed and respectable, I made my way to Lincoln's Inn. Atkins, Mr Rowsell's clerk, was copying a document in the outer room. He greeted me coldly – Atkins never cared for me; I believe he was jealous of my place in his master's affections. I begged the favour of a few words with Mr Rowsell.

'I am afraid he is not here today, sir.'

'He has been called away on business?'

'He has been unwell: there was palpitation of the heart yesterday, and Mrs Rowsell kept him at home to be bled. I believe he is quite recovered but he sent word this morning that he would stay away until Monday.'

'Would he object if I waited upon him at home?'

Atkins's mouth puckered in the pale circle of his face. 'Mr Rowsell is a gentleman who enjoys company, sir.'

I thanked him and walked up to Northington-street. When I rang the bell, the door was opened by a servant but Mrs Rowsell was coming down the stairs, with a gaggle of children behind her. I scarcely had time to open my mouth when she pushed aside the maid and confronted me on the doorstep. I swept off my hat and made my bow.

'Mr Shield,' she said, her face reddening. 'You are not welcome in this house.'

In the chilly silence, the children stared up at me. The maid peeped over her mistress's shoulder. Bransby knew of my connection with Mr Rowsell but I had not anticipated that he would move against me with such rapidity: he must have written yesterday, as soon as he had had the letter from Carswall. Nor had I expected Carswall's malignity to pursue me so far, or so quickly, or my friends to be so little proof against its power.

'Madam,' I began, 'I hope I have done nothing to offend –'

'Go,' she commanded and flung out her right arm as though to sweep me from the doorstep. 'Mr Rowsell will not see you again, either here or at Lincoln's Inn. Nor shall I. Go, Mr Shield, and never return.'

I bowed, replaced my hat and walked away. The door slammed. I drifted, allowing my legs to carry me according to their whim through streets filled with slush and mud and restless crowds. I had lost my position, my good name and even my friends. I had lost Sophie – indeed, had she ever been mine? In the middle of the throng I was as solitary as if I had been a castaway on a desert island.

The currents of the city flung me hither and thither, and at last washed me up among the coaches and wagons in the yard of the Bull and Mouth in St Martins-le-Grand. I hesitated at the open door of the coffee house, the rich smells reminding my stomach that I was hungry. But now I was friendless, I knew I must conserve my meagre stock of money; and I owed it to both my aunt and myself to preserve intact my little nest-egg in the Funds for as long I could.

A plump man was standing in the doorway, haranguing an unseen audience within. He was thinking about money, too. 'Six shillings a day! Have you ever heard the like? God damn it, do they think I'm Croesus? Six shillings a day!'

At the same moment, a lady leaned over one of the balconies that ran round the yard and communicated with the rooms beyond. She called down to her maid, who was taking a parcel to the Cirencester coach. 'Why didn't you pack the pearls?' she cried. 'You silly, silly girl! You know I always take my pearls.'

Six shillings. Pearls.

The words flew together and jogged my memory. A foolish schoolboy pun fell out. Mrs Jem, I had said on the day that Mr Rowsell had informed me of my aunt Reynolds's legacy to me, Mrs Jem, you are indeed a pearl of great price. Mrs Jem lived at 3 Gaunt-court, and she still owed me six shillings from the sale of my aunt's belongings.

CHAPTER SIXTY-SEVEN

A WEEK LATER, on the 29th of January 1820, the old king died: poor mad George III at last made way for his plump and profligate son: and the world shrugged its shoulders and moved on. By that time, I was already beginning to slip into another mode of life – by good fortune, rather than by intention. When one is entirely adrift, it is sometimes wiser not to splash and shout but to lie still and trust to the benevolence of the currents.

In their own way, the Jems were indeed benevolence incarnate. They lived in a tall, narrow building hard by the Strand. Three Gaunt-court was one of a group of dilapidated houses huddling around a dingy court like elderly ladies reduced in income, retired from the world and finding safety and recreation in the company of their kind. When I came to call for my six shillings, I saw a card in the window announcing a room to let. The steps up to the front door had been recently swept, and someone had tried to clean the knocker, though without notable success.

Mrs Jem remembered me. Without my prompting, she unlocked a drawer of the kitchen dresser and brought out a paper containing six shillings. I inquired about the room: she puffed up the stairs and showed me a back garret with a narrow bed. I was tolerably certain that Mrs Jem would not allow anyone to pilfer my belongings. Within a few minutes, we had come to an arrangement which depended on my paying my rent a week in advance, meals and laundry extra.

It was necessary for the agreement to be ratified by Mr Jem, an enormously fat man who spent most of his days in bed, but this was a formality, like Parliament sending up a bill to the monarch for the Royal Assent. Mr Jem had once been a carpenter with men working under him but a mishap with a saw had cost him his right hand.

'A schoolmaster?' he wheezed. 'I have a letter to write. I'd be most obliged if you would assist me, most obliged.' He waved his hook at me. 'I cannot write neatly, sir, not now, not as neatly as I would wish.'

I doubt he could ever write much more than his name. The letter was a petition to a man he had once worked for. The following evening I tried without marked success to show Mrs Jem how to reckon up accounts on paper as well as in her head. Within a few days, and quite without conscious volition, I had become part of a minuscule community composed of the Jems and their lodgers. We were held together by our poverty, and by our need for one another's services.

Jem and Mrs Jem and all the little Jems held sway in the basement and on the ground floor apart from the front parlour, which was rented out to a man who constructed fake Neapolitan mandolins and filled the house with the scent of wood shavings and varnish. In the rooms above nested the other tenants, not higgledy-piggledy, as in the Rookeries of St Giles, but with decent intervals between them. I remember a widow who washed clothes and a man who had a coffee stall in Fleet-street; a one-legged sailor who acted as a gentle and infinitely resourceful nursemaid to the smaller Jems; a Russian couple who spoke only a few words of English, who went in fear of the police, and who were always willing to offer you a dish of tea; and a broken-down clerk who had worked in the City before his health gave way. As for myself, I helped reckon up who owed what to whom, tried to teach the younger Jems their alphabet, and wrote letters for anyone who would pay for them.

No, Gaunt-court was not St Giles: there is more than one way of being poor. Mrs Jem was fiercely determined that her house should be respectable. On Sunday, she took the little Jems to chapel twice a day, and Mr Jem too, if she could contrive it. She ruled her kingdom with Amazonian severity. When she saw the seamstress from the second-floor front parading in her finery up and down the Haymarket one Friday evening, she threw the poor woman and her belongings on to the street. To be both poor and respectable, you must also be ruthless.

Mrs Jem and I got on well enough. She took me on trust: all she knew of was that my aunt had been a decent woman and that I was a college man replete with book learning. I told her I was newly returned to London, having lost my position through no fault of my own. I did not enter into particulars, and there was no need so long as my conduct continued satisfactory.

As time passed, Mrs Jem, whose invisible web of influence spread far beyond the confines of Gaunt-court, found me scraps of tutoring here and letter-writing there among her friends and acquaintances. Like old David Poe, I became a screever, a humble scribe of other people's communications.

So, by and large, my life was tolerably comfortable. I was poor but not indigent. I had useful occupation but not too much of it. I did not eat fine food but my belly was always full. I had a roof over my head and people who thought in a remote but not unfriendly way that I was one of them. From the window of my room I had, on clear days, a vista of slates and chimneys and pigeons; and at night-time the sky glowed an unhealthy yellow with the flaring lights of the West End.

I run ahead of myself. February moved into March. I felt a certain pride in my survival, for I knew that, even a year ago, even six months, such independence and self-sufficiency would have seemed an impossible dream. I had changed. My mind was whole again.

I could not say the same for my heart. Not a day passed but that I thought of Sophie. The humdrum nature of my existence left me plenty of room for reflection, and for dreams. In memory I relived that after-noon in Gloucester a hundred times, a thousand. I tried to recall every word, every gesture, that had passed between us, from our first meeting outside Mr Bransby's school to that cruel moment on my last evening at Monkshill when Sophie had seen Miss Carswall slipping away from the schoolroom.

On most days I would find occasion to visit a tavern or a coffee house and read one of the papers. In this way, I came across a brief account in the *Morning Post* of the inquest on Mrs Johnson. Sir George had contrived matters very neatly, and with great discretion. I learned that Mrs Johnson, the wife of a naval officer serving on the West Indies station, had suffered an unlucky fall, due in part to the inclement weather, in the ice-house on a neighbour's estate. She had struck her head on a grating and been instantly killed. The Coroner's jury brought in a verdict of accidental death. The report was entirely accurate as far as it went, but it did not go very far at all.

So there was a life gone, neatly parcelled up and despatched into oblivion. Early in March, after a decent interval, the engagement between Miss Carswall and Sir George Ruispidge was announced in the London papers. A few days later, I saw a notice to the effect that Mr Carswall and his family had come up to town, where they had taken their old house in Margaret-street again.

Had Sophie and Charlie come with them? Was Edgar back with Mr Bransby? The new term at Stoke Newington had begun on the first day of February. I would have liked to know whether Miss Carswall was sanguine about her future happiness. A prig was always a prig, surely, even though he had a baronetcy and a fortune to lay at her feet.

In this period, I communicated only once with my former associates. On the last day of January, I wrote to Edward Dansey, thanking him for his kindness, without specifying its nature, and asking him to have my trunk packed and stored until I was in a position to receive it. I enclosed a little money to defray his expenses. I did not give him my direction, however, though I added that I would do myself the honour of writing to him again when I was more settled. With this letter, I enclosed a note to Mr Bransby, regretting that circumstances compelled me to resign my position with immediate effect and begging him to accept the salary he owed me in lieu of notice.

Of course, I read the public prints for another reason. To my inexpressible relief, there was no mention of a stolen ring, no mention of a search for Thomas Shield. I reasoned myself into a belief – or at least a hope – that, having frightened me off and cost me my livelihood, Stephen Carswall had decided to leave me alone, perhaps because the pleasure of any additional revenge he might wreak on me was not worth the danger of scandal at this delicate point in his daughter's life. He

357

would not want to put at risk the very existence of his grandson, the hypothetical Carswall Ruispidge, and his golden future.

The only item that still tied me to the past was Amelia Parker's mourning ring. I could not bring myself to drop it in the Thames, which would have been far the wisest course of action, for it was my one remaining connection with Sophie Frant. But I would have returned it to its owner, if I had known who its owner was. In the meantime, I hid it in a deep crack in one of the exposed purlins that ran the length of my room. I masked its presence with crumbling plaster rammed deep into the fissure; and in time a spider built its web across the crack, and I went for days without remembering the ring's existence.

I had cut myself adrift from my own life. I was not happy in those days but I thought myself safe.

CHAPTER SIXTY-EIGHT

THE BUBBLE BURST on a Tuesday in April. It was a fine day, almost warm enough for summer, and in the morning I had walked out to the pretty village of Stanmore, where Mrs Jem had a friend who wished to write a long and carefully worded letter of complaint to her father's executor. When I returned to my lodgings late in the afternoon, I found one of the little Jems waiting for me on the stairs.

'Ma wants you,' she announced. 'Mr Shield, am I as pretty as Lizzie? She says I ain't – she's a liar, ain't she?'

'You and your sister are both incomparably beautiful, each in your unique way.'

I gave her a penny and went down to the basement, where Mrs Jem was usually to be found sitting in an elbow chair placed between the range and the window at the front, which commanded a view of the steps up to the front door. Her fine, dark eyes peered out at me from their swaddling folds of fat.

'There was a man come asking after you before dinner,' she said.

'He wanted a letter written?'

'He didn't want nothing. Except to know if you lived here.'

'So you told him I did?'

'The girls told him. They was playing outside on them steps, the little monkeys. Then I came up and sent him about his business.' She studied my face. 'What you been up to?'

'What do you mean, ma'am?'

'Don't try and gammon me. I smoked you a long time ago. A man of your parts must have a reason to want to live in a place like this.'

'Madam, I told you –'

'I know what you told me, and you don't have to tell me again.' She smoothed her apron. 'You'll say it's none of my business, and in the ordinary way of things it ain't, not if there's no trouble. But he wasn't the sort of man I like to have inquiring about my lodgers. Sharp little runt, with a dreadful knowing way about him. He tried to bully me, too.'

I smiled at her. 'I wish I had seen it.'

Mrs Jem did not return the smile. 'Could have been a runner once, maybe, and now works private. The sort of fellow you'd find sniffing round the servants in an action for crim. con.'

'I assure you, ma'am, that is not the case here.' I felt myself grow warm, nevertheless: if Henry Frant were alive, then what had passed between Sophie and me on that afternoon in Gloucester would indeed have amounted to criminal conversation. 'I – I cannot think what he wanted.'

'He wanted you,' Mrs Jem said. 'That's plain enough. I give you fair warning: I don't want to lose you, Mr Shield, you're clean and obliging and you pays your rent. But I won't have unpleasantness in this house. I have to think of my girls.'

I bowed to her.

'Lord, don't waste your fine airs and graces on me. Just make sure that man don't come pestering us again.' She smiled as she spoke, though, and waved me away as she would have dismissed one of her own children.

I went quickly upstairs to my garret. I had little doubt what this visitor meant: Carswall had found out my direction. I cursed my own complacency. I had known from the beginning that he was a man of strong passions, a man capable of enduring hatred. I wished with all my heart that I had not hidden the ring in my room. Was there still time to dispose of it?

There was a loud knocking on the street door below, followed by voices in the hall, and then the patter of small feet running upwards. Lizzie and Lottie burst neck and neck into my room.

'Oh, sir,' Lottie began.

Lizzie pushed her sister against the jamb of the door, temporarily silencing her. 'There's another man for you, sir, not the –'

Lottie interrupted her sister with a well-directed kick to the ankle. 'No, sir, please, sir, he begs the favour of a word with you.'

As she brought the last words successfully out, a smug smile spread over her freckled face. Her sister pulled her hair. I broke up the altercation, as I had broken up many of their altercations before, by interposing my body between theirs, and marched them downstairs. In a way I was glad it had come to this: the decisions were made for me; there was no need to debate whether to stay or to run, to take the ring or to leave it where it was. As we walked, the children chattered to me, each apparently oblivious of the other's presence. My mouth was dry and I felt light-headed.

In the hall, a man in a black coat stood waiting. His back was turned to me, and he appeared to be studying the drops of dried blood on the floorboards that marked the place where Lottie and Lizzie had fought for possession of a sugar plum on Sunday afternoon. As I reached the foot of the stairs, he turned to greet me. I recognised the plump white face of Atkins, Mr Rowsell's clerk.

'Mr Shield, sir, I trust I find you well.'

While we said what was civil to each other, though without warmth on either side, he examined me with barely concealed curiosity. I thought it probable that he had known of the reception awaiting me at Mr Rowsell's house, but he had not warned me. He felt in his breast pocket and produced a letter.

'Mr Rowsell begged me to give you this. He said that if I found you here, he wished me to wait for an answer.'

I turned aside, broke the seal and unfolded the letter.

My dear Tom

I regret the misunderstanding that occurred when you called at Northington-street in January. Would you be kind enough to allow me to explain the reason for it? It would give me great pleasure if you were able to dine with me any day this week, apart from Saturday. In the meantime, believe me to be

 Your affectionate friend,
 Humphrey Rowsell

I looked at Atkins. 'Pray give my compliments to Mr Rowsell, and Thursday would be quite convenient.'

CHAPTER SIXTY-NINE

MR ROWSELL TOOK me to a tavern in Fleet-street. We drank first one bottle of claret with our dinner and then another. He was as amiable in his manner to me as ever but at first he steered our conversation resolutely towards general topics. He talked in fits and starts, rushing at his words as though he feared they might escape him if he did not hurry, and laughing boisterously at the slightest opportunity. Not that there was much cause for amusement – I remember we talked of the Cato Street Conspiracy against the government, which was then in the news, and the Peterloo Massacre in Manchester the previous summer. For all its wealth and vigour the country was tearing itself apart.

'These are troubled times for the nation,' Mr Rowsell said, as we broached the third bottle. 'I fear there may be a crash, a great crisis in public confidence that will make the collapse of Wavenhoe's seem no more than a trifling upset. So keep your capital safe, Tom, do not be tempted into speculation.'

'Thank you, sir.' I eyed my host's face with some anxiety, for it had grown dark with wine. 'May I ask what you meant in your letter? About an explanation?'

'An explanation?' He shut his eyes for a moment. 'Aye, well, first I must tell you that I have written to Mr Bransby. When I was trying to find you out, he was naturally the first person I thought of.'

'In that case you will know that I have resigned from my position at his school.'

'Yes – he – well, not to beat about the bush – he made a number of allegations about your conduct which I found hard to credit.'

'That is perhaps because they were untrue.'

Rowsell's eyebrows shot up. 'I am glad to hear it, Tom.'

'Theft, philandering and neglecting my duty to his pupils?'

He nodded. 'I reminded the reverend gentleman that there was a law of libel in this country. He did not reply to my second letter.'

'Surely Mrs Rowsell must have known of my disgrace long before you heard of it from Mr Bransby?'

'Yes, yes, Mrs Rowsell – yes, I shall come to that.' His colour darkened still more, and he applied himself to his wine. 'I did not know where you were. I cannot tell you how glad I was when Quintus Atkins came up to me on Monday morning and said he had found you.'

'On *Monday*? Not Tuesday?'

'Yes, it was Monday, I'm sure of it – you would not think it to look at him, but Atkins has a gift for talking to strangers, for asking harmless questions in a way that does not cause offence, and a wide acquaintance. I did not think it likely you would have returned to Rosington, or even left town. I determined to concentrate our search on the vicinity of the Strand – I thought it the most likely part of London for you to choose, you see, because of its long association with your aunt. It was merely a matter of his tramping the streets and asking questions for long enough, and there you were. To be precise, he was introduced to a stonemason in a public house. It turned out you had written a letter for the man. And later Atkins confirmed it by buying a glass of rum for a former sailor who lodges on the floor below you. I may say that both men gave you fine testimonials. So then I wrote the letter he brought you.'

I hesitated, wanting to pursue the matter further but uncertain how best to go about it. 'Forgive me for labouring the point, sir, but I heard that another man came looking for me at Gaunt-court on Tuesday. I wondered whether someone else, perhaps less benevolent than yourself, wished to find me.'

'I'm positive that Atkins told me the news on Monday.' Rowsell frowned. 'Mr Carswall? Could it have been he?'

'It's possible.'

'Do you feel able to tell me more about the circumstances?'

'I left Monkshill-park under a cloud. The cloud was none of my making, and Mr Carswall treated me unjustly. His malevolence pursued me to London, for he wrote to Mr Bransby and made certain accusations – those you have already heard. He manufactured evidence to support the most serious of those accusations. He meant to cost me my position, sir, and possibly my liberty – and even, perhaps, my life.'

'If you were my client, I would advise you not to repeat those accusations in public.' Rowsell dabbed his finger in a circle of wine on the table and drew the outline of a head resembling a fox's. 'He is a wealthy man, Mr Carswall, and one with a certain reputation. He may be an old dog, but he can still bite.'

'I was forewarned of his scheme by a friend,' I continued. 'So I came straight to you, intending to lay the matter before you and ask your advice.'

Rowsell lowered his head over his glass. 'I am sorry. It was most unfortunate that I was not in the way when you called.'

'I went to Lincoln's Inn first, and Atkins sent me on to Northington-street. I concluded from Mrs Rowsell's reception of me that Mr Carswall had reached you before me, and poisoned your mind and hers against me.'

'Very natural, my dear boy. That was not the case, however – the first I heard of what had happened was when Mr Bransby replied to my letter of inquiry. No, Mrs Rowsell's conduct sprang from another source. I hold myself very much to blame. I have not been altogether candid with you, I am afraid, and the fault is entirely mine. Circumstances placed me in an awkward position, and indeed they still do.' He swallowed half a glass of wine. 'That is why I asked you to dine with me here, rather than at Northington-street.'

'If I have distressed Mrs Rowsell in any way, I regret it extremely.'

'No, it is not you who have distressed her: it is I. And of course I have also distressed you. Tell me, did you never wonder why your excellent aunt placed her affairs in my hands? I do not wish to seem immodest, but it must have occurred to you that I am moderately successful in what I do, and that I would not usually attend so assiduously to the affairs of a lady in her circumstances, however amiable she was in her personal character. Mrs Reynolds's estate, as you know, was not large.'

'I had remarked on your kindness many times, sir. You will think me foolish but I had ascribed it to philanthropy, to a natural benevolence.'

'I am reproved. I wish that were true. Though, in fairness to myself, I may state that I assisted your aunt in her legal affairs, and indeed yourself, with no thought of gain. My motives were disinterested but I cannot claim they sprang from general benevolence.' Rowsell broke off to pour more wine. He had neglected his food, which was unlike him, for he was usually a good trencher-man.

I said gently, 'I would not pain you, sir. Whatever your reasons, you were very kind to me when my aunt died and afterwards, and I shall always be grateful for that.'

'Mrs Rowsell,' he said, apparently out of the blue, 'is a great reader of novels.'

I stared at him. 'I beg your pardon. I think I did not quite catch –'

'What I mean to say is this,' he broke in, speaking low and fast and rather indistinctly. 'Her mind has been to some extent formed by the reading that delights her hours of leisure. Nothing gives her greater pleasure than to settle down of an evening with a volume of the latest novel from the library. One could sometimes wish – ah, but no matter; I digress.' He ran out of words and stabbed the meat he had barely touched with uncharacteristic venom.

I said, 'One judges a man by his actions, and yours have been uniformly generous.'

Rowsell swallowed a mouthful of wine. Then he stretched his arm across the table and touched the sleeve of my coat. 'My dear boy. You are so like your mother sometimes. It is quite uncanny.'

I laid down my knife and fork. 'My mother, sir? My *mother*? You have the advantage of me: I did not realise that you knew her.'

'Yes. A lady of great charm and refinement. Indeed, there lies my difficulty, the source of my present difficulty, that is to say, with regard to Mrs Rowsell. You recall that you were to have eaten your dinner with us on Christmas Day, but were unable to join us? It was on that very occasion that I allowed a few ill-timed words to slip out. We were dining with two of Mrs Rowsell's aunts and several of her cousins, and I suggested we drink a toast to you in your absence. With hindsight, I see that this was not altogether wise. It led to Mrs Rowsell's inquiring a little more deeply than before about the – ah – the evident affection in which I held you. I mentioned that I had known both your mother and your aunt when I was a young man. I – I chanced to expatiate at some length on your mother's many good qualities. I realise now, of course, that my enthusiasm was ill judged. Though Mrs Rowsell knew you were the nephew of a valued client, she was not aware that at one time I had been acquainted with your mother.'

'When you say "acquainted" –?'

'Indeed, rather more than acquainted.'

He broke off again, having given the last words a singular emphasis, and looked miserably at me. By now a terrible suspicion was forming in my mind. I helped him to another glass of wine and he gulped it down as though it had been so much water. He took out a handkerchief and wiped his forehead.

'It grows quite warm in here, I find.' He attempted a smile. 'I do not think I have mentioned that, as a very young man, I passed a year or two in Rosington?'

I agreed that he had not mentioned this fact.

'I did not mean to conceal the circumstance: but delicacy urged me to choose with care my moment of revealing it. I went to Rosington to fill a position as a junior clerk to an auctioneers – Cutlack's: you may recall the name?'

I inclined my head.

'Old Josiah Cutlack was then the head of the family. It was at his house that I had the honour of meeting the young lady who later became your mother. She was a friend of Josiah's niece. We saw each other on subsequent occasions and – well, to cut a long story short, I developed a great tenderness for her. And she – she did not look unkindly on me.'

'Sir,' I began, 'are you to tell me that –'

But Rowsell rushed on, propelled by the current of his confession: 'I could not afford to marry – indeed, I could barely support myself – and your grandparents would never have sanctioned such a match. Then a friend of my late father's, an attorney in Clerkenwell, offered me a clerkship. Here, at last, was the possibility of advancement, of attaining a situation in life which would enable me to marry and support a wife. Your mother urged me to seize the opportunity. Though no words were spoken on either side, I confess I cherished a hope that one day, a few years hence – but it was not to be.'

He turned aside to blow his nose and, I daresay, to wipe a tear from his eye. I stared into my glass, attempting to decipher the outlines of my own life, newly shrouded in mist. It seemed that I had acquired a past I did not want and the possibility of a future I did not desire. Was even my name no longer my own?

'We did not correspond, of course,' Mr Rowsell went on. 'There was no engagement; it would not have been the thing. However – a year or two later, I heard of her marriage to Mr Shield: a worthy man, I am sure; and in those days most comfortably situated as well. I met him once at Mr Cutlack's, I believe. It often answers very well for a man to be considerably older than his wife. As indeed I have found myself, with Mrs Rowsell.'

'Sir,' I said urgently. 'A year or two later?'

'What?' He reached for the wine. 'Aye, one year and nine months. And each month passed like a century.'

'And you did not see my mother in that time?'

'No – but I had news of her, every now and then. I corresponded for a while with young Nicholas Cutlack, the old man's grandson; dead now, poor fellow; a fall from his horse. It was he who told me of your mother's marriage. I will not pretend that it was not a bitter blow, but still: a man must look forward, eh, not over his shoulder. I threw myself into work and in the fullness of time my principal invited me to become his partner. And he happened to have a daughter, and we found that we agreed very well together.'

I raised my glass. 'Let us drink to Mrs Rowsell, sir.'

'God bless her,' murmured Mr Rowsell, dashing a tear from his eye. When he had set down his glass, he continued: 'My tale is nearly done. Many years later, I saw your name in the newspapers in connection with that – that unfortunate incident in the Park. It is not a common surname, and one report mentioned that you came originally from Rosington. I inquired, and found that you were indeed the son of my old friend. So I made myself known to your aunt Reynolds – a most estimable woman, by the by, who was wonderfully kind to me when I was at Cutlack's.'

'She knew you? And she did not tell me?'

'The position was extraordinarily delicate, Tom – and on both sides. I wished to be of assistance but I could not be seen to help. I had Mrs Rowsell to consider and Mrs Reynolds was the first to acknowledge this. Your aunt was also extremely jealous of both your mother's reputation and yours. If my part became known, there are many in this world who would rush to place an uncharitable construction on my motives and on your mother's.'

'You place me under an obligation, sir.'

Rowsell dismissed it with a wave. 'I wish with all my heart I did. But Mrs Reynolds was a proud woman. She would accept very little from me. All I could do was lighten the legal burden that she needed to carry after your arrest. And later I was glad to help her put her own affairs in order. As her time drew near, I suggested the possibility to her that I might try to obtain a clerkship for you, but she preferred to try Mr Bransby first. She said she did not think it right to be further obliged to me. And then, by and by, after her death, I came to be acquainted with you.'

'I regret I am become a source of embarrassment to you and Mrs Rowsell.'

'The fault is scarcely yours.' With a tip of a finger he converted the drop of spilled wine from a fox's head to a spider. 'I scarcely know how it was but I had never found the opportunity to mention my previous attachment to Mrs Rowsell. Not that I concealed it, exactly – it was a case of *suppressio veri* rather than *suggestio falsi*. After all, it was so very long ago, you see, and the term "attachment" made more of it than I had any right to claim. There was no engagement between your mother and me, or even an understanding. But, as I say, on Christmas Day, I had drunk perhaps a little more deeply than usual, in honour of the occasion, and my tongue was less guarded, my mind less circumspect than it should have been.'

'Perhaps if I were to write to Mrs Rowsell and explain the circumstances?'

'Thank you, but I do not think it would answer. It was a great misfortune that Mrs Rowsell's aunts and cousins were at table with us. Their presence added salt to the wound. In all events, I regret to say that Mrs Rowsell misinterpreted what I said – quite understandably; the fault was entirely mine – and drew an erroneous conclusion, one which might not have been out of place in one of her novels. It was inexpressibly painful. There were tears – there were accusations – I had betrayed her in her own home – I was taking the bread out of our children's mouths – my character was quite beneath contempt. Mrs Rowsell is a woman of great tenacity, and once she has an idea in her mind, it can be very difficult to shift it.'

Mr Rowsell ran out of words. My first reaction was relief: despite his many virtues, I was glad he had not suddenly become my father. Now I knew the reason for his kindness in the past, I honoured him for it. My mother's heart had chosen wisely though her head had set its veto against it. As for Mrs Rowsell, no wonder my appearance on her doorstep had thrown her into such a passion. I felt sorry for them both: if Mrs Rowsell believed me to be her husband's illegitimate son, brought like a cuckoo into their home, then the bosom of the family could not have been a happy place for either of them since that unlucky Christmas dinner.

'It was cursed ill luck that I was forced to keep to my bed on that day you came to my house. I heard the hullabaloo at the door, though I did not know its cause. The rest you know. I wish it had not taken us such an unconscionable time to track you down. I might have found you sooner had I employed an agent. But once I had heard those absurd accusations from Mr Bransby, I thought it wiser not to involve a third party.'

'May I speak frankly, sir? Two men asked after me at Gaunt-court on Tuesday. The second was Atkins, but the first –'

'You fear that Mr Carswall has set a man to track you down?'

'I do not know what to fear. The first man questioned the children about me. My landlady sent him about his business, though not before he had discovered that I was lodging there. She thought it likely that he was some sort of inquiry agent, perhaps a former Bow-street runner who works for a lawyer.'

'You have done nothing wrong, dear boy: it may be best simply to stay where you are and let events take their course. On the other hand, if Mr Carswall intends to bring an action against you, he must have evidence to support his case.' Mr Rowsell leaned forward, his features suddenly grim: he had become the man of business again, and all trace of the kindly host had vanished. 'There's more to this than meets the eye, I fancy. I saw the reports in the newspapers about a lady who died by an accidental fall in the ice-house at Monkshill-park in January. And of course Miss Carswall is to marry Sir George Ruispidge, no doubt with a very handsome dowry. But I am at a loss to see how all this could affect you, or what possible reason Mr Carswall could have for pursuing you.'

I bent down and hooked a finger between my right shoe and my stocking. I fished out a small bundle, wrapped in a square of linen, which I laid between us on the table. I pulled back the folds of cloth one by one. There, winking up at us, was Amelia Parker's mourning ring.

CHAPTER SEVENTY

'OH PLEASE, SIR,' cried Lizzie as she opened the door to me on my return to Gaunt-court, 'we was watching you coming up to the door. Are you *fearfully* lushy?'

Lottie punched her arm. 'That ain't polite, Lizzie. Say "disguised" instead.'

'Don't be foolish,' I said, and advanced into the hall, stumbling slightly when my legs somehow became entangled with my stick. 'Neither term is apt.'

'I tell you, he's been at the blue tape,' Lizzie continued. 'Just like Pa. Ain't you, sir?'

'Blue tape is a low expression,' Lottie snarled.

I turned and looked sternly down at them. 'I have not had a drop of gin, children. Nor am I intoxicated. I may seem a little elevated in my spirits, but I am as sober as a judge.'

'Oooh,' squealed Lizzie. 'Ain't it lovely? Talks just like a book, don't he?'

Feet shuffled on the basement stairs, and Mrs Jem appeared. She ran her eyes over me. I suspect I was perhaps a little dishevelled, owing to a tumble in the gutter on my way down Fleet-street. When I beamed at her, she gave a shake of her head and said, 'You get along upstairs. Leave your clothes outside your door. I'll send someone up for them.'

There is no arguing with an autocrat. The girls vanished into the back regions of the house. I made my way slowly upwards, flight by swaying flight.

'Mind what you do with your candle,' Mrs Jem called up after me. 'I don't want you burning us all in our beds.'

As I mounted the stairs, my head seemed to clear as the altitude increased. I had drunk a quantity of claret during and after dinner but I had not followed Mr Rowsell's example and rammed home the claret with brandy. The truth was, it was not merely wine that intoxicated me: it was also relief.

Unlike Dansey, Mr Rowsell had been both immediate and unequivocal in his offers of support. At least one person unhesitatingly accepted my word before Mr Carswall's. Of course, I had not told him everything. Only a scrub would have revealed what had passed between Sophie and myself; and I could not be entirely frank about my relations with Miss Carswall.

Nor had I mentioned my suspicions concerning Mrs Johnson's death. Had I done so, it would have led inevitably to even wilder and more dangerous speculations about the identity of the murdered man at Wellington-terrace. Mr Rowsell must have thought me mad if I had blurted out my suspicion that Henry Frant had been not only an embezzler, but also a murderer, and that now he had killed his former accomplice, Mrs Johnson.

No, it would have been wildly indiscreet to confide my worst fears to him. However, Mr Rowsell had lifted a weight from my mind. There was no doubt, he thought, that the ring should be returned to Mr Carswall. Until its ownership should be definitively established, if it ever were, Mr Carswall had the best title to it. My possession of the ring made me immediately vulnerable, and Mr Rowsell was shocked I had retained it for so long.

'Leave it with me,' he had said. 'I will see that Mr Carswall receives it.'

'But your hand must not appear in the matter, sir.'

At that stage, Rowsell still had most of his wits about him. 'It is perfectly simple. If you give me his direction, I will have the ring sent in such a way that the sender cannot be traced. There will be no covering note. The address will be written in capital letters. Stay, we shall muddy the waters still further: I am sending Atkins up to Manchester next week: I shall give him the ring and desire him to post it from there. So you need not trouble yourself in the slightest. Forget you ever saw it.'

Once I reached the haven of my room, I sat on the little bed, which was rocking like a hammock aboard ship, and stripped off my coat, neckcloth, waistcoat and boots. I became aware that pushing through my relief like a green shoot in a flower bed was another emotion: a desire to write to Sophie. It struck me that the return of the ring might even be construed in some quarters as confirmation of my guilt, and it seemed a matter of urgency to make clear, at least to her, that I neither acted like a guilty party nor considered myself to be one.

I realise now – considering the matter coolly and soberly in another time and place – that this argument was barely rational, the flimsiest justification imaginable: I wished to write to Sophie, that was the long and the short of it, and I wished to do so directly. Without pausing for thought, I found pen, ink and paper and sat down at the washstand, which also served as my writing desk.

I was still sitting there when Mr Jem himself toiled up the stairs, tapped on my door and asked me how I did, when church bells struck first the half-hour and then the hour. At last I gave up the struggle to find words which would convey everything I wished to say, both explicitly and implicitly. I wrote simply this:

Pray do not credit the accusations you may hear about me. But believe me to be, at all times, your very faithful friend.

I neither dated nor signed the letter. I folded the paper and sealed it with a wafer. I wrote Sophie's name on the front in a disguised scrawl, but not her direction because I was uncertain whether she had come to town with Mr Carswall. Finally, I raised the letter to my lips and kissed it.

A moment later, I dropped my clothes outside the door, climbed into bed and fell asleep with the candle still burning.

CHAPTER SEVENTY-ONE

THE FOLLOWING MORNING, I woke to find myself dry-mouthed but surprisingly clear-headed. As I lay there, still with the soft tendrils of sleep around me, the thought of Sophie filled my mind so vividly that I felt, with but a minute extra effort, I could reach out my hand and touch the warm, living woman.

I sat up in bed and saw on the corner of the washstand the letter I had written her the previous evening. Before she could read it, however, I had to find her. Though it was probable that she was with the Carswalls at Margaret-street, it was by no means certain. I hoped that if I strolled through the neighbourhood for long enough I might catch a glimpse of her. Perhaps – and at this point my heart began to beat faster – I might even be able to press the letter into her hand. For I dared not trust it to the two-penny post. An hour or so later it would be in Mr Carswall's hands, for every letter to the household was seen by him. I thought him more than capable of reading any that came for Sophie.

My plan was by no means perfect but it had two outstanding merits – that it gave me something to do, and that it gave me a chance of seeing Sophie again. True, there was a danger that I might be recognised by another member of the household. But I had recently purchased a dark green topcoat from the sorrowful Russian gentleman on the second floor, a garment which would be unfamiliar to any who had known me before. If I wore the collar turned up and my hat pulled down, and if I exercised caution at all times, I was reasonably sure that I could avoid detection.

It was a little after eleven o'clock when I made my way northwards from the crowds in Oxford-street and entered Margaret-street from its western end. Mr Carswall's house was on the north side, in the block between Lichfield-street and Portland-street. With my eyes averted, I hurried along the opposite pavement.

It was too early for anyone to be about, apart from servants on errands and tradesmen's delivery boys. Indeed, there were so few foot passengers that I felt myself conspicuous. Never before had I realised that a spy must feel as though his profession were stamped in red upon his forehead for all the world to see.

In a flurry of panic, I turned into Great Titchfield-street and darted south towards the rumble of vehicles in Oxford-street. I spent the next hour perambulating the immediate neighbourhood of the house. I saw the weaselly Pratt, Carswall's creature, in his morning livery, ogling the women as he sauntered through Oxford-market. I ducked into a shop until he had passed.

At last my patience was rewarded. In Winsley-street, I noticed two boys walking ahead of me. I recognised their backs at once, and with an unexpected pang of sadness. I had not realised until then that I missed the boys. A moment later I tapped Charlie on the arm.

'Why! It's you, sir. I say, Edgar! Stop!'

The boys shook my hand vigorously. They were momentarily tongue-tied but I could not mistake the pleasure on their faces.

'Are you come to call on us, sir?' Charlie said at last.

'No. I – I happened to be passing.' I saw Edgar drive his elbow into his friend's side in a manner he evidently believed to be discreet; Charlie's face coloured with embarrassment. 'It is such a fine day. I was taking the air.'

'Yes, sir,' said Charlie. 'Just what occurred to me: it is a beautiful day, perfect for a walk.' He spoke in a gabble but his intention was entirely kind.

'I am surprised you are here,' I said, 'though of course I am very happy to see you. But I had imagined you would be at school. Or at least that Edgar would be.'

'Mr Carswall said Charlie could come back with me after all,' Edgar said. 'So we are both at Mr Bransby's still.'

I nodded. Mr Bransby had been most obliging to Mr Carswall so the latter's change of mind was understandable. 'That must be agreeable for you both. So has Mr Bransby given the school a holiday?'

'Not the school, sir,' Edgar said. 'Only Charlie and me.'

'Yesterday was my cousin Flora's birthday, sir,' said Charlie. 'There was a big dinner, and afterwards there was dancing and cards, and lots of people came. Flora begged for us to be invited, me because I am her cousin, and Edgar because he is my most particular friend. Captain Ruispidge came to fetch us from school. Only fancy! He drives a bang-up curricle gig and we sat squashed up beside him when we drove off. All the fellows were sick with envy.'

'But we return to Mr Bransby's this afternoon,' Edgar put in. 'Mr Allan's clerk will take us.'

'And the bird, to be sure,' Charlie said.

'The bird?' I said.

'A parrot, sir. Mr Carswall gave it me. And we are to take it back to school: Mr Bransby has given us leave. We have just been to buy seed for it. It does not say much yet but we shall teach it.'

'Oh, sir,' Edgar said, after an awkward pause in the conversation. 'There is a new man at the school now, Mr Brown, and the fellows don't like him half so well. They — we — wish you hadn't left.'

'I regret it myself,' I said, realising from this that Carswall and Bransby had not published the reason for my dismissal, or perhaps even the fact of it. Neither of them stood to gain from the scandal being known abroad.

'I beg your pardon, sir,' Charlie said. 'But was there a disagreement between you and Mr Carswall? We could not understand why you left Monkshill so suddenly, and Mr Carswall will not let your name be mentioned at home.'

'There was a disagreement.' I smiled down at them. 'But I need not trouble you with the details. Now, I must not detain you any longer.'

'Should you like to see the bird, sir?' Edgar asked. 'It is uncommonly interesting. And singularly intelligent, too. It keeps saying something, only we do not yet quite understand it.'

'I should like it above all things. However —'

'Edgar and I are to walk with it to Mr Allan's this afternoon,' Charlie said suddenly. 'Mr Carswall cannot spare the carriage. Mama says there is no need to go to the expense of a hackney for such a short walk. If you cared to join us, we should have the pleasure of showing it to you.'

I bowed. 'That would be most kind.' My conscience gave a twinge at the thought of making an unlicensed rendezvous with the boys. All at once, however, I thought of a stratagem which would not only be kind to my scruples but also of practical assistance. 'Pray, Charlie, may I ask a favour of you? I have a letter for your mother here, which I meant to leave at the house as I passed, but it slipped my mind. I wonder if you would be so kind as to give it to her.'

Charlie said he would be delighted to be of service. I noted a look of intelligence passing between the boys, and knew there was no need for me to hint that discretion was desirable. The boys were accustomed to living under tyranny, whether Mr Bransby's or Mr Carswall's, and tyranny nourishes the ability to keep secrets. It was arranged that we should meet in Bedford-square, which lay on the route they would take to Southampton-row since it allowed them to skirt safely to the north of St Giles.

I spent the intervening time constantly in motion, for I was filled with a restless energy that would not let me stand still for a moment. I tramped north, past the new St Pancras Church they were building at the top of Woburn-place and up to Clarendon-square. There I panicked, thinking I might be late, and walked south again as though the devil himself were at my heels, reaching Bedford-square a good twenty minutes before the appointed time. I paced up and down the square and the surrounding streets until at last, at ten minutes past the hour, I saw the two small figures approaching, walking in file. As we drew nearer, I discovered that the boys carried on their shoulders a pole, from which hung a birdcage covered in blue serge cloth. We came together at the corner of the square, and they set down their burden with infinite solicitude.

'When the cover is on, the bird believes it night-time,' Charlie said. 'It falls asleep directly.'

He crouched and slowly raised the cover. Having seen how the cage swung on the pole, I was not surprised to find its occupant already awake. It was an unkempt creature, its plumage dull and ragged, with a wicked look in its eyes. The cage itself, on the other hand, was spotless. Charlie was still in the honeymoon of proprietorship. I desperately desired to know what answer Sophie had given but I knew better than to ask for it.

'Has the bird a name?'

'It has two, sir,' Edgar said.

'His name is Jackson,' Charlie said. 'After Gentleman Jackson, the pugilist. I'm sure the bird would be a doughty fighter if he could. But I said Edgar could choose a name for him too, though he is my bird, for there is no reason why a bird should not have two names any more than a person has.'

'Very true,' I said.

'My name for him is Tamerlane.'

'That is a very grand appellation.'

'He is a very grand bird,' Edgar said gravely. 'I am sure he is intelligent. We shall teach him heroic poetry.'

'He already speaks,' Charlie put in. He poked a finger through the bars of the cage and prodded the unfortunate fowl, which scuttled away to the other end of its perch. 'Come, Jackson, talk to us.'

The bird preserved an obstinate silence. Despite the boys' pleading, it stared balefully through the bars and refused to utter a sound.

'I'm so sorry, sir,' Charlie said. 'You would have enjoyed it enormously. He speaks so clearly – it is just as though he were a real person, only one cannot quite make out what he is saying.'

'It is no matter. Tell me, were you able to give my letter to your mother?'

He looked up at me, his eyes apparently guileless, and as so often with children, I wondered how much he noticed, how much he understood.

379

'Oh yes, sir. Mama sent her compliments, and said there would be no answer.'

I nodded, hoping that my expression somehow implied that this was entirely what I had expected.

'*Ayez peur*,' squawked the wretched bird.

'What did that –?' I began, and choked back the rest of the question.

Edgar clapped his hands. 'There! I knew he would. Is it not quite splendid, sir?'

'Yes, indeed.'

'And does he not sound exactly like a person?'

'Oh, identical.'

'Can you make out what he says?' Charlie said.

'*Ayez peur*,' repeated the bird, and pecked at his seed.

'I believe I can,' I said, 'though he has not perfectly mastered the consonants. Does he not say "I hate beer"?'

'*Ayez peur*,' said the bird for the third time and defecated on the floor of the cage.

'Yes, that is undoubtedly it,' I went on. 'Does he abstain from all liquor, or is it only beer that arouses his disgust?'

My feeble attempt at wit struck the boys as exquisitely funny. We talked for a few minutes more until Edgar touched his companion's arm.

'We must walk on, Charlie,' he said. 'Mr Allan will not be happy if his clerk is kept waiting.'

Charlie bent over the cage and carefully restored the blue cover.

Edgar said, his voice so low that only I could hear: 'Mrs Frant goes to the burying ground this afternoon, I believe. I heard her telling Mrs Kerridge. Mr Frant's headstone has now been set up.'

'There,' said Charlie. 'It is night again. I daresay Jackson does not mind the swaying of the cage as we carry him, for quite probably it reminds him of the swaying of the trees in his native jungle.'

'Thank you,' I said to Edgar, and then again, more loudly, 'Thank you so much for showing me Jackson Tamerlane. I am sure you will soon succeed in teaching him entire poems.'

We shook hands and parted. I stood for a moment watching their little procession hurrying along the pavement towards Southampton-row.

And then I too began to move slowly in an eastward direction, though bearing towards the north, so that I would not follow in their footsteps.

I blundered along, a man in a trance, sometimes brushing against walls and other pedestrians, sometimes stumbling. Passers-by avoided me, gave me disapproving looks. I felt dazed, as though I had woken from a heavy sleep and found myself in a time and place that were entirely strange to me.

In my head I heard over and over again the sound of Jackson Tamerlane squawking out the only words it knew: *Ayez peur, ayez peur*.

CHAPTER SEVENTY-TWO

FROM THE BURYING ground of St George's, Bloomsbury, I heard the cries of children at play, shrill and incomprehensible as the language of birds. Directly to the south lay the stately buildings of the Foundling Hospital, flanked by the gardens of the Mecklenburgh and Brunswick-squares.

Sophie was not here. Perhaps she had already left. Perhaps Edgar had been mistaken about the time or even the place. I tried to summon up her face and for once even that comfort was denied me.

I sought solace in activity. The cemetery looked newly polished in the late afternoon sunshine of a spring day. An attendant loitered by the gate. I gave him sixpence to show me the grave I sought. The headstone was small and plain, raw and unweathered. Here were no weeping cherubs or fulsome inscriptions. Incised in the stone were these words and nothing else:

HENRY WILLIAM PARKER FRANT
17th July 1775–25th November 1819
aet. suæ 44

With his lean figure, Henry Frant had looked younger. The date of his birth stirred a memory: I recalled that according to the tablet in the church at Flaxern Parva his mother Emily had departed this life in the same year: perhaps she had died in childbirth, or from complications arising from it. I had a sudden vision, at once unexpected, intense and unwelcome, of a small boy alone among the servants in that great house at Monkshill; growing up without a mother, and with a father dedicated to dissolute pursuits that took him far away from his child; and, when Monkshill had to be sold, of a boy removed from the comfort of the familiar and sent to live among strangers in Ireland. Henry Frant was, or had been, a gentleman: but perhaps there had been little to envy in his situation.

I turned aside and paced up and down the gravel walks, the refrain of that unlovely fowl never far from my mind. A funeral procession passed me and automatically I uncovered and stood aside. Oh, the awful panoply of death! The last of the mourners went by. And there, hurrying away along a path at right angles to the procession, was the unmistakable figure of Sophie Frant. She was quite alone.

I walked rapidly in pursuit. Widow's weeds often mask their wearers with a layer of anonymity: even when the face is unveiled, one sees the widow, not the woman. There was no mistaking Sophie, though. I recognised every line of her body; I had traced in fact and in fancy the curve of her neck; I knew her posture and I knew the way she walked, with her eyes turning from side to side; for her mind was always alert, always watchful, always interested.

She heard my footsteps on the gravel behind her and stood aside to let me pass, pretending to study an inscription. I drew level and stopped. Slowly her head turned towards me.

I bowed. Neither of us spoke. There we were, four or five feet apart. I was aware of the cortège winding its way to an open grave within a stone's throw of the place dedicated to the mortal remains of Henry Frant. It was a fine afternoon, and there were others visiting the dead. Here, among the graves, a tide of living humanity ebbed and flowed around us.

She pushed the veil away from her face. It was always her eyes that drew me. I took a step nearer, then stopped as though chained to my situation like a dog in a yard. At Monkshill, seeing her every day, dining at the same table, walking in the same grounds – all this had bred a false intimacy between us, in the sense that it had seemed entirely natural for a woman in her position to treat me almost as her equal. But these last three months apart had dispelled this rosy mist of illusion: now, seeing her again, I could not help but be aware of the great chasm that lay between us: of the contrast between my shabby second-hand clothes and the dark elegance of hers. I did not recognise her cloak, or the pelisse or gown I glimpsed beneath.

'Tom,' she said, 'I – I must not see you.'

'Then why did you not write me an answer to my note? Why leave me in suspense?'

She winced as if I had hit her. 'That was not what I intended. I thought a clean, immediate break was best.'

'For whom?'

She looked directly at me. 'For me. And perhaps for you. Besides, further intercourse between us would not be kind to my cousin.'

'To Miss Carswall? But what has she to do with it?'

'You should know that better than I, sir.'

I felt myself grow warm. 'Sophie – my dear, please: if you mean that last evening in Monkshill, Miss Carswall came to the schoolroom merely to wish me goodbye and to lend me some money for my journey. It was an act of kindness, nothing more.'

She turned her head away, and her hat and veil obscured her face. 'Even if that is true, there is another reason why I must not see you or write to you.'

'Is this because of the accusation Mr Carswall has fabricated against me?'

She shook her head. 'I knew that was nonsense. So did Flora.'

'He had someone sew the ring into my greatcoat. I suspect it was Pratt. By great good fortune, I found it there when I reached London. I have made arrangements for it to be returned anonymously.'

'I have been so anxious. I did not know where you were, or how you were.' Sophie spoke more quickly now, and her face was alive with animation. 'Mr Carswall changed his mind about withdrawing Charlie from Mr Bransby's. But you are no longer there, I collect?'

I nodded. 'Mr Bransby and Mr Carswall came to an understanding. I resigned before I was discharged.'

'How do you live?'

I saw her looking at me, and knew the figure I must cut in my battered hat and threadbare coat. 'I live very well, thank you. I am not without friends.'

'I am glad.'

'And you?'

Her shoulders twitched. 'I live with my cousins, as before. Mr Carswall sees to everything. He pays Kerridge's wages, and Mr Bransby's bills. I want for nothing.'

'Sophie, there is still –'

'I am looking for Mr Frant's grave,' she interrupted, and her interruption was a form of reproof. 'The headstone was set up only last week. I thought I should see it.'

I pointed. 'It is over there.'

'Mr Carswall paid for that, too.'

Uninvited, I paced in silence beside her. I indicated the headstone and we stopped. Sophie stared at it for a moment, her face pale and still. I do not think there was any trace of emotion in her countenance. She might have been studying a bill of fare.

'Do you think he is at peace?' she said suddenly.

'I do not know.'

'He was always restless. I think he would have liked to be at peace. To be nothing. To want nothing.'

Her right hand gestured towards the grave, and the movement brought to mind the way a mourner throws a handful of earth on top of the coffin before it is covered over for ever. There was a finality about it. Without looking at me, she walked away. I replaced my hat and followed.

'Sophie,' I said, because after what had happened between us I would not call her Mrs Frant. 'Will you listen to me?'

'Pray do not speak.' Her eyes were bright. 'Please, Tom.'

'I must. There may not be another opportunity. You cannot stay where you are.'

'Why not? The Carswalls are my cousins.'

'What will happen when Miss Carswall marries Sir George? You will be alone with that foul old man.'

'That is my concern. Not yours.'

'It is my concern: I cannot stand back and leave you there unprotected.'

'I do not want your pity, sir.'

'I do not wish to give you pity. I wish to give you love. I cannot give you much, Sophie, but I believe that I could through my exertions preserve you and Charlie from absolute want, even now. If you would let me, I would offer you my hand with all my heart.'

'I cannot entertain such a proposal. It is quite out of the question.'

'Then let me support you without marriage.'

'As your mistress, do you mean?' she said sharply. 'I had not thought you –'

'No, no. I mean as a sister, as whatever you wished. My lodgings are perfectly respectable, and I would put you under the protection of the woman of the house and move elsewhere.'

'No, sir, no.' Her voice had become gentler. 'It cannot be.'

'I know we should be poor at first, but in time I hope to earn a modest competence. I have friends, I am willing to work. I would do all in my power –'

'I do not doubt it, Tom.' She touched my arm. 'But it cannot be. When my year of mourning is up, I am to marry Mr Carswall.'

I stared appalled at her for a moment, my mouth open like an idiot's. Then I grasped her hand and said, 'Sophie, my love, no, you must not –'

'Why not?' She moved aside, pulling her hand from mine. 'It is for Charlie's sake. Mr Carswall has promised to settle a considerable sum on him on the day we are married, and to provide for him in his will.'

'It is damnable. Carswall is a monster. I –'

'It will be a perfectly respectable arrangement in the eyes of the world, and in the eyes of our family and friends. We are cousins. There is a disparity of age but that don't signify. I have no doubt we shall do very well. Charlie will be provided for, and I shall live in comfort. I cannot pretend these considerations mean nothing to me. And, as I have accepted Mr Carswall as my future husband, I must respect his wishes. Any acquaintance between you and me must come to an end.'

I looked aghast at her pale, determined face. Something inside me shivered and broke. I turned and ran. My vision shimmered. Tears chilled my cheeks. I pushed my way through a knot of mourners who had attended the cortège and burst through the gates of the cemetery.

Drawn up outside was a row of carriages. I glimpsed a face I recognised at the window of the nearest one, a hackney. Mrs Kerridge was waiting for her mistress.

I ran on. In my mind, the cry of that damned bird ran round like a jingle.

Ayez peur, ayez peur.

CHAPTER SEVENTY-THREE

I MUST HAVE walked more than thirty miles that day, from one side of London to the other and then back in great zigzags. At nine o'clock of the evening I found myself in Seven Dials. It had come on to rain, but that did not deter the drinkers and the prostitutes, the beggars and the hawkers.

By this time, I was long past the surge of misery that had enveloped me as I left the graveyard. I was cool, entirely rational. I was no longer blind to the need for self-preservation, that most resilient of instincts. I had a firm grasp on my stick, avoided dark entries and kept a wary eye on those I met.

I had walked so far with a simple purpose in mind, that I might sleep eventually, for a weary body is the best of all soporifics. I had come to Seven Dials with a purpose, too. A drowning man will catch at a twig and hope against hope it will bear his weight.

Ayez peur, ayez peur.

I turned into Queen-street. A moment later I was strolling past Mr Theodore Iversen's shop. There was a light in the window. I crossed the road and went into an alehouse a few doors further down. I ordered a pint of porter, pushed my way through the crowd and leaned against a wall beside a grimy window that gave me a view of the other side of the street.

I drank slowly, rebuffing attempts at conversation. I was caught on the horns of a dilemma. I did not wish to make my interest in the shop too obvious, but unless I went closer, there was no possibility of my finding what I sought. It soon became apparent that there was a good deal of coming and going at Mr Iversen's – both at the shop door and at the passage leading to the backyard, where the men had attacked me. Respectability was an uncommon quality in Seven Dials, but all things are relative and I gradually came to the conclusion that those who patronised the shop were, taken as a whole, less disreputable than those who came and went by the passage.

In general, the better sort of Mr Theodore Iversen's customers emerged from the shop with a package or a bottle. Apart from the ghostly movements I sometimes discerned on the other side of the glass, all I saw clearly of the interior was revealed in the moments when the door opened. However much I peered, my vantage point would not allow me to see into the back of the establishment.

Someone touched my arm. I wheeled around, twisting my features into a scowl. For an instant I thought there was no one there. Then I lowered my gaze and saw in the dim light of the taproom what at first I took to be the pale, dirty face of a child with ragged ginger hair hanging loose to her shoulders. A moment later, I realised that the shape beneath the torn shift she wore was womanly, and almost at once I recalled her identity.

'Mary Ann,' I said. 'I – I hope I find you well.'

The little dumb woman uttered the high, bird-like sound I recalled so well from our meeting in the yard behind Mr Iversen's house. Her face was working with fear, and perhaps anxiety. She seized the cuff of my coat with grubby hands and pulled me towards the door. For an instant I resisted, fearing that she was leading me into a trap. A ripple of notes, as pure as a chorister's, burst out of her. I allowed her to tow me into the street.

'What is it? What do you wish to show me?'

This time her cry was sharper, even with an edge of anger. She gestured vigorously with her right arm, pointing towards the end of the street, and motioning with her other hand, as if to reinforce the urgency. Then she pushed me away from her, and as she did so, her eyes slid across the road to the shop. I saw the fear in her face, this time quite unmistakable. She bunched her hands into fists and pretended to punch me in the chest again and again and again, the blows light, meant for show, not for harm: to tell me something.

'They are coming to find me?' I said. 'They mean to hurt me?'

Her mouth opened into a great oval, showing the rotting teeth within. Her squeals became louder. She passed the flat of her hand across my windpipe.

Cut-throat.

'Tell me one thing before I go.' I felt in my pocket for my purse. 'Has Mr Iversen still got his bird? The one that says *ayez peur*, the one he used to keep in the shop?'

She shook her head and shooed me, as if I were a wandering chicken.

'What happened to it?' I opened the purse and showed it to her. 'Where did it go?'

She spat at the purse, her spittle spraying on my hand.

I cursed myself for a fool. 'I'm sorry. But when did the bird go? Within the last week?'

In the dull evening light, dusk contending with flaring lamps and torches, Mary Ann's face grew even paler and the freckles stood out like typhus spots. She was looking not at me but across the road. Two heavily built men in black coats had emerged from the passageway beside the shop. One of them glanced at me and I saw him touch his companion's arm.

At the same time, I saw something else, something so wholly unexpected I could hardly believe it. Passing in front of the two men, impeding their rush across the road at me, was a small, lopsided but intensely powerful figure. He pushed open Mr Iversen's door – by some acoustical freak I heard the jangle of the shop bell – and vanished inside. But I recognised him. It was the tooth-puller, the man called Longstaff, who lived with his mother in Lambert-place, quite a different neighbourhood from this; the man who had given me the satchel containing the severed finger.

Mary Ann screeched and ran away down the street. I walked hurriedly in the opposite direction, towards the crossroads that gives Seven Dials its name. I glanced back and saw the men plunging across the roadway, careless of the traffic. I abandoned dignity and broke into a run.

For the next quarter of an hour, we played fox and hounds, and all the time I made my way south and west. In the end I lost them by ducking into an alley off Gerrard-street and working my way along the backs of the buildings till I could emerge at the eastern end of Lisle-street. I slowed to a more comfortable walk and took my time strolling among the bright lights of Leicester-square. I did not think they would dare attack me there, even if they had been able to follow me. I made two leisurely circuits of the square, enough to convince me that I had thrown them off.

At last I made my way back to the Strand and Gaunt-court. I was exhausted, and faint with hunger for I had not eaten since long before I met Sophie. Far worse than weariness and sore feet, though, were the anxieties that weighed down my spirits.

A hackney was waiting near the entrance to Gaunt-court, its driver huddled under his greatcoat on the box. The glass was down and the smell of a cigar wafted out into the evening air, its fragrance momentarily overwhelming the smells of the street. I had a glimpse of two eyes, their whites quite startling in the half-light of the evening, and heard a deep, familiar voice.

'Well met, Mr Shield,' said Salutation Harmwell.

CHAPTER SEVENTY-FOUR

A T MR NOAK'S lodgings in Brewer-street, Salutation Harmwell provided me with a sandwich and a glass of madeira. The refreshment was welcome, but its effect, combined with the warmth, the lateness of the hour, the softness of my chair and above all my tiredness, was my undoing. As we waited in the big, shabby room on the first floor, I fell into a profound sleep.

A rapping on the street door brought me suddenly to my senses. In that instant, poised between sleeping and waking, a bed of red roses glowed and pulsed like embers in a dying fire, and time stretched into the dark, illimitable wasteland around them. Then the roses became tufts of wool, a faded carpet shimmering in the lamplight: time was no more than the ticking of the clock above the fireplace and the expectation of the sun rising.

I heard footsteps below, the rattle of a chain and the withdrawing of a bolt. In some confusion, I sat up and cleared my throat. I had an uneasy suspicion that I had been snoring.

'I beg your pardon,' I said. 'I had fallen into a doze.'

Salutation Harmwell, still as a hunter, silent and alert, was seated bolt upright on the other side of the fireplace. 'It does not matter in the least, Mr Shield,' he said, rising from his chair. 'The fault is ours, for bringing you here at this hour. But now at least your wait is over.'

There were footsteps on the stairs. The door opened, and Mr Noak bustled in. He advanced towards me with his hand outstretched.

'It is good of you to come, Mr Shield. I am sorry you have had such a delay. I was dining with the American Minister, and I found he had invited several gentlemen expressly to meet me. I could not with decency leave Baker-street until I had talked to them all.'

I protested automatically that he had not inconvenienced me in the slightest, wondering a little at the civility he showed me. Mr Noak waved me back to my chair. He himself took the seat that Harmwell had vacated. The clerk remained standing – attentive to Mr Noak, as always, but never subservient – his dark clothes and skin blending with the shadows away from the circle of light around the fireplace.

I said, more abruptly than I had intended: 'May I ask how you found my direction, sir?'

'Eh? Oh, my London lawyers recommended an inquiry agent who does that kind of work.' He glanced at me over his spectacles. 'You did not give him a great deal of trouble.'

I fancied there was a hint of a question in his words but I chose not to hear it. I said, 'When did he find me?'

'Earlier this week.' After a pause, he added, his voice suddenly sharp, 'Why do you ask?'

'He was noticed at the house where I lodge.'

'Yes. I shall not employ him again. He was less discreet than I would have wished.' Noak hesitated, and then continued, 'You see, when I commissioned him to find you, I was not sure when – or even whether – I might wish to see you. But today there have been a number of events which make renewing our acquaintance a matter of urgency.'

'For whom?'

'Oh, for both of us.' The American sat back in his chair and a spasm of pain passed over his face. 'In my opinion, that is to say. You of course must be the best judge of your own interests.'

'It is difficult to be the judge of anything when one has no idea what is happening, sir.'

He inclined his head, as though acknowledging the force of my argument, and said in his flat, quiet voice: 'Murder, Mr Shield. That is what has happened. And now there are consequences.'

'You mean Mr Frant's murder?'

Noak said: 'We go too fast. I should have said: murders.'

The plural form of the word filled the room with a sudden, uncomfortable silence. It is one thing to articulate a theory in the privacy of your own mind; it is quite another to hear it on the lips of someone else, particularly a man of sense.

I pretended ignorance. 'I beg your pardon, sir – I do not catch your meaning.'

'The man who lies in St George's burial ground had lost his face, Mr Shield. The law decided he was Mr Frant but the law may sometimes be an ass.'

'If he was not Mr Frant, then who was he?'

Noak regarded me in silence for a moment. His face was perfectly impassive. At last he sighed and said, 'Come, come. Let us not fence with one another. You and Harmwell found Mrs Johnson's body. Both Sir George and Mr Carswall had pressing reasons to treat her death as the accident it seemed, at least superficially, to be. But there is no reason why you or I should delude ourselves. What on earth would a gentlewoman be doing in her neighbour's ice-house in the depths of a winter night, a gentlewoman dressed in her husband's clothes? You will recall the poisoned dogs, I am sure, and the mantrap that was sprung in East Cover. I think Harmwell drew your attention to the sound of a horse when you were carrying back the boys that night. And I am sure you will recall the ring that you and he found the following morning.' He gave a dry, snuffling sound which I think was a sign of mirth. 'I am a tolerable judge of character, by the by. I have never credited Mr Carswall's allegations about you.'

'I am heartily glad of it, sir. Surely, though – and I admit I know little or nothing of the law – even if there are two murders rather than one, and even if the victim of the first was not the man he seemed, it is not easy to change the verdict of a coroner's jury? Not, at least, without irrefutable evidence.'

'Two murders?' said he, ignoring my question. 'I did not say two murders. I believe there has been at least one more.' Mr Noak leaned forward, his elbows on the arms of the chair, and I saw the twinge of pain once again pass like a shadow over his face. 'That is the reason for my involvement. But I've already told you something of that.'

He peered at me. It took a moment for his meaning to sink in. When it did, I felt an unexpected rush of pity.

'Lieutenant Saunders, sir? Your son?'

Noak stood up. He walked slowly across that red rectangle of carpet until he reached the fireplace. He put out a hand and rested it on the mantel-shelf and turned to face me. I was startled by the change in his face. Now he seemed an old, old man.

'You recall that I mentioned him at Monkshill?' he said. 'It was partly to judge the effect of his name on the company when I revealed the connection. It is not generally known, even in America.'

He had also told me that I resembled his son, and that the day was the anniversary of his son's birth. I remembered, too, that he had said something in my private ear about the manner of the young man's death.

'I think you told me that he died in an accident?' I said.

'Another accident.' Noak gave the last word a vicious, hissing twist. 'And it was clumsily done. They found him in a muddy alley at the back of a hotel that was no better than a brothel: face-down in a puddle, stinking of brandy and drowned. They even found a woman who swore he tried to lie with her. She said she had taken his money but found he was unable to fulfil his part of the bargain because he was so drunk. According to those of his fellow officers I was able to question, my son was not a brandy drinker, and he had no business in that part of Kingston. Nor was he known as a man who frequented prostitutes.' He paused and looked inquiringly at me, indeed almost imploringly, which confused me.

'A young man's friends may not wish to tell the unvarnished truth about him to his father.'

'I am aware of that, and have made allowance for it. But I do not believe my son died by accident. And if he did not die by accident, then how and why did he die?' Noak gestured at the shadows on the left. 'Harmwell is convinced my son was killed to keep him silent.'

'Sir, I regret your son's death extremely. But you will forgive me if I say that I do not understand why you have sought me out, or why you have brought me here at such a late hour.'

'The link that binds us, Mr Shield, that binds my son's murder with those others, is Wavenhoe's. The bank was active in Canada during the late war. Mr Frant oversaw its operations there in person for the first year or two, until 1814. There is always money to be made in wartime, if you do not mind the risks. A contractor found himself in difficulties, and the bank came to the rescue and exacted a price for doing so. Wavenhoe's took over the firm's ownership, and Mr Frant assumed its direction. Originally the contract was for fodder for artillery horses, I believe, but Wavenhoe's expanded the sphere of operation considerably. They did very well for themselves, too. But then Mr Frant's desire for profits outran both his commercial acumen and his patriotic scruples. Many sorts of men are drawn to the army, and not all of them are averse to making a private profit, especially if it involves no more than turning a blind eye on occasion. What are they defrauding, after all? They do not think of their fellows, or any individuals, as their victims, but some faceless, formless thing such as the War Department or the government or King George. They tell themselves it is not stealing at all, simply a legitimate perquisite of their office that everyone has and no one talks about. So they sign for goods they have not received, or for damaged articles, or they contrive to lose the necessary paperwork – all of which means that the contractor has a pleasing surplus to dispose of, and in many cases – and this I know for a fact – Mr Frant found a ready market across the border, in the United States.'

'But that is treason,' I said.

'Profit has no nationality,' Noak replied. 'And it follows its own principles. I believe that once Frant had established a channel linking British North America with the United States, he discovered that it could be used for information as well as goods. Information leaves far fewer traces of its passage and it is much more lucrative.'

'You have proof?'

'I know that such intelligence was received in the United States, and I am as sure as I am of my own name that Mr Frant had a hand in it.' Mr Noak stopped suddenly, swung round and extended his arm at Mr Harmwell. 'Were you aware that Harmwell enlisted in the Forty-First when my son was commissioned into it? That was at the start of the war, in 1812. Tell Mr Shield, Harmwell, tell him what you saw.'

Harmwell stepped out of the shadows. 'Lieutenant Saunders did me the honour of confiding in me,' he said sonorously, as though reading a statement in a court of law; and his rich voice reduced the memory of Noak's to a thin whisper. 'He believed the regimental quartermaster to be engaged in peculation in concert with a contractor. Two days before his death on the sixth of May, 1814, he took me with him as a witness to a meeting between the quartermaster and a gentleman at a coffee house. I did not learn the gentleman's name on that occasion, but I did see his face.'

'You understand?' Noak cried. 'The possibility of proof. Harmwell subsequently identified the man whom the quartermaster met as Henry Frant. You were present on the occasion of his identification yourself, as it happens: when we arrived from Liverpool, and called at Russell-square, and you had come to take Frant's son back to school.'

'But can you prove the gentleman was involved with the fraud?' I asked.

'My son was convinced of it,' Noak said. 'He told Harmwell so.'

I could have pointed out that hearsay fell a long way short of proof. Instead I said, 'Mr Frant welcomed you. You seemed an honoured visitor.'

'But why should I not be? He was not aware of my connection with Lieutenant Saunders, or of my true reason for visiting this country. A mutual acquaintance had written to advise him of my arrival. Frant knew me simply as a wealthy American with money to invest, and a number of friends who might be useful to him. I had gone to considerable pains to ensure that we would be welcome guests.'

'You wrote Carswall's name on the back of your card when you sent it in to him.'

Noak frowned. 'You have sharp eyes. That was to give Frant an additional reason to welcome me, and to do so without delay. The coolness between the two of them was common knowledge, so I said I wished to consult him about regaining a bad debt from Carswall. A man is disposed to look favourably on one who has the same enemy as he: I have always found it a sound principle. And I may say that Harmwell recognised Frant at once.'

'But Mr Harmwell's identification does not amount to proof that he was guilty of anything.'

'Of course it don't,' Noak said. 'I will not beat about the bush, Mr Shield: I believe my son was murdered on the orders of Mr Frant, because he threatened to expose the sordid foundations of the scheme that was making him rich. But I cannot prove it.'

'Surely if you approach the authorities –?'

'With what? With wild allegations supported solely by the word of a Negro? Harmwell is a most respectable man, but – well, I need say no more, I am sure. And you must bear in mind the fact that I am an American citizen. Believe me, I have tried and failed to pursue the matter by orthodox means.'

Not entirely failed, I thought: for Noak's attempts had helped to float the rumours in the City that Rowsell had heard.

'However, there are other methods.' He caught my look of astonishment and went on, 'Always within the law, Mr Shield. I disdain to sink to their level. To put it in a nutshell, in my own mind I was perfectly certain of Mr Frant's guilt in the matter of my son's death – but wholly unable to prove it. However, my inquiries about his character and activities in England suggested that he was vulnerable in other ways, that it might be possible to bring him to justice for other offences. Moreover, I wished to come here for another reason, to establish whether Mr Frant had been acting on his own in Canada or on the orders of a more powerful patron.'

There flashed before my eyes a picture of the misery that had been caused by the collapse of Wavenhoe's at the end of last year. 'Am I to understand that you brought about the bank's ruin, and that of its depositors and their dependants, so that you might have a private revenge on Mr Frant?'

'I did not cause the collapse of the bank, sir,' snapped Mr Noak. 'That is quite inaccurate. The collapse was inevitable once Mr Carswall withdrew his capital and Henry Frant took over the direction of the bank's affairs. I merely hastened it, and made sure that Frant would be implicated in the ruin, and his embezzlement exposed.'

'You bought bills at a discount and presented them for payment?'

'I find you are surprisingly well informed. Yes, that and other tactics. For example, I encouraged Mr Frant to believe I was contemplating a substantial investment in an English bank – that was what we were discussing when we dined together on the night of Mr Wavenhoe's death. The intelligence I gained was remarkably valuable. When one has a little knowledge, much can be achieved by sowing a word in the right ear. A bank is like a hot-air balloon held in the air by the gas of public confidence. If the balloon is punctured, then the machine tumbles to earth.'

'And so we come to Mr Frant's murder,' I said flatly.

Noak regarded me in silence for a moment. 'It was very convenient, was it not? It saved him and his family the mortification of a trial, and the public hanging which would inevitably have followed. It also meant that a number of questions were left unanswered because only Henry Frant could answer them. For example, there was a considerable sum in securities that was never recovered. His confidential clerk gave me a list of the missing bills that were in the possession of Wavenhoe's Bank at the end of August.'

'Arndale? Was it not he who identified his master's body at the inquest?'

'You imply that he may not be an unimpeachable source? Possibly. But I have confirmed at least some of his information elsewhere, and I am inclined to think that he no longer has any motive to conceal the truth. But to return to the securities: Frant might have gambled them away or sold them at a discount before his presumed death on the twenty-fifth of November. But I do not believe it.'

'They could be turned into ready money? Even now?'

Noak nodded. 'They were all negotiable by bearer. You would need to know what you were doing, and of course the transactions would leave a trace.' He walked back to his chair and sat down slowly. 'Two weeks ago, one of the bills on the list was presented for payment in Riga. The sum involved amounted to nearly five thousand pounds. It was not presented directly but through a local intermediary.'

'It is nigh on six months since Mr Frant died,' I pointed out.

'Or disappeared.' Noak glanced at Harmwell, who had retreated into the shadows. 'I think it likely, however, that Frant did not have the securities at his disposal until some way into January this year.' He paused and looked steadily at me.

I said, 'You believe he deposited them at Monkshill?'

Noak stared impassively at me.

'He knew Monkshill and its environs intimately,' I continued. 'As only a boy who had grown up there could have known it.' I stared back at Noak, and thought I saw an almost imperceptible nod. 'The recess in the ice-house sump, where Mr Harmwell and I found the ring. It is the sort of hiding place that an inquisitive little boy might have found.'

'What age was Frant when he left Monkshill? Do you know?'

'Ten or eleven.' I remembered Sophie telling me on the night of the ball, as we sat beside the fire at Fendall House. I yearned with sudden urgency to have her beside me now. 'I have it from an unimpeachable source. Or perhaps he discovered it later. When he was at school in England, he often stayed with the Ruispidges at Clearland-court. It is no distance for an active youth. He might well have revisited the scenes of his childhood.'

'Ah.' Noak pulled back his lips, exposing his gums. 'So – if we allow this – why should Frant have not retrieved the securities before January?'

'Because when he deposited the securities, he must have reached the sump by the drain. The ice-house was full and he could not reach it from the chamber above, could he? He could not have foreseen the accident of the autumn gales, of the landslide which blocked the shaft down to the drain.'

'Quite so, Mr Shield. And why Monkshill? Why Monkshill, out of all the hiding places in the world?'

I smiled at him, for suddenly I sensed that I knew as much as he did, that for once we were on an equal footing. 'Mrs Johnson.'

'She was his confederate,' Noak said flatly. 'There is no shadow of doubt in my mind on that score.'

'I saw her in London in October, hard by Russell-square. Miss Carswall glimpsed her in Pall Mall. But at Monkshill she denied having been in town.'

'I believe the woman was his mistress.' There was a rare note of passion in Noak's voice, as though adultery disgusted him more than theft and murder. 'When Frant saw ruin staring him in the face, I suspect he set aside a collection of portable valuables and that he or Mrs Johnson hid them at Monkshill. It is possible that he entrusted her with them on the day you saw her, and that she carried them down to Monkshill. No doubt their intention was to wait until the hue and cry had died down, and then slip abroad under false names. When the blocking of the drain prevented them, they were compelled to wait until the time came to clear out the ice-house, when the sump would become accessible from the chamber itself. On the night in question, they poisoned the dogs and went to the ice-house from Grange Cottage to retrieve what they had left there. And something went wrong – a lover's quarrel that turned sour, perhaps, or even a simple accident – and Mrs Johnson died, leaving Frant with no choice but to take what he had come for and make good his escape. Either way, he would have been hanged if he was caught.'

'This is speculation, sir.'

'Not entirely: and what is speculation is well supported by the evidence.'

I cast my mind back over the events of the last few months. 'This does not explain your interest in Mr Carswall.' My voice was hoarse, and I was tired and growing angry. 'Nor indeed your interest in me.'

'Mr Carswall.' Noak's lips tightened as he gathered his thoughts. 'My inquiries both here and in North America have established beyond any doubt that until a few years ago Frant was Carswall's creature. When Frant joined Wavenhoe's as a young man, he had nothing in his favour except his birth, and even that was tainted by his father's excesses. Yet he prospered, and with enormous rapidity, because he found a patron in Carswall who was then an active partner in the bank. Carswall had sold his West Indian interests just before the abolition of the Trade and invested much of his capital in the bank. George Wavenhoe, even then, was not the man he once was, though the bank's reputation still rested on the City's knowledge of his integrity, both moral and financial. In theory, it was George Wavenhoe who sent Frant to Canada during the late war, to look after and extend the bank's interests there. In practice, however, I have no doubt that it was Carswall's decision. Frant's clerk tells me he took it for granted it was so.'

'Then the question must be: was Carswall fully cognisant of Frant's activities in Canada, and of the murder of Lieutenant Saunders?'

'Precisely. My investigations have pointed the finger again and again at Carswall, but I cannot prove it. And I will have justice, Mr Shield, not revenge: within the law, always within the law.' The blood had rushed to his face, and his hands clutched convulsively at the arms of his chair. He said nothing for a moment and then continued in a quieter, suddenly weary voice. 'You will recall that Carswall and I were negotiating over some warehouses in Liverpool. That served a double purpose. On the one hand, it gave me a reason to prolong our stay at Monkshill-park, and on the other it allowed my lawyers to examine the records at the warehouses. These are Carswall's personal property, these warehouses: and there is no doubt that goods destined for Frant's contractors in British North America went through them, and that Carswall charged a fat fee for the privilege. But of course this does not amount to proof of collusion with Frant, or even corruption. And the matter is enormously complicated by the fact that Frant and Carswall quarrelled when Carswall withdrew his capital from the bank five years ago – after Frant had returned from Canada and become a partner at Wavenhoe's. Carswall's departure made the bank's crash almost inevitable, particularly given Frant's loose, expensive way of living. Frant tried to stave off his ruin with embezzlement, but it could not answer for ever. So he and his mistress laid their desperate plan.'

'If it was not Frant who was murdered at Wellington-terrace, then who was it?'

Noak shrugged. 'Does it matter? Scores of men go missing in London every day. No doubt Frant found some unfortunate about the same age and build as himself, spun him a tale, and murdered him. I suspect Mrs Johnson played Lady Macbeth's part. My impression of her was of a strong-minded, ruthless woman. She would stop at nothing to get what she wanted.'

It was more than plausible. But Noak still did not know everything that I knew.

'So now we come to the present,' he said, and his thin voice was hoarse with tiredness and talking. 'One of the missing bills has changed hands. So we may deduce that Frant is almost certainly abroad, living under a false name and moving from place to place. But Carswall is still here, and I believe him to be as responsible for my son's death as Frant, as the man who pressed his head down in the puddle. If I cannot prove his collusion in my son's murder, then I shall find something else he has done, something he cannot so easily conceal, just as I did with Frant. In these months before his daughter's marriage, his position is particularly delicate.' Noak paused, his jaws moving soundlessly and methodically as though chewing the problem to digestible pulp. 'And there is yet another possibility that would make his position even more precarious: if we could show that he and Frant, far from being mortal enemies, were in fact acting in concert.'

'That can hardly be – they hate each other.'

Noak ignored my interruption. 'Even now, it is not impossible to kill two birds with one stone. What gives me hope is the bill that was changed in Riga. I have looked into the circumstances which led to its being presented for payment, how it passed from hand to hand. It is like a chain – one end attached to the bill, each link corresponding to a person through whose hands it has passed. But the chain breaks in February. The bill plunges into obscurity until it re-emerges on the schedule that Arndale prepared for me. None of those links has anything to do with Henry Frant. But one of them, a notary in Brussels, is a known associate of Stephen Carswall's.'

The reasoning was too fragile for its conclusion. I concealed a yawn and said, 'The inveterate hatred between Mr Carswall and Mr Frant must surely argue against it, and there are other reasons as well.'

'I shall deal with those in a moment,' Noak replied. 'In the meantime I shall merely observe that necessity makes strange bedfellows. It would not surprise me to find that Frant found it difficult to operate with sufficient anonymity, even abroad. The money market is not a large place, you understand: it may span the globe but it presents many of the characteristics of a village.'

I shook my head. 'I do not see why Carswall should be content to run such enormous risks for a man he so recently loathed.' A man, I thought but did not add aloud, whose wife he desires so ardently that he will overlook her lack of dowry and the crimes of her former husband.

'Ah!' Noak sprang up, as though so bursting with vitality that exercise had become essential. 'That is the beauty of it. They hate each other still, I daresay. But each has something to gain from renewing the association, and each knows the other dares not betray him. Frant needs to realise his ill-gotten capital; he must find somewhere to live in safety; he must at all costs avoid the gallows that await him in England. Carswall, on the other hand, would charge handsomely for his services in converting whatever Frant saved from the wreck of Wavenhoe's into ready money. But he has no temptation to betray Frant. In the first place, he too needs the money, rich though he is. Sir George Ruispidge is a very fine catch for his bastard daughter, but a baronet like Sir George comes at a high price. In the second place, Frant would feed him the bills one by one so Carswall would have no incentive to bilk him. And in the third place, if Frant were proved to be alive, he would stand between Carswall and what I fancy he now desires most of all – and desires with all the force of an old man's obsession.'

'I must beg you to enlighten me, sir,' I said coldly.

'I allude, as you must know, to Mrs Frant. As far as the law is concerned, her husband is dead and she is free to marry again. Should Mr Frant choose, however, he could reverse that state of affairs with a few strokes of a pen, written from the safety of a foreign sanctuary. No – as matters stand – the whole complex business is perfectly balanced. Perfectly but precariously.'

It had long since occurred to me that Mr Carswall was not the only elderly gentleman in the grip of an obsession. I said as gently as I could, 'Sir, you have erected a prodigiously impressive edifice. But I am not persuaded that its foundations are firm enough to bear its weight.'

Noak drew near to me in my chair, and, small though he was, towered over me. 'Then help me test its strength.' Such was his passion that he sprayed a few drops of moisture on my upturned face. 'If my hypothesis is correct, Mr Shield, if their fears and their desires are so precariously balanced, then the smallest jar, the slightest shock, will serve to overset them. And who better than yourself to administer it?'

CHAPTER SEVENTY-FIVE

IT WOULD NOT be true to say that I stormed out. I was entirely civil, if a little chilly. But I did leave without further delay. I declined point-blank to hear any further proposals Mr Noak might have, or to listen while he advanced his carefully wrought reasons why I should help him. Nor would I allow Mr Harmwell to fetch me a hackney from the stand, or to accompany me on my way home.

A gentle rain was falling. I picked my way through streets still crowded with revellers and those that prey on them. Hat in hand, I paused by the workhouse at the bottom of Castle-street and stared up at where the stars would have been in another place. I felt the cool refreshment of rainwater on my cheek. It was at that moment that I at last accepted the truth which should have been evident to me since Sophie left my little chamber in Fendall House: I had lost her. Indeed, except in a narrow carnal sense, I had never possessed her, so she could not truly be said to be mine to lose. She had merely lent herself to me, for reasons of her own; and like so many loans, the transaction was for a brief, fixed period, and the rate of interest was higher than the borrower anticipated.

A few minutes later I reached the Strand. I walked slowly, so tired that I was hardly aware of fatigue, so careworn that I did not concern myself with the possibility that I might be followed. I had the illusion that I was floating above the pavement, cushioned on the pain of my swollen feet, the left one of which was wet because the sole of my boot had developed a hole.

As I walked, I turned over in my mind what had passed in Brewer-street. My thoughts had the misleading limpidity that so often accompanies fatigue. Mr Noak had been remarkably frank, I believed: which might be due to the strength of his fanatical desire to avenge his son's death, to his despair of making progress, to old age and the consequent decay of his intellectual faculties, or to any combination of these. Alternatively, every word, every hypothesis, every apparent confidence, had been carefully planned for the purpose of achieving an unknown end.

This evening's events were only the latest in a long series. From start to finish in this sorry business, I had been led by the nose – by Henry Frant, Stephen Carswall and now Mr Noak; by Flora Carswall and even, perhaps, by Sophie – though my partiality for her struggled to persuade me that she had been as much a victim as myself. It was undeniable that I had come very close to falling in with Mr Noak's proposal since it appeared to accord so well with my own wishes. But among all the drawbacks to the plan was this: I could not rid myself of the knowledge that if anyone had a motive for murdering Mr Frant, it was Mr Noak himself.

I stopped to lean against a railing. In some part of my mind I became aware that a set of footsteps behind me had also stopped. A moment later I moved on, and so too did the footsteps. I repeated the experiment and obtained the same result. London is a busy city but at night it contains pockets of silence so profound that one may hear a pin drop on the pavement. The footsteps should have put me instantly on the alert. But my body was too weary, and my mind too full of other anxious thoughts, for the possible significance of the footsteps to register as a cause for alarm.

Mr Noak's grand scheme to confound his enemies had come to this: he wanted me to spy on Sophie, and through her on Mr Carswall. Mrs Kerridge, it had appeared, was happy to oblige Mr Harmwell with information upon occasion, and she had reported my meeting with her mistress at the burying ground that afternoon. Noak had also learned from her the real reason for my departure from Monkshill-park. From this, and from his own observations, he had inferred quite correctly that I had a tenderness for Sophie Frant. He had made a further deduction at an earlier stage of my acquaintance with Mr Carswall that I had been employed by him for confidential business. That was why he had set Harmwell to follow me on the occasion of my going to Queen-street that first time, in search of the man who was either David Poe or Henry Frant. It had been fortunate for me that he had done so – Mr Harmwell had been my rescuer when Iversen's hired bullies assaulted me, and now Noak wanted me to pay a price for it.

So tonight Noak had dangled the hope of reward in front of me: if I could turn Sophie into his spy, he had hinted, I might hope to win Sophie for myself. Were Carswall disgraced, she would have no one else to turn to. Noak promised me that, if all went well, he would put me in the way of earning a competence so that I might support her. But the promises were vague and I had no guarantee that he would fulfil them. I thought he would have promised me anything if I could have ensured the downfall of Stephen Carswall and discovered the identity of the man in Wellington-terrace. In the end, I did not trust the American, which was why I had not told him of the finger I had been encouraged to find at the tooth-puller's, or of today's discovery that the tooth-puller was among Mr Iversen's customers.

With immense effort of will, I abandoned the support of the railing and staggered down the Strand. Movement had become a form of torture. Worse than the woes of my body, however, was the despair that depressed my spirits. Noak's offer had given me the possibility of regaining Sophie. It had been as alluring a temptation as any I had ever faced. I might have justified succumbing to it, too, on the grounds that it might save Sophie from Mr Carswall, whom I knew to be the worst of men.

I heard the footsteps behind me, slow and dragging like an echo of my own. Nemesis pursued me and knew she need not hurry.

The stumbling block was this: in the past six or seven months, I had learnt too well the lesson of what it felt like to be manipulated by others, to have no more control over one's destiny than Mr Punch in his puppet show. Were I to accede to Mr Noak's proposal, I would seek to make

Sophie my puppet. In agreeing to marry Mr Carswall, she had made a perfectly rational choice. He was rich and she was poor. He was old and she was young, which at least had the advantage that the marriage was unlikely to be a long one. On her side it could not be a love match. On his, I doubted that the emotions that made him desire her had much to do with love as it is generally understood; for a desire to possess, to be a person's master, is not love. But each would gain by the arrangement. Marriages have been happy without love before now, but not without money. As Flora Carswall had pointed out, love in a cottage didn't pay the bills. You cannot eat and drink love; you cannot wear it, and it will not provide for your children.

I reached the entrance into Gaunt-court. There was no gas illumination here, of course, only the fitful glow of the oil lamp on the corner. Nothing had changed, I told myself, since Sophie had given me my *congé* this afternoon.

At the head of the steps up to the front door of number 3 I stopped and, supporting myself on the railing, turned to look back down the court. I heard in the distance a carriage passing along the Strand, the clop of hooves, the jingle of harness and the rattle of wheels on the roadway. I did not hear the sound of footsteps. At some point in the last few minutes, they had stopped. I told myself that London is a city full of dramas played out every night, and there was no reason in the world to believe that these footsteps had belonged to my little tragi-comedy. But now the footsteps had stopped I felt inexplicably uneasy.

Ayez peur, I murmured to myself, *ayez peur*.

CHAPTER SEVENTY-SIX

THE FOLLOWING MORNING I left the house in search of coffee. I was unwashed and unshaven. I had slept late and my mind was still fogged with sleep.

A small, closed carriage, painted black and rather the worse for wear, was standing at the corner by the lamp-stand. As I drew near, the door opened and a swarthy man dressed in shabby black clothes leaned out and asked me the quickest way to Covent Garden.

Simultaneously, a second man, also in black, came round the back of the carriage and seized my arm. The first man grabbed my lapels. Between them, they pulled and pushed me into the carriage. The second man followed me in, shutting the door behind him. The carriage moved off with a jerk.

With three of us inside, there was barely room to move, let alone to struggle. The blinds were down and there was scarcely any light. The first man had his arm round my neck, drawing my head back. I felt the prick of a knife at my throat.

'Stay still, cully,' he murmured. 'Stay still or we've got a nasty accident on our hands.'

As the carriage rattled and bumped through streets filled with the noise of a London morning, a ritual was acted out inside it. I use the word ritual with care. My captors knew so precisely what they were doing that there was a negligent, familiar ease about their movements.

The second man tied my wrists in front of me, inserted a filthy rag in my mouth, and finally lashed my knees together.

By now I was huddled in the corner of the seat, still with the tip of a knife at my throat. Neither man spoke. The confined space was filled with the sound of our breathing and the smell of our bodies. I tried without success to bring my mind to grapple with my situation; but fear inhibits rational thought. Over and over again I cursed my own folly at remaining in the house at Gaunt-court, and not seeking refuge under another name and in another city. Once again, and in far more brutal circumstances than before, I had become a mere cypher in my own life.

We came to a halt again. I felt and heard our driver jumping down from the box, the sound of voices and of heavy gates being unbarred and drawn back. Then the horses began to move again. At that moment my head was roughly seized and a bandage placed over my eyes. The carriage door opened. A current of fresh air swept inside. One of my companions jumped down. Between them they dragged me out of the carriage. In a moment I found myself in the open air with a man on either side to hold my arms.

Owing to the bonds around my knees, I could not walk. Grunting and swearing, the men dragged me across cobbles, my boots bumping up and down, and pulled me into a place that smelled strongly of sawdust and varnish. It was at this point that my nightmare entered a still more terrible phase. Without warning my feet were lifted away from the ground and I felt myself hoisted aloft on strong arms, my body moving from the vertical to the horizontal. I was raised and then lowered. There was a glancing blow to the back of my head. It was followed by a laugh, expressive of unforced merriment and wholly unexpected in that grim setting.

'The cove's too long,' someone said. 'Have to cut off the feet again.'

'No,' said another man. 'Take his boots off – that should do it.'

My boots were roughly removed. I was now lying on my back, with my elbows, the crown of my head and the soles of my stockinged feet touching hard surfaces. A heavy object fell on my leg. I twitched invol-untarily. Something else fell beside it and then the third item. I stretched down my bound hands and made out the shape of a boot-heel.

'Hey, lad,' said the voice of the first man. 'There's air holes. You can breathe. Not very big holes, though. If you was stupid enough to make a row, you'd need more air, and you couldn't get it, could you? So keep quiet as a mouse.'

At first I could not understand him, for there was plenty of air, albeit laden with the scents of sawdust and varnish and an underlying tang of horse manure. Then I heard a great clatter a few inches above my head and sensed a sudden enclosing, a diminution of the light. All at once, a terrible racket broke out about me. My ears filled with the sound of hammering, so close that the nails might have been driven into me. There must have been two or three of them wielding hammers, and in that confined space, which acted like a drum, it seemed like a multitude. They were nailing me up in a box no larger than a coffin.

All at once, the terrible truth burst over me. I recalled what I knew of the dimensions of the box, and put them together with the black carriage and the rusty black clothes of the two men. I realised that the box was not like a coffin: it was a coffin.

CHAPTER SEVENTY-SEVEN

I WAS TO be buried alive. I had no doubt of it whatsoever. I faced the prospect of a lingering and horrible death.

My captors transferred me to another conveyance, probably a closed cart. We drove for what seemed like hours but might have been as many minutes. Time means very little without a way of measuring it.

I tried to struggle – of course I did. Yet the dimensions of the coffin, the presence of my boots and hat with me, the shortage of air, and above all the tightness of my bonds made it almost impossible for me to move at all. All I could manage was the faintest of whimpers from my parched throat and an ineffectual knocking of my elbows against the sides of my prison. I doubt if the sounds I made could have been heard by anyone sitting directly on the other side of the coffin, let alone by those in the street.

My intellectual faculties were equally paralysed. I wish I could say that I faced what lay before me with calmness. In the abstract, it is perfectly true that if you cannot avoid death, you might as well look it in the eye. But the needs of the moment swamped such lofty considerations. To continue to breathe – to continue to live – nothing else mattered.

We came to another halt. I half felt, half heard a great clatter and then a jolt. There was a knocking on the roof of my little prison. Someone laughed, a high sound with an edge of hysteria. The coffin swayed and bumped and banged. It tilted violently to a sharp angle. This, together with a series of irregular thuds, told me that we were mounting a flight of stairs. The coffin levelled out and a few paces later I heard a man's voice, but could not make out the words.

The coffin groaned and screeched: someone was raising the lid. Currents of air flowed around me. The tip of the crowbar came so far inside that it grazed my scalp. I felt a burst of intense happiness.

'Remove the gag,' said a man whose voice was familiar. 'Then the blindfold.'

I retched when they pulled the rag from my parched mouth. I tried and failed to say the word 'water'. A hand gripped my hair and pulled up my head. Fingers tugged at the knot of the blindfold. Light flooded into my eyes, so bright that I moaned with the shock of it. I could see nothing but whiteness. I closed my eyes.

'Give him a drink,' said the voice. 'Then leave us.'

A hand cradled the back of my head. A container made of metal rattled against my teeth. Suddenly there was water everywhere, flooding down my face, finding its way between my cravat and my neck, filling my mouth and trickling down my throat and making me gag. The mug withdrew.

'More,' I croaked. 'More.'

The mug returned. I was so weak that I could not satisfy my thirst.

'Leave us,' the man commanded.

I heard footsteps – two sets, I fancy – on a bare floor and the sound of a door opening and closing. There was water on my lashes, and I did not know whether it came from the metal cup or from my tears. My eyes were still screwed shut against the light. Slowly I opened them. All I could see was a sagging ceiling, fissured with cracks, with the lathes exposed on one side where the plaster had crumbled away.

'Sit up,' said the voice.

I hooked my bound hands round the rim of the coffin and eventually managed to bring myself into a sitting position. The first thing I saw was a great, grey mass of hair below a black velvet skull cap, like a hanging judge's. I lowered my eyes to the face, which was on the level of my own. Recognition flooded into me with a sense of inevitability.

413

'Mr Iversen,' I said. 'Why have you brought me here?'

'You will be more comfortable in a moment.' He leaned forward in his wheeled chair and studied my face. 'Wriggle your limbs as far as you are able. Now lean back a little, now forward. Does that not feel better? Now, more water?'

I drank greedily this time. Mr Iversen refilled the mug from a jug on the table beside his chair. The cripple was attired as he had been before, in a black, flowing robe embroidered with necromantic symbols in faded yellow thread. His crutches were propped against the bottom of the coffin. On the table was a pocket pistol.

My eyes travelled on, and I discovered we were not alone. Seated by the window with his back to us was another figure in a dusty suit of brown clothes and an old-fashioned three-cornered hat.

'You're a fool,' my host observed in a friendly tone. 'You shouldn't have come back. You should have gone far, far away. Seven Dials is not a safe place for the inquisitive. I tried to give you the hint on your last visit. Still, one cannot expect old heads on young shoulders, I suppose.'

'A hint?' Anger spurted through me. 'You call those bullies of yours a hint? What do you want of me, sir?'

'The truth. Why did you come back here yesterday?'

All my words might win me was a kinder way of dying. I was tired of the lies, so I told him the truth. 'I came back because of that bird of yours.' I saw understanding leap into his eyes. 'The one that says *ayeʒ peur*.'

'That damned fowl.' Iversen's fingertips tapped the butt of the pistol. 'I put up with it for the sake of the customers, but I could stand it no more. I hoped I had seen and heard the last of it.'

'I've drawn up a memorandum,' I said. 'It covers all the circumstances of this business, including my visits to Queen-street, since I first met Mr Henry Frant.'

'Ah yes. And you've had it witnessed by a brace of attorneys and sent a copy to the Lord Chancellor. Come, Mr Shield, don't play the fool. You would have gone to the magistrates long before this if you had intended something like that.'

He was in the right of it. I had indeed begun to write such a

414

memorandum on my last evening at Monkshill-park. But it lay unfinished in my room at Gaunt-court.

'No,' Iversen went on. 'I do not believe it for a moment. Not that it matters. We shall soon have the truth out of you.'

Neither of us spoke for a moment. The room was heavy with a strange, sweet odour. I looked at the two figures before me, Iversen seated beside the coffin, and the old man in an elbow chair by the barred window. I heard as if at a great distance the sound of the world going about its business. There were noises in the house, too, feet on the stairs, a tapping from below and a woman singing a lullaby. There was life around me, and it was full of wonders, a sweet thing that I could not bear to part with.

'Sir,' I said to the man in brown. 'I appeal to you. I beg you, help me.'

The old man did not reply. He gave no sign he had heard me.

'His mind is on other things,' Iversen said.

I turned back to him. 'If you wish me to answer your questions with any coherence, sir, you would find me in a better condition to do so if I had something to eat. And I would be obliged if I might use the necessary house.'

Iversen laughed, exposing a set of false teeth made of bone or perhaps ivory, and clearly expensive; they reminded me of the tooth-puller and curious possibilities stirred once more in my mind. 'You shall have your creature comforts, Mr Shield.' He levered himself to the edge of his chair, thrust himself upwards by exerting pressure on the arms and in one, practised movement seized a crutch and placed it under his right shoulder. For a moment he stood there, swaying slightly, gripping the side of the coffin with his free hand, with an expression of triumph on his face. He was a big man and he loomed over me like a mountain. 'But first I must relieve you of the contents of your pockets.'

His big hands worked deftly and rapidly through my clothes. He removed my pocketbook, my purse, my penknife and the red-spotted handkerchief which the boys had given me on the eve of my departure from Monkshill. He gave each item a brief examination and then dropped it in the pocket of his robe. At last he was satisfied.

'I shall desire them to bring you a pot directly. And something to eat.'

'They will not expect me to stay here – in this coffin?'

'I can see that would be inconvenient. There is no reason why you should not be lifted out. They will keep a watch on you, after all.'

'It will not be easy for me, or for them, if they do not untie my hands,' I pointed out.

'I do not think untying you will be necessary, Mr Shield. A little inconvenience to you or even to them is neither here nor there.' Mr Iversen picked up the pistol from the table and dragged himself towards the door. He glanced back at me. 'Until we meet again,' he said with something of a flourish, a gesture that raised the ghost of a memory deep within my mind.

He dragged himself on to the landing, leaving me alone with the old man in the fading light of an April afternoon. I listened to his hirpling progress along the landing, and his clumping descent of the stairs.

'Sir,' I hissed at the old man. 'You cannot sit there and permit this to happen. He intends to kill me. Will you be an accessory to murder?'

There was no answer. He did not stir a muscle.

'Are you Mr Iversen's father, sir? You would not wish your son to stain his soul with the blood of a fellow human being?'

Apart from my own ragged breathing, I heard nothing. The room was suddenly brighter, for the sun had come out. Motes danced in the air before the window. The arms and rails of the chair were grey with dust. A suspicion grew in my mind and became certainty. The man in brown could help no one.

I waited for relief for well over a quarter of an hour, to judge by the distant chimes of a church clock, while my need for the chamber-pot grew ever more pressing.

At length the door opened and the two men dressed in rusty black entered. They had kidnapped me today; and I believed that they had pursued me yesterday evening, though I had not seen their faces clearly so I could not be completely sure. I wondered whether they had also attacked me on my visit to Queen-street in December. The first man bore the chamber-pot, swinging it nonchalantly as he walked. The other

416

carried a wooden platter on which was the end of a loaf, a wedge of cheese and a mug of small beer. He put the platter on the windowsill, close to the elbow of the man in the brown suit. Both men were clearly used to his silent presence, for they did not give him a second glance.

'Is that a waxwork?' I asked in a voice that trembled.

'You won't see one of them at old Ma Salmon's.' The first man put the pot on the table. 'That's Mr Iversen, Senior, sir, at your service.'

They heaved me from the coffin, which was resting on a pair of trestles. They derived a simple and ribald pleasure from my fumbling attempt to use the pot. Fortunately, in a moment they were distracted by something they could see from the window.

'You wouldn't think she had such white skin,' said one of them.

'It only looks like that because of the cuts,' said the other, jingling a bunch of keys in his pocket. 'If you was nearer, you'd see the blemishes, you take my word for it.'

They continued discussing the subject in a detached and knowledge-able manner while I buttoned my flap as best I could with two hands tied. Their remarks were delivered with such an air of assurance that they might have been a pair of critics contemplating a portrait they did not much care for in the Exhibition Room at Somerset House. Still hobbled at the knees, I shuffled a little closer and found that, craning over their shoulders, I could look down into the yard.

There were two women below, one old, one young. The elder was tall, with a curved back like a bow. She was a grey shadow over the other, who was as small as a child, and whose gown and shift had been pulled down from her shoulders so she was naked from the waist upwards. I knew at once that she was not a child because I saw the swell of her hips and the curve of a breast. A moment later, I recognised her as Mary Ann, the dumb woman who lived in the kennel at the back of the yard.

'He did it this morning,' one of the men said. 'Wish I'd seen it.'

'Did she faint?'

'Once: but they threw water over her until she woke and then he began again.'

I found it hard to suppress a gasp of horror as I stared at the network of weals on that white back. Mary Ann winced and trembled as the other

417

woman applied what I assumed was a healing ointment to her wounds. The back of her shift was a mass of blood, some rusty, some fresh.

'Stupid bitch,' said the first man. 'No better than an animal.'

He rattled the window, a casement, until one leaf of it flew open. He pushed me aside as though I had been a chair and picked up the chamber-pot. The bars were fixed horizontally and there was just space between them to allow the chamber-pot to pass through. He extended it to the full length of his arm and turned it upside down.

'Gardy-loo,' he cried, and he and his friend bellowed with laughter.

I was now too far back in the room to see down into the yard; and I was glad. I forced myself to pick at the bread and cheese, knowing that I needed nourishment, for I had eaten nothing since the sandwich Mr Harmwell had given me. The men stayed by the window, hooting with mirth. Gradually their laughter subsided, and I gathered the women had spoiled their sport by taking shelter in the kennel.

It had gradually been borne in upon me that both of them were very drunk. The smell of spirits filled the room, slicing through the unwholesome blend of other odours. Men such as these might always be a little drunk; but their behaviour now was clearly a long way from habitual tipsiness. One of them lowered his breeches, lifted his coat-tails and placed his posterior on the windowsill, no doubt hoping that the women below would be looking at him. But as one grew more boisterous, the other became quieter, and the colour gradually drained from his face, which was scarred with the pox. At length he murmured some excuse and bolted from the room. His colleague dragged me to the window, upsetting my beer in his hurry, and lashed my bound hands to one of the bars with a length of rope.

'Now don't run away, my pretty,' he said hoarsely. 'I got an errand to run, but I won't be a minute. You tell me if the ladies come back, eh?'

He clapped me across the shoulders in the most good-humoured manner imaginable and left the room, slamming the door behind him and turning the key in the lock. I waited for a moment. The yard below was empty. The door of the kennel was closed. Blank walls of smoke-stained brick reared like cliffs on every side. The man had spoken of an errand, and I thought it likely he had gone to fetch more gin, perhaps from the establishment across the road where I had waited yesterday evening.

I flexed my hands. The knots that held my wrists tied together were as firm as ever. But this latest knot, fastening the cord which passed between my wrists and round the bar of the window, was a more slap-dash affair. For a start, the position was wrong, for the cord had not been drawn tight, allowing my hands at least a limited mobility. In the second place, the knot itself was far from impregnable. I contrived to curve one hand round until the fingers had a grip on part of the knot, while I tugged at another part with my teeth. With my ears straining to hear the sound of footsteps outside the door, I worried away at the coarse, tarred cord, which chafed my skin like glass-paper. The precious minutes slid away. At last the knot loosened; and a moment later I pulled my hands away from the bar.

My wrists were still bound together, so tightly that the flow of the blood was impeded, and held with a knot that I found impossible to undo with my teeth. My legs were still tied at the knees, with the knot beyond my reach at the back. I was able to move only with painful slowness, shuffling and hopping with noisy inefficiency across the floor, an inch or two at a time.

It took me an age to reach the door. I tried the handle and confirmed it was locked. I bent my head down to the keyhole and saw that my captor had withdrawn the key so there was no possibility of my pushing it through the door and somehow retrieving it from the floor of the landing. It was a stout door, too, reinforced with iron, which made me wonder whether Iversen used it as his strong-room.

I hobbled over to the window and looked out. Mary Ann had emerged from the kennel and was now huddled in the doorway with a smouldering clay pipe in her hand. The casement was still slightly ajar. I heard foot-steps immediately below, which meant I dared not call out to her.

I glanced about me. There was no fireplace in the room. Apart from the two chairs, the trestles, the coffin and a large iron-bound chest, there was no furniture. My eyes came at last to the body of Mr Iversen, Senior. He sat with his legs slightly apart, his yellow, sunken face towards the window, and his gloved hands resting on his thighs. The fabric of his coat was riddled with moth-holes and both the man and his coat were covered with a fine, feathery powdering of dust. The coat was undone, revealing the waistcoat beneath. My eyes lingered on the old man's left-hand waistcoat pocket. The stub of a pencil protruded from it.

I eased the pencil gently from the pocket. There was still a point on it, albeit a blunt one. I looked wildly round the room for something to write on. My eyes returned at last to the corpse. I touched a corner of his hat gently with my finger. It did not move. I took a grip with both hands and lifted it, hoping I might find a label attached to the band. The wig rose a few inches and then parted company with the hat and fell back on to the bald skull, sending up a puff of dust. The movement dislodged a few yellow flakes which drifted down to Mr Iversen Senior's shoulders.

I glanced inside the hat and discovered that it had been wedged on to the head with scraps of paper. All were brittle, some had crumbled, but a few were still whole. I picked out the largest fragment and gently unfolded it. It was a receipted bill, attesting to the fact that Francis Corker, a butcher, had received the sum of seventeen shillings and three pence three farthings from Mr Adolphus Iversen on the 9th of June 1807. The other side of the receipt was blank.

I smoothed out the paper on the windowsill, holding down one corner with the platter and most of one side with what was left of the cheese. I would not have believed it possible to write with one's hands tied, but desperation is a fine teacher. Letter by letter, word by word, I scrawled this message:

If the bearer takes this to Mr Noak or his clerk the Negro Harmwell they will receive the sum of £5. They lodge in Brewer-st, north side, second house west from Gt Pultney-st. I am held captive at Iversen's, Queen-street, Seven Dials.

I pushed the window as wide as it would go. Mary Ann still sat smoking, her face turned away from the house. I heard voices below, though whether from the yard near the house or through an open window or door I could not tell; in any case, I dared not call out to attract her attention. I tried waving my bound arms from side to side, standing as close as I could to the window, in the hope that the movement would register at the edge of her vision. Then, to my horror, I heard heavy footsteps on the stairs and approaching along the landing.

I had nothing to lose. I pushed my arms through the bars and let the note flutter from my fingers. As I did so, Mary Ann turned her head, perhaps attracted by a burst of laughter or a sudden movement from the door to the back kitchen. As she turned, she saw me and her eyes widened. The paper fluttered from my fingers and her eyes followed its fall.

The key turned in the lock. The door burst open. The man who had left me tied to the window shouldered his way into the room. His bloodshot eyes roved swiftly over the room, taking in the changes that had occurred since his departure. He lurched across the floor and gave me a backhanded blow that sent me sprawling across the coffin.

'Get back in there, you God-damned swab.' The words were harsh but he spoke in a whisper, as if he were afraid of being overheard, that his dereliction of duty might be discovered. 'In there, I say.'

He bent down and manhandled me back into the coffin, cramming me in so I lay awkwardly on my side. He pushed my head down, catching my nose on the wood, and the blood began to flow. I heard him scurrying around the room in his heavy boots. I raised myself on an elbow. He restored the wig and the hat on to the corpse's head, sending up another cloud of dust as he did so. He did not notice the pencil. He looked out of the window, but saw nothing there to cause him anxiety.

As he turned away, however, he knocked against the outstretched left leg of the corpse. The blow dislodged the dead man's gloved hand from his thigh. There was an audible crackling sound, like tearing cloth. It was not much of a movement, but enough for the hand to hang down below the seat of the chair.

One would expect an embalmed body to be rigid. It was only some time later that I realised the significance of the movement, of the fact that it was possible when so little force had been brought to bear. The rigidity of the limb in question had already been broken. The first time, it had not been an accident.

At first, my captor did not realise what he had done. He felt the blow, of course, and turned back, looking askance at Mr Iversen, Senior as though he suspected the old man of hitting him.

The glove was slipping downwards. It was clearly much larger than the hand – perhaps the latter had shrunk – and it fell to the ground, leaving the hand beneath exposed. I saw yellowing, waxy skin, long nails, and spots of what looked like ink on the fingers. In some corner of my mind, some corner that remained remote from my present anxieties, I knew I had observed something very similar to that hand before. Then, my vision clearing, I saw with the kind of clarity which is almost like a physical pain that the top joints of the forefinger were missing. All at once I remembered the tavern in Charlotte-street, and the contents of Mr Poe's satchel on the scrubbed table top, and the maid's gasp of shock.

A rare specimen of *digitus mortuus praecisus*, lent me by the professor himself. Except that now it was no longer quite so rare.

CHAPTER SEVENTY-EIGHT

THAT NIGHT THE men who had brought me to Queen-street re-enacted the grim charade of the morning, this time under the supervision of Mr Iversen. His presence miraculously sobered them. As they were about to nail the lid, he waved them away from the coffin, and peered down at me.

'Pray do not disturb yourself,' he said. 'It is only for an hour or so. Try to rest, eh? To sleep, Mr Shield: perchance to dream, eh?'

He gave a signal, and the men nailed the coffin lid, the hammer blows pounding through me like artillery fire. They took me down the stairs and loaded the coffin on to the conveyance, presumably the one that had brought me here, waiting in the street. We drove away, moving much more quickly at this time of night, despite the darkness. At first I heard the noise of the streets, albeit very faintly, and once I distinguished the cry of a watchman calling the hour. Gradually these sounds died away, and we picked up speed.

We had two horses, I thought, and to judge by the smoothness of the ride we were travelling on a turnpike road. This suggested they were taking me either north or west because to go east or south would have meant a longer, slower journey through the streets. Sometimes the rumbling of wagons penetrated my wooden prison, and I guessed they formed part of the night-time caravans bringing food and fuel into the ever-hungry belly of the metropolis.

That journey was a form of death, a foretaste of hell. My wrists and knees were still bound; and I had been gagged again and wedged in place with my hat and boots. To be deprived of sight, of movement, of the power of action, even of grounds for hope – all this is to be reduced to a state that is very nearly that of non-existence. As I jolted along in that coffin there were times when I would have given anything, even Sophie, even my own life, to be transformed into an inanimate object like a sack of potatoes or a heap of rocks, to be incapable of feeling and fearing.

My discomfort grew worse when we left the turnpike road and jounced along rutted lanes with many sharp bends, as fast as the driver dared. At one point our conveyance lurched violently to the left and came to a sudden halt that set the unsecured coffin sliding forwards and sideways until it, too, came to a stop with an impact which left me more bruised than ever. I guessed that our nearside wheels had fallen into the ditch along the side of the road. I prayed that we had broken a wheel or an axle – anything to increase my chance of rescue. Alas, a few minutes later we were on our way again.

The first indication I had that we were nearing our journey's end came when the surface beneath the wheels changed to hard, bone-shaking cobbles. We slowed, swung to the right and stopped. The cessation of movement should have been a relief to me: instead it increased my awareness of my plight. However I tried, I could not make out what was going on around me. I grew colder and colder. My body was racked with spasms of cramp.

Desperate for air, for light, I hammered on the lid of the coffin, on the roof of my tiny cell. A memory came to my mind, of lying wounded in the dark, crushed by the weight of a dead horse, on the field of Waterloo: and I screamed as past and present glided like lovers into an indissoluble embrace. Panic was a creature in the coffin with me, an old ghost who would smother me if I let him. I fought him, forcing myself to breathe more slowly, to unclench my muscles.

There came a muffled crash, which sent a tremor through my wooden world. The coffin was dragged out of the vehicle. I heard crashes and bangs. Nausea rose in my gorge. The coffin pitched forward. I plunged feet first down a steep slope and came to rest, still at an angle, with a jolt that was worse than any I had previously experienced. But I had no time to recover, for the coffin moved again, twisting round and then descending with another shattering blow to a horizontal position.

A crowbar dug into the join between lid and coffin. The nails rose from the wood. I saw the first glimmer of light I had seen for hours. It came from a pair of flickering tallow candles yet to me, for a moment, those candles were brighter than a pair of suns. By their light, I made out two huge shadows looming over the coffin, which had been placed on the floor. Above me was a lattice-work of joists and floorboards. There was a deafening clatter as the lid was cast aside.

I tried to sit up and found my limbs would not answer. A man laughed, and the familiar smell of gin assailed my nostrils. I managed to pull myself up so my head at least was out of the coffin. I was in what seemed to be a low cellar with walls of brick. I recognised my captors as Mr Iversen's men, each with a candle in his hand. One of them stooped and picked up the crowbar. The other pulled out the gag. Then, ignoring me, they scuttled like black beetles up a steep flight of open wooden stairs to a trap-door.

'Sirs,' I croaked. 'I beg you, for God's sake leave me a candle. Tell me what this place is.'

One of them paused, the one who had removed the gag. He glanced back. 'You'll not need a candle, mate,' he said. 'Not where you're going.'

The other laughed. A moment later the trap-door slammed down, leaving me once more alone in the darkness.

But not quite as before: I was no longer pinned motionless in a box. I could not doubt that they had brought me to this lonely spot in order to kill me. But at least I could make their job difficult.

There followed one of the most exquisitely painful experiences of my life. I threw out my hat and boots to give myself more room. Slowly I hauled myself to a sitting position. Clinging to the side of the coffin, I raised myself up to a crouch. I swayed from left to right with increasing vigour until I had achieved enough momentum to pitch myself inelegantly out of the coffin. Sobbing with pain, I lay huddled on my side on what felt like damp and filthy flagstones.

Gradually I straightened up, as uncertain as a child taking his first steps, until I attained a kneeling position. I found my boots and managed to put them on. My situation was almost as bleak as before. I feared that I had merely exchanged one prison for another, albeit a larger one. I examined it as well as I could in the darkness, which was not easy bearing in mind the fact that I was still bound at the knees and at the wrists. I paid particular attention to the stairs and to the trap-door. The latter was close-fitting but I believed I could discern a trace of light at one corner. I tried to heave it up with my shoulders but it would not budge.

When I stepped back from the stairs, I trod on something that seemed to snatch at my foot. With a muffled cry I sprang away and there was a clatter on the floor, as though there were an equally terrified animal in the cellar with me. Reason came immediately to my aid. The sole of my left boot had caught on the point of a nail protruding from the upturned lid of the coffin.

I knelt down and with cold, clumsy hands swept the floor until I found the lid. I ran my hand along its edge, touching the sharp points and the squared edges of the tapering nails. There were six of them in all. I brought my bound wrists down on the nearest one and began to saw.

I scarcely knew what drove me. In the conscious part of my mind I had already half-surrendered to whatever fate had in store for me. But there was another, deeper part of my being that continued to struggle. It was this that drove me to ignore my aching knees and my bleeding arms; to rub and hack at the cord that bound my wrists with the tips and sides of the nails.

I had no means of measuring the time. It might have been an hour before I felt the first strand part. For a time, this pushed me on to work with renewed vigour, but it was another age before I felt another strand give. I sawed the cord against the edges of the nails, I poked their iron points into the knot and worked it to and fro, and sometimes I merely snarled and tore at my bonds with my teeth, hoping if they were not vulnerable to one method then they would be to another.

I was in so much pain from the chafing of my skin and the many times I had accidentally dashed a nail against my arm rather than the cord that I barely noticed when the rope gave way. My hands flew apart. I sat back on my heels and wept, raising my arms and stretching them as far behind me as I could, as if I were arching a pair of wings. I looked up as I did so, and for the first time glimpsed a crack of light filtering between the boards. The night was ending.

I drove myself to work at the knot that bound my knees, which had been previously inaccessible to me, since it was at the back. I could not use the nails for this, and my hands were feeble. I had hardly begun when I heard footsteps above my head.

I hobbled quickly to the stairs and slumped on the floor against the wall near the foot of the stairs. A bolt was drawn. With a creak, the trap-door rose and fell back against a wall. Light flooded into the cellar. The day was more advanced than I had thought. Heavy footsteps descended the stairs.

A hand fell on my shoulder and shook me. With all the strength I was capable of, I spun round, straightening my knees, and jabbed my outstretched fingers at the face of the man looming over me. He gave a shriek, for one of my nails had caught his eye, stepped back incautiously and tripped over the coffin. I hauled myself up the stairs towards the rectangle of light with the fallen man screaming imprecations behind me.

'Mr Shield,' said a rich, husky voice behind me as my head and shoulders emerged through the trap-door. 'This really will not do.'

I turned. Not four feet away from me Mr Iversen was seated in a chair by a table, with a pistol in his hand. He had changed his professional robe for a brown travelling coat. The crutches were propped against the table.

'Raise your hands in the air, if you please,' he continued. 'Climb the stairs slowly. No, no, Joseph' – he addressed the man below – 'leave him alone for now.'

I ascended with ungainly hops into a room fitted out as a kitchen, with a great range at one end and a dresser at the other. I struggled to my feet and looked about me. The place was indescribably dirty. I must have presented a sorry spectacle – unwashed, unshaven, with my coat torn and my cuffs and breeches bloody from my efforts to untie my hands during the night. I turned back to Mr Iversen.

He was no longer in the chair. Instead he was standing, pistol in hand, in the middle of the kitchen. The crutches were still against the table. He saw the surprise on my face and his mouth twisted into a smile.

'It is a miracle, is it not, Mr Shield? How truly edifying. You will find a pump in the yard. Joseph and I will come with you.'

They took me out into a yard beyond the kitchen, watching me hop and stumble through the mud to the privy, which I was obliged to use with the door open. From the seat of ease I saw, over the roofs of the outbuildings at the far side of the yard, the chimneys of two large, modern buildings some sixty or seventy yards away. Mr Iversen noted the direction of my gaze. 'No one is within earshot,' he observed. 'You might as well save your breath.'

'Where are we?'

He shrugged, evidently deciding he had nothing to lose by answering my question. 'We are to the north of the village of Kilburn, in the middle of a large tract of land set aside for building. This was once a farmhouse and in former times much of the surrounding land belonged to it. The establishment over there with the tall grey chimney-stacks is a madhouse. They are used to the sound of screams and calls for help. The building next door – you see it? with the belfry? – is the workhouse. It is a most convenient plan, I understand, for the inmates may pass from one to the other as their guardians see fit. This parish is run on the best rational lines.'

I rose and buttoned my trousers. 'I do not understand what you want with me. I beg of you to let me go.'

He ignored these words. 'They even have their private cemetery. Look through the gateway. You may catch a glimpse of its wall behind the limes over there. Madness and poverty share this characteristic, that they commonly end in death sooner rather than later. Consider the tender feelings of the village people, what is left of them; consider the inhabitants of the brave new streets and squares and crescents that one day will spring up on this spot: they would not care to await the Last Trump in the same burial ground as these unfortunates, would they?

But with this private cemetery, everyone is happy, and everything is convenient. Admirable, do you not agree?'

'Why have you brought me here?'

'All in good time, Mr Shield. The burial ground has its own sexton, an admirable fellow, though not a polished one.'

'And does he provide the coffins for his employers too?'

Iversen glanced at me and gave a quick, approving nod.

I said, 'No doubt with the assistance of the men who brought me here?'

'You are perfectly correct. Do not judge by their appearance.' He glanced at the man standing in the kitchen doorway. 'Eh, Joseph? They are good-hearted men at bottom. They will even help the poor Sexton fill in a grave if he is hard pressed with other duties.' He pointed at the limes. 'There is a gate in the wall. The Sexton and his helpers can pass quite privately through it into the burial ground.'

Iversen allowed me to use the pump, to splash water over my face and drink my fill. He had told me quite clearly, in so many words, that he had it within his power to have me interred in a cemetery for the poor and the insane, and I doubted if it would matter to him whether I were dead or alive when my coffin was lowered into the open grave.

'Sir,' I said as we began our slow, halting progress back to the house. 'May I speak with you in private a moment?'

'Nothing would give me greater pleasure.' He stopped and motioned Joseph towards him. 'Is the other horse saddled?'

'Yes, sir.'

'Ride back to town. You should return with Elijah in the cart this evening, at about six of the clock. But first you will bind this young fellow's hands behind his back. Then cut his legs free.'

Joseph obeyed, and I think he took a fiendish pleasure in making the cord as tight as possible. When he had left us, Iversen nudged me into the kitchen with the barrel of the pistol.

'Well? What have you to say?'

'There is much I do not understand about this whole business,' I said when we were inside, my eyes flicking to and fro to find a possible weapon. 'Indeed, at times I doubt I understand any of it. However, I know enough to make me wonder whether we need be on opposite sides.'

He smiled at me. 'That is a bold suggestion.'

'If it is a matter of money –' I began.

'You have many natural advantages, Mr Shield, but I do not think possession of a fortune is one of them.'

'I believe I know a man who would pay handsomely for intelligence, for the right sort of intelligence.'

'The little Yankee and his tame nigger?' Iversen's vowels changed their character, became flatter and bolder. 'No, I do not think it would answer.' He reverted to the cultivated speech he had used before. 'We are gone too far in this business. A man does not change horses in mid-stream if he has any choice in the matter.' He motioned with the pistol towards the open trap-door. 'I wish you to return to the cellar for a while.'

I had no choice but to obey. When he had shut me up in the darkness, I tried half-heartedly to free myself, but Joseph had done his job too well. I do not know how long I sat on the lowest tread of the stairs, turning over in my mind various arguments I might advance to Iversen, only to discard each and every one of them. Footsteps moved to and fro above my head, and once Iversen sang a few lines of a sentimental ballad. On two occasions I thought I heard hooves, but I could not tell whether they were coming or going, passing or stopping.

At length there were footsteps again overhead, followed by the scrape of metal and a rapping on the trap-door.

'Mr Shield? Mr Shield?' Iversen called. 'Pray answer me.'

'I hear you.'

'You may come slowly up the stairs. I have unbolted the trap-door. But no rash movements, if you please.'

I emerged, blinking like a mole, into a room filled with morning sunshine. Iversen was waiting at a prudent distance from the trap-door. He required me to turn my back on him so that he could examine the cord around my wrists. Then he led me through the kitchen into a passageway and thence to a room furnished as a parlour according to the rustic taste of the last century. No sunshine penetrated here once

430

the door was shut, for the shutters were closed and barred. Most of one wall was filled with a great fireplace where logs burned in a brazier. The only other light came from half a dozen candles.

There were two people already in the room. One was Mary Ann. She was bound to a chair. Even her mouth was gagged, the mouth that could speak no words, only trill like a bird. She stared at me with huge, unhappy eyes.

The second person, sitting with his watch in his hand on a high-backed wooden settle close to the fire, was Stephen Carswall.

CHAPTER SEVENTY-NINE

'*AYEZ PEUR*,' I said, and watched a glance dart from Iversen to Carswall.

'You've taken leave of your senses, Shield,' said Carswall.

Iversen pushed me to a stool opposite the settle and stationed himself by the door.

'The connection between you is known,' I went on, pressing what I hoped was my advantage.

'Known by whom?' Carswall said. 'Noak? A man may buy a parrot, may he not? For a boy who is about to become his stepson?' He gave the last words a peculiar emphasis and shot a look of mingled triumph and hatred at me. 'Why were you pestering Mrs Frant over her husband's grave?'

'How did you know I met her there?'

'She told me.' Carswall stared around the room as if the ramshackle wainscoting were an admiring audience. 'She sent you off with a flea in your ear, eh?'

I shook my head. 'It was Mrs Kerridge, wasn't it? She serves two masters, you and Mr Noak. And that's not all she told you. She learned where I lodged from Salutation Harmwell and passed it on: which is how Iversen's bully-backs could find me so quickly.'

Carswall shrugged. 'How far has Mr Noak penetrated this business?'

'I am not in his confidence.'

'Let us put that assertion to the test. Have you seen a man's hand crushed in a door?'

I did not reply.

'It is not a pretty sight. It is prodigiously painful, too. Yet it is so simple. One holds the hand between the fixed edge of the door and the jamb, one finger at a time if one pleases. Then one closes the door. As any mechanic will tell you, you do not need strength if you have leverage. A child could do it, so long as there were someone present to hold the hand in the appropriate position.'

'You are a monster.'

Carswall said, 'Necessity knows no law. Isn't that one of your tags, Mr Tutor? I take the world as I find it. You are a double threat to me: to the reputation of my affianced wife and to the success of a business transaction.'

I did not speak. I clasped my bound hands and thought of the flesh, sinew and bone beneath the skin.

Carswall nodded to Iversen, who cocked his pistol and took a step towards me.

'Not him,' Carswall said. 'The girl first. Let him see the effect of his silence before he feels it.'

Iversen nodded and untied Mary Ann's wrists. Leaving her bound around the legs, he hooked his arm through hers and dragged her towards the door. She was still gagged but she made a gargling noise in the back of her throat that was more painfully eloquent than any quantity of words.

'Stop,' I said. 'There is no need for the girl to be hurt.'

Carswall leaned back on the settle and opened his watch. 'I will give you a minute to convince me.'

'Will you set her free?'

'Perhaps. It depends how honest you are.'

I had no choice in the matter. I said, 'Mr Noak believes that Henry Frant was responsible, directly or indirectly, for the murder of his estranged son in Canada during the late war. He believes that Lieutenant Saunders died because he threatened to expose corrupt dealings on the part of Wavenhoe's Bank, or rather on the part of Mr Henry Frant.

Furthermore, he suspects but has not yet succeeded in proving that you yourself, Mr Carswall, were Frant's partner in this corruption, and are therefore, to some extent at least, a party to Lieutenant Saunders's murder.'

Carswall puffed up his cheeks and blew out a gust of air. 'What evidence has he?'

'Nothing that confirms your guilt. However, Mr Noak's investigation uncovered Henry Frant's embezzlement since he took over the direction of Wavenhoe's. Mr Noak took steps to hasten the collapse of the bank and Mr Frant's ruin.'

'But the matter did not end there,' Carswall said softly.

'No, sir, it did not. Mr Noak struck up an acquaintance with you. His negotiations over the proposed sale of the Liverpool warehouses convinced him that you had an active involvement in the Canadian operation, though it did not prove you had a hand in his son's death.' I hesitated. 'And then there was the business of Mrs Johnson and the ice-house.'

I felt the atmosphere suddenly change in the room when I mentioned those last words. Iversen let out a tiny sigh.

'It was an accident,' Carswall said with a sniff. 'The Coroner said so.'

'An accident, sir? But I think the Coroner was unaware that she was not alone. There was a man with her.'

'I should have thought it an unlikely time and place for a romantic assignation.'

'That was not their purpose. Henry Frant and Mrs Johnson had concealed certain items of value in the ice-house, in the hope that they would be able to build a new life for themselves after the bank's collapse, perhaps abroad and under assumed names.'

Carswall raised his great eyebrows. 'I can conceive of nothing less likely.'

'They left behind the ring. Or rather he did.'

'The ring? The ring you stole?'

'The ring you had a servant conceal in my coat, to give colour to the false accusation you made against me.'

'False? False, you say? Then where is the ring?'

'I cannot tell you that. But I can tell you that it will soon be delivered to your house in Margaret-street. But to return to Mr Noak: he obtained a list of the securities that went missing when the bank collapsed. They included a bill that was recently cashed in Riga.'

'And how does Mr Noak explain this?'

'He believes that Henry Frant contrived his own murder, and is still alive, and that you and he have come to an arrangement.'

Carswall cleared the phlegm from his throat. 'Pray enlighten me.'

'You assist him to convert the securities and perhaps other items into ready money. Mr Frant dares not do this himself, even abroad, because not only is there the question of the embezzlement hanging over him, but also that of the identity of the man murdered in Wellington-terrace. Mr Noak has established that the bill cashed in Riga had passed through the hands of a notary in Brussels, a man you do business with.'

'So do many others, no doubt. And what advantage do I derive from this ludicrous arrangement?'

'You, sir?' I said. 'Why, you have a share of his profits, do you not, and the opportunity to enjoy Mr Frant's wife.'

Carswall's colour, already dark, deepened still further. He studied the face of his watch, his chest heaving up and down. 'I have rarely heard anything so nonsensical,' he said at last.

'It has the merit of explaining why the four of us are together in this room.'

Iversen coughed, reminding Carswall of his presence.

Carswall swivelled towards him and pointed at Mary Ann. 'Give the drab a taste of her medicine.'

'To what end, sir?' Iversen asked. 'It seems to me the young gentleman is chatty enough as it is.'

'What's it to you?'

'The girl's a servant of mine, sir, and wonderfully discreet on account of her affliction. If I crush her hands, she'll be no good to man nor beast.'

I said – at random; urgent to distract Carswall from his purpose:

435

'There is another question that Mr Noak would give a great deal to have answered.'

'Eh?' Carswall pressed the repeater button on his watch, which emitted a minute ping. 'The man is a fool: what profit does his infernal Yankee meddling bring him?'

'He wishes to know whether you realise what a laughing-stock you make of yourself when you pursue that canting hypocrite of a baronet with your bastard daughter and your ill-gotten money. Whether you know how the world sneers at you for your desire to ape the gentry. Whether you will die of natural causes, sir, or go to the gallows as you so richly deserve.'

My voice rose as I spoke, as the passion welled up from a hidden recess in my being. Noak had not asked these questions: but I did, for now there was nothing to lose that was not already lost. After I had finished, a moment of complete silence descended on the frowzy room. Iversen was watching Carswall, and on his face was an expression of detachment, almost amusement. Blotches of angry pallor appeared in the old man's cheeks. I heard, quite distinctly, another tiny chime from his Breguet watch.

With a great bellow, he rose from the settle.

'You rascal! You knave! You God-damned scrub!'

'You must know that Mrs Frant hates and despises you,' I said softly. 'I wonder at the strength of your desire to possess her. Is it because she was the wife of Henry Frant? Did you hate him so very much? Did he make you feel he was your master? Yes, sir, your *master*.'

Carswall shook his fist at me, the one with the watch in it. 'I shall see you suffer, I assure you. You there!' He addressed Iversen now. 'Hold his hand in the door, damn you. I shall break every bone in his body. I shall – I shall –'

He broke off as a great surge of passion ran like electricity through his body, making him vibrate, and jerk, and twist like a sheet in the hands of a laundry maid. His mouth opened but no sound emerged. He stared fixedly at me but there was no longer any anger in his eyes: his face was puzzled, confused, even imploring. Then he gasped, as if he felt an unexpected pinprick. His left leg gave way and he fell into the hearth, bringing down a set of fire irons in his fall with a rattle like grapeshot.

I struggled to my feet, my eyes still on the stricken man.

Iversen screamed.

I turned sharply towards the sound, almost overbalancing. As I did so, I heard a clatter. The pistol had fallen to the floor. By a miracle it had not discharged itself and was still cocked. Now silent, Iversen bent over Mary Ann and pummelled her with hands balled into fists and then wrapped his arms round her waist.

I fell to the floor, rolled and scooped up the pistol in my bound hands. Iversen threw Mary Ann across the room. She tripped over Carswall's legs and sprawled on the bare boards, giving a great cry as her back, still raw from the flogging, collided with the leg of a chair. I wrapped my hands round the pistol's butt. My finger found the trigger. Wrenching my left arm almost out of its socket, I arched my back and rested the pistol on my right hip. The muzzle pointed at Iversen.

'Stand back,' I commanded. 'Raise your hands in the air and move towards the corner.'

For a moment he looked at me, showing no signs of panic or fear. Whatever else he was, he was never a coward. A drop of blood fell to the floorboards. I saw that he was wounded in the wrist and realised that Mary Ann had spat out her gag and bitten him there, the shock of which had caused him to drop the pistol.

'Back, sir,' I repeated. 'Back, I say.'

Slowly he raised his arms and retreated into the corner.

The reversal was so sudden that for a moment I did not know how best to profit from it. Mary Ann showed no such hesitation. Without so much as a glance in my direction, she knelt by Carswall. Cooing and trilling, she went through his pockets, tossing the contents on the floor, turning him over this way and that as if he were nothing more than a huge baby. He was perfectly conscious, I believe, for his eyes were open and they moved and watered as she busied herself with him. Yet he could not move. He lay there, a beached whale, an island of blubber in a fine coat now smeared with the ashes of the fire.

Mary Ann found a penknife and brought it to me with an expression on her face like that of a dog who knows she has done well. While I covered Iversen with the pistol, she sawed the cords at my wrists with the little blade, taking care not to block my line of fire.

I felt a sudden increase of pain. The cord round my wrists had broken the skin in places. I took the knife from her with my left hand and cut her own bonds.

'We must summon help,' I whispered. 'The other men may still be here.'

She shook her head.

'They have gone back to town?'

She nodded.

I thought quickly. I dared not send for a constable. One look at us, and at Mr Carswall lying in the hearth, would be enough to prejudice him against us.

I put a hand on Mary Ann's arm and felt her start. 'That letter I threw down to you yesterday, when you were in the yard at Mr Iversen's, were you able to pick it up?'

She nodded vigorously, then mimed a frown, pointed first at Iversen, then at herself, and finally drew a finger across her own throat.

'You were discovered? That is the reason you were brought here? To be murdered?'

'Her wits are disordered, Mr Shield,' Iversen said. 'You cannot trust a word she – that is to say, what the poor girl implies.'

I ignored him. 'The letter was to an American gentleman residing in Brewer-street. If I gave you money, could you take another letter to him?'

Mary Ann moved away from me and crouched by the hearth. She extended the forefinger of her right hand and wrote the word NOAK in the ashes.

'Good God! You read the note! You can read and write?'

She nodded and unexpectedly grinned at me. Then she smoothed away Noak's name and wrote instead: GIG IN YARD. I DRIVE.

'You could take a letter directly to him yourself? You can manage a horse?'

She nodded and rubbed out the words. Next she wrote: WRITE LETTER SERVANT ON ERRAND.

This exchange between us was slow and awkward, not merely because of the medium she used to express herself but also because of the necessity to keep an eye on Mr Iversen in his corner. Before we went any further, I decided to move him into the cellar which had so lately served as my own prison. Mr Iversen seemed happy to oblige. First I held the pistol to his head while Mary Ann patted him to ensure he did not have another weapon concealed about his person. Then, at my signal, he preceded us out of the room, his hands raised in the air, moving slowly, just as I had requested.

'Well, well,' said he as he descended the steps down from the kitchen. 'So the girl is a scholar. Who would have thought it? She has been with us these six months and no one had the remotest idea. You will leave me a candle, will you not? No? Well, I suppose I should not be surprised.'

'Where are we? What is the easiest way for the girl to take to town?'

'Left out of the yard, right at the crossroads, and in less than a mile you come to the high road through Kilburn to London itself.'

'Whose is the gig?'

'Mr Carswall hired it from an inn – you will find the bill in his pocketbook, I believe. He drove himself, of course. If he had travelled in one of his own carriages, the whole world would have known what he was up to, and where. There are two horses in the stable, by the way – the brown mare is mine.'

'You are very obliging.'

'And why not, pray? You may trust my advice entirely, Mr Shield – after all, I have no reason to lie to you, not now, and everything to gain from obliging you in any way that lies within my power. Besides, I am hoping you will allow me a candle. I truly dislike the darkness.'

Iversen was so determined, it seemed, to bear his misfortunes philosophically that I nearly acceded to his request. But Mary Ann spat neatly on his head as he reached the foot of the stairs, slammed the trap-door down with great force and laughed as she rammed home the bolt.

We conducted a rapid search of the premises. These consisted of a large cottage with a yard on one side containing several barns and a stable and the usual offices, most of them in a dilapidated condition. It had never been an establishment of any size, to judge by the buildings; and now the buildings were all that was left, apart from the remains of a small garden at the front, with a paddock and an overgrown orchard beyond. The land round about was used principally for rough grazing while it waited for the contractors to sow bricks and raise their crop of houses.

The kitchen and the parlour were the only partly habitable rooms. The remainder of the cottage was in a parlous state, with rotting boards spattered with bird-droppings, the plaster crumbling from the walls and, in the largest room upstairs, a place where the ceiling and part of the roof above had collapsed, giving a view of a blue sky. There were three coffins stacked up in one of the barns. Another contained the gig, and the horses were in the stable beside it.

Carswall was too heavy to move very far. Between us, Mary Ann and I dragged him away from the hearth. I loosened his breeches and his neckcloth, tied his thumbs together in case he was shamming, and covered him with a horse blanket from the stable. Among his possessions was a pocketbook and a pencil. Mary Ann tore out several leaves and put them and the pencil in the pocket of her dress.

Even then I realised she had become quite a different person – which was evident not merely from the way she behaved, but also from the way I behaved towards her. When she could express herself only in bird-like trills and primitive sign language, I had unconsciously treated her as little better than an idiot: as if her inability to talk was due to a wider intellectual deficiency. Now she had found her voice, and I realised that the deficiency had been mine rather than hers.

I sat at the table in the kitchen and dashed off a note to Mr Noak, explaining as concisely as I could the situation we were in and begging his assistance and his discretion. I helped Mary Ann harness the horse to the gig and watched her drive out of the yard.

I went back to the parlour and threw another log on the fire. Carswall was breathing heavily. His eyes were still open. Every now and then his lips would tremble, but no words emerged. His cigar case was among the heap of his possessions. I took a cigar and lit it with an ember from the grate.

I bent down and uncurled the fingers of the old man's right hand, for they were still folded round the open Breguet watch, as if time itself were the last thing he would let go. His eyes followed every movement. I put the watch to his ear and pressed the repeater button. The tiny chimes rang out.

'*Ayez peur*,' I said aloud. I stared at the old man's fleshy and decayed face. 'Can you hear me, sir?' I asked. 'Can you hear the chime of the repeater?'

There was no response. His intelligence was imprisoned, as Mary Ann's had been, but unlike her he could not even write in the ashes. I closed the watch and pushed it into his waistcoat pocket. I left him to count the minutes, the hours, the days, and went back to the kitchen, where I knocked on the trap-door.

'Mr Iversen? Are you there?'

'I am indeed, my dear sir, though I cannot hear you as clearly as I would like. If you were to be so good as to open the trap-door a trifle —'

'I think not,' I said.

'There has been a good deal of misunderstanding in this sad business,' Mr Iversen said plaintively. 'Misunderstanding piled upon misunderstanding, one might say, heaping Pelion upon Ossa as Homer so —'

'You would oblige me extremely if you would explain the misunderstandings.'

'Ah, yes, Mr Shield — but would I oblige myself? In a perfect society, all men would be honest, all men would be open: but alas, we do not live in Utopia. Nevertheless, I will do my utmost. I am the soul of candour.'

'You gave that parrot to Mr Carswall, I collect?'

'Indeed I did. The boy was mad for a bird, Mr Carswall said, a bird that talked, and as it happened I was able to oblige. I like to oblige, when possible.'

I blew out a plume of smoke. It was at that moment that a dazzling light broke over me. As a child, I remembered, I would sometimes puzzle for minutes, even for hours, at a passage my master had set me to translate: then, with a similar shock of revelation, I would see the thread of meaning that ran through it and, following it, I would have the sense in a trice. Just so, now: the clue that resolved this whole confusing matter was this, that it was only a little leap between a parrot that talked French and a rare specimen of *digitus mortuus praecisus*. Did it not follow from this simple observation that Mr Iversen had been obliging not only to Mr Carswall but also to Mr Frant?

'Do I smell tobacco?' Mr Iversen inquired.

If the finger I had found in the satchel had belonged to the embalmed body of Mr Iversen, Senior, then there was no reason to suppose that the body I had seen at Wellington-terrace had been anyone other than Henry Frant. In that case, only one person truly benefited from the confusion and uncertainty.

As any actor knows, we rarely study the faces of those we encounter. We remember them by their salient features, which are often accretions, not essentials. Thus, for example, we do not have a clear mental image of a person's face: instead – for the sake of illustration – we see a tangled beard, a pair of blue spectacles, a wheeled chair and a robe embroidered with magical symbols. In my mind, I stripped away the accretions and considered what I knew of the essentials.

'I believe, sir,' I said in a voice that shook, 'that I have the honour of addressing Mr David Poe as well as Mr Iversen, Junior?'

I strained my ears to hear the reply. The seconds passed. Then, at last, I heard the sound of a low chuckle.

CHAPTER EIGHTY

THE WHOLE TRUTH about David Poe, late of Baltimore, Maryland, and Mr Iversen, Junior, late of Queen-street, Seven Dials, did not emerge on that morning. I do not suppose anyone will ever know it. Nature may have framed Mr Poe to be candid but life had taught him to dissimulate.

'What's in a name, Mr Shield? Time is not on our side at present. Let us not quibble about trifles. I have in my pocketbook a document that –'

'But you are Poe, are you not? You are Edgar's father?'

'I cannot deny either charge. Indeed, having seen the lad, I challenge you to find a prouder parent in Christendom. I do not wish to appear importunate, but –'

'Mr Poe,' I interrupted, 'even if Mary Ann meets no obstacles on her way, we shall be able to enjoy each other's company for hours. I think we should occupy ourselves with your story. We have nothing else to do.'

'There is the matter of the document I mentioned.'

'The document can wait. My curiosity about you cannot.'

I sat smoking on a chair by the trap-door, and never did a cigar taste so sweet. From below my feet came David Poe's rich, drawling voice – now Irish, now American, now genteel, now Cockney, now whispering, now declaiming. Principally from that conversation, but also from later

443

observations and information provided by others, I believe that at last I built up a tolerably accurate picture of his life, though by no means a comprehensive one. It goes without saying that he was a loose and vicious man who cared not how low he had to stoop in pursuit of his own base ends. But we are none of us made of whole cloth. Like the rest of us, he was a quilt made up of scraps from many materials, some of which sat well beside their neighbours, some of which did not.

Yes, he was cruel and dissolute and often a drunkard. He was also, I believe, a murderer, though in the case of Henry Frant he claimed to have acted in self-defence, a plea which may have some truth in it. The death of Mrs Johnson he attributed to an unlucky accident, and this I found harder to credit.

Nor do I find it likely that David Poe and Mr Carswall intended that Mary Ann and I should remain alive. Poe told me that the coffin had merely been a method to bring me discreetly from Seven Dials to this place where Stephen Carswall might interrogate me without fear of prying eyes. I believe it was to have served a further purpose. It would have been easy enough to slip another coffin or two into the private burial ground attached to the workhouse next door; the Sexton was Poe's creature, and in an establishment of that nature it is never long before there is a need for an open grave where two may lie as comfortably as one.

I have leapt ahead of myself. The point I had begun to make with my talk of quilts and cloth is simply that Mr Poe could be an agreeable companion if he wished. He was a man of parts, who had travelled the world and observed its follies and peculiarities. Of course he had every reason to make himself agreeable to me while I had him imprisoned in the cellar.

His story, in brief, was this. As a young man, his father had put him to study the law, but it had not answered and he had become an actor instead. He had married Miss Arnold, the English actress who became the mother of Edgar and of two other children. Alas, an actor's life is a precarious one, with many temptations. He had been very young, he told me, and he had quarrelled with managers and critics. He had drunk too deeply and too often. He had failed to husband his few resources.

'And I was not, perhaps, as good an actor as I thought myself. My Thespian talents do not shine at their brightest on the boards, sir: they are better suited to the wider stage of life.'

The open mouths of his young family added to his cares. At length, the young man could shoulder his burden no more. At that time he and his wife were in New York. A chance-met acquaintance in a tavern offered to procure him a berth on a boat sailing for Cape Town where, he was told, there was such a hunger for dramatic entertainments that no actor worth his salt could fail to make himself a fortune within a very short time indeed. There was not a moment to be lost for the ship was to sail on the outgoing tide. According to his account, Poe had scribbled a note explaining his intended absence to his wife and had entrusted it to a friend.

'Alas! I trusted too well. My letter was never delivered. My poor Elizabeth went to her grave a few months later not knowing whether I was alive or dead, leaving my unfortunate children to depend on the charity of strangers.'

David Poe's misfortunes had only just begun. The ship in which he was to work his passage to Cape Town was a merchantman sailing under British colours – at that time, our two countries were not yet at war. But the Union flag proved Mr Poe's undoing for the ship was snapped up by a French privateer out of Le Havre. Mr Poe was reticent about how he had spent the next few months, but by the summer of 1812 he had moved to London.

'I know a man of your sensibility, Mr Shield, will have no difficulty in picturing my distress when I discovered, by a circuitous route, that my beloved Elizabeth had died. My first impulse was to rush to the side of my motherless children and provide what comfort a poor widowed father might bring. But on second thoughts, I realised that I could not afford the luxury – I might say the selfishness – of indulging in my paternal sentiments, not for my own sake but for the sake of my children. To get a passage to the United States at that time would not have been easy, since Congress had declared war on Great Britain in June. I understood, too, that my children were being cared for by the most amiable of benefactors: indeed, even if I could get to the United States, their material circumstances would immediately worsen. I blush to admit it, but there had been a little temporary embarrassment just before I left New York, in the shape of unpaid debts. No, though every generous feeling urged me to rush to the side of my children, prudence restrained me.' Here I imagined him on the other side of the trap-door, standing at the foot of the stairs with his hand on his heart. 'A father must place his children's welfare above his own selfish desires, Mr Shield, though it break his heart to do so.'

Fortunately, the grieving widower was not obliged to grieve in solitude. He had wooed and won the heart of a Miss Iversen, who lived with her father in Queen-street, Seven Dials, and assisted him in his business.

'She was not in the first flush of youth,' Mr Poe told me. 'But then nor was I. We were both of an age when one woos with the head as much as with the heart. Mr Iversen's health was failing and he was anxious to secure the future of his only child in the event of his death. She was a most amiable lady, with the additional attraction that she brought not only her delightful self to our connubial bower but also a means of earning my living – by honest toil, the sweat of my brow, but I did not mind that. There can be no higher calling than to heal the ills of one's fellow men. I firmly believe we have had more success in that department than the entire College of Physicians. We doctor their souls as well as their bodies.'

'You tell fortunes?' I inquired. 'You give them coloured water and pills made of flour and sugar? You interpret their dreams, sell them spells and help women miscarry?'

'Who is to say that is wrong, sir?' Mr Poe replied. 'You would not believe the cures I have effected. You would not credit the number of sorrows I have soothed. I give them hope, sir, which is better than all the money in the world. In my way I am a philanthropist. Tell me, which is worse? To live as I do, an honest tradesman, a broker of dreams. Or to prey upon widows and hard-working men, and prise away their little fortunes and give them nothing in return. A splendid establishment and a carriage with a crest on the door are no guarantee of moral probity. I need refer you only to Mr Henry Frant and Mr Stephen Carswall as evidence of that.'

I believed him – or rather, I believed some part of him meant what he said: no man is a monster to himself, not entirely. And he spoke no more than the truth: the distance between Seven Dials on the one hand, and Margaret-street and Russell-square on the other, is shorter than the world realises.

When old Mr Iversen died in 1813, his daughter had been plunged into a melancholy so profound that her doting husband had feared she would never emerge. She could not bear to be parted from her papa. In the end Mr Poe had suggested that his body be embalmed.

'It is done in the best families now. And the old man, despite his trade, was an out-and-out Rationalist. Why should he wish for the grave or the attentions of worms? And of course the solution was also eminently practicable. My patrons are, by and large, a superstitious crew. They do not care to play foolish tricks on a man whose father-in-law keeps guard for all eternity in a room above the shop. Better than a pair of mastiffs, eh? Those dogs at Monkshill were no use as guards when they were dead, but with my late wife's father being dead was in fact an advantage.'

Mr Poe had taken over not only the business of the old man but also something of his identity. 'Only an American, sir, can truly appreciate the value of tradition.' He called himself Mr Iversen. He wore his father-in-law's professional garb – that is to say, the gown with its strange symbols and the skull cap; he even pretended to be crippled, as Mr Iversen, Senior, had been.

'There is much to be said for distinguishing one's professional activities from one's private life,' Mr Poe said. 'If I slip on a beard and a pair of blue spectacles I become another man altogether. People come and go in Seven Dials. In a year or two, most of them had forgotten there had ever been another Iversen, especially after my poor Polly followed her pa to the grave.'

He was understandably reticent about the precise extent and nature of the business he had inherited from his father-in-law and then built up himself. I think it probable that there was a great deal more to it than quack medicines and spells for the credulous. I cannot forget the bully boys in their rusty black clothes, the firm of undertakers who worked so assiduously for him, and the tumbledown farm so close to a work-house, a lunatic asylum and a private burial ground.

In all probability, David Poe would have continued to prosper in Queen-street if he had not learned that Mr and Mrs Allan were in London, with their foster son Edgar. Over the years he had naturally paid attention to the news from America, and in particular to Americans visiting London. According to his own explanation, he had been possessed by an overpowering desire to see his son, whom he had last laid eyes on when the boy was not much beyond two years old and still in petticoats.

I see no reason to doubt at least the partial truth of this. As I said, we are all a patchwork of emotions. Why should David Poe not have felt a sentimental attachment to the children he had seen so little of? Absence and ignorance encourage such tender feelings. But an act may have more than one motive. Knowing Mr Poe, I suspect that he may also have borne in mind the possibility of deriving pecuniary advantage from Mr Allan, for he must have known that Allan was accounted a rich man.

Whatever his purpose, Mr Poe visited Southampton-row, where I unwittingly confirmed his son's identity, and where he learned that Edgar was to be found in Stoke Newington. Later he came to the village, where he accosted the boys and had his altercation with me. He had indeed been more than a little tipsy on this occasion – 'if ever a man had need of refreshment, it was I on that day.' Another layer of confusion was added by the fact that Mr Poe was short-sighted, and his vision was further hampered by the blue glasses: therefore he found it hard to distinguish between Edgar Allan and Charlie Frant, which brought about the initial assumption that the object of his interest was not Edgar but Charlie. It was this misunderstanding which led, through my good offices, to his acquaintance with Mr Frant.

Frant saw what David Poe wished him to see: an Irish-American with a taste for gin and no visible means of support; no threat to Frant or to anyone else. Frant saw all this, and he also saw that David Poe was approximately the same height, weight, age and build as himself. Leaving aside the superficial dissimilarities, Poe made a perfect substitute for

Henry Frant in the rôle of murder victim. Urged on, no doubt, by Mrs Johnson, he retained Poe's services. In the late afternoon of Wednesday 24th November, Frant lured Poe up to Wellington-terrace with the intention of murdering him.

'He told me we were to meet a gentleman there, and gave me a suit of his clothes, saying I must look the gentleman, too, or the design he had in mind would be doomed. By God, he thought me a prime flat, but in truth it was the other way about. He told me to get to Wellington-terrace early, where he would explain the design. So I walked there from the turnpike road, and he sprang on me, with a hammer in his hand.' David Poe coughed. 'I had been half expecting it. We had a bit of a set-to, and I happened to get hold of the hammer. I didn't mean to kill him, as God's my witness, but he would have killed me given half the chance. I must have hit him a little harder than I thought. There I was, Mr Shield, in something of a difficulty, as I think you will agree.'

'You did not mean to kill him?' I cried. 'Mr Poe, you forget I saw the body.'

'On my honour, Mr Shield, I had no more intention of killing him than I have of killing you, as you will see when I explain those injuries. When he died, he was almost entirely unmarked, apart from the back of the head, that is. But I knew that no jury in the land would believe that my blows had been struck in self-defence, that I had not wished to kill him. While I considered what to do, I searched him, and I struck lucky with his pockets, at least. Frant planned to run away, you see, after he'd killed me. He was carrying plenty of money, a case of jewellery, and also a letter from his fancy woman down at Monkshill. Shockingly indiscreet, she was, sir, quite shocking.'

'So you knew what they planned?'

'Not then. I didn't have time to read the whole, but I saw enough to discover what my part was to be, enough to realise there was plenty of money in this, far more than Mr Frant had in his pockets. I was to stand in for Frant himself – Frant as a dead man, you understand, so that he would not be pursued. Can you credit such evil ingenuity! Of course I needed time to contemplate the pros and cons. Anyway, the long and the short of it is, I decided my best course of action was to follow at least some of the design that Mr Frant had laid out for me. So I knocked his face and hands about so his own mother couldn't have been absolutely sure who he was – I had to do the hands, because of the finger – and then I slipped away. I knew there'd be questions asked, and I'd have to find a way to deal with them. With your assistance, Mr Shield, as it happened.'

Mr Poe had laid the trail for an investigator to follow, the trail that led to the finger in the satchel at the dentist's. 'Maria at the Fountain in St Giles is one of mine. If anyone came asking for Frant, she was to direct them to Queen-street and ensure I knew they were coming. And along you came, Mr Shield, not Mrs Johnson or a runner, as I'd been half-expecting. So we played out our charade – I thought it a neat touch to have Mary Ann give you the drawing that led you to my dentist, eh? If you had not asked to see the girl, she would have accosted you as you left. Then off you went to find the satchel with the finger.'

'It was only when I saw your late father-in-law in Queen-street, when a glove fell off his left hand, that I realised what had happened.'

'I needed a finger,' Mr Poe said with a trace of embarrassment. 'His was to hand, if you excuse the vile wordplay. I regretted the necessity of removing it, of course, but the result was so particularly ingenious that I could not resist: it suggested, did it not, that the body at Wellington-terrace was indeed mine, whoever I might be, and that Henry Frant was alive and well – and not only an embezzler but a murderer.'

Having secured his own safety, as far as was possible, Mr Poe then turned his attention towards Monkshill-park. By that time he had studied Mrs Johnson's letter. She had not only made it clear that she and Mr Frant hoped to elope, and that their nest-egg was hidden somewhere in the vicinity of the ice-house at Monkshill-park and unlikely to be accessible until January: she had also dropped a broad hint about the value of the nest-egg, a sum so substantial that, as Mr Poe put it, 'even the angels would have been tempted.'

So Mr Poe had travelled down to Monkshill-park, arriving on St Stephen's Day. His had been the face that had peered at me through the window of Grange Cottage on the day that Edgar sprained his ankle.

'You gave me quite a fright, sir,' he said reproachfully. 'All in all, I did not have a happy day. You had hardly left the cottage when a chaise called for Mrs Johnson and took her away, and I knew by her luggage that she planned a visit of some length. The servant locked up and walked up to the village. I explored the garden and the outbuildings, and later I slipped into the park with the intention of discovering the ice-house. But a gamekeeper took me for a vagrant and threatened to set his dogs on me.'

Later, Mr Poe learned from alehouse gossip in the village that Mrs Johnson was spending a fortnight with her cousins at Clearland, a circumstance which made a private conference with her difficult, if not impossible, to achieve. Urgent business called him back to London. But after the two weeks had elapsed, he returned.

'I hired a hack in Gloucester and rode over. You will imagine how mortified I was to find the cottage quite deserted. I slipped away –'

'Not before you were seen,' I said. 'I came over to the cottage myself to look for traces of you.'

'If only I had known,' Mr Poe replied courteously. 'I should have been only too glad to renew our acquaintance.'

On his return to Gloucester, however, a solution to his difficulty presented itself. The assembly at the Bell was only two days away and not unnaturally it formed the principal topic of conversation at that establishment. Mr Poe supped there on the Monday evening and discovered that a party from Clearland-court was among those expected to grace the occasion. It did not take him long to establish where the Ruispidges lodged. He witnessed their arrival on Wednesday and sent up a note to Mrs Johnson, begging the favour of an interview.

'I mentioned in my letter that I had something to communicate in relation to Mr H.F. – a matter of life and death, and discretion was of the utmost importance. I ventured to suggest we met on the morrow, but in her reply she insisted on an interview that very evening, and proposed that we meet in the gazebo at the bottom of the garden of the house where the Ruispidges lodged.'

Mrs Johnson had been in a pitiable state, not knowing whether Henry Frant were alive or dead. Indeed, it was by playing upon the possibility that Frant was still alive that Mr Poe was able to induce her to co-operate with him. He told her that Frant had been attacked by a ruined creditor; that Mr Poe had acted the Good Samaritan and come to his aid; that Frant was lying dangerously ill in London, unable even to write; and that he had begged Mr Poe to fetch both Mrs Johnson and what was hidden in the ice-house.

'This was cruel indeed, sir,' I said. 'To play upon the poor woman's weakness.'

'Upon my life, sir,' Mr Poe protested, 'she received only what she deserved. The letter I discovered in Mr Frant's pocket enabled me to form the opinion that Mrs Johnson was the originator of the scheme to have me killed in Mr Frant's place. Both she and Frant were ruthless and reckless, sir, and as impulsive as children; but she was immeasurably the stronger character. I can safely assert that it was she who was truly to blame for those ghastly events at Wellington-terrace.'

'Did you tell her who you were?'

'Indeed I did not! That would have been the height of folly. The success of my scheme depended on the lady believing that it was I, Poe, not her lover, who had been murdered, just as she had planned. I led her to understand that I was a former associate of Mr Poe's, a man who had reason to hate him, a man who could be trusted as long as he was generously rewarded.'

Mrs Johnson had needed desperately to believe him because he alone offered her the hope of finding Henry Frant. She agreed to return to Grange Cottage after the ball, not to Clearland as she had previously intended; Mr Poe would join her there to retrieve what was in the ice-house. As they talked in the gazebo, however, she became much agitated, and also very cold and, according to Mr Poe, suggested they take some refreshment. Her cloak and hood granted her anonymity, and they patronised a hostelry at a distance from both the Ruispidges' lodgings and the Bell.

'But the liquor went to her head,' Mr Poe cried. 'She wept on my shoulder! She became quarrelsome! She led me a merry dance! And then at last you and Mrs Frant appeared and I feared that all was lost.'

Fortunately for him, Mrs Johnson had kept her own counsel, and he had come to the cottage according to plan. I myself had seen him on his skewbald mare. Mrs Johnson took a daily walk to the lake to ascertain when the men began to empty the ice-house.

'Her lover had given her a key to the door, which she had concealed in a secret compartment at the bottom of a small jewel box. Now I come to a most curious circumstance, my dear sir: I had the identical twin of that box in my own possession! But I shall return to this in a moment.'

All had at first run smoothly on the night of their expedition. According to Mr Poe's version of events, their difficulties had begun only after Mrs Johnson had retrieved the valuables from the sump of the ice-house. In her excitement, she had missed her footing on the ladder and fallen to her death in the pit. To add to his troubles, he had nearly perished when he blundered into a mantrap on his way back to Grange Cottage.

'What could I do?' Mr Poe cried. 'I am naturally law-abiding, and my instinct was at once to lay the matter in its entirety before the nearest magistrate. But nothing could bring my charming hostess back to life. I knew that circumstances were against me. All in all – for Mrs Johnson's sake – for the reputation of the illustrious family to which she had the honour of being connected – it seemed wiser that I should slip modestly away. My presence would have served only to confuse matters.' He chuckled, as though challenging me to disagree with this interpretation of events; Mr Poe was a great tease.

'I did not have an opportunity to examine what Mr Frant and Mrs Johnson had concealed in the ice-house until I returned to London. I had expected gold – I had expected banknotes – I had expected more jewellery: and in all these I was not disappointed. I had also anticipated that there would be bills and other securities, though with less interest because I knew these would not be easy for a man in my position to realise for anything like their true value. But there is a profound irony here: the most valuable item of all was already in my possession, and it had been since November. That little box I found in Mr Frant's pocket.'

'Would it have been made of mahogany, by any chance?' I said, remembering something Sophie had once asked me. 'Inlaid with tulip wood, and with a shell pattern on the lid?'

'My dear Mr Shield! I find you remarkably well informed! Yes, Mr

Frant must have had two of them made, one for his wife and one for his mistress. I had already removed the items of jewellery that Mrs Frant's contained. But I had not suspected the existence of a secret compartment until Mrs Johnson had revealed the one in hers. If only Mr Frant had known! How delighted he would have been!'

David Poe paused and cleared his throat. He was an artist as well as a tease. He waited for me to say something, to encourage him to reveal what he had found. I tapped ash from what was left of my cigar and waited.

'The compartment held a letter,' Poe said at last. 'Its contents were wholly unexpected. I immediately realised it altered everything. It brought great possibilities in its train. But in order to bring those possibilities to fruition, I would have to act, and act soon. There is a tide in the affairs of men, as the Bard so aptly says, which, taken at the flood, leads on to fortune.'

CHAPTER EIGHTY-ONE

L IFE IS A topsy-turvy affair at best, and David Poe's secret history was by no means life at its best. Here is the worst, and saddest, part of his narrative and mine.

You may picture me, sitting by the trap-door in the kitchen of that squalid little farmhouse with a pistol in one hand, a cigar in the other, and the acrid flavour of fear still twisting and turning in my stomach; and all the while the sound of Mr Poe's whining yet oddly mellifluous voice, as beguiling as the serpent's in Eden, was insinuating itself up through the cracks between the floorboards.

'Mr Shield,' said he, 'none of us can argue with the immutable decrees of Providence. Fate has put you on one side of this trap-door and me on the other. But that is no reason why we should not discuss our situation like rational beings. I have a letter in my pocket which could bring you considerable benefit. Material benefit. It is of no use to me now. You, on the other hand, might derive much advantage from it.'

'I do not wish to listen to you.' I rose to my feet and ground out the cigar with my heel.

'Pray, Mr Shield – this will not take a moment. You will not regret it, I promise you. I may whet your interest by revealing that the letter is addressed to Mrs Frant.'

'Who was Mrs Frant's correspondent?'

'Mr Carswall's natural daughter, Miss Flora Carswall. She wrote the letter when she was little more than a child. She was then at a school in Bath whose address is at the head of the letter, as is the date, which is a circumstance of importance. October 1812. The contents of the letter suggest that during the summer she had spent several weeks with her father on a tour of various properties he owns, or owned, in Ireland.'

'I fail to see the significance.'

Poe's voice rose in his excitement. 'The letter is not such a letter as a daughter should ever write about her father, Mr Shield. No one who reads it can doubt its meaning. I shall be blunt – this is no time for delicacy. By my computation, Miss Carswall was at the time no more than a child of fourteen or at the most fifteen. Her letter suggests strongly that, one night when her father was inebriated, he had taken a terrible advantage of her innocence – indeed, one can place no other construction on it – and as a consequence of this she feared that she was with child. The motherless girl was clearly distraught, and she had nowhere else to turn – so she sought the counsel of her friend and cousin, Mrs Frant.'

For a moment I did not know where to find words to say. I felt horror, of course, and also a twisted anger towards that hulk of a man lying in the parlour next door. Most of all, though, I felt pity for Flora. For if this was true, it made clear much about her I had not understood before. I write *if this was true.*

'Show me the letter,' I said. 'You may slip it between the boards.'

'Not so fast, my good friend. If I pass it to you, I pass you my sole means of negotiating. I have no wish to harm the reputation of the unfortunate lady, but you must see that I am in a difficult position myself.'

'Does Carswall know you have it?'

'Of course. He has known since February.'

'You were blackmailing him.'

'I prefer to say that we arrived at an agreement which benefited both of us.'

'It was he, perhaps, who arranged for a certain bill to be cashed in Riga?'

'Precisely.'

'What do you want?' I asked.

'Why, that you should let me go free. I ask for nothing more. If you wish, we shall contrive a struggle and make it look as if you had no choice in the matter. That is entirely up to you. You give me my freedom: I give you this letter, which will enable you to make what terms you wish with Mr Carswall, if he recovers his wits and his powers of speech, or with Miss Carswall, if he doesn't.'

'Why should I strike a bargain with you, Mr Poe? I have it in my power to compel you.'

'With that pistol? I think not. You do not strike me as having the temperament that allows one to kill a man in cold blood.'

'I would not be obliged to. Once help arrives, you can be overpowered and searched without any need to shed your blood.'

Mr Poe laughed. 'I see two difficulties with that plan. In the first place, if a committee searches me – yourself and Mr Noak – that nigger of his, perhaps, the slut, the constable and any Tom, Dick or Harry who happens to be in the vicinity – then the whole committee will read the letter. Miss Carswall's name will be sullied for ever and to no purpose. Is that really what you wish? In the second place, and this argument is even more cogent, if we cannot strike a bargain, I shall simply threaten to destroy the letter. It is only a sheet of paper, and not a large one. By the time you raised the trap-door and reached me, it would be in a dozen pieces and descending into my stomach.'

'Perhaps that would be best for Miss Carswall.'

'It would depend entirely on whether I had in fact carried out my threat. You could not be absolutely sure that I had eaten the letter without searching me, and for that you would need your friends' assistance. Also, if the letter had been destroyed, there would be no chance of your deriving any benefit from it.'

'I do not understand you, sir.'

'I think that you do, Mr Shield. Forgive me if I trespass in places where I have no right to be, but I do not think you have prospered of late. This letter would give you the power to change all that.'

I felt light-headed, and as dry as a man in a desert, a man who sees a mirage trembling before him. 'I would be a fool to let you out without seeing this letter. I have only your word that it even exists.'

457

'Ah – spoken like a man of sense. I applaud your caution. I believe I have a suggestion that will deal with the point you raise. Suppose that I tear the letter into two pieces of unequal size. I shall push the smaller portion through the crack. It will contain enough to confirm what I have said, though for it to be of any use to you, you will also need the larger portion, which I will happily surrender up to you when you release me. You will of course have me covered with the pistol at all times, so there will be no danger to you whatsoever.'

Poe's audacity astonished me. Here was a man who had kidnapped and mistreated me, who almost certainly intended to have me killed, and who now was proposing in the coolest way possible that I should set him free in return for a compromising letter which would enable me to blackmail a lady. I licked my lips and longed for a pot of strong coffee.

I said, 'Very well. Let me see part of the letter.'

He passed a scrap of paper through to me. It was four-sided, but only one side was straight, and contained a few scrawled words, the ink blotched as if with tears.

> —ut Papa flew
> —he fault was mine
> — be whipped for

When I read those words I abandoned prudence. I wanted the whole of that letter. At that moment, I had no thought of self-advantage. I wanted the letter so I could avert the danger of others reading it. I wanted to show it to that old man lying in the parlour and kick his helpless carcass.

I opened the trap-door. Mr Poe blinked up at me. After that, matters moved swiftly and I observed them as one in a dream. A little later, I remember how Mr Poe leaned down from the horse and shook my hand with the utmost cordiality. 'God bless you, my boy,' he murmured.

It cannot have been much more than twenty minutes after Mr Poe left the cellar that I found myself standing in the yard behind the farm-house listening to a distant bell striking one o'clock in the afternoon. Nearer by far was the sound of hooves on the lane, gradually receding.

The sun came out and turned the mucky water in the horse trough and the puddles between the ruts into things of beauty. I turned and went back into the house. In the parlour, Stephen Carswall had not moved. Whistling and squeaking as the air slid in and out of his lungs, he lay on the floor near the dying fire. His eyes were open; they followed my movements. He knew what I was about.

I held up the letter so this rotting mound of flesh and bone could see it by the flickering light of the last candle. 'I know,' I said. 'I know.'

I crossed the room to the window, threw open the shutters and flung wide the casement. I looked across a little garden which had been given over to brambles, nettles and thistles. There were buds on the trees of the overgrown orchard, and somewhere a blackbird was singing.

CHAPTER EIGHTY-TWO

APRIL GAVE WAY to May. I remained at Mrs Jem's house in Gaunt-court. I earned enough for my keep and a little more. I should have been happy, for a great fear had been lifted from me, but I was not.

I dined once or twice with Mr Rowsell who thought he might be able to put me forward for a clerkship with a friend of his. It would be respectable employment, with the hope of something better in the long run. I saw Salutation Harmwell on several occasions — we would stroll through the parks and watch the world go by, neither of us feeling the need to speak very much.

It was Harmwell who told me that Mr Carswall's life was no longer despaired of. But the old man had not recovered the use of his limbs, and he was still unable to speak. His physicians believed it probable that the apoplexy had affected his mind as well as his body.

'He has become a great baby now,' Harmwell said. 'He does nothing but lie in his bedchamber. Everything is done for him.'

'And Miss Carswall's marriage?'

The Negro shrugged. 'She and Sir George are still willing, but it is now a question of settlements and of who is to assume the direction of Mr Carswall's affairs. A matter for the lawyers, in other words. So in the meantime Miss Carswall and Mrs Frant remain with the old man in Margaret-street. Though how long that will last for I cannot tell.' He hesitated and added, 'Mrs Kerridge tells me that Captain Ruispidge is in town and has called on several occasions.'

The world knew nothing of what had transpired in that tumbledown farmhouse beyond Kilburn. It was given out that Mr Carswall had hired a gig and taken Mr Noak to view the building land nearby, as a prospect for a joint investment. Mr Carswall had been taken ill on the way, and the two gentlemen had found shelter in the farmhouse. No one questioned this story. No one had any reason to do so.

Early in May, Mr Noak invited me to dine with him in Fleet-street, at the Bolt-in-Tun. We ate a frugal meal of mutton chops and caper sauce, washed down with thin claret. Mr Noak looked careworn.

'There is no news of the man Poe,' he said abruptly as he pushed aside his empty plate. 'I have had a constant watch on the premises in Queen-street and instituted other inquiries. The place is in great confusion – the bailiffs have been in. But the man himself has vanished. I suspect he has fled abroad.'

'What of the stolen bills?'

'I have found no trace of them. We must presume that Poe took them with him. None has been presented for payment since the one in Riga earlier this year. I am tolerably certain how that was managed, by the way. Carswall has – or had – a man of business in Paris. He has a clerk named Froment: and it was a Monsieur Froment who passed the bill to the notary in Brussels, who then passed it on to the others whom I had already traced. But of course Poe does not have the advantage of Carswall's commercial connections on the Continent. That is –' He leaned across the table and said in a low, urgent tone, 'You are perfectly convinced as to the identity of the man in Kilburn?'

'Yes, sir.' I was saddened by the desperation I detected in his voice. 'There is no possible doubt. The man I talked to was David Poe, not Henry Frant.'

Noak leaned back against the settle. 'It is a thousand pities you allowed him to escape.'

I smiled, affecting a nonchalance I did not feel. 'He tricked me, sir. But perhaps it is for the best. What matters, surely, is that the finger I was encouraged to find in the satchel had been removed from the hand of the corpse of his father-in-law. There can be no doubt about that. In that case, it was simply designed to throw me off the scent, to make me believe it possible that the corpse in Wellington-terrace was not that of Henry Frant. But of course it was.'

'I wish I had brought Frant to the gallows as he deserved,' Noak said after a silence. 'I shall regret it always. My son's murderer unpunished.'

I repressed a shudder. 'If you had seen Mr Frant's body, sir, you might not think him unpunished. All in all, he did not have a happy ending. He had been reduced to a bankrupt, an embezzler in fear of the gallows: and then, at the last, he lived to see his schemes confounded, and when he died he was beaten to a pulp. No, he did not die an easy death.'

Noak sniffed. He took up a toothpick and toyed with it for a moment. Then he sighed. 'Carswall, too: I do not think I can touch him.'

'Surely Providence has already judged him? He is living imprisoned in his own body, and under sentence of death.'

Mr Noak did not reply. He summoned the waiter and paid our reckoning, carefully counting out the coins. I thought I had angered him. As we were walking out into the Strand, however, he stopped and touched my arm.

'Mr Shield, I am sensible of the great service you have done me. The matter has not turned out exactly as I would have wished, but I have achieved most of what I set out to do, one way or the other. I shall return to America in a week or two. And what do you intend to do with your life?'

'I do not yet know, sir.'

'You cannot afford to leave the decision too long. You are a young man of parts, and if you should find yourself in the United States, I may be able to put you in the way of something. I will write to you before we sail, and give you my direction.'

I bowed and began to thank him. But he turned on his heel and without even a handshake walked rapidly away. In a moment he was lost to sight among the crowds.

CHAPTER EIGHTY-THREE

A T THE END of May, after Mr Noak and Mr Harmwell had sailed from Liverpool, I presented myself at the house in Margaret-street. I was freshly shaved, my hair was trimmed, and I had bought a fine black coat in honour of the occasion.

The door was answered by Pratt. I saw doubt flare on his thin, sallow face; perhaps there was a tinge of fear, too. I took advantage of his hesitation and stepped past him into the hall. I held out my hat and gloves and, without thinking, he received them.

'Is Miss Carswall at home? Pray give her my compliments and inquire if she can spare me a moment or two.'

He considered me for a moment, his eyes narrowing.

'Do not delay,' I said softly, 'or I will reveal to her the lengths you were prepared to go to satisfy Mr Carswall.'

He dropped his eyes and showed me into the parlour where Mr Carswall had questioned me, and drunk his wine, all those months ago. Though the furnishings were unchanged, the atmosphere had altered entirely. The room was lighter and airier. The masculine paraphernalia of cigars, glasses and newspapers had been swept away and the furniture was uncluttered and freshly polished. I had not waited more than a couple of minutes when the door opened. I turned, expecting Pratt, and saw Flora Carswall.

Careless of convention, she was alone. She closed the door behind her and advanced towards me with her hand outstretched. 'Mr Shield, I am rejoiced to see you. I find you well, I trust?'

We shook hands. She sat on a sofa, and patted the seat beside her. 'Pray sit here, where I can see you.' She was dressed soberly in grey, as befitted her situation, but there was nothing sober about her face and she had an assurance about her that was new. 'Charlie is at school, of course – he will be mortified to miss you.'

She did not mention Sophie.

I asked after her father, and learned that his condition was unchanged. Miss Carswall went on to volunteer the information that both Sir George's lawyers and Mr Carswall's were sanguine that the marriage would be able to proceed on the terms previously agreed.

'As for Papa,' she went on with a gurgle of laughter, 'I have such a delightful scheme for his welfare. When I am married, of course, I shall have to devote myself to my husband. But I have arranged for Sophie to stay with him, and play the daughter's part when I am not there.' She smiled at me, and her lashes fluttered most becomingly. 'Is that not a delightful plan? Poor Sophie will have a home and dear Charlie, too: and as for Papa, he always doted on Sophie.' She glanced sideways at me. 'After his own fashion.'

I could not conceive of a scheme more calculated to bring distress to the two principal parties concerned. I said, 'And Mr Carswall? Does the plan please him?'

'I do not mean to be unfeeling, Mr Shield, but I have no idea. He simply lies there, up in his chamber, without moving. Three times a day, they raise him up and give him broth or something of that nature. He can still swallow, you know. Whether he knows what – or even *that* – he is swallowing is another matter. It is very sad, of course, particularly when one remembers the man he was, so vigorous, so determined!' She smiled. 'So amiable, too! One must make the best of it, however, must one not? But to turn to happier subjects, I am so glad that little misunderstanding of my father's concerning the mourning ring has been dealt with. He was sometimes inclined to be hasty, particularly when agitated. I know Papa felt Mrs Johnson's death keenly – as did we all, of course – and no doubt it affected his judgement.'

'I saw the account of Mrs Johnson's inquest in the *Morning Post*,' I said. 'A sad accident.'

'Indeed.' Miss Carswall's face was suitably grave. 'The family was so worried about Lieutenant Johnson – he doted on her, you know – and he was always inclined to melancholy. But Sir George made interest with the Admiralty, and soon the poor man will have a ship of his own. Quite a little one, I understand, but at least it is something, and it will take his mind off his sorrows, will it not?'

We sat in demure silence for a moment. The Ruispidges were admirably thorough. They had taken steps to ensure that Lieutenant Johnson would be accommodating about the matter of his wife's death and the verdict of the Coroner's inquest. I was not altogether surprised by Miss Carswall's next remark.

'I was saying to Sir George only the other day,' she said, 'that a young man of your education and character is too valuable to lose sight of. You must be sure to leave me your direction before you go.' Here she edged a little closer to me on the sofa. 'Sir George may be able to assist you in the world.'

'Miss Carswall, may I lay a suggestion before you?'

She smiled broadly. 'By all means, Mr Shield.'

'It concerns Mrs Frant.'

She drew herself up. 'I do not think I understand. What have you to do with Mrs Frant?'

'The suggestion does not concern me, Miss Carswall. It concerns you. You will remember that in the autumn of last year I witnessed a certain codicil.'

She stared at me with an expression very like her father's. 'Of course I remember it.'

'It occurred to me that it would be remarkably becoming if you were to resign your interest in Mr Wavenhoe's legacy in favour of Mrs Frant, who I understand was the original legatee.'

'Becoming, sir, perhaps. But hardly wise.'

'Why not? You are a lady of great wealth now, in all but name. Soon you will be married and you will be even wealthier. And such a gesture could not but win the world's approval. It would be generous indeed.'

She snorted. 'I can think of another word for it.' She put her head on one side. 'Why? Why do you suggest this?'

'Because I was not altogether happy with the circumstances in which that codicil was signed.'

'Then you should have said so at the time.'

'My situation did not make that easy. The fault was mine, I own. Still, it is not too late for me to rectify that. I know Sir George is an honourable man. Perhaps I should lay the matter before him and ask his advice.'

'I am surprised at you, Mr Shield.' She stood up, and I followed suit. In her anger, she had an unexpected dignity. 'I must ask you to leave.'

'You will not entertain the notion?'

'Pray ring the bell. A servant will show you out.'

'Miss Carswall, I beg you to consider. The Gloucester property would mean nothing to you. It would be everything to Mrs Frant and Charlie.'

'Very touching, I am sure.' She wrinkled her little nose. 'Still, you don't fool me, Mr Shield. I am sure there's advantage in this for you, as well.'

'No. There is nothing whatsoever.'

'You want her,' she said, flushing. 'Do not deny it.'

'Why should she ever look at me?' I said.

'I knew it!' she cried. 'You do. I knew it from the first.'

'Miss Carswall, I believe it would be cruel and unfeeling to leave Mrs Frant and your father together, to leave her as nothing better than a hired nurse for him. You know that she hates him.'

'Then she should fight to suppress such an unworthy notion. She is a Christian, is she not? So her duty is to nurse the sick. Besides, my father is her cousin. And you may not know that, had my father not fallen ill, the connection would have been even closer.'

I ignored this flight of moral logic. 'If you will not agree, Miss Carswall, you compel me to use another argument.'

Her lips lifted, exposing white, sharp teeth. 'Will you force me to ring the bell myself, sir?'

I interposed myself between her and the bell rope. 'First hear what

466

I have to say. I must tell you that a letter has come into my possession. I do not think that either you or Sir George would be happy to see it made public.'

'Blackmail, is it? I had not thought you would stoop so low.'

'You leave me no choice.'

'You shall not impose on me, sir. There is no letter.'

'You wrote it to Mrs Frant,' I said. 'You were living in Bath at the time, and she was in Russell-square. The date on the letter is the 9th of October, 1812. You were not long returned from a tour of Ireland with Mr Carswall. You referred in it to an incident that took place in Waterford.'

'What are you talking about?' She spoke mechanically, in the form of a question but not in the tone of one. She went first to the door, as if to confirm that the latch had engaged, and then to stand by the window. After a moment she turned back to me. 'How did you get it?' she asked in a low voice.

I ignored her questions. I said, 'I do not wish to reveal the contents to anyone. I wish to give you the letter so you may destroy it.'

'Then give it to me now.'

'I shall give it to you when you have transferred Mr Wavenhoe's bequest to Mrs Frant. Consider: on the one hand, certain disgrace and the possibility of clinging to a little property you neither need nor deserve; and on the other, perfect peace of mind, the knowledge you have done right, the gratitude of your cousins, and the approbation of the world.'

She stamped her foot. 'No! You are infuriating! Do not preach to me, sir!'

I waited.

She went on, 'How do I know you are telling the truth? How do I know you really have such a letter? Will you show it me?'

'No. I do not have it with me. If you wish, I will send you a copy, word for word, so you may be sure that I am speaking the truth.'

She swallowed. 'I – I do not think that will be necessary, upon reflection. I – I shall consider the matter, Mr Shield, and I shall write to you with my decision.'

I took out my memorandum-book, scribbled Mr Rowsell's address and tore out the page. But for a moment I did not give it to her. 'I have two minor conditions, which I should mention at this juncture, though I do not think either of them will be of any difficulty to you.'

'It is not your place to lay down conditions,' she said.

'First,' I said, 'I wish the deed of gift, or whatever legal instrument is necessary to transfer the property, to be drawn up by a lawyer of my choosing: he is a gentleman named Humphrey Rowsell, of Lincoln's Inn; you will find he is perfectly respectable. This is his address, and you may write to me there. In the second place, I do not wish Mrs Frant to know that I had any hand in this matter. I wish her to believe that your generous nature is the sole reason for the gift.'

Flora Carswall approached me and came to a halt where our bodies were no more than a few inches apart. Her bosom rose and fell. She looked up at me, and we were so close that I felt her breath on my cheek. 'I do not understand you, Mr Shield. Truly, I do not understand you at all.'

'No, I do not suppose you do.'

'But if you were to try to understand me – and I were to try – and if –'

Her voice seemed to wind its way into my mind like a silken snake. With an effort of will, I tore myself away from her and pulled the bell rope.

'I will look forward to hearing from you by the end of tomorrow.'

'And if not?'

I smiled at her. There was a knock, and Pratt entered. I bowed over her hand and took my leave. At the door, however, I stopped.

'I had almost forgot.' I took a paper sealed with a wafer from my pocketbook and laid it on a side table. 'It is for you.'

Her face softened. 'What is it?'

'The repayment of a loan. You were so kind as to lend me five pounds when I left Monkshill.'

A moment later, as I was descending the steps from the street-door to the pavement, I met Captain Jack Ruispidge, as glossy as a rich man's hunter.

'What are you doing here?' he asked abruptly, for he no longer needed to play the smooth, condescending gentleman with me.

'Is that any business of yours, sir?'

'Don't be impertinent.' He stared up at me, for I was still on the steps. 'Mrs Frant is not without friends, you know. If you pester her again, I shall know how to deal with you.'

CHAPTER EIGHTY-FOUR

O N MAY 23RD, I received a letter, brief to the point of rudeness, addressed to me care of Mr Rowsell and brought to me by Atkins. Mrs Frant begged to inform Mr Shield that, if the weather was fine, she usually walked in the Green Park between the hours of two o'clock and three o'clock in the afternoon. It was an invitation in the form of a statement.

I at once decided I would not meet her. If a man scratches an itching scab, the wound will reopen and start to bleed again.

Instead I snarled at Mrs Jem's children when they stumbled over their lessons. I sent away a man who would have paid me well to write a begging letter to his uncle because I thought him grasping and odious. I could not concentrate for more than a moment or two at a time on any one thing or any one person. My mind would think of nothing except the implications of that curt little note.

Shortly after midday, I went up to my room. An hour later, I left the house: I was scrubbed, scraped and polished, and looked as much the beau as my limited resources would allow. I reached the Green Park shortly before two o'clock. The Season had begun, so its walks were sprinkled with the fashionable and the not so fashionable.

I saw Mrs Frant almost at once. She was pacing slowly along the line of the reservoir at the park's northern corner, opposite Devonshire House, in the direction of the fountain at the end. She was not attended by a maid. I approached her, watching her while for a moment she was unaware she was observed. Her eyes were on the water, which flashed gold and silver in the sunlight. She was still obliged to wear mourning for Mr Frant but she had pushed aside her veil and her weeds were not at all out of place in that fashionable throng. I remember with exactitude how she looked, and how she dressed, because it showed me in an instant the chasm that lay between us, that would always lie between us.

I went up to her and bowed. She gave me her hand but did not smile. My scab was picked: my wound began to bleed once more. She suggested we walk away from the roar and rattle of Piccadilly and the crowds who promenaded at this end of the park. We paced slowly southwards. She did not take my arm. When we had gone a little way, and there was no possibility of our being overheard, she stopped and looked directly at me for the first time.

'You have not been frank with me, sir. You have worked behind my back.'

I said nothing. I stared at the white skin of her arm between glove and cuff, noting the smudge of London black.

'My cousin Flora has restored my uncle Wavenhoe's legacy to me,' she went on.

'I am rejoiced to hear it.'

'She said she would not have done it, had it not been for you.' Sophie glared up at me. 'What did you do for her, pray? Flora does nothing for nothing.'

'I told her I was unhappy with the circumstances in which your uncle signed the codicil. If you remember I witnessed his signature. Miss Carswall's generous nature did the rest.'

She moved away and I followed her across the grass. Suddenly she stopped and turned back to me. 'I am not a child to be kept in the dark,' she said. 'There is more to it than that. A lawyer from Lincoln's Inn called on me with the necessary documents. As he was leaving, I asked him point-blank if he knew you. He tried to avoid the question, but I pressed him, and in the end he said he did.'

'I wished Mr Rowsell to deal with the transaction because I trust him implicitly. So I recommended him to Miss Carswall.'

'That suggests you do not trust my cousin.'

'I did not say that, ma'am. In affairs of the law, the advice of a disinterested party is always worth having.'

'Oh, stuff!' She glared at me. 'And how was it that you were in a position to dictate to my cousin?'

'I did not dictate to her. I merely tried to explain the desirability of following a particular course of action.'

'Then why did you tell her that you did not wish it known that you had – had advised her, if that is what you call it? Come, sir, I have a right to know why you took it upon yourself to interfere in my affairs.'

I turned over in my mind all the answers I might make. In the end, only the truth would do: 'I did not wish you to be obliged to feel gratitude.'

Her face blazed. 'You are insufferable, sir.'

'What would you have had me do?' I realised I had raised my voice. I took a breath and continued more quietly, 'I beg your pardon. But I did not like to think of you trapped with that terrible old man.'

'I am sure your concern does you credit. But you need not have worried. I will not pretend that the prospect of living with him was agreeable to me. But I would not have had to endure it long.' She raised her chin. 'Captain Ruispidge has done me the honour of asking me to marry him.'

I turned away. I could not bear to look on her bright face any longer.

'He asked me before my cousin Flora told me of her design to transfer the Gloucester property to me. His motives were of the purest.'

I glanced over my shoulder. 'I do not doubt it. I hope you will be very happy. He is a worthy man, I know, and I am sure it is a most prudent course of action.'

Sophie came a step nearer, forcing me to look again at her face. 'I have been prudent all my life. I married Henry Frant because it was prudent. I lived in my cousin Carswall's house because it was prudent. I am sick of being prudent. It does not agree with me.'

'You have not always been prudent.'

We looked at each other for a moment. In my mind I saw that little room in Gloucester, I saw her dear self wantonly displayed for my delight. Her face softened momentarily. She began to turn away but stopped and glanced up at me through her lashes. A coquette might have made the same movement, but she was not a coquette. I think she was afflicted by a sudden shyness.

'I was not prudent when Captain Ruispidge asked me to be his wife,' she said. 'I told him I was deeply sensible of the compliment he paid me, and would always consider him my friend, but that I did not love him. He said that did not matter, and he renewed his suit. I told him I wished to have time to turn his offer over in my mind before deciding.'

'So you might be prudent after all?'

'I had to think of Charlie.' She hesitated. 'I still do. Then Flora told me that she was going to make over the property to me and – and I wrote to Captain Ruispidge with my decision. Flora heard I was not to marry him, and that was when she told me it had been at your suggestion that she had made over the legacy to me. And you had asked her to conceal your part in the matter. I ask you again: why did you do that?'

'My answer is the same: I did not wish to put you under an obligation.'

'I am under a much greater obligation to my cousin Flora.'

'I do not doubt it.'

'She has made over what amounts to an income of nearly two hundred and fifty pounds a year.' Sophie looked up at me. 'So – tell me then: why should I not be grateful to you, as well as to her?'

'I had no intention of deceiving you. I wished to help you secure an independence, nothing more. If you had felt beholden to me, if you had known that I was concerned in any way – I – I feared it might cloud your judgement.'

'With regard to what?'

I did not answer. As if by common consent, we walked on, towards St James's Park, and it seemed to me that she walked a little closer to me than she had before. I could not see her face because of her bonnet, only the plumes nodding and swaying above her head. She murmured something. I was obliged to ask her to repeat it.

She stopped again and looked up at me. 'I said thank you. You showed true delicacy. I would have expected no less of you. Yet there are occasions when delicacy outlives its purpose. It is a virtue, undoubtedly, but it is not always appropriate to exercise it.'

I said, 'In that respect, it sounds strangely like prudence.'

We stood for a moment watching three magpies squabbling over a piece of bread and emitting their raucous, grating cry, like beans rattling in a gourd.

'How I detest magpies,' Sophie said.

'Yes – scavengers, thieves and bullies.'

'But do you know the rhyme that country people have about magpies? One for sorrow, two for mirth –'

'Three for a girl and four –'

'Three for a girl?' she interrupted. 'That was not what they said when I was a child. Besides four must be boy and it would not rhyme with mirth. No, when I was a child it was always three for a marriage.'

The magpies took fright and flew away.

'And four for a birth,' she added in a very low voice.

'Sophie?' I said, and held out my hand to her. 'Are you sure?'

'Yes,' she replied, and laid her hand in mine. 'Yes.'

APPENDIX

9th June 1862

The foregoing account came into my hands after the death of my sister-in-law, Flora, the Dowager Lady Ruispidge, on the 21st of October last year. She had deposited a number of items in the strong-room of the lawyers who had served both her and her father.

'I do not trust banks,' she told me once. 'But lawyers go on for ever.'

The items included a small wooden box, bound with iron hoops and secured with two locks. It was brought to my house at Cavendish-square to await the services of the locksmith. But there was no need, for the keys were found in a writing chest my sister-in-law kept by her, and which she had by her bed when she died. The box held a thick, closely written manuscript, divided into numbered sections. At the bottom was a five-pound note enclosed in a sheet of paper inscribed with the name 'Miss Carswall'.

As I sat by the library fire after dinner, I skimmed through the manuscript's pages, by turns amazed, fascinated, distressed and disturbed. Time does not heal all wounds and there are some indeed which fester and grow worse as the years slip by.

The identity of the author was evident to me from the beginning. When I met him, in the last weeks of the reign of George III, Thomas Shield was a schoolmaster. He records that meeting, in the churchyard at Flaxern Parva, and also our last encounter a few months later, when we passed each other at the door of the Carswalls' house in Margaret-street. (Until now I had no idea of the significance of his visit. How I regret that I allowed myself to speak so intemperately.)

It was not long before I realised that Shield's narrative threw a new and often shocking light on the Wavenhoe scandal and, in particular, on the American associations of this dark affair. Few remember it now but it was one of the precursors of the great banking crisis of the winter of 1825–6; over forty years ago, it set London by the ears and brought ruin to a number of families. The manuscript also tells us something of the unhappy sequels in Gloucestershire and later in London, though these episodes attracted little attention at the time.

Many questions have, perforce, remained unanswered until now; and questions that should have been asked have never been posed. There is small wonder in this, for much information was never put before the public. For example, the rôle of the little American boy was never mentioned, then or later, despite the mingled fame and obloquy his career subsequently attracted. Contemporaneous accounts also ignored the parts played by other North Americans, among them Mr Noak of Boston, Massachusetts, and the Negro Salutation Harmwell from Upper Canada. Yet, without them, events could not have unfolded as they did. Until now, I believe, not a whisper has emerged of the connection between the failure of a London bank in 1819 and that sad and unnecessary conflict which had divided the two great English-speaking nations, Great Britain and the United States of America, a few years earlier.

In other words, the Wavenhoe scandal was like the Breguet watch that Stephen Carswall cherished as he never did a child: simple enough on the surface, but its apparent simplicity concealing a complex arrangement of hidden springs, wheels, checks and balances; organised according to rational principles, to be sure, but too delicate and complicated a piece of machinery to yield its secrets to the profane. Carswall's watch lies before me as I write, still keeping perfect time, its inner workings as mysterious to me now as on the day it came into my possession.

Tom Shield was right, in one way at least, and so was that hardened reprobate Voltaire. We owe respect to the living, but to the dead we owe only truth.

II

How did Thomas Shield's narrative come into the hands of my sister-in-law? We may safely assert that he would not have given it to Flora of his own free will. I questioned her servants as discreetly as I could, but none of them could shed light on the matter. There was no hint in her letters or other papers. She did not keep a diary. Her lawyers knew nothing.

The little writing chest by her bed also contained her account book. Throughout her life, my sister-in-law recorded how her money ebbed and flowed, for she knew the value of money; she was her father's daughter in this and much else. I found in a drawer of her bureau a set of account books stretching back to her schooldays in Bath. It occurred to me that perhaps her accounts might hold a clue to the manuscript's provenance.

I believe I was right, though it took me many hours to find the trace of it. (But what else have I to do, now I am old? After all, this is a story of old men's obsessions, and what is one more obsession among the others?) In the June of 1820, there began a series of small irregular payments, never more than five guineas. These were identified only by the initials QA. In May 1821 there was a much larger payment of £80. After that date, QA continued to receive a payment of seven guineas each quarter. This arrangement continued until August 1852, after which it abruptly terminated. Occasionally the later payments were to 'Q. Atkins' rather than 'QA'.

Surely this was the link I sought! For I had stumbled upon a Q. Atkins in Shield's narrative – Quintus Atkins, to be precise, Rowsell's clerk, a man who seems to have disliked Shield. The name is sufficiently unusual to place the identification beyond reasonable doubt. As Flora knew, Rowsell was Shield's lawyer. If Shield communicated with anyone other than Sophie after his disappearance, it would have been Rowsell. Atkins had acted as their go-between before, and perhaps had done so again.

Here at least is a solid foundation for a hypothesis: that Flora suborned Atkins, paying him what the lawyers call a retainer to feed her scraps of information about Shield and poor Sophie. More than scraps, I fancy – on one occasion a veritable banquet: for I cannot resist the conclusion that Flora's acquisition of Shield's narrative is connected with her payment of £80 to Quintus Atkins.

In her account book for 1819, Flora recorded the loan of five pounds to Thomas Shield in January. Later she put a line through the entry and added the words *Debt repaid*. But she kept the five-pound note in the box with Shield's manuscript.

I used to believe that the only person Flora loved was Sophie Frant. I was wrong.

III

I have before me a certified copy of the entry recording the baptism of Thomas Reynolds Shield in the Parish Register of St Mary's, Rosington. It is a strange, unsettling thought that Shield – or someone close to him – may have kept himself informed of my path through the world. The principal events of a man who moves in my sphere of society inevitably make their way into the public record. By now, however – considering the matter purely from the viewpoint of an actuary – Shield is more likely to be dead than alive. Indeed, almost all of those most nearly concerned in the Wavenhoe affair have gone to answer for their conduct before the highest judge of all.

I do not know whether Shield believed the story he tells to be, as far as he knew it, the truth. Much of what he writes is at least consonant with my own, more limited knowledge of the affair. I remember several incidents he describes, albeit in much less detail and with a number of differences. But I can confirm the essential accuracy of his descriptions.

Nevertheless, he may have had an ulterior motive in writing this account. It is impossible, at this remove, to corroborate the majority of the information he provides with material from other sources. (By its very nature, much of his story can never be corroborated.) Moreover, memory itself may, without conscious volition or awareness, clothe the naked form of truth in the garb of fiction. Why did Shield compose the narrative in the first place? To while away the days and weeks before Sophie was ready to leave with him? As a justification? As an *aide-mémoire*, in case the authorities took a further interest in the activities of Stephen Carswall, Henry Frant and David Poe?

Shield's language appears artless, yet I wonder whether its superficial simplicity may not conceal an element of calculation, a desire to manipulate the truth for purposes unknown. At some points I have suspected a want of frankness, at others a willingness to embroider. I find it hard to believe that he could have recalled the precise words of so many conversations, or the nuances of expression on others' faces, or the restless manoeuvring of his own thoughts.

It irks me almost beyond endurance that so many questions remain unanswered. On the first page, Shield plunges his reader *in medias res*; and on the last page he abandons him there almost in mid-sentence. By accident – or design? Does his story break off at this point for the simple reason that Atkins stole the manuscript?

I shall never know. If truth is infinite, then any addition to our knowledge of it serves also to remind us of what remains unknowable.

IV

Carswall's Breguet watch ticks on, as it has for more than half a century. In the end, time is always our master. It is we who run down, we who wear out, we who stop.

There is much in these pages which has the power to shock a modern mind. It is regrettable that Thomas Shield did not moderate some of his language and draw a veil of modesty over some of the thoughts, words and actions that he records. Some passages reveal a want of taste which at worst degenerates still further into impropriety. It is true that he wrote at a time that was both more robust and less fastidious than our own but often he betrays a vein of coarseness which can only offend.

The publication of Shield's narrative, even in a very limited, private sense, is out of the question. I would not care for my wife or my servants to read it. But I do not intend to destroy his story. My reason is simply this: as Voltaire suggests, there are occasions when we must weigh carefully the competing demands of the living and the dead, when the former must yield precedence to the latter.

Does it not follow from this that, if we owe a duty of truth to the dead, then we also owe it to those who will come after us? It occurs to me now, as I write the sentence above, that perhaps Divine Providence has sent me Tom Shield's account in order that I may add to it.

V

Flora's generosity in resigning the legacy in favour of her cousin was widely praised. Even my brother George, not the most open-handed of men, saw the justice of it; and he was not blind to the advantages of being so closely allied to such a philanthropic gesture. He and Flora were married, in a private ceremony, some months after they had originally intended.

By that time, Mrs Frant had left Margaret-street. After some months in the country, she settled at last in a pretty cottage in Twickenham, near the river. Her old servant, Mrs Kerridge, remained to nurse Mr Carswall. I now realise that Mrs Frant must have become aware of Mrs Kerridge's duplicity. The woman had been providing information about her mistress to both Salutation Harmwell and Mr Carswall.

As the year 1820 drew to its close, I visited Sophie in Twickenham, and ventured to renew my suit. She refused me. In Margaret-street, I had hoped that she was beginning to look kindly on me. But that was before Flora's gift and (as I now know) before that fateful meeting in the Green Park.

Nothing happened suddenly. I found Sophie at home in March 1821, but when I called at the cottage some three weeks later she was gone. The front room was shuttered and the furniture shrouded with dust covers. A little servant remained to look after the place. The girl was dumb. Now I can hazard a guess as to her name and history. She wrote me a note in a surprisingly neat hand to say that her mistress had gone away for a while and she did not know where. When I next passed by, in May, there were new tenants; and Mrs Frant had left no forwarding address.

I have not seen or heard from Sophia Frant from that day to this. In the first six months after her disappearance, I was sedulous in my attempts to discover her whereabouts. Flora said she had heard nothing of her cousin, and promised she would let me know if she did; she professed herself as puzzled as I.

Charlie had long since been withdrawn from Mr Bransby's in Stoke Newington, and they knew nothing of his present whereabouts at the school he had briefly attended in Twickenham. I tried Mr Rowsell, who informed me he was unable to put me in communication with either Mrs Frant or Mr Shield. When I passed through Gloucester on my way to Clearland, I inquired after Sophie's property, only to learn that the freeholds in Oxbody-lane had recently changed hands. I hired the services of others better qualified than I to make inquiries, but they were equally unsuccessful.

You must not fancy from this that my subsequent life has been one long, dying fall, that I have done nothing except mourn the loss of Sophia Frant. It would be true to say that I have always been aware, in some corner of my being, of her absence. I have found it fatally easy to dwell on what might have been: if, for example, I had had the courage to propose to her at Monkshill, despite her lack of fortune, despite her son and despite her first husband's notoriety. George and our mother had united to dissuade me, pointing out, though not in so many words, that I did not have enough to live comfortably as a married man, that I must look for a wife with a little money of her own, and that in any case I would be unlikely to find happiness in the arms of an embezzler's widow.

So I joined our diplomatic service and served first at several of the smaller German courts and later in Washington, a post which the climate of the American capital sometimes made profoundly disagreeable. While I was in the United States I met Mr Noak again, increasingly eccentric but so wealthy that he could not help but wield considerable influence. A year later he was dead, and it was found that he had dispersed the bulk of his enormous fortune to a number of charities, with the exception of one substantial legacy to his former chief clerk, Salutation Harmwell.

My diplomatic career, never distinguished, came to an end when my brother unexpectedly died in 1833. His marriage had been childless – and Mr Shield's narrative, of course, hints at a possible reason for that, as it does for other qualities that distinguished my sister-in-law. I was my brother's heir.

With a title and a fortune, I found myself the eligible bachelor. I married my second cousin, Arabella Vauden, a match considered advantageous for both parties. Our union has not been blessed with children, and when I die the title and the entailed part of the estate will pass to a cousin in Yorkshire. My wife regrets this circumstance extremely.

Flora did not remarry, though she had several offers. She could afford to please herself. She passed most of her long widowhood in London, where she entertained widely if not wisely in her house in Hanover-square. When she died of inflammation of the lungs, much of her wealth passed to me by the terms of her marriage settlement. Now she lies where we have laid her, in the cemetery at Kensalgreen.

I run ahead: I must not forget her father. As soon as the law allowed, Flora closed down the house in Margaret-street and moved Mr Carswall and his nurse down to Monkshill. The mansion-house was let, so she settled them at Grange Cottage, where Mrs Johnson had dragged out the last years of her unfortunate life.

Stephen Carswall never recovered his powers of speech and move-ment. I saw him twice in his decline and he was as useless as fruit rotting on the tree. Mrs Kerridge bullied him mercilessly, and at the time I wondered that Flora did not intervene. He lingered for seven long years, until February 1827. At his demise, his fortune was found to be much depleted.

I come now to David Poe, Mr Iversen, Junior, of Seven Dials, the father of the American boy who when he grew to manhood was buffeted by fame and misfortune in equal measure. Having read Mr Shield's manuscript, I instituted inquiries about this gentleman, both here and in America. I found no *certain* trace of him whatsoever. As far as the world knows, he vanished in 1811 or possibly 1812.

But I did uncover an intriguing hint that, many years earlier, Mr Noak had attempted to trace David Poe's later career, and that the old gentleman had learned that there were those who preferred to let sleeping dogs lie. One of these was Mr Rush, who in 1820 had been the American Minister in London, a man with whom Noak had many dealings while he was in England, and whom he certainly would have pressed for information concerning David Poe.

Another gentleman who wished David Poe to remain buried in obscurity – and here we come at the matter from quite a different angle – was General Lafayette himself, the venerable hero of both the American and French Revolutions. Though of course Lafayette had no official standing in the United States, his reputation and achievements gave him influence in the most unexpected places.

My correspondent in the United States drew my attention to the fact that Lafayette and David Poe's father had been comrades in arms in the great revolutionary struggle. The connection between the two men was clearly close. When the old General visited the United States for his triumphal tour in 1824, he visited Baltimore, Maryland, where he singled out for particular attention the wife of his old comrade, who had died some years earlier. A few weeks later, Lafayette was in Richmond, Virginia, where he was assigned a guard of honour composed of boys in the uniform of riflemen; one of these was Edgar Allan Poe.

These are facts, but they prove nothing except that Lafayette had a kindness for the Poe family. But, if one takes this in conjunction with hints and whispers from other directions, it is impossible to ignore the suspicion that several surprisingly prominent gentlemen were perfectly happy that David Poe should remain a lost sheep.

It was, I suppose, the worst of ill luck for Henry Frant that his villainy led him to an even greater villain than himself. God knows, he paid heavily for his vices and suffered for his crimes. Before I allow David Poe to return to obscurity, however, I must record one speculation that occurred to me. Shield seems strangely well informed about David Poe's life. Is it possible that there were subsequent meetings between the two men?

VI

I come at last to the American boy. Edgar Allan Poe was like the pintle of a hinge – barely visible, yet the still point around which the whole business revolved. He waits at almost every twist and turn of Shield's narrative.

The American boy knocks on Mr Bransby's door on the occasion of Shield's very first visit to the Manor House School. He is Charlie's particular friend and indeed champion. He is the unwitting cause of his father's introduction first to Tom Shield and then to Henry Frant, and hence brings Frant to his murderer. He is in the ice-house at Monkshill-park, desperate to search it for treasure. He and Charlie make their midnight expedition to the ruins, without which the events of that night must have turned out very differently. He helps to carry Charlie's parrot across London, and the bird with its cry of *ayez peur* is the clue that draws Shield back to Seven Dials and provides the link between Carswall and David Poe. It is Edgar who whispers to Shield that Sophie may be found visiting her late husband's grave in the burying ground of St George's, Bloomsbury. All in all, it is hard to quarrel with Shield's assertion that the boy 'acted as the proximate cause of much that had happened'.

I have followed Edgar Allan Poe's subsequent career as a poet and critic with interest. I heard with regret of his tribulations in later life and his death. I wondered whether traces of his boyhood experiences in England may be descried in some of his work. With the help of American correspondents, I even attempted to explore the circumstances of his death, which was shrouded in mystery. I failed to dispel the mystery. But I did acquire a piece of information that Flora never had.

The facts, such as they are, appear to be these. On the 26th of September 1849, Edgar Allan Poe dined at a restaurant in Richmond, Virginia. Friends and associates believed that on the following day he intended to set out for Baltimore, a voyage of some twenty-five hours by steamer. Not only is the precise time of his departure disputed, but so are his means of travel and the time of his arrival.

In short, Poe vanished. There are no confirmed sightings of him whatsoever between the evening of 26th September in Richmond and his reappearance, a week later, in Baltimore. A printer named Walker noticed him at Gunner's Hall, a tavern in East Lombard-street. The city was in the throes of an election which brought with it a drunken orgy of corruption and intimidation. Gunner's Hall was one of the polling stations.

Poe was 'in great distress', and asked Walker to notify a friend, Joseph Snodgrass, who arrived in due course with several of Poe's relations. They assumed that Poe was drunk. 'The muscles of articulation seemed paralysed to speechlessness,' Snodgrass recorded in 1856, 'and mere incoherent mutterings were all that were heard.'

They arranged for Poe to be taken to the Washington College Hospital where he was treated by the resident physician, Dr John J. Moran. According to a letter Moran wrote a few weeks afterwards to Poe's aunt

Mrs Clemm (the sister of David Poe), his patient was at first unconscious of his condition. Later his limbs trembled and he was seized with 'a busy, but not violent or active delirium – constant talking – and vacant converse with spectral and imaginary objects . . . ' By the second day, he was calm enough to listen to questions but 'his answers were incoherent and unsatisfactory'.

Dr Moran tried to cheer his patient by saying that soon he would be well enough to receive friends. Edgar Allan Poe 'broke out with much energy, and said the best thing his friend could do would be to blow out his brains with a pistol.' Soon he became violently delirious – despite his weakness, two nurses were required to hold him down.

Poe continued in this state until the evening of Saturday the 6th of October, 'when he commenced calling for one "Reynolds", which he did through the night up to *three* on Sunday morning.' Then, 'enfeebled from exertion', he became quieter for a short time. At last, 'gently moving his head he said *"Lord help my poor Soul"* and expired!'

The precise cause of death is unknown – no death certificate was issued. No one, then or now, knows who 'Reynolds' is or was. My agents state that, while neither Snodgrass nor Moran may be entirely trustworthy as a witness, there seems no reason to doubt the essential veracity of their accounts. They add that Poe appeared in good spirits in Richmond, where he had lectured to great applause and become engaged to be married. They also drew my attention to rumours current in Baltimore to the effect that when Poe arrived in the city he fell in with old friends, who persuaded him to take a drink to celebrate their reunion. Poe had eschewed alcohol for some months, and it is said that he was yet another victim of *mania à potu*.

Perhaps. But may there not be another explanation for Edgar Allan Poe's disappearance and for the extraordinary prostration that led to his collapse and death? Remember Poe's despair – his wish for suicide – his repeated calls for 'Reynolds'. Remember that according to the Parish Register, Tom Shield's middle name was Reynolds, the surname of his mother's family.

Was Shield in Baltimore in 1849?

As a man, Edgar Allan Poe was frail in mind and body. What if he had suddenly learned the true history of those months in England in 1819–20? Above all, what if he had come face to face with the terrible truth about his father?

It could drive a stronger man to drink. It could drive a stronger man to death itself.

VII

It is time to lay down my pen. I shall lodge this narrative with my lawyers and leave instructions that it is to be opened by the head of the family seventy-five years after my decease. After such an interval of time, neither Shield's account nor these notes I have appended to it will have the power to hurt anyone.

The older I become, the more I wonder about Sophie herself. Is she alive? Is she with Thomas Shield? If they were lovers, and I think there can now be little doubt of that, did they marry? If they married, what became of their lives? Which continent gave them a home? Are there children, grandchildren? Is she happy?

Mr Carswall's watch has informed me with its tiny chime that it is two o'clock in the morning. If I blow out the candles and pull back the curtains of the library's bow-window, I shall look out over mile after mile of nothing, a night without boundaries.

I wrote earlier that if truth is infinite, then any addition to our knowledge of it serves also to remind us of what is unknowable. And that of course brings me back to what might have been, to Sophie, for ever unknowable, for ever hidden in the illimitable darkness.

JRR
Clearland-court

A HISTORICAL NOTE ON
EDGAR ALLAN POE

'NOVELS ARISE OUT of the shortcomings of history,' wrote Novalis, a remark Penelope Fitzgerald chose as the epigraph to her novel about him, *The Blue Flower*. The history of Edgar Allan Poe is littered with shortcomings and also richly overlaid with myths, speculations and contradictions. It would be irresponsible wilfully to add to them: hence this attempt to describe where the history ends and the novel begins.

Poe's grandfather, David, Sr, was born in Ireland in about 1742. The family emigrated to America, eventually settling in Maryland. David became a shopkeeper and manufacturer of spinning wheels. During the Revolutionary War he was commissioned as Assistant Deputy Quartermaster General for Baltimore, and given the rank of major. In 1781 he used his own money to buy supplies for American forces under Lafayette, and his wife is said to have cut 500 pairs of pantaloons with her own hands for the use of his troops. In David Poe's old age he may have taken part in the defence of Baltimore against British attack in 1814, during the War of 1812.

Poe's father, David, Jr, was born in 1784. He made an abortive attempt to study law but in 1803 became an actor. In 1806 he married Elizabeth Arnold, a widowed Englishwoman who had made her debut as an actress ten years before in Boston, Massachusetts. Edgar, the second of their three children, was born on 19th January 1809. What evidence survives (mainly from hostile theatre critics) suggests that David Poe was a mediocre actor, hot-tempered and often intoxicated. On the other hand in his six years on the stage he played one hundred and thirty-seven parts, some of them important ones, which suggests that he was neither incompetent nor unreliable.

David Poe was commended by the editor of a Boston theatrical weekly in December 1809. Afterwards we are left with hearsay. He was reported in New York in July 1810. It is probable, but by no means certain, that he deserted his wife in 1811.

Elizabeth Poe died in Richmond, Virginia, on 8th December 1811. No one knows where or when her husband died, which has not prevented biographers from providing at least three specific dates for his death over a period of approximately fourteen months. All we know for sure is that David Poe drops out of recorded history at some point after December 1809.

In other words, Edgar Allan Poe's life began with a mystery, still unsolved.

After his mother's death, Edgar took the fancy of a childless couple, Mr and Mrs John Allan. Born in Scotland, Allan was a prosperous citizen of Richmond, and a partner in a firm of tobacco exporters and general merchants. Though the Allans never formally adopted Edgar, he took their name and it was generally understood that he was not only their son but their heir.

In June 1815, John Allan sold Scipio (one of his slaves) for $600 and set sail for Liverpool with his little family. He intended to set up a London branch of his business. For five years, between the ages of six and eleven, Edgar Allan Poe lived in England. He was the only important American writer of his generation to spend a significant part of his childhood in England, and the experience marked him profoundly.

At first Allan prospered. He took a house in Southampton Row – number 47; in the autumn of 1817, the family moved to number 39. It is clear from surviving correspondence that Mrs Allan's health was a constant source of worry – and perhaps, for Mr Allan, a source of irritation as well. The Allans paid at least two visits to Cheltenham, on the second of which they stayed at the Stiles Hotel. Here Mrs Allan could take the waters and benefit from the country air.

While they were at Cheltenham in 1817, a parrot ordered for Mrs Allan arrived at Liverpool. This was a bird reputed to speak French, and was designed to replace a parrot left behind in Virginia (who had been able to recite the alphabet in English). In his 'Philosophy of Composition', the adult Poe revealed that when he was planning 'The Raven' his first thought was that the bird should be a parrot.

At some point in the first six months of 1818, John Allan withdrew Edgar from his school in London and, despite business reverses, transferred him to a more expensive establishment, the Manor House School in the nearby village of Stoke Newington. The schoolmaster was the Reverend John Bransby. 'Edgar is a fine boy,' Allan wrote to one of his correspondents in June that year, 'and reads Latin pretty sharply.'

The Manor House School is long since gone, but we know what the roadside façade looked like from a contemporary sketch and a photograph of 1860. We also have a photograph of a portrait of Bransby. Several of Master Allan's school bills have survived, which reveal among other things that Allan paid an extra two guineas a term for Edgar to have the privilege of a bed to himself. We know from other sources a good deal about life in English private schools of the period.

Best of all, we have Poe's own short story, 'William Wilson', which contains a fictional version of the Stoke Newington school, complete with its own 'Reverend Dr Bransby'. The story is particularly interesting, because it concerns a boy haunted by a schoolmate who appears to be his double.

Years afterwards, a former pupil at the Manor House School questioned John Bransby about the school's most illustrious old boy and, in 1878, published his memory of those conversations. Mr Bransby was reluctant to talk about Poe, perhaps because of the way he had been portrayed in 'William Wilson'. But he is reported as saying: 'Edgar Allan was a quick and clever boy and would have been a very good boy if he had not been spoilt by his parents, but they spoilt him, and allowed him an extravagant amount of pocket money, which enabled him to get into all manner of mischief – still, I liked the boy – poor fellow, his parents spoilt him!' On another occasion Mr Bransby added: 'Allan was intelligent, wayward and wilful.'

John Allan's firm continued to suffer from financial difficulties. On 2nd October 1819, Allan's landlord in Southampton Row dunned him for rent. But Allan was still willing and able to pay Edgar's school bills – the last one that survives is for 26th May 1820. On 16th June 1820 the Allans and their foster son sailed for New York aboard the *Martha* from Liverpool. The American boy was going home.

Lafayette did indeed visit Baltimore in 1824, where he asked after his old comrade and called on Edgar Allan Poe's grandmother. According to a later account in the *Philadelphia Saturday Museum* (4th March 1843), the General knelt beside the grave of David Poe, Senior, and said, '*Ici repose un coeur noble!*' A few weeks later Lafayette was in Richmond, where Edgar's friend Thomas Ellis recorded his pride in seeing Edgar among the distinguished visitor's guard of honour.

Edgar Allan Poe's life began with the mystery of his father's disappearance and ended with the mystery of his own. The account given in the Appendix to *The American Boy* is substantially accurate. No one knows where Poe was between 26th September and 3rd October 1849. When he reappeared in Baltimore, he had lost his money and he was wearing cheap, dirty clothes which were not his own; but he was still carrying a malacca cane he had borrowed from a Richmond acquaintance.

The most detailed evidence, and probably the most reliable, comes from the earliest accounts of Joseph Snodgrass, the friend who rescued Poe, and of Dr Moran, the physician who attended him in his last illness. Neither was an unbiased witness. Snodgrass was an ardent Temperance campaigner and regarded the story of his friend's death as an illustration of the perils of alcohol. Moran was one of Poe's posthumous supporters, and his story became increasingly embroidered as the years went by. However, he wrote the passage quoted only a few weeks after Poe's death; it uses the plainest language of all his accounts; it mentions both Poe's cries for 'Reynolds' and his desire for death. Moran is also the earliest source for the suggestion that when Poe arrived in Baltimore he fell in with 'some of his old and former associates'.

Several theories have been advanced to explain Poe's condition. The main ones are: the effects of alcoholism; 'cooping' – a violent election-eering practice which involved intoxicating voters and then forcing them to vote repeatedly; and – an imaginative late entry into the field – the bite of a rabid dog. They are no more than theories.

After his death, as Poe's reputation continued to grow, the facts of his doomed and mysterious life continued to be obscured by the enthu-siastic modifications of his many supporters and detractors. His work has found admirers all over the world, including Abraham Lincoln and Josef Stalin.

Anyone wishing to know more about him cannot do better than to start with Arthur Hobson Quinn's *Edgar Allan Poe*, originally published in 1941 and still the best biography available. A hoard of essential biographical source material relating to Poe has been assembled in *The Poe Log* (1987) by Dwight Thomas and David K. Jackson. Finally, the Edgar Allan Poe Society of Baltimore, Maryland, maintains an admirable website at www.eapoe.org: scholarly, detailed and well-organised, it is a pleasure to use.

ACKNOWLEDGEMENTS

I would like to thank the small army of people who have helped this novel find its way into the world – so many that it is only possible to name a handful of them: Vivien Green, Amelia Cummins and others at Sheil Land; Julia Wisdom, Anne O'Brien and their colleagues at HarperCollins; Patricia Wightman; Bill Penn; and the long-suffering members of my immediate family to whom the novel is dedicated.

A historical novel inevitably depends on the unwitting assistance of the dead. I wish to record my particular gratitude to Clarissa Trant (1800–44), a remarkable woman whose journals deserve to be far better known than they are.

The Ashes of London

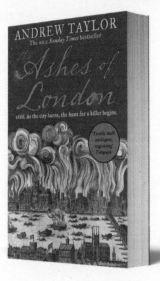

A CITY IN FLAMES

London, 1666. As the Great Fire consumes everything in its path, the body of a man is found in the ruins of St Paul's Cathedral — stabbed in the neck, thumbs tied behind his back.

A WOMAN ON THE RUN

The son of a traitor, James Marwood is forced to hunt the killer through the city's devastated streets. There he encounters a determined young woman who will stop at nothing to secure her freedom.

A KILLER SEEKING REVENGE

When a second murder victim is discovered in the Fleet Ditch, Marwood is drawn into the political and religious intrigue of Westminster — and across the path of a killer with nothing to lose...

The Fire Court

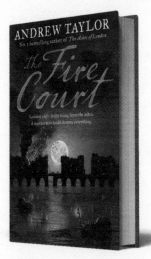

SOMEWHERE IN THE SOOT-STAINED RUINS OF RESTORATION LONDON, A KILLER HAS GONE TO GROUND…

The Great Fire has ravaged London, wreaking destruction and devastation wherever its flames spread. Now, guided by the incorruptible Fire Court, the city is slowly rebuilding, but times are volatile and danger is only ever a heartbeat away.

James Marwood, son of a traitor, is thrust into this treacherous environment when his ailing father claims to have stumbled upon a murdered woman – in the very place where the Fire Court sits. Then his father is run down and killed. Accident? Or another murder…?

Determined to uncover the truth, Marwood turns to the one person he can trust – Cat Lovett, the daughter of a despised regicide. Marwood has helped her in the past. Now it's her turn to help him. But then comes a third death… and Marwood and Cat are forced to confront a vicious and increasingly desperate killer whose actions threaten the future of the city itself.